NINE O'CLOCK HORSES

NINE O'CLOCK HORSES

A Mystery

A.E. Ewing

For Johanne & Whitman, with all my love.

Acknowledgments

This story is based on the truth of the nine o'clock horses in Leicester, England. The factual information about WWII is accurate to the best of my knowledge.

My parents and my siblings, who are the real characters in the book, are now deceased, allowing me to reveal my mother's suicidal personality, my brother's sexual abuse, and my life, growing up in the fragile atmosphere of war. This writing began twenty years ago, and it has been a cathartic journey into my past to try to assuage my own guilt, of which there is a lot!

I could not have finished this book without support from my Writers Group: Georgia Cockerham, Sandra Garber, Dan Gray, and Karl Sandstrom, who never failed to encourage me to keep going even when the emotions and memories were so overwhelming that my writing was put away for months on end. My gratitude goes to Leslie Wolf, who kept my wayward punctuation under control, and to Sonia Gray for the monumental task, (at least for me) of formatting this book for print. Available from Amazon for Kindle and in print from Amazon.com and bookstores worldwide.

Cover design: Kenneth Greg
Author's photo: Magdalena Huybreghs

Authors Notes

Great Britain has long been besieged by other nations who have wanted to claim and dominate a tiny island no more significant than the State of Oregon. Its history is long and complicated.

Centuries before the birth of Christ, the island, surrounded by three seas — the North Sea, the Irish Sea, and the Atlantic — was inhabited by savage tribes who lived in grass huts and caves.

It was the Celtic peoples of Central Europe who invaded the island and gradually introduced agriculture and farming to uneducated inhabitants. A branch of the Celts, known as the Gaels, introduced the Gaelic tongue to Wales, Scotland, and Ireland. They were barbaric and worshipped strange gods and practiced human sacrifice. Skilled in building, they had laws set down by religious chiefs, the Druids, who were supposedly the builders of Stonehenge, the famous ring of stones on Salisbury Plain.

But it was the Romans, who invaded Britain in 55 B.C, who had the most influence. The city where I was born, where my early story takes place is a Roman town. Leicester still boasts remains of Roman baths and mosaic pavement discovered beneath modern shops in the High Street.

The first parliament of England was held in Leicester's Guild Hall long before London became the capital.

The Romans gave Britain their laws and government. They were the ones who taught Latin to the general populace and advanced trading with the Saxons from Northern Germany. It was the Saxons who ruled England for centuries. After them came a Germanic tribe, the Angles, and the name, 'England.'

There were more invasions from the Normans, the Vikings, the Danes, and the Jutes. Each left their mark and part of their heritage, which defines Britain today: a mongrel race, dominated by warring tribes, and yet maintaining their style of life and their ability to become — once upon a time — a world power.

Over the centuries, civil wars have divided Britain into separate Kingdoms: England, Scotland, Wales, and Northern Ireland, now known as the United Kingdom. Not so long ago, it was war and unrest between England and Ireland. Recently Scotland requested a split; now they have their own parliament.

But the interesting thing to me is the fact that Britain's heritage is German. Even our Royal family are descendants of the House of Hapsburgs, a German aristocratic family who ruled European royal dynasties for centuries. Our own Queen Victoria married Albert of the German Saxe-Coburg-Gotha house. With WWII imminent, the royal family changed their name from Saxe-Coburg to Windsor. This was considered a politically correct thing to do since WWI had severed so many ties to European monarchy.

I mention the history of England now, only because it brings to mind the close association with Germany throughout history, and yet, they were our enemies in that dreadful war we know as WWII.

Part One

England 1940-1961

"Victory at all costs.
Victory in spite of all terror.
Victory, however long and hard the road may be;
for without victory, there is no survival."

WINSTON CHURCHILL
Speech May 13, 1940

Prologue

Leicester, England

Vickie Norton lit the oil lamp on the narrow mantelpiece in the children's bedroom. She blew out the match and looked heavenwards. "I know you're up there," she whispered. She moved to the window wanting to draw back the curtains to look outside. No, she couldn't do that. The enemy up above the treetops would see even the light from the oil lamp. Her two daughters, Amelia, two, and Pauline, ten, were asleep. Douglas, six, her favorite child, was in the cot by the wall.

Heat rose to her cheeks as she suddenly recognized the sound of the engines. German! When the wham, wham, wham, of the engines suddenly stopped, she inhaled a sharp breath and flung herself over Pauline, her arms like wings. When the sharp whistle pierced the air, Vickie Norton knew they would all die.

The explosion came seconds later. Earsplitting. Deafening. Bricks clattered down the chimney in a cloud of soot. The oil lamp went out. The Jesus picture clattered to the floor. Curtains billowed into the room. Pieces of the windowpane, hanging by yellowed tape, thrust jagged shards into the room. Pauline cried out, "Mummy?"

"It's all right, love. Be still." Vickie waited; she expected the floor to collapse beneath them. Instead, there was an eerie silence broken only by the occasional tinkle of glass falling to the floor. Was it safe to walk on? Were the stairs still there? How would they get out?

A sudden gust of wind blew the tattered curtain into the gloom as she made her way to where the window had been. The frame dangled beneath her at an odd angle. She called to Pauline, "Get your shoes on. Be careful; there's glass everywhere. Douglas, stay where you are, love."

Voices from below, "Are you all right?"

Men in the street looked up as Vickie looked down. She gasped. The house next door, the Clayton's, where she and Margi had spent many evenings with gin and tonic, was just a pile of bricks and rubble. Dust hung in the air like a pall over everything.

One

A Sunday afternoon. The living room was quiet except for the rhythmic click-click of my mother's knitting needles. Occasionally, she raised her head to focus her gaze intently upon my father as he sat at the dining room table reading the newspaper. I watched her frown when she suddenly stopped knitting. "Edward," she said, breaking the silence of the quiet afternoon, "Are you aware that the Yanks stationed on the park are making out with our local girls?"

"It is wartime, you know," my father said quietly. "Our boys would be the same if they were in a foreign country."

"Oh, you would say that, Edward, but I think they would be more respectful than these Yanks if they were away from home. What are they doing in the park, anyway?"

"The soldiers?" He turned the page of the newspaper, then ran his finger down the crease to hold it flat. "These *Yanks,* Vickie," he said, raising his eyebrows, are from the American 82nd Airborne division training to be parachuted into France. And you know," he hesitated for a minute, "you know, they may be giving up their lives for us even though it's not their war. Not all of them will come back."

Mother carried on as though she hadn't heard him, "Can you believe it? Sherry's daughter is expecting, and it won't be her husband's baby, I can assure you of that! Poor sod's been in France for over a year, but here *she* is, prancing around with a good-looking black man."

Edward said, "I'd rather you didn't talk like that about the soldiers, Vickie. I know most people around here have not seen a black person before, but they are good men. They work hard for us, and if you talked to them, you would agree they are an asset to us, regardless of color. They are good chaps." He folded his newspaper, pushed his chair back, and walked to the window smoothing his neat mustache. "I guess winter is here at last," he said. "The last leaf is finally gone from on the Malus Baccata."

Mother resumed her knitting, "You're not listening, Edward."

"Ah, yes. I see the lawn has a lot of Trifolium again. Best get that out."

Mother sighed, "Some of us didn't learn Latin, you know."

My father glanced at me and winked. At six years old, I had learned to listen and watch all that went on in my family. Even as a child, I was conscious of the atmosphere in the house. And, although I didn't know it then, I found out — when I was an adult — that to see colors around people, was unusual. The auras of my family were evident to me. I thought everyone saw what I did. Mother's aura was often deep purple or red. My fathers were always pale, compared to hers, which probably showed a great deal about the disturbance of her mind.

When a sudden chill swept through the room, Mother paused her knitting again. "Feel that?" she said, "It must be our Lennard."

My father turned to look at her, "Vickie, stop that. Your brother died at Dunkirk."

"Well, you don't need to remind me of when he died, but he still visits me."

My father raised his eyebrows and looked at me, "It's all right, love," he said.

Maybe he thought I would be afraid of her words, but I knew my mother often talked to herself, or someone who wasn't there. I didn't think it was strange. I'd never known her to be otherwise.

The grandfather clock in the hall suddenly gave its usual prestrike clunk before four heavy strikes on the bell. It wasn't a melodious bell, like our wall clock in the living room with Westminster Chimes, but, as my father explained, it was an ancient grandfather clock with lead weights and a bicycle bell that had replaced the original one.

Mother glanced at the clock on the wall, rolled up her knitting and pushed it into the cloth bag by her side. "I wonder where our Pauline is," she said. "I bet she's in the park, and it'll be getting dark soon."

Father turned from the window and walked to the fireplace to poke at some coals, which spurted green and blue flames. "She's almost fifteen," he said. "She knows where she lives."

Mother sighed and glanced at me, "Oh, Amelia, there you are." It seemed to me that she had forgotten I was there. "Can you go outside to see if you can find our Pauline? Tell her to come in."

I stood on tiptoe to the turn the knob on the front door. Pauline was just about to knock. She rushed by me into the living room. "Guess what?" she said, her face all aglow, "I've been to the park with Nancy, and one of the Yanks gave me some chewing gum."

Mother frowned, "Now, you just spit that nasty stuff out. Right now. Chewing gum indeed! I want you to stay away from those men. Is that clear?"

Pauline shrugged, "Mum, they're nice to us."

"Just stay away from them. There's plenty of other places in that park for you to play. Now, why don't you go and feed the chickens before it gets too dark?"

Our two chickens were in a wire pen at the very bottom of the garden. Chickens were only allowed during the war in a suburb of a city, and only then if there were enough scraps from the dinner table. The rooster was Ike, named after General Eisenhower; a brown hen was M, his driver. Next to the pen was my father's workshop, a favorite place for me to hang out. The smell of the sawdust and the little pieces of curled wood on the floor enchanted me. Among the tools that were arranged neatly on the walls were some bits and pieces from an American pilot who flew the B-17's at the aerodrome where my father worked. He had arrived home with a leather jacket for himself and a pair of nylon stockings for my mother. She was furious, "You just give them back. Damn Yanks."

My father said sharply, "You do realize that Britain is low on funds for armaments? The Americans are helping with that; they are here for us."

"Yes, but you know as well as I do, they would *not* have joined us if it hadn't been for Pearl Harbor."

"Regardless of that, Vickie, we have to be strong and get through this war."

"Just like the Claytons next door? We could be next, you know."

My sister, Pauline, knew everything. She told me it was a miracle we'd survived that bomb because the same wall joined the two houses. One half of the house was completely gone, the other half where we lived remained intact, although there was a lot of plaster that dropped off the wall in the bedroom.

✻✻✻

The windows of our house were streaked with tape, yellow and brittle from the sun, making it impossible for us to see out, but assuring us we would not be killed by flying glass should a bomb be

4

dropped nearby. In the narrow hall, raincoats and umbrellas shared the same hook with the gas masks, which were always carried when we left the house. A reminder that German warfare could include gas bombs. There were ration books and flashlights on a small mahogany table by a door that led into the living room, and despite the bright coal fire, dampness pervaded the room from the clean laundry hanging on a clothes horse in front of the fireplace. Heavy curtains lined with black made the room gloomy even on a sunny day.

In the backyard, there was a concrete dug-out six feet deep covered with corrugated tin, an Anderson Shelter, my father said. But we hadn't used it since Pauline's pet rabbit got out of its cage and drowned in the foot of water. Then Mother declared she would rather die from a bomb than from pneumonia.

It was evident by 1944; the war was changing the landscape, the attitudes, and the hopes of the British people. Fear of the Germans landing on British soil was on everyone's mind, according to the newspapers. Articles relating to the precautions that were being put into effect to prevent the Germans from landing became a frequent topic. One morning at breakfast, my father announced that since it was inevitable that Hitler would invade England, he had a plan that needed to be discussed after tea that night.

I was sent to bed early, but I crept out of bed and sat on the third step from the bottom, where I could see my father standing behind his chair at the dining room table holding court. He announced dramatically, "I've purchased a handgun from one of the pilots at the airfield." Pauline shrank back when he laid the gun on the table. He looked at her and then at Mother, "No need to be afraid of the gun; it won't go off on its own. But this is very serious. We shall not be captured. I will take care of everything. You cannot ever be in harm's way as long as you are under my roof."

Pauline's lips began to quiver. Mother looked at her, then at my father. "Edward," she said, "Mr. Churchill said we —?"

"I know what Churchill is saying, but we're not winning yet. Everybody is talking about Operation Sea Lion. The barbed wire on the beaches and the mines, just in case Hitler comes? Yes, and let's not forget the piers that were demolished in Eastbourne and Brighton. Why would they do that if they didn't expect the Germans to try and land here? You should try reading the newspaper sometimes, Vickie." He went on and on about Russia and how Hitler was concentrating on that country. "But wait," he said, "just wait, he'll try to get here, but he won't get to us." He looked at Pauline, who was dabbing her eyes with her handkerchief.

She said quietly, "Why would the man come to our house?"

Father stared at her before a frown creased his brow, "What? Not here to this house, Pauline, *to this country*. This man, Hitler, is a maniac. He invades countries, so he can gain control and make every one German. When he took France, they had to fight for survival. His tanks and armies can go from city to city in every country on the Continent." After a moment's pause, he smiled and looked at everyone over the top of his glasses. His voice shook with emotion, "The problem for Hitler is you see; he's got the English Channel to deal with! So far, he's got his air power and he's done his best to bomb us out of existence. If it was not for the fact that we are an island, we'd be in trouble, but he wants England badly, and he's going to try to land here, make no mistake." He hesitated for a minute before looking directly at Vickie, "You have to be brave now. Remember what I'm telling you. I am going to put this gun into the bookcase for safekeeping. You cannot touch it." He waited for her reaction. She just looked at him with a blank stare. He turned to Pauline, "Listen, love; this gun is not to be played with. I'm putting it here, see?" He walked over to one of the bookcases, lifted the glass door, and placed the gun on top of a row of books on the very top shelf.

I didn't understand why having a gun in the house would help if this man, Hitler, came to England. It was much later I learned my father intended to kill us all, rather than be ruled by such an evil man, or live under his regime.

Soon the gun was forgotten, or so I thought, except I caught Mother taking it from its hiding place once. She held it for a moment, inspecting it carefully. I couldn't understand why she would go against Father's instructions.

When a neighbor came to the house one morning to ask if Mother would like to work at the munitions factory downtown, sewing parachutes, Mother shook her head, "Oh, I couldn't be responsible for the life of an airman."

"No, you'd be sewing. You know, the seams in the chutes. You wouldn't be expected to fold and pack them. That's done by military personnel, and there's always someone to check our sewing. Quality control takes care of things like that." She ended the conversation by saying, "You're good at sewing. Please come. We need you. You can sit next to me."

Mother nodded, "I'll give it a try."

One morning at the factory, when the air-raid sirens began and then ramped up to their crescendo, all the women ran from the room to the shelters down below, except my mother. She didn't move. After the all-clear, she was found curled up in a parachute, under the table where she worked, in total shock, struck dumb and seemingly deaf.

For weeks after, she sat in her chair by the fire mumbling to herself. I often saw her close her eyes and put her hands over her ears as though blocking out noise from somewhere. Once, she shouted, "If you don't come in now, the nine o'clock horses will get you."

I was the only one in the room with her, but I didn't dare ask her what she meant. I was afraid of her answer because she looked so frightened when she said it. The color around her was grey-black. I had become quite used to colors around people that indicated whatever their state of mind was at that time. I mentioned the color to Pauline, who frowned and said, "What colors are you talking about, Amelia?

"She's so sad," I said. "All that darkness around her."

Pauline looked at me in a strange way, "Mother is just not well, that's all."

One evening after dinner, when my father was out with the Home Guard on the park operating the anti-aircraft guns and the searchlights, Pauline asked Mother, "Why did you stay behind, Mum?"

She answered quietly, "It was my turn to die."

My sister's eyes grew wide. She opened her mouth to speak, but nothing came out. She grabbed my hand, and we both fled upstairs to our bedroom. Pauline wouldn't talk to me. She just sat and bawled. I didn't know those words my mother had uttered would be installed in my brain to re-emerge many times during my life.

That night I had a dream. I am my mother, tall and slim with dark hair and blue eyes. In the dream, I am sitting at a sewing machine, the silk slippery beneath my fingers. Then, above the noise of dozens of sewing machines, the sirens start-up low, winding up, rising in pitch, until there is a long wail of warning, just as she had said. I knew everything she'd felt and done because she'd told us so many times about it.

I stand up, ready to run out of the room with the other women, but I can't move a muscle. I'm rooted to the spot. Then I hear another sound besides the siren. The noise is coming from outside, and I look down at the courtyard below to see the apple tree from our garden. A man stands by the tree with an ax in his hands. He hauls it back almost over his head, ready to swing at the tree. "Oh, no," I cry out, "Don't cut the tree down!" I'm banging on the glass. "Oh, please, please don't cut the tree."

The man hits the tree again and again. Petals swirl up in the air and float softly to the ground. I open the window just in time to hear a sound like a crack of thunder as the tree falls. A flurry of pink and white petals cascade past the window like snow, and I reach out for a petal. When I look closely, it is not a petal, but a feather from one of our chickens.

As I'm looking at the feather in my hand, I feel someone shaking me. Pauline is pulling the sheets away from me. Her eyes are wide. "Didn't you hear it, the gun?" She's shouting now, "Amelia, get up. Get up. I can't leave you here with Mum. She's got the gun. She's gone barmy."

Two

Pauline hustled me down the stairs. She didn't look in the living room or say a word to me as we left the house and walked quickly down the dark street. There were no street lights for fear of alerting enemy planes to our existence. Pauline's torch shed a low light on the path ahead of us.

"Where are we going?" I asked, running beside her to keep up.

"To Nancy's. Her mother will let us stay the night."

Nancy's mother made us comfortable with some blankets on the floor of the living room. Pauline started to explain things, but she couldn't continue because she was sobbing so much and could hardly get her breath. Nancy's mother put an arm around her. "Shush. Don't cry," she said gently. "It's going to be all right. Just keep this to yourselves. It wouldn't do for all the neighbors to hear about the gun. Guns are illegal, you know. Of course, the men in the Home Guard are allowed a few between them."

I worried all through the night, and I was scared when we went back home the next morning. Father opened the door. He didn't say anything as Pauline went upstairs to change for work. After a minute, he knelt beside me. "It's all right, love," he said. "Your mum has had a nasty turn. She'll be okay in a day or two. Off you go to school now." He reached up to the hook on the clothes-stand, retrieved the gas mask in the small box, and made sure the strap was snug on my shoulder, "There. All set?" He smiled, "All right, then?"

When I got home from school, I expected Mother to be in bed, but she was making tea and had already made a cake. She was always so smart with managing to swap eggs for butter or sugar; with rationing on, it wasn't easy to find the things we'd always had. I missed the ice-cream and the oranges. My parents had often remarked it would be good to have meat once in a while. We had fish a lot and chicken sometimes. My father said that we might have to eat one of our chickens but keep the rooster. Mother said, "Over my dead body. I need the eggs to swap for other stuff." I think my father was joking because he liked chickens.

Pauline asked my father why there wasn't much food in the shops. He said it was because the Germans were sinking the ships that brought food and goods from Europe. It was their idea of starving us so we wouldn't win the war. I didn't understand that at the time, but apparently, Hitler had his U-boats all around Britain, preventing all the imported goods we needed from reaching us.

The gun episode wasn't mentioned in the house, but one day, when I was sitting in the living room sewing a dress for my doll, I happened to glance up at the small round hole in the ceiling and the plaster around it like a spider's web. Mother followed my gaze and gasped. She cried out, "Oh God. What did I do?" She ran from the room, out through the kitchen into the back yard. I hurried to the window to watch her stand by the entrance to the air-raid shelter. For a minute, I thought she was going in it, but instead, she fumbled for her Will's Woodbine and matches in her apron pocket. When she tried to light the cigarette, her fingers shook so much she gave up and threw the match and the cigarette on the ground.

I couldn't bear to see her like that. Her aura was purple and red. She was afraid, I knew. I went out, took her hand, and led her back into the house. She didn't say a word, but she did hold tight to my hand.

I thought a lot about my mother's reaction when she looked at the hole in the ceiling, and when Pauline came up to bed, I told her about it. She shook her head, turned away, and buried her head in her pillow.

"Pauline?"

"What's the matter now?"

"I can't stop thinking about the gun."

"Well, stop thinking about it. It's over."

"But we were told not to touch it. Why do you think Mother did?"

Pauline sat up and hugged her knees. "She wanted to kill herself," she whispered.

"Kill herself? Why would she do that?"

"I don't know. How should I know?"

Then I noticed her red, puffy eyes and tears glistening on her cheeks.

I said, "I know what it is. She doesn't like us anymore."

"Don't be daft. That's not it." Pauline pulled her handkerchief from under her pillow and blew her nose. "Amelia, our mum loves you and me. She stood in line for hours at the downtown shop at Christmas to buy your best doll. Nobody's manufactured toys since the war started. Dolls are hard to find. She spent hours sewing clothes for it when you were in bed. She needn't have done that you know. Anyway, she misses our Doug."

"Why did *he* have to go away?"

"Lots of kids have been evacuated. The twins from down the street went to live somewhere in the country, out of harm's way."

"Why can't we go, then?"

Pauline shrugged, "It's the government's idea. It's called Operation Pied Piper. They send some kids away depending on their age, I think. You're too young, and I'm too useful around the house and looking after you."

"I hope Douglas is safe," I said.

"Yes. I bet he misses us, just as much as we miss him. Now go to sleep."

Three

It was a blustery evening in November. The wind whipped the branches of the Hawthorne against the window like chalk on a blackboard. Father was out with the Home Guard as usual, and Pauline was at night school, so Mother and I were alone. When the side gate suddenly slammed shut, opened and slammed shut again, she turned up the radio until it boomed through the room. A voice interrupted the classical music hour from the Palm Court Orchestra, "Germany Calling. Germany Calling." A British spy who called himself Lord Haw-Haw was the educated voice the Germans used nightly. Mother listened to every word. The man made it very clear that Britain was being wiped out. Aircraft were shot out of the sky. British ships were being sunk, and casualties were rising. The whole program was intended to deflate the resolve of the British people, to fill them with the news that would lower their morale. The ploy worked with my mother. When she turned off the radio, she said, "If we're alive tomorrow, it'll be a miracle." She poured the last of the sherry into her glass. "You know," she said, "there's a quarter of a million people homeless now in London, we'll be next or dead."

When the side gate to the backyard slammed shut again, she turned to me, "Oh, for God's sake, Amelia, go outside and latch that damn gate, will you?"

I stood on the stool in the hall to reach my woolen coat hanging on the coat stand. It was Pauline's old coat that had a hole at the elbow which had been darned over and over. I hated the feel of the rough wool, anything harsh against my skin. I still do.

As I closed the front door behind me, I looked around the garden that was illuminated by moonlight so bright I could see the bushes and trees. It was a full moon, stars bright and brittle in the night sky; glittering pinpoints of light, a phenomenon rarely seen in the industrial smog-filled city of Leicester. Only when there was a strong wind could we see the stars. The air around Leicester was always smoky with the mix of ground-fog that left smudges of black on the Monday morning lines of washing.

I heard the crunch of gravel on the path and turned to see Mr. Johnson, the Irish Night Warden.

"Is that you, Amelia?"

"Yes, I'm trying to get this gate to stay closed."

"Your dad needs to fix this," he said. "The latch is bust. Let's see if we can wedge it shut for now with something." He picked up a large rock from the rockery. "That should do it. By the way, there's a chink of light coming from the front bedroom window. Gotta keep the blackout curtains closed tight, all right? We don't want those Gerry planes to see us, do we now?"

I said, "They're going to kill us, aren't they?"

"What? What's that?" Mr. Johnson squatted down and pulled me to him, "And where on earth would you get that notion?"

"Mother said."

"Well, Miss Amelia, you get it out of your head right now. You're safe with me around. Always will be, and don't you forget it."

"Thank you for helping with the gate."

"It's all right, lass. How is your Ma doing? Your sister? Have you heard from your brother?"

"Pauline is at night-school tonight; she's taking typing lessons. We haven't heard from Douglas." I didn't mention Mother.

Suddenly, there was a hum in the air like a swarm of bees. The humming grew louder and louder until the air was vibrating with the drone of engines above us. Mr. Johnson straightened. We looked up. The sky was black, with hundreds of planes moving steadily overhead, droning on and on for a long time. He took off his hat as he looked heavenwards, "They're ours. Thank God, they're ours. Look at 'em all. Poor buggers. I wonder how many of them will come home." He raised his hands to his mouth and yelled into the night, "God Speed, lads. God Speed."

We both stood looking up at the waves of bombers that filled the sky, droning on and on. "Are they all going to Germany?" I asked.

"Oh, yes. But, tonight, well, the poor blighters in Hamburg or Berlin won't get much sleep with that lot."

"Why did they go out tonight? Everybody can see them. It's so bright, like the day."

"Aye, lass," he said, his voice slightly hushed. "Aye, it's a bomber's moon, all right. A bomber's moon." Mr. Johnson walked away, still gazing upward as the sound faded away into the distance.

I looked around again at the moonlit garden, and since the next-door house was now just a pile of rubble, I had a clear view of the street and the front door of Mrs. Mansfield's house. I always remember her as the blonde-haired lady who always wore very red lipstick. The door opened, and I saw the familiar figure of a man step out of the house. I stood there transfixed as he put his arms around the woman and hugged her. Just the way he moved was enough to tell me it was my father. I wanted to run away and hide. How could he do that? I watched him walk to the gate, turn, and wave. Then, to my horror, Mrs. Mansfield ran to him and threw her arms around his neck. He kissed her on the lips! As I turned to go into the house, I looked up at the bedroom window, just in time to see the chink of light Mr. Johnson had mentioned suddenly disappear as the curtains were pulled together. My heart sank; could Mother possibly have witnessed the same scene? I fled into the house just as she was coming down the stairs. She walked past me and said nothing. But I could feel her anger, see it around her.

The tea was a silent affair, and as soon as we had finished our baked beans on toast, my mother set upon my father, "I saw you with that floozy," she yelled.

My father looked at her over the top of his glasses. "Vickie," he said quietly, "let's talk about this some other time, and it's not what you think, either."

"What is it then?" Her eyes were wild. "What trivial little tale are you going to drum up to cover your arse?"

He strode over to my mother and pushed her into her chair. "Listen carefully," he said, leaning over her. Christine Mansfield has just lost her son. She had a telegram today. You know I have always been a friend of hers and her husband before he went to the war. He's dead, and now Tony. She had to tell somebody. She asked me in. For God's sake, I was just comforting the poor woman. I hugged her. What's so wrong about that?"

Mother stared at him for a minute before she rose and pushed him out of the way. She went to the door, "I'm going to bed."

I wondered if she'd seen the kiss.

My father sat down at the table and opened the newspaper in front of him; then he pushed it away. He leaned his elbows on the table and held his head in his hands. I went to him and reached up to touch his cheek. I felt his warm tears on my hand. He looked down at me, then scooped me up to sit on his lap. We rocked back and forth. I buried my head against his shoulder, and I could smell the sweet aroma of Cherry Blend tobacco mixed with soap.

Four

Hamlin Road Infant School was at the very top of Overpark Avenue. I went there from 9:00 to 3:00 p.m. Daytime air raids seemed to be less now, but we knew the drill when we heard the sirens warning of bombers coming. The shelter was adjacent to the school building. It was a room built underground with benches along the walls. Shelves were equipped with extra gas masks and torches.

When we arrived, there was a slight tremor, but no explosion. The teacher told us to go home since lessons were over for the day. I ran down the street, my gas mask in its little box swinging from my shoulder. I was almost at my gate when I noticed several men in uniform on the park opposite. They were busy constructing a fence of some kind around what appeared to be a hole in the ground, although I couldn't see exactly. One of the men must have seen me looking because he came over the road to talk to me.

"You live here, m'dear?" he asked.

"Yes."

"See that circle where the fence is being put up?"

"Yes."

"Now, you don't you go nosing around it. That clear?"

"Why?"

"It's very dangerous. Just stay away. You understand?"

"Yes," I said, not really understanding. I kept turning around to see what was going on as I walked up the path to the front door. I knocked, expecting to hear Mother coming along the hall to open the door, but there was no sound. I knocked again, but there was silence. I decided she must be out because she wouldn't be expecting me home yet. I was earlier than usual.

I knew there was a key hanging on a nail behind the letterbox, but I wasn't tall enough to reach it, so after a minute or two, I walked back to the front gate to watch the men in the park and noticed Mrs. Mansfield was standing in her garden smoking a cigarette. She, too, was looking at the activities across the road. I decided she probably wouldn't mind pulling the key out for me so I could go into the house. I hadn't seen her since the bust-up between my parents. I still wondered why she and my father had seemed so friendly with each other. I could never have imagined him being with someone other than Mother, although I did think Mrs. Mansfield was pretty with her blonde hair and bright lipstick. I thought I might make my hair blonde when I grew up.

"Hello," I said, "What are the men doing in the park?"

"Oh, there's an unexploded bomb, but don't worry, pet, they'll get the experts in tomorrow and take care of it."

"Could it go off now?"

"Oh no, they have it all under control."

"Can you come and reach my door-key, please, it's behind the letterbox, but I can't reach it?"

"O'course."

We walked down the street, still looking at the men in the park, and before we reached the front door, Mrs. Mansfield threw her cigarette on the path and stepped on it, "Your mum out, is she?" she asked.

"I think so, or asleep."

Within a second or two, she had pulled the key on the piece of string through the letterbox and opened the door. "There you are, pet," she said. She hesitated before stepping quickly into the hall. "Goodness me, your mum has gone out and left the gas on; best we switch that off, eh?" She laughed. "Good job I didn't bring my fag in with me, we could have been blown sky-high with this much gas. Phew! Can you open some windows, pet, while I get to the kitchen?"

I could smell gas even in the living room, and then I heard her voice, "Oh! No! What the…oh, bloody hell."

I ran to the kitchen and saw Mother lying on the floor; her head was resting on the edge of the open door of the oven.

Mrs. Mansfield switched off the gas and knelt beside my mother. She sounded angry when she spoke. "Oh, for Christ's sake, what has she gone and done? Mrs. Mansfield was coughing, and she put her hand to her mouth, "Amelia," she managed, "get that back door wide open and get some wet towels. Right now."

I opened the door, then I picked up the tea towel from the rail by the sink, stood on tip-toe, and managed to reach the tap.

"That's it. Good." Mrs. Mansfield rose and turned toward the door. "Now, you get on your knees and wipe your mum's face," she said. "Don't stop. I'm going to my house to telephone for an ambulance."

"But Pauline will be home soon," I said. "Shouldn't we wait for her?"

"No. Best we get some help now."

I sat down beside Mother, wiped her face as instructed, not knowing what was happening. The smell of gas was still strong, and I thought she might be dead, but I could feel her breathing. After a few minutes, she opened her eyes wide. With a deep breath, she cried out, "They're here. The horses. I can hear them." Her breath came in ragged bursts. I wanted to run out of the room. Instead, I just sat there and cried. Mother held on to me and cried too.

Pauline came home just as the ambulance arrived outside the house. I told her how I had come back early because of the air-raid, and Mrs. Mansfield had come to open the front door and found Mother.

Pauline hugged me. She said, "Well, it looks like for once, Hitler saved a life. You wouldn't have come home if there hadn't been any sirens, would you? Then where would we be?"

"Without a Mum?"

"Yes. That's right."

Mother was taken away in the ambulance to the mental institute on the edge of town, *The Tower's Hospital*, referred to by local kids as the loony bin.

Five

My Aunt Dorothy and Uncle Walter Moore lived in the village of Foxby, seventeen miles from Leicester. I had visited them almost every month, usually as a passenger on my father's big motorbike, which I loved. Now I was sent to live with them. The village didn't have thatched cottages, crooked half-timbered houses, or golden stone cottages that are the quintessential essence of England. Only the Saxon church with the Norman arches gave any indication there must have been an historical past. The pond in the square was well scattered with ducks, and the small school, built of local grey stone, boasted a large playground surrounded by wrought iron railings. On Main Street, constructed snugly up against each other, were the shops: a newsagent, post office, hardware and general store, a bakery, and the ubiquitous fish and chip shop.

Small brick-built houses boasted pretty gardens and brightly painted front doors on the lane known as Cowcluss, where cows plodded up and down from Furnival's Farm to be milked twice a day at the bottom field. My Grandmother Louise and her spinster daughter, Olive, lived in the house next door to my Aunt's. The two houses, joined together, known as semi-detached, were in a prominent position at the very top of the lane where a wooden gate opened to a muddy, narrow footpath that meandered through a long stretch of rippled fields separated by Hawthorne hedges. The ridge and furrow fields around Foxby had been there, unchanged since horse-drawn plows tilled the land in the seventeen hundreds.

✳✳✳

The family, to which I now temporarily belonged, didn't have to worry about food rationing. They had their own cow; they made butter and cheese. Chickens roamed around the garden and left their eggs in strange and unlikely spots among the hedgerows.

My Aunt's house was much more beautiful than ours in Leicester. It was not a council house, and that was the difference. Council houses had sprung up in large estates during and after the war when thousands of people had been left homeless. The homes were then cheaply and hurriedly constructed with no moisture barrier. The outer walls in our house were often damp to the touch. Even the wallpaper in the living room on one wall had peeled off in places. My aunt's house was dry and warm with a kitchen where large hams hung on a rack to dry in front of a huge range, which was always kept lit.

My cousin Elise, or Ellie, as everyone called her, was two years older than me. At ten, she had a high opinion of herself, always taking charge to show me how things were done around the house and the garden. Uncle Walter Moore was a market-gardener. He had two enormous greenhouses at the very end of the village, one for exotic ferns and orchids, the other for seedlings and flowers which he used for bridal bouquets. Ellie knew the names of all the flowers.

24

She taught me how to disbud the rose bushes, so only one bud would remain to develop into a beautiful bloom.

Freesias were my favorite. When they were in bloom, I sat on one of the high stools to breathe in their heady perfume. The greenhouse exuded an aroma of promise, new growth, earthy, and clean, unfettered by the vagaries of the wartime existence in the city. In those rare moments of solitude, I thought about my brother, sister, and my father, but most often, my thoughts would turn to my mother. I was torn between a feeling of disappointment and abandonment. Young as I was, I wondered why she was so unhappy most of the time. Was it just the war, or were there some underlying events that would cause her to want to end her life? Or, was it the noises she could hear in her head?

The answers eluded me until I started to spend more time with my Grandmother Louise and Olive. Instead of the well-worn, comfortable soft furniture in my aunt and uncle's home, grandmother's house was elegantly furnished with beautiful antiques, upright chairs, and a sofa with carved wooden arms. Shelves of books lined the walls of the so-called library; a fire always burned brightly in the front room, and apart from the steady tick-tock of the grandfather clock in the corner of the living room, the whole place seemed hushed to me. Everything seemed to be always in place. One would never expect to see a wilted bloom among the artistically arranged flowers on the dining-room table. The silver tray on the sideboard with the glass decanter and two or three crystal glasses was always highly polished.

I soon learned why everything was so orderly. Ellie explained with great aplomb that Grandmother and Grandfather Norton had been in service at the Manor as maid and butler when they were young. Lord and Lady Kilby had imparted to them a genteel way of life they had followed all their married life.

I now believed this reverence for order, and gentility had rubbed off on my father. He was always Mr. Norton to the neighbors, never Edward, or heaven forbid…Ed. Of course, in those days, children did not call their elders by their first name. My father carried with him an air of authority with a mustache that curled up neatly at the ends, and he tended to look down his nose when speaking. I concluded that the aura of superiority he exuded was an irritant to my mother, causing her to belittle him when a discussion arose about his parents and her own, or if they had visitors for tea. Her sarcasm was rampant at times, especially after the second glass of sherry. Those situations were probably exacerbated by the fact that my father appeared to take it in his stride, looking at her over the top of his glasses and smiling in his condescending fashion. His use of Latin, which seemed to crop up quite often, usually ended up with some sarcastic remark from Mother suggesting he thought himself better than everyone else, and that he was a show-off with his Grammar School learning.

I was always aware of the interaction between my parents, and one incident depicted - to me anyway - my mother's disdain for my father. It was a Sunday lunchtime. Pauline had set the table with place-mats and freshly ironed linen serviettes. Mother brought the hot dishes of food from the kitchen and placed them on the larger mats already there. Everything was ready to serve.

Aunt Hilda, who wasn't really my aunt, was often with us for Sunday lunch. She was a friend of Mothers and had been for a very long time. It seemed to me she had a lot of influence over my mother with her remarks about my father and living in a council house of all things. Hilda had snuff in a tiny silver box. I'll never forget the smell.

Every Sunday, Yorkshire pudding was served as the first course with gravy. Since meat was not often on the menu, it was a treat to have a small roast; leg of lamb, or pork. Father would place one or two slices carefully on everyone's plate. It was ceremoniously carried out; everything was done in the right order with little conversation. On this occasion, Mother took it upon herself to help serve. I watched her as she placed a small portion on Hilda's plate, Doug's, Pauline's, and mine before taking a huge spoonful of mashed potatoes and slopping them on my father's plate, almost over the side. Her act was ferocious.

My father closed his eyes and winced as though he'd been struck. He looked at my mother just for a second before he rose from the table and left the room. Even as a little girl, I could feel his hurt. A blue color enveloped him. His sensitivity to all things crass left him speechless. But it was the look my mother gave to Hilda as she tucked into her meal that made me wonder what else she had up her sleeve to get a reaction like that from my father with Hilda's help.

Six

When I attended the local village school in Foxby, I felt like a fish out of water. Everyone called me a 'Townie.' Their accents were different from mine. I was a foreigner, even though I had lived in the city only seventeen miles away. Accents and dialects in England varied from town to town and village to village. The children might not have liked me much, but I decided the English teacher did. She often asked me to read aloud any poem I knew by heart, and since my father and I often read together, I remembered a lot of poetry. My favorite was *The Tyger* by William Blake. Everyone clapped, and I knew I had been accepted, sort of.

One afternoon, after school, a boy followed me up the lane kicking a stone along the street from side to side like a football. I remembered seeing him in the school playground, but I didn't know his name. When he caught up with me, he asked me why I was living with the Moores. I found out everyone knew the family because of the flower nursery. I told him I was visiting my aunt and uncle while my mother was in the hospital. When we got to the top of the lane, he opened the gate as wide as it would go. He smiled then waved to me before letting it close behind him with a loud thud. There was a rubber tire nailed to the gate, but the noise was enough to arouse the curiosity of my grandmother, who always checked on the comings and goings of the villagers. He laughed merrily when her face appeared at the window, then he waved again, turned, and ran fast along the path to his parent's farm by the bridge.

I was surprised when, one Saturday morning, he knocked on the front door and asked me if I'd like to go to the canal to watch the barges. I said, yes. Then I wondered what Aunt Dorothy would say. She had made it clear she did not want me to go to the canal; there had been reports of a child drowning recently.

She smiled when she came to the door, "Well, look who it is! Colin Hadley. How is your mother?"

"She's fine, thank you."

She invited him in, and I watched him as he drank a glass of orange squash and ate three chocolate biscuits. He seemed so polite, and I could tell by the way my aunt talked to him she liked him.

I'd never been out with a boy before. It was a strange feeling. We ran through the field, up to one ridge and down the other, Colin leading the way. When we got to the Hawthorne hedge that separated the ridged field from the meadow, I noticed the soft dirty sheep's wool clinging to the thorny growth. I decided it would be perfect for stuffing the pincushion I was making for my mother for Christmas.

The canal, referred to by the locals as 'the Cut,' was built to transport coal from Newcastle to the factories in Leicester, Birmingham, and Coventry. The waterway cut through the heart of the English countryside, and barges plied the still waters every day pulled by horses along the towpath. The first time I saw a barge coming along led by a horse, I was fascinated. When they reached the bridge, the horse was unhooked from the line attached to the barge. The horse was led over the bridge to the towpath on the other side of the canal and re-hooked to the barge. I wondered what would happen when they got to the tunnel. I asked Colin. He said he didn't know, so I asked my uncle that evening. He said the horse would be led over the top of the tunnel by one of the men, and the other men on the barge would lie on top of the roof of the barge and push along with their feet. It was hard for me to imagine that, but apparently, there was no other way it could be done.

Horse and barge remained an efficient way to haul bulk cargo from coal to cast iron between cities and villages in the Midlands of England well into the 1950s.

✳✳✳

I had been living in Foxby for a year. Phone calls from Pauline and my father were vague about my mother. "She's getting better," or "She's okay, having some treatment or other," was their usual response to my questions.

Sitting with my cousin one morning after a breakfast of fried bread, bacon, and egg, my aunt called to me from the hall, "Amelia, dear, there's a phone call from your sister."

I hurried to the telephone, "Hello."

"Hello, love. How are you?"

"I'm all right."

"My new boyfriend has *a car,*" Pauline said, emphasizing the word, *car*. "He and I are going to the hospital to see Mum. Do you want to go with us?"

At that moment I wasn't quite sure. I had hidden those terrible memories of the time I had found her in our gas-filled house. It was another world away, somewhere on an alien planet, nightmarish, a place I did not want to be.

Pauline's voice interrupted my hesitation, "Well? Do you want to come or not? Richard said he didn't mind driving to Foxby to pick you up. He's really nice."

At sixteen, my sister had had several boyfriends. None of them had a car, but Richard was nineteen and was used to driving a company car before buying his own. It was a big deal to have an automobile.

"So? You coming, Amelia?"

"Oh, all right then."

"We'll pick you up around two," Pauline said firmly. "Be ready, will you, because they don't allow visitors after five."

It was the smell of the place that made me shudder. Strange sounds came from closed doors along the corridors that were painted a sickly green known as Eau-de-Nile, the water of the Nile.

I reached for Pauline's hand, and we walked into a room where upright wooden chairs were arranged in a large circle. No one was sitting in the ring. A few women in armchairs sat around the perimeter of the room. It was in one of these chairs that my mother sat staring into space, and I could feel my heart race as we went to her.

My sister kissed her cheek. Mother smiled up at her. "Hello," she said softly. "How nice of you to come."

She didn't smell like my mother anymore when I reached to hug her. Her eyes were almost black, not the lovely blue I remembered. When I stared at her for a moment too long, Pauline gave me a nudge and motioned for me to sit down.

"So, how have you been?" my sister queried, as she settled herself into a chair next to my mother.

Mother nodded, "Fine, fine. They've got me on something."

"Medicine?"

"Yes. So, where's this new boyfriend you mentioned?"

"They only allow family."

"Oh."

My sister leaned forward, "What are they giving you? What is happening? Are you feeling better?"

"Electric shock treatment and hypnotism, that's what they do here. Electric shock treatment and hypnotism. Try to make you remember things."

"And do you?"

"Well, I told them about the nine o'clock horses."

Pauline looked at me and raised her eyebrows.

She turned back to Mother, "What horses?"

I remembered the times she had spoken about the horses when she thought I wasn't listening, but I didn't say anything at that moment because suddenly, a vacant look came over her face. "I was little, and I saw them coming," she said dreamily. "I heard the bell. I should have gone home. Then the men with the horses and the drays came with all the big bins. One grabbed me...."

Her hands dropped to her side, and she closed her eyes.

"Mum," Pauline said, shaking my mother and rousing her, "Mum."

Mother's voice suddenly rose, "They were always there ready to get me. I should have listened."

I started to cry. The room was dark, sinister, horrifying to me, sitting there with this woman who seemed to be in a world of her own. She wasn't my mother. What had they done to her? I said, "I want to go home, Pauline. Let's go; please let's go."

Mother looked at me, her glare hostile. She wasn't asleep now. "You go, go back to your father, and that fancy women he has. You and him, you're just alike."

As I was running from the room, I heard my sister say, "For goodness sake, she's just a kid. She's staying with Aunt Dorothy and Uncle Walter now."

I waited at the door, wondering if my mother would answer. She did.

"Well, isn't that a surprise! Of course, she's with his precious relatives. Edward wanted me to live in that village, you know. Did you know that? I wouldn't mix with that lot. They all laughed at me when I went to see them for the first time, me in my lovely dress and high heels. I wasn't a country girl. I wouldn't want to be among that cow-shit."

My sister fled from the room, and then we were running down the green corridor and out into the late afternoon sunshine to Richard sitting in his car reading a newspaper. We sat silently on the way back to Foxby. I thought about the nine o'clock horses. Pauline said she had no idea what she was talking about.

I was beginning to understand my mother's fears of hearing things in her head, but not the reason she seemed to dislike me. I was to find out much later.

One Saturday morning, Ellie came with me to the bridge to meet Colin. When we saw a family of ducks paddling around, Colin and Ellie recited together the rhyme from *Wind in the Willows: "All along the backwater, Through the rushes, tall, ducks are dabbling, up tails all."* They had read the same book to read in school. Colin said, "Kenneth Graham wrote that."

A rare variety of yellow long-stemmed primrose grew in the meadow by the farm: Cowslips. Colin would often help me to pick a few blooms to take back to my aunt or his mother. But the day Ellie went with me to the field, I noticed that Colin opted to sit on a bank to watch us. I wondered if he believed Ellie would think him less of him if he picked flowers. Did it matter to him what she thought? At that moment, I felt a pang of jealousy and decided he liked her more than me.

When I asked Ellie if she liked Colin, she said, "He's all right." Her lack of enthusiasm when she said his name led me to believe that Ellie thought herself far too high and mighty to be associated with a farm boy. But, she included me in most of her activities, and for that, I was grateful, even though I knew it was because she felt sorry for me. It was apparent she thought I was of a lesser breed being from the city, a Townie, and especially with a mother who was a bit daft in the head. Aunt Dorothy was wonderful, as was Uncle Walter. I loved them both. I learned what it was like to be in a household where laughter and love exist between husband and wife. I wanted to be part of that always, and when my father called my aunt to say he was coming to pick me up because Mother was home, I ran to the bridge and wept. I wondered if I would ever live in such a lovely place again.

Colin came to the house to see me off, and just as I was getting into my father's car, the first one he'd ever owned, Colin handed me a book, *Wildflowers of England*. In between a folded sheet of paper in the middle was a pressed cowslip. It was dry and flat, but it had retained most of its color. Colin waved as we sped away.

I knew then I loved him.

Seven

The war was over. It seemed that life should have resumed as it was before, but rationing was still on; debris from bombed-out houses and factories were constant reminders of the death and destruction that had affected our lives for six years. Sadly, there was no money to rebuild. It was years before the ruined buildings were cleared away to make room for modern factories and homes.

For me, after living in a village where the air was full of the soft sound of sheep, I was not prepared for life in the suburbs of a busy city. Even though the park opposite was green and open, I missed the long walks we used to take through the grassy meadows and fields of Foxby. Sadness and fear overwhelmed me. Would I be trapped in the city with my parents and their rivalry, never to escape to the quietness of the village I had grown to love?

My mother had adjusted to what I imagine was her role before the war. There was no mention of her attempt to commit suicide. My father said we should never talk about it, so we didn't. She'd begun to play the piano again, and it wasn't until she reached the problematic part of Beethoven's *Für Elise* and hit the wrong notes, that she was upset beyond all reason. At those times, she would squint at the music, throw her hands in the air, then slam the lid of the piano down with such force the keyboard would vibrate. If she wanted our attention, she got it. She would march out of the living room, through the kitchen to the back door and out into the garden. Sometimes I wondered what she was thinking when she stood for several minutes beside the cedar tree with a cigarette burning in her fingers. I remembered the day I had gone out to her and held her hand. This time I just watched her stroll casually through the garden, round and round to inspect every flower.

Before marrying my father, she had been employed by a clothing manufacturing company making sample garments for their sales department. The samples, of course, had to be perfect for potential buyers, and she was considered one of the best sample-hands in the company. Now, the corner of our living room overflowed with her sewing equipment. She loved making wedding attire, and it wasn't unusual to find a half-finished wedding dress hanging from the picture rail. Pieces of the thread found their way into every part of the house and on to everyone's clothes. Pauline complained that it would be nice to leave for work without white thread clinging to her black skirt.

My sister and I still shared a bedroom, and one early morning as I watched the play of the dawn light casting shadows on the floral wallpaper, she rose from the bed next to me and went to the open window. Snapping it shut, she said, "I can't understand why we have to keep the window open when it's so damn cold."

Since the only source of heat came from the coal fire downstairs, little warmth ever permeated the upstairs bedrooms.

Pauline stared out of the window. "Look at that," she said, her nose pressed to the glass. "There are hills out there somewhere behind all that smoke. Richard and I can't wait to get away from this place."

"Away. Where? Where would you go?"

"Well, I wasn't supposed to say anything, but I can tell *you*," she said. "You know that Richard has worked for Singer Sewing Machines since he left school. He's such a good mechanic, and he's a good manager. They have asked him if he would go to Africa to open a factory there. I shall go with him."

"Africa? Isn't that a long way away?"

"Oh, yes. Let me show you where it is." She reached up to the top shelf of the wardrobe and took down a rolled map. Spreading it out on her bed, she said, "See, this is Lagos, in Nigeria. It will be exciting, a new start away from this place."

"You mean you'll go away and leave us forever?"

"I'll come back sometimes. The climate is too hot for white people to live there for long without coming back to England for a few months. Anyway," she said, as she rolled up the map, "you should think about leaving when you get older, this place is no good for anyone. I mean, look outside. The air is very unhealthy. Patricia Fleming and her sister down the street had T.B."

She reached up to put the map away. I suddenly felt afraid. What would I do without her? She was my friend, my confidant. It was then I realized my only true friend beside Pauline, was Colin. I saw him almost every weekend, although my parents never approved of me traveling alone on the bus to Foxby. I liked it because it stopped at the village square in Glenford for ten minutes, giving me time to explore and buy an orange drink at the village post office across the road.

Pauline and I were on our way downstairs, dressed and ready for breakfast, when the doorbell rang. My father opened the door to find Mr. Johnson on the step, accompanied by a tall, good-looking young man in a peaked cap and rough work clothes. Mr. Johnson shook my father's hand. "Edward," he said, "this German chap is going to clear away your bomb shelter. He's a good lad, won't be any trouble. He's decided to stay on over here."

"Is he legal?" Father asked, looking closely at the young man.

"He wants to be, and we need good chaps to help us clean up. We lost too many of our boys over there. We won this blasted war. Don't forget that."

My father went out and led the way down the side of the house to the backyard. I heard him telling Mr. Johnson he'd already cleared away most of the earth above the corrugated tin roof of the shelter.

Pauline and I hurried to the kitchen window to watch the foreigner. She was looking over my shoulder. "I don't know why we should have a German in our yard," she said. "You never know what they might be up to. I hate them."

I watched the young man take off his jacket and look around the yard. "He doesn't look like a bad person," I said.

Mr. Johnson waved his arms about and pointed to all the tools lying nearby. The German seemed to know what the man was saying because he looked at the shelter, walked around it thoughtfully, and then picked up a large metal bar. He stood for a moment, as though deciding how to tackle the job of prying the roof away from the concrete that lined the six-foot-deep hole.

My sister turned away from the window, "The Germans are wicked. Look what they did next door. They killed thousands of innocent people everywhere in Britain."

Just then, my father came into the kitchen. He had overheard what my sister had said, "Now don't you go on like that, Pauline. The war has ended. It's all over and done with. We killed a lot of Germans too, don't forget that. It was just as bad for—"

He was interrupted by an ear-splitting screech from the backyard. A cacophonous din echoed through the neighborhood. The horrible sound of scraped metal set my teeth on edge.

"Oh, blimey," my father said, making for the back door. "After the last bomb dropped, the chickens didn't lay for a week. God knows, if he keeps that up, we'll be out of eggs for months."

We looked at the hen house. Chickens were flying around the pen. Feathers flew.

My sister suddenly giggled as my father stomped back into the yard, "How does he expect the bloke to pull the thing down without making any noise?"

We watched him as he waved his hands in the direction of the henhouse. We couldn't hear what he said, but the man looked at the chickens, looked back to my father, and shrugged.

Pauline laughed, "Oh gosh, that's funny, that is. Poor dad."

My father came in swearing under his breath, "He didn't understand a bloody word about the chickens." When he saw my sister's face, he grinned. "I know," he said. "How can he do it without making a racket?" He sat down at the table and stared out the window. "I bet he's only a bit older than you, Pauline, eighteen maybe, in a strange country, on his own. Perhaps we should offer him a cup of tea."

My mother appeared at the door. "Let's not go that far," she said. "We should leave well enough alone. Forget the damn chickens."

Her tone of voice alerted us to the fact that something had upset her. We tiptoed out of the kitchen and Pauline put her finger to her lips, "Something's up with her, so don't say a word."

When I returned home from school that afternoon, it was raining. It was usually my task when I got home to check for eggs. I went out into the back-yard and stopped to watch the young man swinging wildly at the corrugated tin of the roof. The noise was deafening. I noticed chicken feathers stuck to the wire fence of the henhouse, and I wondered if the poor things were still alive.

The young man stopped in mid-swing when he saw me. He nodded, "Guten tag."

His face, shiny with rain, was the most handsome I had ever seen. Blonde curly hair stuck out from under the front of his cap.

I walked over to him, sloshing through the mud. "It's too wet for you to be out here," I said.

"I have a good raincoat, ya?" He smiled down at me.

When Pauline found me in the backyard still talking to the German, she marched over to me. "Amelia, you come in right now. You shouldn't be fraternizing with the likes of him." I think she emphasized the word *fraternizing* because she knew it sounded grown-up.

The man looked at her, let the hammer fall to the ground, picked up his jacket and walked out of the yard.

"That wasn't very nice, Pauline," I said. "Fritz is lovely."

"Oh, it's Fritz, is it? It didn't take you long to get acquainted."

She went back into the house, leaving me standing in the rain. As I started for the door, I spotted something shining among the debris on the ground. It was a man's watch with a broken leather strap.

I took it upstairs into my bedroom and hid it in the drawer of my bedside table. That night, I took it out of the drawer. I was trying to read the inscription on the back when Pauline came into the room. She looked at the watch, "Whose is that?" she asked.

It belongs to Fritz. The strap broke, so he dropped it."

"Let me look." She took the watch and turned it over, "It says Fritz, and I know Mütti and Vati. That's mother and father."

"Ah, then I shall give it back to him tomorrow."

"Why would you do that? Finders keepers."

"No. If it was a present from his mum and dad, I'm giving it back to him."

The next day was Saturday. The sky was dark with black clouds that threatened rain again. My father said the German boy would not be here until the mud dried up a bit, but when I looked out the window, Fritz was there searching the ground. I ran upstairs to retrieve the watch. When I went back downstairs, Pauline was at the kitchen window. She said, "He's looking for that watch. Are you going to give it back?"

"Of course."

"I'll give it to him," she said, snatching it from my hands. She marched outside, and I saw him smile as she approached. He took off his cap and nodded to her. Pauline handed him the watch, and to my horror, I heard her shout, "I hate Krauts."

The young man stared at her for a moment. His face turned bright red as he put the watch in his pocket. Then he put his cap back on and headed for the gate. My sister turned quickly and ran back into the house. "That told him," she said.

I couldn't believe my sister. I wanted to rush outside and apologize for the words she had uttered. Then I noticed her lips were trembling. She looked at me and was suddenly weeping. "He's so beautiful when he smiles," she said. "He's got such lovely blue eyes. How could I have said that? What will I do?"

"Why don't you tell him you're sorry?"

"I can't."

"I'm going to tell him, and you can come with me."

For once, Pauline walked behind *me*. Fritz had already disappeared around the side of the house and was almost at the front garden gate. "Fritz," I yelled. "Wait. We are sorry, honestly."

He stopped, turned, stood to attention, smacked his heels together smartly, and saluted. "Heil Hitler," he said.

Pauline was sobbing, "I deserved that."

They stood quietly, looking at each other. I could tell my sister didn't know what to say. She was dabbing her eyes with a handkerchief.

I went to Fritz and took his hand. He held it tightly, and we both stood to look at her.

"The watch," she finally asked, "Was it a present from your parents?"

"Ya, Mütti and Vati, day are killed in Berlin."

I could see the horror on Pauline's face. I gripped Fritz's hand more tightly.

"I'm…I'm so sorry," she stammered. All at once, she thrust her hand out to him, and he let go of mine to grasp hers. He stepped forward, wiped a tear from Pauline's cheek, and pushed a curl back from her face. She took his hand and led him into the house. "Come on," she said. "Let's have some tea."

My parents were in the kitchen. They nodded to Fritz as my sister busied herself filling the kettle. Mother surprised me when she asked if he would like some cake.

"Danke," he said. He sat down, and we watched him quietly as he drank two cups of tea and ate three pieces of mother's freshly baked sponge cake. Then he was gone.

Pauline had a dreamy look on her face.

"You like him now, don't you?" I quipped.

"I don't know him, do I now, so what makes you think that?"

"Because he's better looking than Richard, isn't he?"

"No, I wouldn't say that; he's just different."

My father was looking at Pauline over the top of his glasses, "You thinking of marrying the chap?"

"You mean Richard?"

"Is there someone else?"

42

Pauline giggled, "Maybe Fritz? Her eyes sparkled as she looked at each one of us. "Oh, of course, I want to marry Richard and, I might as well tell you now; we are going away after we marry."

"Well, that's good," my father said. There's not much room in this house for both of you. But let me tell you, young lady, you are too young to think of marrying or going away right now."

"Dad, we are planning to go to Africa."

My parents answered in unison, "Africa?"

"Yes," Pauline put on her exaggerated English accent." Yes, first I'm going to go to Italy. I'm going to study with Maria Montessori. It's a new method of teaching for young children, which means I'll have my work cut out teaching African kids."

My mother opened her mouth to say something, then closed it again. She glanced at my father, who took his glasses off and laid them carefully on the table before he spoke, "So, Pauline, you have the money for these classes in Italy and this new career? Of which," he added, "we have heard nothing. Tell us what part of Africa are you planning to live?"

"Richard is going to be setting up Singer Sewing Machine factories all over," she said smugly. "We'll go first to Lagos in Nigeria and then Accra in Ghana."

"The Gold Coast…white man's grave," My mother whispered, "White man's grave."

"What does that mean?" I asked.

My mother answered, shaking her head, "It's called that because there's so much malaria out there. It's a deadly disease, malaria."

Pauline wasn't fazed by the reaction of my parents regarding the health problems associated with Africa. She was young, and I suppose like most of us at that age, invincible. No matter what, or where, she had decided she was going to become a Montessori teacher, and she was going to Africa with Richard.

My father eventually gave in and paid for the school in Italy, but he stood firm on Pauline getting married and going to Africa. He talked to Richard about it, and reluctantly, Richard agreed that it was best to wait. In the end, it was the Singer Sewing Machine Company who decided it was too risky to send anyone out there with the political unrest.

Eight

When my brother turned eighteen, he was called up for his two-year stint in the Army. In the immediate post-war political landscape, Britain had considerable obligations and only a limited number of men still in service. Between 1945 and 1963, two and a half million young men from all over Britain were compelled to do their time in National Service. Military bases had to be manned in Germany, Austria, Palestine, and Aden. Plus, the Suez Canal Zone and a chain of lesser military bases.

As I write my story, I remember feeling very glad that Douglas had gone away. I have hesitated to mention the times when he and I were alone in the house. He liked me to listen to his records in his bedroom. It was a brotherly thing to do, and I loved it because I used to dance around the room, and he always watched me intently. I thought he played music just for me. But it wasn't dancing that excited him. He was after something much more personal. I was about to be initiated in the world of grownups and particularly of men and their sexual appetites.

I sat on his bed, happy to be with him, swinging my feet. I loved my brother.

"I…I want you to do something for me, Sis," he said.

"What?"

"Touch me."

He never hurt me, and I suppose, to have his approval, I did what he asked.

∗∗∗

Colin was about to leave Grammar School. He was already thinking about college or being an apprentice with an engineering company in London. I had another year before leaving school, although I would not yet be sixteen. Sadly, I had Scarlet Fever when I was eleven and missed the critical eleven-plus examination. I would be destined to attend a school for students with lower I.Q.s. I would have to attend a Secondary Modern School that did not prepare students for college, unlike High Schools or Grammar Schools. But, I did excel at Folville Girls School about three miles from our house. There were no school buses, no bus route close, so I walked every day there and back and thought nothing of it. It was just the way it was in England at that time. I was a top student in most of the classes, and I thought the uniforms were smart. Navy blue tunics, white blouses, and black and white striped ties. But the thick black woolen stockings were awful. After school, if I had arranged to meet my friends, I would slip into the school bathrooms and change into nylon stockings, purchased at great expense from Marks and Spencer's. After all, we had to be dressed in our best togs to go to see Doris Day in a movie in the city, Betty Hutton, in *The Greatest Show on Earth* with Cornel Wilde. Sometimes, I went to Joanie's house to listen to the radio. America's latest song hits Johnnie Ray, Nat King Cole, Bing Crosby, Al Martino, and Frankie Laine. They were the idols of my time, and my very favorite film star was Charlton Heston. Who could forget him?

It was a nuisance to have to change back into the woolen stockings before I went home, but I knew my mother would have a fit if she saw me in sheer stockings. "Nice girls don't wear see-through stockings to show off their legs," she said.

Despite the so-called poor education standards at Folville, there was an excellent drama teacher, her name was Miss Grace. I loved acting. I could be anyone I wanted to be on stage. I liked playing someone other than myself. To be another person on stage suited me and seemed to impress Miss Grace. She made it her business to enroll me in the *Belvoir Acting & Dance School* in Leicester. I took advantage of the elocution lessons that were offered. Leicester's dialect was not charming. I had acquired it, not from my parents, but my contemporaries at school.

It was the end-of-term school play, open to parents and the public. I was playing the lead part as a princess. The back of the hall was full of adults as usual. Toddlers and very young children were seated in the front rows. As I stood at the edge of the stage, ready to speak my well-rehearsed lines, I could see the children looking up at me expectantly in my shimmering pink princess dress. Toward the end of the play, I gazed over the edge of the stage, "Fish, fish, you that know me," I quoted, standing on tiptoe. "Dimly shimmering fins below me, thirsty throats that no draft can slake. Go and drain my father's lake."

All the children rose from their seats to look for the fish. The applause filled my mind, and, at that moment I knew my destiny was to be an actress.

In the audience was Steven Connery, a blustery, large man with a ruddy complexion. He was the director of the Kirby Players, a local drama group that performed plays every month. He asked me if I would join. What a thrill for me. So, I began my amateur acting career, and I was surprised and delighted when I was accepted at Leicester's new BBC2 radio station to take part in their radio dramas.

✳✳✳

At that time, the Baptist church Pastor who had listened to one of the radio dramas in which I'd taken part, came to the radio station to ask if I would be in a play he had produced. I was thrilled. He cast me as Ruth in a Biblical play that ran for three weekends on the stage of the local theatre. Because of this man, I became fascinated with the Bible and read it from cover to cover. I went to the church three times a week just to be near him, and I blushed whenever he spoke to me. The crush I had on him changed one evening when I was sitting in the front pew looking up, adoringly, at this sandy-haired man whom I admired so much. He looked directly at me and pointed his finger in my direction. His eyes seemed to search my soul as he announced dramatically, "You are a sinner." I wasn't to know he intended those four words to apply to all his congregation, but I took it to heart and wept as I walked home. What had I done for him to suggest such a terrible thing? When I told my mother why I was so upset, she swiped the tea-towel she was holding against the counter, sending one of our best china cups and a saucer flying to the floor. As she swept up the broken pieces, she said, "You are no more a sinner than the man in the moon." With the brush pointing in my direction, she said, "You shan't go back to that church. Is that clear? I won't have your mind filled with such Cod's Wallop."

I never did go back, but I never quite got over the fact that somehow I had sinned against this God, whom the sandy-haired pastor talked about so often.

Later, I attended an evening class at Vaughn College in Leicester; I had the privilege of being a student of Sir Mortimer Wheeler, the archaeologist, for one term. He talked about the theory of evolution, Darwinism. At least that made sense to me.

✳✳✳

After Pauline's Montessori training in Italy, she returned to England, and when she was twenty-one, she married Richard. She carried red carnations and stephanotis. She had intended to carry red and white carnations, but my mother put a stop to that, "Not red and white together. That's blood and bandages." Mother's superstitions ruled our lives at times.

I was a bridesmaid. Uncle Walter gave me a small bunch of Freesia to carry. He remembered how much I loved them.

✳✳✳

Colin had applied to be a draftsman with an engineering company. His apprenticeship was to be in London. And with Pauline now married, I didn't have much to do at weekends. Perhaps my father noticed that, and when he suggested he and I go to Sadler's Wells Ballet that was on tour in Nottingham, I was delighted. Mother laughed, "Fancy a man liking ballet."

In the evenings, my father worked on tapestries as seat covers, one each as a gift for his brothers and sisters. "Good gracious," Mother whispered, "Cross-stitch is not much of a masculine pastime for a man, is it?"

But I believed my father was very talented. I loved the fact that he liked to carve intricate designs on the bellows he gave away to his friends. He was an excellent carpenter, creative as an architect in his younger years and he was always aware of the beauty in nature. He taught me so much about art in all its forms, and in the summer months, I spent weekends in the allotment garden learning about flowers, their names, and the Latin names that stuck with me forever. My father grew vegetables as well as flowers. He supplied the neighbors with produce, and seemed happier in the garden than being at home in an atmosphere permeated by my mother's discontent.

Everyone who lived in a council house owned by Leicester City had the opportunity to rent an allotment. There were acres and acres of land designated for extra gardening space during and after the war. My father's garden was immaculate. Rose bushes grew each side of the long grassy path that led to a little shed where all the tools were kept, plus a journal for making careful notes of what had been planted and on what date. I loved it there in that little hut. I made it into my home away from home with curtains at the windows. I bought pretty teacups and a teapot from the Leicester market. My father built a fire pit at the bottom of the garden, and we had what I called *smoky tea*, sitting on a log under the gnarled branches of an ancient apple tree. He talked about his childhood in Foxby, and when he was a farmer at Furnivall's Farm leading a plow behind a horse, milking the cow named Daisy.

Sipping our smoky tea, I asked him how he had met my mother.

"She was a beautiful woman," he said, smiling. "Yes, lovely dark hair, incredible blue eyes. Unusual."

"And what else," I asked.

"I thought she understood me."

By the way he looked into space as he was talking, I suspected there was more to this story, so I asked, "You don't think she does, understand you I mean?"

"Vickie is complicated," he said, shaking his head. "She was brought up so differently from me. Her mother scraped a living taking in washing. I had left Furnivall's Farm because I wanted to study architecture. The university in Leicester was costly to attend, and rather than relying on my parents, I found a menial job, believe it or not, collecting rents."

"You mean going door to door."

He nodded, "Yes. I was in a boarding house close to the University - just one room - but it was convenient to go out in the evenings for a few hours. Gray Street, where Vickie lived, was on my route. I asked her out, and she seemed eager for my company. We went for walks around the park. She liked to sit in the pub-garden with a glass of cider. Women weren't allowed in the pubs, but they could sit in the garden. We just met now and then. Things just went on from there."

"Doesn't sound very romantic," I said.

"Ah, yes. Well, I'd had my romance with Violet."

"Violet? I've not heard of her."

"No, that was in the past. She had red hair…"

"You had an affair with her?"

He nodded, "Vi was Mr. Furnivall's daughter."

As he told me, I began to imagine the scene:

Louise and Frank Norton had nine children. By the time diphtheria and tuberculosis had taken the lives of the four youngest, my father, Edward, was the eldest of five, with brothers Bill and John and two sisters, Ida and Dorothy.

When Louise and Frank left Kilby Manor, where they worked for sixteen years as maid and butler, Frank worked at Furnivall's Farm. A house was provided for him and his family at the top of the lane that led to the fields. As long as a member of the family worked at the farm, the house would remain for them to live in.

Edward was sixteen when he left Grammar school with high expectations of becoming an architect. His parents suggested that since his father was getting too old to work the horses with the plow, Edward would be needed to learn to be a farmer. Otherwise, they would be homeless. Edward had to step into his father's shoes.

Before long, he had become friends with Violet. They were the same age and seemed to have similar interests. At first, they would just take walks along the perimeter of the big field where yellow Celandines grew in abundance under the Hawthorne hedges, talking about what they were going to be when they left school. Violet was planning to go to university in Cambridge to study horticulture. Edward told her after his brother Bill was old enough to take his place at the farm, he was off to University also. They both had dreams that would lead them to a wealthy life if they had the necessary degrees. World War I was just about to end, and the future looked bright for both.

Violet was a girl who liked boys, and she wanted to experience sex. She encouraged Edward to join her in the big barn near the outhouses in the evenings. With testosterone running rampant at seventeen, Edward was very eager to comply. He was entranced by this beautiful red-head who was so willing to give herself to him without reservation. Edward thought she was heaven-sent and prepared to ask her father for her hand in marriage.

He told Violet many times that he loved her, and he wanted to marry her. At first, Violet would tease him, "Oh, Edward, we are just having fun, aren't we?"

Edward thought she loved him and that they could have this sort of fun forever if they were married.

After a hot love session in the barn one late afternoon, Edward proposed. He begged her to be his wife.

Violet sighed as she rose from his side, "Oh Edward, dear Edward, I couldn't marry you. My father would not allow it. I mean, let's face it," she said, smiling brightly. "He owns all the cottages in the lane and half the land in the village. Why would he ever agree to me marrying you? Your parents were in service at the manor. They were a maid and a butler! Can't you see? We are miles apart in every sense of the word."

Edward could not believe what she had said. "Don't you love me?" he finally managed.

"Don't be silly. Love has nothing to do with what we do together. We have fun, don't we? Let's not spoil it."

But it did spoil it for Edward. The love affair was over, leaving him with a broken heart.

For a long time, I thought about him as a young man with a girl who didn't want him. It must have been traumatic. I knew my father so well, I could feel his sadness.

I said, "Did you ever see her again?"

He shook his head, "No, I left the farm. My parents never knew the reason, and my dad had to stay until he was far too old to be a farmer. He developed asthma, which eventually did him in. I didn't care if I never saw the farm again. That's when I went to live in Leicester and met your mother."

"Did you ever find out what happened to Violet?"

"I heard that she did go to Cambridge, but she was later killed in the Blitz."

"Poor Violet. What a sad story," I said. "How were your parents able to keep the house when your dad couldn't work at the farm?"

"Well, I'd like to think it was Vi who persuaded her father to let our family stay. A new agreement was drawn up, and if one of our family stayed in the house, even if they didn't work on the farm, it would be rent-free. It still is to this day. That's why your grandmother and aunt live there."

"Does Mother know all this?" I asked.

"God, no. She wouldn't understand."

"Really? Don't you think she got the short end of the stick at that time?"

"Maybe. Yes, maybe. But you see, I knew she was on the rebound too."

"Oh?"

He nodded, "I doubt she'll ever tell you, but I got to know everything from her mother about a man named Jack Rush?"

More skeletons, I thought. Who was Jack Rush?

Nine

My brother was back from his stint in the Army. He appeared slimmer and somewhat withdrawn to me. He seemed to want to be alone in his bedroom with his record player. I didn't join him ever. I was so relieved.

Mother remarked that something was not right with him. My father suggested that Douglas went into the service as a boy and came out as a man. From eighteen to twenty seemed a short time for that to happen, but my mother agreed that perhaps he had been around a lot of other men, and now he was adjusting to being with his family.

Meanwhile, I had been working in a chemist shop as a sales assistant until I was accepted to the *Royal Central School of Speech and Drama* in London. When the letter finally came, I was ecstatic. I had assumed that Douglas would take my place to bring in monthly money for room and board at home just as I had done since he'd been away. It soon became apparent that I could not possibly go to London, "What are you thinking?" Mother asked. "Dreams are great, but you have to earn a living. Acting won't do that, will it?"

I went into my bedroom and wept. There was no way I could live in London and afford the horrendous costs associated with the academy. My father suggested that if I really wanted to do that, I should work in a factory for a while where I could earn a lot of money and save it.

I got a job in the factory downtown wiring jigs for radar screens. After six months, I was bored to tears with the repetition of it, although Elsie, the supervisor, said my work was much neater than some of the other girl's work. Piece-work means speedy work. My fingers were sore from the twine used to bundle the colorful wires together, and soldering little transistors was not my forte even though I was fast.

When I discussed my tedious job with Colin one weekend, he suggested that I could go to evening classes at the Pitman Secretarial College in Leicester. It seemed like a good idea, but I had to give up the radio drama and most of the other stage events that were so important to me. Mother said, "I don't know why you worry so much, You'll be married before long and supported by a husband. Why worry about a career? Just earn enough money to get by on until then."

I had added, "And to pay my room and board."

Colin was enjoying his apprenticeship in London, but he was looking for employment in Leicester. At weekends, when he was in Foxby with his parents I stayed with my Aunt and Uncle, although Colin and I spent most of the weekend together. I noticed, at those times, his kisses were different. He even suggested that I stay with him in London some weekends so we could make love. I really did not want to have sex with him until I had a gold band on my finger. This, apparently, according to my friends, was because I was a prude or very old-fashioned. I didn't care about that, but I did wonder if there was something wrong with me. I was afraid to have a sexual relationship with Colin. Try as I might, I could not separate the experience with my brother and his aggressive commands to Colin's sweet approach to sexual intimacy. I wondered if I would feel repulsed. Was it normal to have these fears? Was I normal? All these questions surfaced and stayed with me. Of course, the other worry was that I had known a couple of my girlfriends who had to get married, and I knew they were not happy. Getting pregnant outside of marriage was not looked upon kindly in those days.

If you were married, it was an acceptable and welcomed event as it was when Pauline visited us at home to tell us she was pregnant. However, there was the proverbial fly in the ointment when Richard announced that the ban to go to Africa was lifted, and he'd been waiting for the opportunity to go. Still, now, with Pauline expecting, he was going alone. Pauline would have to stay in the UK until the baby was born. He said that Africa was too much of a third-world country, and he had no idea what their hospitals were like. He feared that native women probably gave birth to their children in the middle of the jungle.

At least Pauline had Mother and me. We accompanied her to the clinic every month. In fact, it was on one of these occasions that I was, once again, reminded that my mother really did not like me.

On the bus, she was talking to a lady sitting in the seat in front of her. Pauline sat beside her. I was in the seat behind. I heard my mother say to the lady in front, "Yes, this is my daughter, Pauline, she's the sweet one, not like the one sitting back there." The remark left me with another scar that never went away.

✳✳✳

I stayed at the factory for the year while I was at Pitman Secretarial School in the evenings, and in the fall of that year, I had my degree. I was hired by Services Watch Company, a short bus ride away, to work in the secretarial pool.

It was my second day there. I was extremely nervous, sitting in front of Mr. Babbitt with my notepad and my pencil poised. He was a thin, pale-faced man with a goatee. One of the girls told me they called him 'Babbitt the Scrappitt.' This man apparently dictated letters to soothe irate customers, then he threw the typed letters away.

Mr. Babbitt was not a friendly man. He appeared to resent the fact that he had to apologize to customers. Perhaps he thought Services Watch Company never did anything to be sorry for. When I sat with him, he talked so fast I thought I would never keep up, but I soon got used to his pace of dictation. It was when I realized that some of the verbiages he used in his letters were not very polite or respectful to unhappy customers, and I made the mistake of changing the wording to read a little more kindly.

One late afternoon, just before I was ready to go home, he called me into his office. With his elbows on his desk, rubbing a pencil between his hands, he smiled up at me as I stood by the door waiting for him to hand me the letters I had typed earlier, "You know, dear," he said, "We are swamped downstairs in the manufacturing plant, would you mind helping out there just for a few days?"

I must have looked shocked, because he reiterated, "Just for a few days, dear?"

"Well," I stammered, "I…I'm a secretary. I spent a year at night school learning shorthand and typing. I don't want to work assembling watches."

He placed the pencil on the ink-blotter pad, stood up, and pushed his chair against the desk. He straightened his jacket, then turned and stared at me for just a moment before he said, "Right then, young lady, find yourself another job, you're fired."

I didn't cry, but my mouth dropped open. I couldn't believe my ears. I stood motionless for a few minutes before I turned and walked out the door in a trance. I heard his loud voice, "Nobody, but nobody knows about customers better than me, or changes my words."

It was a rude awakening for me to know that not every boss was going to appreciate me correcting their letters.

I caught the bus home looking out the window but not seeing anything. What now? I didn't tell my parents. They had told me I should never leave one job until I had secured another. Any lapse in my room and board money would be a hardship for the family, even though Douglas was now working as a dental technician at a local dentist's office and was presumably paying his share of room and board.

I went straight to my friend Maggi's house and used her typewriter to write a new resume, with the intention of going door to door to the offices downtown.

The next morning, I caught the early bus to the city without breakfast, something I usually would never do. When the bus arrived at the town center, I felt a bit light-headed and decided a cup of tea and a sticky bun at the café in the new department store, Rushkin & Thurman, would ease my hunger. The awful thought that I might be unemployed for a long time hung over me like a black cloud.

On the way through the dress department on the ground floor, I bent down to inspect a gorgeous ballroom dress on a mannequin. Unfortunately, a very tall man came around the corner of the counter and almost fell right over me. The folder he was holding went flying; papers drifted everywhere. As I scrambled to pick up the papers, I mumbled my apologies.

"No problem," he said politely.

I ordered a cup of tea and a scone in the café and sat there thinking about my next move. It was just a matter of finding offices and dropping off a resume to each one. What else could I do?

The tall man with his folder came in and sat at a nearby table. I watched him running his fingers through his already tousled hair as he sorted through the papers. He wrote something on each sheet and shook his head. He was obviously very frustrated at what he was reading.

The waitress, an older woman, very plump and pretty, smiled at the man as she set a cup of something in front of him, "Having trouble with your secretary again, Lionel?"

"Claudia, I am going out of my mind. Stella is a nice girl, but her typing leaves a lot to be desired."

My heart started to pound as I rose from my seat and went to his table, "Pardon me," I said, "Er…I'm a secretary. Can I help?"

He sat back and squinted at me before grinning. "You were eavesdropping?"

"Yes," I said, feeling my face flush. "I'm looking for a position in this company."

"Sit down, let's talk about it."

He was still laughing when I left the café with his promise to employ me as his secretary. I was thrilled. I was told to be at the store in two weeks at eight-thirty in the morning and be ready when the store opened promptly at nine.

Rushkin & Thurman was a high-class department store that sold everything from fine ladies' wear to haberdashery. It was all very plush with glass countertops and beautifully displayed windows that were changed every month by a professional interior decorator. All the floors were carpeted except the third-floor café.

I waited for the bus home outside the Granby Halls every evening after work. I noticed, every Wednesday evening, music floated out of the windows of a dance studio. The rhythmic sounds made me tap my feet. I'd always loved dancing around the living room when no one was at home imagining I was on the stage, but I hadn't learned ballroom dancing. Colin never wanted to be seen at the Palais De Dance that was popular among my school friends. I had not even thought about lessons.

Instead of getting on the six o'clock bus home, I went inside to listen to the music. A group of men and women were in the process of learning the waltz. As I was about to sit down to watch, a man swept me up and spun me around in a fantastic sequence of steps. It seemed magical to me that I could be led around and keep time with the rhythmic one-two-three counts of the waltz just like that. I stayed for the whole evening.

One night a week soon turned into three at the dance studio. I loved it. Just the music and the company of other like-minded men and women was fun.

The dance instructor partnered me with Kevin Walker, a tall, sharp-featured man, much older than me, who took dance lessons very seriously. He was a strong leader, and even though he was much taller than a dance partner of mine should have been, it seemed to work. Meeting three times a week gave us lots of time to talk and get to know each other. I learned that he was thirty, unmarried, and an accountant with a large firm in the city.

It became a habit for him to drive me home in his old car, a Humber Super Snipe with leather interior, a huge steering wheel, and a dashboard of polished mahogany.

He lived with his elderly parents in one of the big houses on London Road. It was an upscale area of Leicester, and when I knew where he lived, I felt embarrassed. A council house was not the best address. My mother was always unhappy with her status. "Why, Edward," she would ask, "do we have to live here? It's so common."

Father would just shake his head, "Because we can't afford to buy a house, that's why."

After the war, seventy percent of households in England and Wales were under the Rental Housing Act of 1919. Money was not available during the first three years of the war for anything but armaments. Afterward, England owed so much to America, banks were limited to a loan for anything related to housing. In the country, wealthy people owned their own homes and purchased other properties as investment, to rent to people like us.

✳✳✳

One evening, after Kevin had dropped me off, I noticed the house was dark. Obviously, everyone was in bed. Not wanting to disturb my parents, since the only bathroom was upstairs next to their bedroom, I went into the kitchen to wash. We had an *Ascot* heater, and the water was always hot, so it was no trouble to have a strip wash standing at the sink. I was just drying myself when my brother appeared in his pajamas.

"What are you doing up," I asked.

"Waiting for you."

"Why?"

"I worry about you out at this time of night."

"You don't need to. Kevin brings me home."

"I bet Kevin expects a bit more than a kiss, doesn't he?"

"No, he doesn't. He's not like that. Go back to bed, Douglas. We are not going through that again. I'm not twelve now."

He reached for me, "Oh, come on, please, Sis."

I pushed past him and raced upstairs, still holding the towel to my chest. I had left my blouse on the chair in the kitchen. Reaching my bedroom, I closed the door firmly behind me. I leaned against it. My heart was thumping in my ears, and I could feel myself starting to sweat. What was happening to me again in my own home? It was a

62

nightmare I had to keep to myself. But, I made up my mind to leave the dance early from now on, so I could be in bed before my parents. I doubted Douglas would come to me in my bedroom. I locked my door every night and was wary of being alone with him in the day, but as the weeks passed, it seemed all was forgotten. I reasoned that if I got home in the evenings early, I would be safe. My father retired to bed early, and my mother stayed up late listening to radio plays or music. Television was still not popular in some families, and certainly not in mine. My father believed if we needed to be entertained, a good book was the answer.

I couldn't dwell on my predicament, and I daren't discuss it with Colin because I knew he would probably want to kill Douglas, or at least make trouble for me at home. In retrospect, I should have told him, and I should have let him say something to my parents, but I didn't say a word. I decided if it never happened again, it would be just my secret and best forgotten. But, the incident reminded me of the sad tale of one of my old school chums who had been raped by her cousin. When she found out she was pregnant, she aborted the fetus with a knitting needle and bled to death. I reasoned that this sort of behavior only happened to girls in the more impoverished council estates. Now I wasn't so sure.

Ten

My mother was very superstitious, "Don't cross knives in the sink or on the tabletop, Amelia," or "Oh dear, did you see the new moon through glass? That's bad luck; better throw some salt over your left shoulder." If I forgot something when I left the house and went back inside, I was told to sit down and raise my feet off the floor. Bad luck would follow us if we didn't abide by the rules. However, the rituals of her superstitions did not usually include her leaving the house two or three evenings a week. Now it seemed to be a regular occurrence. I assumed it was because she had recently been approached by the local church and was attending their meetings. When I asked, she said it really wasn't my business to know. After that, I was worried. I seriously considered stalking my own mother until one evening, she came home with a lovely gold brooch to show me. "Isn't this beautiful," she said, turning the vintage jeweled piece over and over in her hand. "It belonged to Alice McDonald down the street."

"She gave it to you?" I asked.

"Oh no, she's dead. Her sister gave it to me to see if I can get in touch with Alice."

She must have noticed the blank look on my face because she said, "You didn't know I could get in touch with spirits, did you? They tell me I have a gift."

"I know you talk to people who are not there," I said. "But to get in touch with dead relatives of people you don't know, seems a little weird to me."

"Everyone wants to know about their loved ones."

"When they've passed away?"

Mother smiled, "Oh yes, I can get through to Alice by holding this brooch in my hand. She talks to me. There's nothing strange about it, you know. Did you really believe that life on earth is all there is?"

I was at the door ready to leave the room and all the strange talk when she said, "My mother talks to me all the time. We communicate often. It's comforting to me."

At that moment, a tingle of the old fear crept up my spine. Was she really mentally ill? After all, she had been in a mental hospital.

"I'll tell you one thing," she said. "My mother has helped me a lot. And, she's even said she was sorry that when I was a kid, she frightened me with the nine-o'clock horses."

The nine o'clock horses had been a mystery to me, and even though it had always been something I wanted to ask about, I had never dared broach the subject. I went back and seated myself opposite her. I had given it a lot of thought and had decided she must have experienced something as a child that had frightened her like the boogeyman under the bed, or the monster in the cupboard. "Tell me about it," I said.

Seated in her chair, staring intently into the coal fire, she finally looked up at me. "It's awful," she said.

I could see she was uncomfortable talking to me now. I wondered if I should just leave and tell her that it was all right, that I didn't need to know, but then she frowned, "Oh those horses…charging down the street at nine o'clock…every night the dreadful sound of them coming along hell for leather on the cobbled stone streets, and the bell."

My curiosity was really peaked now, "What bell?

"You don't understand." She said, running her hands through her hair. "I was just a child, only seven or eight. I loved to play whip-and top in the street in the summer. There was a bell at nine o'clock. Curfew, you know. Mother would call out to me, 'If you don't come in now, the nine o'clock horses will get you.' The problem is, I still hear the bell in my head, and the horses. Can you imagine the terrible racket they make?"

"What was the curfew for?" I asked.

"I don't know."

As I studied her face, I could see she was slipping away from me to another time and place. I raised my voice, "I think that was cruel of Grandma to say that to you. Why were they there, the horses?"

She looked up, obviously trying to concentrate on me. It took her a moment. "You know how narrow Gray Street is? The men with the barrels on the dray were coming to take me away. Coming for me! One of them grabbed me and tried to put me in the cart. I bit him, and I got away. I still hear the bell and the horses, though." Again, the vacant look, eyes unblinking. It was just how she had looked when I saw her in the mental hospital.

For the first time in a long time, I felt compassion for her. Whatever the childhood memories were, they still plagued her. I leaned forward to hug her. "No men were trying to kidnap you," I said. "It was all in your imagination. Can't you just forget them?"

She looked at me for a minute, then turned her eyes away as though she couldn't reveal something she'd hidden away for so long. She closed her eyes and said softly, "I was a little girl. It was a past life. Do you believe everyone has a past life?"

The question took me by surprise. "No," I said. "Never really thought about it. Anyway, how would I know?"

"Déjà vu? Ever experienced it?"

"Yes, occasionally."

"Well, that's because you have lived before on earth, and you have unfinished business. I was a child when I was kidnapped and taken away to work on a farm. I still have nightmares about the men who took me. But it was in one of my past lives."

"Past lives?"

When she opened her eyes, she was staring at me, "You do believe me, right."

I know my eyes grew large as her words penetrated my brain. I stammered, "I don't know."

She suddenly rose from her chair, "Let's make some tea."

With the uneasy thoughts about her pulsing in my head, I tried to understand what she had told me. It was all so upsetting to think that maybe she was insane.

✳✳✳

For a few weeks, my mother's predicament filled my mind, and I tried to forget the problems I'd experienced with Douglas until a month later when I arrived home late from the dance. The hall light shone through the leaded glass panel on the front door, and I prayed that my mother was still up. I tiptoed into the living room for a few minutes, and was just about to go to the kitchen when I heard the creak of the third step on the stairs. Oh. No!

Douglas closed the living room door softly behind him. He stood there in his pajamas, staring at me. Then he smiled; a sly smile that sent chills up my spine.

"Oh, for goodness sake, Douglas. Please stop all this," I said firmly. I hoped I didn't sound as frightened as I was.

"You know what I want," he said. "Let me do it, Sis? Please" His voice was soft, persuasive. "Please."

I could feel the heat rise to my cheeks, "Douglas, leave me alone. If you come any closer, I'll scream. I'll wake everyone."

"I promise it'll be nice for you. You are so pretty, I've always wanted you, you do know that, don't you. I had your photo on the wall when I was away. I thought of you all the time."

"Stop it," I hissed. "You're my brother, Douglas. Don't you see how wrong it is?"

"I know, but I can't help my feelings."

I was almost in the corner of the room. There was no way past him, and then, in one swift movement, he lurched at me. I lost my balance and staggered back until I fell onto the sofa. I was straggled half on and half off. My legs were trapped beneath him. I tried to push him off, but he was so heavy. I had to think about what to do. Not to panic. Oh, God, not to panic. I reached over my head and felt for the pile of books I knew was on a table behind the sofa. I managed to pick up the top one and swung it at his head with all my might. It wasn't a heavy book, but it made him blink and shake his head. For a minute, his weight lessened. I rolled over on to my side, heaved myself up, raced for the door, up the stairs, and into my bedroom. I locked the door and threw myself on the bed. My heart was racing. What to do? I didn't sleep. I just kept thinking I should get up and leave right now. Where would I go?

In the morning, my mother said, "You look as though you slept in your makeup."

I said, "I did." I almost told her about my brother and his immoral behavior to me, but the scenario of what I would say didn't sound truthful even to me. Of course, she would not believe her precious son would be capable of anything untoward. It would be my fault. She had already hinted that my bleached blond hair and my berry-pink lipstick attracted the wrong type of man. Colin and Kevin had told me I was pretty, but maybe my mother had been right. Blonde hair, bright lipstick. Did it give the wrong message to men? I didn't want to find out.

I started to look at ads in the newspaper for available rooms to share, flats to let that I could afford. Every evening for the next week, I made it my mission to travel to various areas in the city where I saw lots of dingy rooms to share and flats too expensive for my budget.

Kevin came to see me at work to ask if I was okay. It was not like me to miss any dance classes, he said.

It was my lunch hour. We walked down the crowded street among the shoppers. I was so full of angst that I blurted out the truth about what had happened. Kevin didn't speak for a long time; he shook his head. Then, he stopped and turned me around to face him. "Look," he said, "my folks' house is huge. We have three extra bedrooms. Why don't you come and live with us?"

"Really? That's kind. I'll think about it but… I am scared to go home at night."

"Tell you what," he said, "After the dance class next week, I'll wait outside the house when I take you home. You signal with the light on and off when you are safe in your bedroom. Your room is at the front of the house, isn't it?"

"Yes, oh, thank you; that would be good."

The following week after the class, as promised, Kevin dropped me off at the house. I could see the lights on in the living room and hear the radio as soon as I got to the front gate. Mother was still up. I was safe. I waved and thanked Kevin for the ride home.

The radio was on full blast; music blared into the room. I watched my mother pouring sherry into her glass until it slopped over the side. She said, "I saw you in the car with that man. He's too old for you."

"He's just my dance partner."

"What about Colin? Doesn't he mind you are out every night with another chap?"

"It's not every night, and Colin is still in London. You know that. Anyway, he doesn't like dancing."

I realized we were shouting at each other. I went to the radio and turned it down.

"Leave it," she said, turning it back up. The music was even louder.

I said, "You'll wake everybody up. I have to go to bed. Please turn it down."

"Just leave it." Her eyes were blazing. "I'm surprised you don't ask your father to go dancing with you. He's going to ask you to go with him to the Gun Club dinner, he told me."

"What dinner?"

"His precious club with all his stuck-up friends. It's their annual do."

"I don't know anything about that."

"Oh, he's always been nice to you because he knows I never wanted you. You were an accident. After Pauline and Douglas, I never wanted any more kids." She lit up a cigarette and took a deep draw before she went on. "I'd already left him, you know, your father. We were separated. I had rented a room in one of those houses on Woodman Road. He knew where I was, and he got what he wanted. He was a randy old sod, and he liked sex. I got pregnant. You were the reason I had to come back to this place, a council house!"

Her words cut me like a knife. I physically winced. I knew now why my mother did not like me. Suddenly angry, my temper took over like a tidal wave, and I yelled, "I'm sorry I was born to you, but now I'm going to bed, and I'd like it quiet, please." I walked out of the room and went to the pantry in the hall. With a snap, I turned off the electricity off at the meter. There was a bizarre system of paying for electricity in council houses. The meter had to be fed with shillings for so many hours of power. It wasn't unusual to forget, and the lights would suddenly go out.

I heard my mother come into the hall. She shoved me aside and turned the switch back on. "You bitch," she said as the lights came back. The music from the radio boomed across the room. Almost at the same time, there was a loud knock at the door. I opened it thinking it might be the police with all the shouting going on. Kevin stood there. His tall, lanky body filled the space. "Get your suitcase," he said firmly, "you're coming home with me." He had heard the music and the diatribe between my mother and me.

I rushed up the stairs and into my bedroom. There was a suitcase under my bed, one too large for packing just a few things, but I didn't care. As I was flinging stuff into it, my father appeared at the door. "Amelia," he said, "I just heard what your mother said about you not being wanted. It isn't true. She didn't mean it. She loves you just as much as I do, but she's not herself right now. Please don't go."

"It's okay, Dad. This is for the best." I could feel the tears coursing down my face. I kissed him quickly on his cheek. "I'll see you soon."

I fled down the stairs and out into the car. I could still hear music blaring. Kevin didn't say anything on the way to his home, and he said it was too late to meet his parents. They were already in bed. He showed me the guest room with a single bed, all dressed up in a floral bedspread. He opened the door to the bathroom just across the hall and laid out fresh towels from a neat, orderly kept cupboard.

"Goodnight, Amelia," he said. "You can sleep safely tonight."

I sat in a comfortable armchair and looked around the room. There was a small dressing table, a table with an electric hot-plate and a small sink. I breathed a sigh of relief even though my heart was broken. I was not wanted by my mother, and I believed it. I slept little that night, with senseless dreams coming and going until I finally gave up and had a bath trying to soak away the feelings of sadness.

It was a surprise to see my father waiting for me outside when I left my office the following day. "Do you fancy having a drink with your old man?" he asked.

"Dad," I tried to laugh, "you don't go into pubs."

"I used to, Amelia. How about the *Red Lion* near the clock tower?"

"Okay."

It was strange to see my father in a pub ordering drinks, a Babycham for me and Cider for himself. He seemed to know the ropes.

"Now," he said as he sat down opposite me, "Let's get this sorted. I'd like you to come back home right now. You are too young to be at that man's home."

"Kevin is my dance partner, and he's a decent person."

"I don't like it, Amelia. You've been acting strangely lately, and I want to know what's wrong."

"I…I just think it's best I'm not at home at the moment, that's all. You'll never change Mother, and she's never liked me."

"That's so unfair of you to say that. You know it isn't true."

I could see my opportunity was now to talk about Douglas. Again, I couldn't bear the thought of what it would do to him if he thought his son had approached me with sex on his mind. It was all so ugly.

He was waiting for me to talk, and when I didn't, he said, "Well, since you are eighteen, I suppose I have no control over what you do." He shook his head. "Vickie has never been well since the war. She really needs psychiatric help, but she won't go."

"Well, I don't know what she's talking about half the time, these days," I said. "She told me she was kidnapped by men in the street and worked at a farm when she was little. Where did that all come from? Her imagination is running wild. Surely none of it is true, the horses and all that. I think she's losing it. Did she ever talk to you about things like that?"

He smiled, "Surely, you jest. Your mother doesn't talk to me about anything, but I do know some things. The records a hospital doctor shared with me, although how it is related to her life, past or present, is beyond me.

"Tell me about it," I said.

"It was a couple of hundred years ago, in Leicester. Like all big cities, domestic waste was thrown into the streets. Cholera was rife, plus other diseases, of course. Anyway, farmers came to collect all the nasty stuff for fertilizer. It made sense to do it. They were called the night soil men."

"But Mother said that these men tried to take her away. Why would they want to take kids away if they were only doing their job?"

"Cheap labor was needed. Why not children?"

"Really? Is that true?"

"Oh yes, that's why they had a nine o'clock curfew in those days. The bell, I suppose, was to alert mothers to get their children into the house."

"Yes, now I remember, her mother would call to her, 'You'd best come in, or the nine o'clock horses will get you.'

I stopped to think and said, "Surely, if Mother was born in 1901, there would be sewers by then?"

"Yes, that's where there's a question of her...shall we say... sanity. She's convinced she was abducted by the night soil men and taken to work on a farm somewhere. She hates the country. That's why she never wanted to live in Foxby."

"Oh, dear," I said, "it seems spooky to me."

My father nodded, "Indeed."

We sat in silence for a while. It was comforting to be with my father in a pub.

He suddenly smile, "I do want you to go with me to the gun club dinner dance. Will you do that?"

"Are you sure?" I asked. "It won't do much for your relationship with Mother."

"I know, love, but I have my life to live, too."

I leaned forward and hugged him. The familiar smell of soap and cherry blend tobacco enveloped him, "I'd love to," I said.

"Good." As we were leaving, he pressed a ten-pound note into my hand, "A new dress, okay?"

✳✳✳

The dress was a hit. I could tell by the way some of the men looked at me. The halter-neckline cotton summer dress made my waist look very small. I was one of the youngest girls there; most appeared to be older married couples, but the way the women flirted with their partners, I'm not so sure about the married bit. There was a lot of wine served in different glasses for an aperitif. Sherry before, wine with dinner, and Port afterward. We were still sitting at the long table after a five-course delicious dinner when I saw my father smile. A young woman passed the table. Her hair was auburn. He looked at me and nodded, "She looks a lot like Violet, an older version, perhaps."

"Ah, yes," I said, "Violet."

He nodded, thinking for a minute, then he said, "It's funny how I mark time with our wars. The Great War — WWI, 1917 is when I worked at Furnivall's Farm and met Violet."

"What was that war all about?" I asked.

"I suppose it was because of the balance of power in Europe and unresolved territorial disputes." He shook his head. "Can you imagine sixteen million young men died in that war in the trenches, and seven million civilians? You should read up on all that sometime."

"Do I need to know about war? It's all so depressing."

"It is our history, though." He sighed, "I'll never forget her."

I was suddenly overwhelmed by a feeling of sadness for him. He was a good man trying his best to provide for his family despite the odd relationship with my mother.

"Do you ever think about a divorce from Mother?" I asked.

"What?"

"Well, you have put up with a lot of weird things with her. No one would blame you if you split up. Everyone knows how she is."

He was obviously shocked that I should propose such a thing because he raised his eyebrows then frowned at me. "There's never been a divorce in my family, not ever in the Norton family."

"Does that matter?"

"It matters to me."

"So, you'd rather live in misery than try and have some happiness with someone else. You're not that old. I'm certain you could find another woman."

"Now, you are ridiculous. How would your mother manage on her own?"

I couldn't help smiling at that, "Well," I said, "you've been led quite a dance with Mother as far as I can see. I mean she has tried to kill herself twice, and she does act a bit strange, don't you think? Talking to dead people. I think that is really scary."

He was quiet as I continued, "You know, Dad, you may think I was too young to remember when you told her not to touch the gun, but she did. In fact," I turned to him, "when I think about it, it was cowardly of her to try to end her own life. My God, I was only about six or seven years old when she did that."

He put his hand on my arm, then turned my face to his, "Amelia, perhaps you should know the truth. She wasn't trying to kill herself. She was trying to kill me."

I stared at him, "What?"

"Pauline had it all wrong about the gun," he said, obviously noticing my confusion. "She didn't see what happened because she was just coming into the living room from the kitchen. I can only assume she saw me when I grabbed your mother's wrist, so the gun wasn't in my face. Of course, it went off when I did that. The bullet lodged in the ceiling. Pauline was terrified and ran upstairs for you. She was the one who decided Vickie was trying to do herself in."

"I don't understand," I said. "Didn't you see Mother get the gun from the bookcase?" I was searching his face for answers.

"Why would I? We all went to get a book from the bookcase now and then. You know how I am when I'm reading. I'm not watching what's going on in the living room. Jesus Christ, it's a good thing Pauline didn't see the whole thing. In her mind, I think she could accept the fact that her mother was having a nervous breakdown, but imagining her mother was about to commit murder…." His voice trailed off as he reached for the last drops of the Port wine shining deep red in his glass. Then he straightened his tie and sighed heavily.

I said, "She could have gone to prison."

"No, it would have been me. Handguns are not allowed in Britain. I didn't have a permit. Anyway, I buried it."

"You buried the gun?"

"Yes."

"Where?"

"Never you mind. I didn't want it in the house."

I sat there, thinking about his words. What other skeletons would I hear about from my family's closet? "Well, you're a better man than I," I said.

He patted my hand, "For better or for worse."

Eleven

Kevin's home was lovely with a lot of rooms and a well-cared for garden looked after by an elderly gentleman who came once a week to trim all the bushes and prune the roses. Kevin's parents were very gracious to me, and I appreciated that. They were older than my folks. His father, Alistair, had retired from business in banking. His mother, Eva, had never worked a day in her life. They were not overly fussy people, which seemed appropriate because they were upper-class. The polished antique furniture and all those things reminded me of my Grandmother Louise's home with everything properly arranged. Kevin laughingly said, "Yes, a place for everything and everything in its place. That's my parents."

I grew fond of my room with a hot-plate and a little electric fire. It was quiet after the storms of my home life, and surprisingly, Kevin was eager to take me to places like Warwick Castle and Stratford-Upon-Avon, to Shakespeare's birthplace. He even treated me to a performance of *Midsummer Night's Dream* at the Royal Shakespeare Theatre. I liked Kevin because he didn't get amorous or make a move on me or anything that led me to believe we were anything but friends. I was comfortable with him, and when Pauline announced baby Louise was now an excellent age to travel to Africa, and had booked airfares to Africa, Kevin drove us to Heathrow in London, which was over a hundred miles away from Leicester. The first permanent passenger terminal had just been constructed at what was then known as Heathrow Aerodrome. Only British Overseas Air Corporation (BOAC) and British European Airways (BEA) were in service.

BOAC had a plush waiting lounge with a dark green carpet and a bathroom full of beautiful cosmetics. Air travel was possible only for the elite at that time, and, consequently, the airlines pampered their wealthy travelers with luxuries that now do not exist in this frantic world of travel. There were no jets in those days to accommodate the hoi polloi; turboprops manufactured by Rolls Royce were used in the fifties for most air travel.

Pauline said she would write every week or so and let me know how it was in Ghana. Richard had told her it was hot and humid, but that Singer had provided them a large home, and he'd already decorated one of the bedrooms for the baby. Pauline was excited, even though she did shed a few tears when her flight was announced over the loudspeakers. "You'll come to visit?" she asked as she gave me a hug.

"I'll save my pennies, I promise," I said.

While we were in London, we visited St. Paul's Cathedral. Kevin was quite the historian and explained that it was built by Sir Christopher Wren in 1675 after the original was destroyed in the Great Fire of London after the plague. "The dome is a whispering gallery," he said, "You stand here, and I'll go to the other side, and you can whisper into the wall." It was magic.

The following week at the pub after work, my father told me that he had received a telegram from his sister, Olive, and that his mother had developed pneumonia after a fall. He asked me if I wanted to go with him to see her. I said I would.

I didn't know Grandmother Louise very well, although I had lived next door to her and Olive. She had always been polite but somewhat distant, and I wondered what I would say to her on this occasion. It turned out that she was very ill and didn't even know we were there, or so I assumed. I waited for my father in the hall, and I heard Olive whisper to him, "It's almost time." It was only then I noticed both she and my father didn't seem upset. I thought it was perhaps they accepted the fact that their mother was near death, and it had to be expected at her age of eighty-six. I tried to analyze that lack of feeling, and concluded that it wasn't that they didn't feel deeply about things, it was just the English upbringing of keeping emotion of any kind under control, and more so if you were upper-class. It wasn't true of my other grandmother. She had lived a far different life than my father's mother. Poverty-stricken, she had lost her husband in WWI and took in washing for a living. She was a fussy lady, hugging and kissing us when we visited, and always with a tin of chocolate biscuits at the ready. She had had very little education, but I never heard her speak unkindly of anyone. She didn't grumble about having to clean the steps outside large homes. She was known as a Charwoman and was paid a pittance for her hard work. Her house on Gray Street was in the center of the city, close to all the factories, on a very narrow cobblestoned street where houses were joined together in rows of five or six. There was an alley that ran at the back of all the houses, and a gate led to the garden of each home. As the name suggests, the street was drab and colorless, with gas lights used to light the slim side-walk, and inside the house, everything was miniature. One room with a tiny kitchen in the corner and steep, narrow stairs went directly into an equally small bedroom. Hard to imagine her raising three children in that house. The toilet was outside in the postage size backyard. I'm not sure what we used for toilet paper, probably newspaper, or sometimes tissue paper that had been wrapped around oranges imported from Spain. The garden was full of dark red Peonies. To this day, when I see the almost black Peonies that are so beautiful, I smell gas.

✳✳✳

Colin had promised that he would be home at weekends, but after a few months, his visits became fewer and fewer. It seemed to me that he preferred being with his new friends in London, and although I was a little hurt, I had Kevin, and he took me to some beautiful places around Leicester in his Humber Super Snipe.

One summer day, we were visiting Belvoir Castle and sitting in a pleasant outdoor café. Tables were arranged on a lawn, which was obviously once part of the formal gardens. I could hear peacocks in the next garden. I was enjoying the scones with jam and cream and just being in the middle of the beautiful countryside. Kevin leaned toward me and smiled. For a moment, he seemed to study my face, and then he said very quietly, "Amelia, I know I'm older than you, but would you consider being my wife? I do love you, you know."

I was so shocked I dropped the teacup. It landed on the grass, and as I picked it up, I tried to compose myself. The cup was intact, but I wasn't. What was I to say to this kind man who had rescued me from an awful place? I finally managed, "Oh, dear, dear, Kevin; you know I…I'm almost engaged to Colin. I'm his girl."

"I see," he said quickly, "Forget it. I just got carried away."

"I'm so sorry." I rested my hand on his. "I didn't know you felt that way about me. Oh, goodness! I didn't know, honestly."

"It's all right," he said. "It's all right. Please forget it."

But it wasn't all right. There was an immediate distance between us and in his demeanor, which changed utterly. He no longer offered to take me to visit out-of-town places in the country where a car was a necessity. But, since I'd never even kissed him or led him on in any way, I wondered what had encouraged him to feel anything but friendship. It must be a man thing I decided.

When it got to the point that he avoided me when I was at the house and barely said anything when we were at the dance class, I realized how uncomfortable it was for both of us. I had to move, but to where?

In Pauline's last letter, she had sounded happy and had said I should visit sometime. She had enclosed a photograph of an African woman with a Singer sewing machine balanced on her head. Apparently, the women there carry cumbersome things that way, and wealthy Africans buy sewing machines for their daughters because it adds to their dowry and makes them a more valuable catch for a husband.

I wrote to her, hoping the mail would be quick to ask if it would be a good time for me to visit, but she wrote back promptly, saying that it was such a third-world country, very primitive, I wouldn't like it. I wondered why that would matter if I was just visiting, but she sounded quite firm. In the end, my refuge, I decided, would again be my aunt's place in Foxby. Then sadly, I learned from Uncle Walter that Aunt Dorothy was ill and that it wasn't convenient to have me there. The news upset me a lot, not because my uncle said it was not a good time, but because I had shared my aunt's life when she was a vibrant young woman. She had never ever complained about ill-health. Uncle Walter was obviously under a lot of pressure, trying to keep his market-garden flourishing, and worrying about her. He suggested that since Grandmother Louise had died, Aunt Olive, who now lived alone, would probably welcome my company. She did.

Within a week, I had packed my suitcase at Kevin's home, said a tearful goodbye to him and his parents, given them a large bunch of flowers, and thanked them profusely for letting me stay with them. I knew this was the end of another phase in my life. I couldn't go to the dance hall for the classes because I had to catch an early bus to Foxby every night. Kevin fell out of my life as quickly as he had come into it, and I was sad about that. He had stood by me through my problems.

***

I moved in with Aunt Olive, feeling like a nomad, wandering from home to home, but she made me very comfortable in a lovely bedroom that was once Grandmother Louise's. Olive shared her meals with me, and made sure I was up early in the morning to catch the first bus from the village to Leicester city. She amused me with stories about her life and her siblings, including my father. Their life, when they were growing up, seemed to me to have been idyllic in the peaceful country village where everyone knew everyone else in the farming community and in the church. Now, I was part of that place, among a small cluster of houses on muddy lanes and a few shops. A country village that I soon learned to love.

I enjoyed the whole atmosphere, and the walk through the fields to the canal. I walked to the locks about a mile away along the towpath even when the day was overcast and dark.

I do remember one glorious summer day, with nary a cloud in sight to filter the sun, that I set out to meet Colin. The gate, with the rubber tire nailed to it, clunked shut behind me. I walked along the narrow path through the fields to the bridge over the canal, where I stopped to think about the time I had been there before. I was eight when Colin and I had stood on this bridge to watch the coal barges towed by horses. Now, they were gone. The waterways of England had been forgotten. Steam engines began transporting coal to the factories. Canals became choked with weeds and overgrown rushes. Barges carrying goods to factories were rare. If they came, there were no horses, just engines purring, leaving a brown wash of water that slapped noisily against the overgrown banks.

I saw Colin walking through the fields from the farm. He was wearing his Harris Tweed jacket with the leather elbow patches. When he waved, my heart began to beat a little quicker. "Hello, sweetheart," he said, giving me a hug and a kiss. He turned to look down at the water below. A family of waterfowl of some kind suddenly appeared at the water's edge and then he glanced at the yellow field. He smiled and turned to me, "Remember when Ellie was here with us that day when you two went off to pick Cowslips. I sat on the bank?"

"I remember," I said.

"That's when I knew you and I would always be together."

I didn't tell him that was when I had experienced a pang of jealousy because I thought he liked her better than me. He turned to me and took me in him arms. When he kissed me, his lips were soft and warm against my own, "I do want you," he said. "You know that, don't you?"

"You mean, that way?"

"Yes, don't you think it's time?"

"Well, I don't know… I mean, I just don't know. Shouldn't we wait until we're married?"

He looked at me, turned away and laughed, but there was sadness in his big brown eyes. "Oh, it's all right, lass," he said, hugging me again. "I just want to be sure we would really like each other that way."

Maybe he was right. It would be awful to find out that you didn't like making love with your husband. I began to wonder if he would seek sexual satisfaction with someone else if I didn't acquiesce to his desires. After all, he had been living in the big city of London where there would be lots of beautiful girls, surely. He was a good-looking man, and I suspected he'd been tempted by women there. I was finding out that most women were ready and willing if asked.

✳ ✳ ✳

The fields were alive with the hum of bees. We were lying in a hollow where Cowslips grew in profusion; their scent surrounded us. Colin gently twisted my hair in his fingers.

I wanted to distract him, "I love these flowers, don't you?"

"Yes, I do, and I love you. And, just remember, these Cowslips will never be gone from this field. You must remember that." As he put his arms around me, I could feel he was aroused, and when he put his hands gently on my breasts, I melted. I knew I suddenly wanted him, all of him. It was easy to be swept up at the moment. His energy and his need filled me with such intensity, I cried afterward. We lay silently for a long time. He suddenly reached out and plucked the long stem of a cowslip and held it to his nose. He said, "*The Cowslips tall her pensioners be; In their gold coats spots you'll see; Those be rubies, fairy favors; I must go seek some dewdrops here And hang a pearl in every cowslip's ear.*"

Then, he was leaning on his elbows looking at me, "*A Midsummer Night's Dream,*" he said. "You like Shakespeare, don't you?"

"Some," I said. "Some, How about, '*Where the bee sucks, there suck I, In a cowslip's bell I lie?*'"

"*The Tempest,*" he exclaimed, "I know it."

He kissed me again, then rose and pulled me to my feet. "We'll remember these moments," he said, holding me close, "when we're old and gray."

Of course, as I write this story, I remember everything that Colin and I did together. He was the center of my world.

* * *

That evening we went to the Black Bull Inn. I had always liked the friendly atmosphere in country pubs. I had ordered a Pimm's Number One, a gin-based liquor with fruit juices. Colin had a pint of bitter ale.

Colin was sipping in silence and I asked him what he was thinking. He looked at me and smiled before leaning his elbows on the table, "You know I've been at Atkinson Engineering for five months now. It's all right, but I was talking to one of the guys there. He says he's planning to live in America. He's already got a prospective job, and I think I could be hired by Bell Telephone Company. I did some research. They are hiring Brits who have engineering degrees for their drafting department. Would you consider going to the States?"

"What?"

His brow creased, "Well, would you?"

"Wow. I don't know, Colin. I mean, it's a long way from England."

"Well, yes. Think of the opportunity, though, to make a better life for ourselves. Amelia, this is our chance. Our time. What do you think?"

My mind was ticking over as to why and how. It could not be that easy. "But," I said, trying to sound smart, "secretaries must be like pennies in a pound out there. Why would they hire me?"

"Ah, ha! Hmm! Yes, that's a point. Yes, that's a point." He sighed, "Still, we could try. Or, I could go first and then sponsor you as my wife."

I looked across the table and studied his face, "Your wife? Are you proposing?"

"Yes, I suppose I am," he said, looking away for a moment. "I suppose I am. I want to marry you; you know that."

He took hold of my hands as I rested them on the table. His warmth seemed to permeate through my whole body. "I love you," he whispered, "and now, after this afternoon, I know you love me."

For a minute, I was stunned. Was sex the key to showing a man you loved him? Having such close bodily contact with a man, feeling his skin against mine was almost overwhelming, but I couldn't say it was love. Love was emotional. Was sex supposed to enhance that? It didn't seem that way to me. Again, the thought that perhaps there was something wrong with me. I had literally opened myself up to this man, and it made me feel vulnerable, almost used. Not quite sure why. And, some questions needed to be answered. Colin had said he *supposed* he wanted to marry me. What did that mean?

To test him, I said, "I think we should set a date for the wedding, don't you?"

"Well, we should wait a little while, lass. I guess we can get engaged, though."

I answered more sharply than I intended, "You… guess? If you feel that way, perhaps we should wait until you're sure."

"Amelia!"

The thought came to me that maybe the incidents with my brother, the feeling of helplessness, the angst of having to keep a secret had somehow skewed my ideas about men. Perhaps I should have told Colin, I thought. I couldn't imagine even for one minute, he would have blamed me or even think I had encouraged my brother in any way. I had told Kevin because he was more a part of my life at that time than Colin was. He was on the spot; Colin wasn't.

It was as though Colin began to read my mind. I noticed a smile hovering around his lips. He said, "Of course, maybe Kevin stole your heart, I mean you did live with him. He took my hands in his and said thoughtfully, "You told me he had money; you might want to rethink your decision to marry me."

I said, "Well, that's true. I'll let you know." We both laughed.

The next Saturday, we met again at the bridge. I noticed the field of Cowslips next to the farm glowed in the sunshine, and when Colin presented me with a gold ring with tiny diamonds, all my doubts about him disappeared. "Everyone loves a June wedding," I said.

Colin answered quickly, "Hold on now. We really must be practical, lass. I can't afford to buy a house right now, or even to rent one, so here's my thought. Why don't we wait until I get the go-ahead to get to the States? That way, we don't have to try and find a house to rent, which neither of us can afford. Quite frankly, my parents are in a bit of a bind right now. They've helped me through my apprenticeship expenses. I'd like to pay them back at least something now I'm going to be working. You like it with your Aunt Olive, don't you?"

Again, the doubts about our relationship surfaced. I tried to reason. I said, "Why don't we wait until we can both go to the States. I'm sure there's a way I could go with you?"

Colin said, "Well if I have a job offer, I'd be stupid not to take it, don't you think? He put his arms around me and held me close. He said, "Look, I know it sounds as though I'm putting off our wedding, but don't you think I should take advantage of a job in the States if it comes my way?"

Of course, he was right. I knew Colin was ambitious and that I should be grateful to have a man who wanted to do well for himself. "Yes," I said, "You should."

Colin smiled and pulled me to him. He said, "I know my mum and dad really can do with the income I'm bringing in to them. If I can pay them back for everything before I go, that's what I want. That's my goal."

There didn't seem much more I could say after that. Colin was right.

Twelve

It was wonderful being a private secretary to Mr. Lionel Godfrey. I had my own office on the top floor with a view of the city. He encouraged me to change the wording of his letters if I felt it necessary, unlike Mr. Babbitt at Services Watch Company. Maybe that's what made me totally loyal to him. I came into the office early every day and left late, and then only to catch the 6:30 bus to Foxby in the evenings. Eventually, he gave me the responsibility of answering all the business correspondence, even if he wasn't around. He was the best boss I ever had. Then, in the late spring of the following year, he announced he had been promoted to regional manager of a large store in the north of England and would be leaving Leicester soon.

The luxury I'd experienced with him. — being able to take care of his work, disappeared. My office became Mr. Cole's. He was a pompous individual with thin lips. He scowled rather than smiled, and he ran the whole store like a military operation. He wasn't liked by most of the older staff members who had been there since the store opened. They began to grumble, especially after the man decided to put everyone on a time clock. It had always been an honor system as to when we started our day to prepare for the store opening time. I hated having to 'clock in' every morning, just like being at the factory. Time cards were not for me.

One by one, the experienced sales ladies left. Mr. Cole hired young girls, all pretty to look at, and the atmosphere of genteel politeness to customers disappeared. I gave my two-weeks-notice without finding another job first, something I never thought I would ever do.

I had saved some money, and I felt secure financially for a few weeks, but only for a few weeks.

Colin suggested a vacation in Portugal on the Algarve. He said it was becoming 'the place to go.' He said that now Portugal's tourism was booming after the many years under communist rule, the political arena had changed for the better with a democratic government, and it was now the most popular destination. And of course, since the Continent was only a couple of hours away by plane, it seemed to be a good idea.

I remember I was entranced by Lisbon, where history abounds with castles and churches. I was enthralled by Portugal's southern coast: the Algarve, which stems back to Roman times, the Visigoths, the Moors, and the Arab influence of the buildings, and the beautiful ornate chimneys.

We rented a villa in a new large resort at the top of a cliff. The resort was isolated from the nearest fishing village of Alvor by three miles of magnificent beach shaped like a crescent moon. At the very end of the bay, forty miles to the west, was Cabot de St. Vincent, the most westerly point of all Europe. The red and white lighthouse seemed to cling precariously to a promontory of brown treeless earth. On a clear day, from the clifftop near our villa, we could see the winking light from the lighthouse that shone its beacon sixty miles out to sea.

Rugged outcrops of red rock, eroded by centuries of wind and rain, had formed craggy rock formations along the cliff edge and the beach below.

I cannot remember why I was alone that day walking along the river to the quaint fishing village of Alvor for a late lunch, but I do remember it was hot, and I was wearing very short shorts and a thin blouse to cover my bikini top. After a bowl of Caldo Verde - lettuce soup - and a glass of Vino Verde, I left the café and walked to the quayside to watch the fishermen bringing in their catch for the day. I was on my way back to the villa when I noticed the river doubled back on itself, creating a narrow isthmus of sand dunes about half a mile wide separating the river from the ocean. I also discovered a path, flanked on either side by gorse and grass protecting it from the wind, so quiet after the roar of the ocean. Egrets sauntered through the shallows, and only the occasional drone of a fishing boat winding through the deeper channels disturbed the silence.

The path led directly to the beach from the river but was hidden from view in both directions.

Delighted to find a shortcut late in the afternoon, I turned on to the path, enjoying the warmth that was reflected from the sand. After a few minutes, I became aware that I was not alone. A man in a red plaid shirt was behind me. He was short and stocky; his ruddy leather-like complexion indicated to me that he was a fisherman. He caught up with me and spoke in Portuguese.

"*Não comprendo*," I said, "I do not understand."

He kept talking, rambling on and on, his words flowing over me as I tried to grasp a concept or two that made sense. I smiled and said, "Sorry, I don't understand Portuguese." We walked together in silence, an, after a while, I found myself relaxing as I heard, but could not see, the ocean ahead. When I glanced his way, I noticed he was looking at my legs. It's not unusual for tourists to wear shorts, but they were never worn by Portuguese women, who dressed, even in summer, in garments that covered them from head to toe. The first hint of fear ran through me as I contemplated what might be running through his mind. I was young and alone, in an isolated part of the dunes.

I quickened my step. He kept up with me. Then, without warning, he grasped my arm with his right hand, pointing to the ground with his left. He released my arm and sat down on the side of a dune. I took the opportunity to run and only turned to look back when I heard him shouting, "*Faz favour, Faz favour,*" He was saying please, and waving his wallet at me. He was offering to pay!

What did he think I was? "*Não, não.*" No. No, I shouted, now desperate to escape.

I couldn't get my footing in the loose sand, and in a minute, he was up at my side and caught my wrist, his hand rough against my skin. I couldn't think of any words to say in Portuguese and I was beginning to panic.

My mind was a total blank, and my heart was pounding in my head as I attempted to move faster. I felt as if I was in a nightmare, running, but not going anywhere. Was it a dream? Would I wake up soon? No, this was real.

He grabbed my arms from behind and dragged me along backward, trying to pull me down. I screamed loudly and kicked back at his legs, my arms flailing helplessly in his vice-like grip. I could feel myself falling, and I thought I was going to faint. Could this really be happening to me?

Then my anger rose to the surface. I felt a surge of strength. How dare he? I twisted out of his grip and skipped away as he lunged at me. Down he went, sprawling to the ground. In an instant, I turned and kicked sand into his face. He was blinded for a moment. I took the opportunity to run, but my feet had turned to lead. Again, I was in a dream of dragging along in slow motion.

Finally, I saw the beach ahead of me. "Dear God, please let someone be there."

As I emerged into open space, the sea sparkling before me, I realized, to my horror, there was no one in sight. It was still two miles along the beach to our villa. When I turned to see where my assailant was, he was looking up into the sky. Only then was I aware of the whirring of a helicopter. Like a big blackbird, the helicopter came down the beach, hugging the shoreline. On the side of it, in large white lettering, were the words: *Luftwaffe*. Even in my panic, I remembered there was a German Airforce base in Lisbon. I jumped up and down in near hysteria. "Help, help," I shouted. I rationalized they probably could not hear me. How stupid of me to think they could do anything up there, but to my astonishment, the big throbbing bird turned and came back. At that moment, I glanced back to the dunes, just in time to see a flash of red as the man disappeared behind a mountain of sand. Surely it was a coincidence that anyone in the helicopter could have seen the exchange among the dunes. Perhaps redshirt had decided to quit stalking me and had left of his own accord. And, what could the men in the helicopter have done anyway? To my astonishment, the helicopter hovered over me, right up above me, for several minutes before swinging into a wide arc over the sea, then back to the shoreline to proceed down the beach. Its engines grew fainter and fainter until it was out of sight.

I kept glancing back to see if I was being followed, but the sand dunes were empty. Only the breeze riffled the tough dune grass, and high clouds cast dark and light shadows on the sand.

I was still running more smoothly this time. My feet pounded on the wet firm sand close to the gentle surf. Tears came in a torrent. I was talking out loud, "It was my fault, wearing shorts. What a fool."

I was still running fast on the empty beach. What if he came after me? There was no one in sight, and my head was beginning to feel light as though I was floating, weightless. The sounds of the ocean were fading away.

When I slowed to a walk, I glanced back again, almost expected to see the red shirt behind me. Up ahead, I could see a young couple walking toward me, laughing, and chatting. They passed me, arms around each other's waist. "*Guten Tag*," they chorused together. The Germans are everywhere, I thought. Thank God.

I went inside to the bar at the resort and ordered a brandy. My shaking had stopped when I finally left. My heart had slowed to its regular beat.

I was afraid to tell Colin about my experience, but when he asked why I was so quiet, I told him. I thought he'd tell me I was a dumb broad, asking for trouble wearing very short shorts in a country where women rarely show any skin even in summer. Instead, he said, "If you see him again, let me know. I'll strangle the bugger."

✳✳✳

After the fortnight in Portugal, Colin worked on his C.V., which had to be impressive. He was sure now he was heading for a better life in the States. Suddenly everything was wrong with England in his book, There was nothing to look forward to with the Labour Government, and the Trade Unions sticking their noses everywhere. They had nationalized the coal, rail, and docks industries. Colin was incensed about that.

I had my own worries about finding employment. It took two weeks before I was lucky enough to find The Wycliffe Brokerage Company, who agreed to hire me at a little higher salary. It was a plush establishment on a quiet side street near the town center.

Although I didn't have my own office, I liked the atmosphere among the other secretaries. I began to learn the vocabulary associated with stocks and bonds and stock-market lingo. It was exciting to discover a different mentality around me. My parents had never discussed money, or the value of it, other than the fact they never seemed to have quite enough. Here, at this office, words like dividends and profit margins and annuities crept into the every-day conversation.

Happily, there was good news from the States. Colin received a letter of acceptance from Bell Telephone Company in New York, with the proviso that he produced a clean medical report and completed the necessary verification that he was a legal resident alien with a 'green card.' I began to catch his excitement. I had no doubt that as soon as he was settled there, he would send for me. He could sponsor me.

Desperate though I was to accompany Colin to America, I knew being just a secretary was not good enough. Plenty of American girls for that. But if I was transferred to an affiliate brokerage office in New York as a trained secretary in Mutual Funds, surely that would be the answer. I was already becoming familiar with the terms used in that department, and I had noticed the bosses were in contact with the New York Stock Exchange every day. It seemed like a reasonable request to ask the boss, Mr. Trevors. He was an astute businessman and a kindly soul. He was white-haired and gentle in his ways with me. I felt comfortable talking to him about Colin and my plans. He must have realized I was serious about emigrating, because he said, their affiliate company on Broad Street, Lerner, Hutchinson Corporation, was a member of the New York Stock Exchange. Yes, they had accepted secretaries in the past.

Colin was excited when I told him about the conversation with Mr. Trevors. "Oh, that would be great," he said, swinging me around. Once again, he voiced his opinion, "Let's face it: England is going to the dogs, going downhill. We've already lost most of our empire. In fact, Africa, where your sister went, is already getting their independence. America is the place to be."

I was just as excited as Colin, but it was exhausting to face what we would have to go through to get there. I wondered how my parents would take the news.

One evening after work, I decided I had to tell them.

After a cup of tea, I said, "You should know that I'm thinking of going to live in the States."

There was a stunned silence. My mother spoke first, "America? Why on earth would you go there?"

"Because I think Colin and I could have a better life, a car may be, and a house of our own. It is the land of opportunity."

Mother shook her head, "You do come up with hare-brained ideas, Amelia dear. What about all the crime, guns and such, Al Capone and his gangs."

"Al Capone?" I said. "Al Capone? Mother, for goodness sake that was in the 1930s. We are in the sixties now, or hadn't you noticed?"

"Well," she argued, "that mentality still exists there. Anyone can get a gun. Anyone. More people get murdered in America than anywhere else in the world. It's the wild-west, you know. It still is." It crossed my mind that my mother had obviously dismissed the fact, or forgotten, that she had used a gun.

When my father finally spoke, his tone was deliberate and final, "I reckon if Amelia believes England is such a terrible place to live, she should go."

I was upset by his words, but I knew it was because he was hurt that I would want to leave. On the other hand, I was resentful that when Pauline had gone away, everyone seemed okay with it.

I said, "You didn't seem angry when Pauline left England for Africa, and that's a third-world country."

My mother raised her eyebrows, "Well, she had a husband."

My father sighed, "Oh, Amelia will be all right. She can come back if it doesn't work out. Although, I agree she should get a job first." That was typical of my father, always the pragmatist.

Thirteen

Colin received a letter from Bell Telephone Company within a very short time, and he was excited. In the letter, he read about the process of attaining a green card. He was to have an examination at the medical offices of the Immigration Department in London. My boss suggested I go at the same time. "Why not be ready?" he said. "You know we will do our best for you. I'm checking every day with the boys in New York. If they hire you on our say so, it will happen quickly."

Colin and I took the seven a.m. train to the American Consulate Immigration Department in Grosvenor Square. We were ushered into a small room with long tables and metal chairs. No luxury there. The man in charge instructed us to fill in the questions in the paperwork provided. "Just routine," he said. Some of the questions seemed trite to me. '*Why do you want to go to the United States of America to live? Do you have relatives who live in the USA? Do you intend to have a family? Will you be gainfully employed and seek health care so that you will not become a ward of the State? Are you a Communist?*

One of the questions made me laugh. '*Do you intend to practice prostitution in the USA?*' I wondered what the response would be if I answered yes!

After about two hours, we were instructed to go to another department to take our medical examinations. It was in a different building a few blocks away from the consulate. We found a place to have a quick lunch, and then the rest of the day was taken up by a thorough medical examination by two doctors and questions relating to health.

***

I think we were both anxious just waiting for some kind of correspondence from the Immigration Department. Still, as with so many things associated with the government and bureaucracy events, things moved slowly. It was eight weeks before Colin received a letter from the American Consulate. The letterhead was embossed in gold. Very impressive. He had passed the medical. A full report would be mailed to him forthwith, and it could be presented to an employer in the States along with other necessary paperwork if it was completed within six months of receipt of the letter.

I joked with Colin, "Best not to get sick in six months then, or you'll have to start the whole process all over again."

I was finally light-hearted. I knew my report would be good. I was as healthy as Colin, and now it would be up to my boss to set things in motion. I had no doubts this would be a big move and the most exciting and meaningful something in my life.

When the letter arrived for me almost ten weeks later, I wasn't worried because I felt there was nothing that could go wrong. My boss had been on the phone to the Brokers in New York. Everything was going as planned.

I studied the envelope and the return address. The *Consulate of the United States of America*. I opened it eagerly and began to read.

It started with a thank you for considering the possibility of immigration to the United States of America.

Then, after reading those first few lines, I almost passed out: *We regret to advise you that because of a Class "A" Medical Condition, we must render you inadmissible to the United States of America. We recommend you seek a doctor's attention immediately.*

You can imagine what went through my mind. What the hell did that mean? It was brief and frightening because there was no explanation. Why would any doctor send out a letter without some good reason for turning me down?

I soon found out when I went to my doctor. I had tuberculosis. My sister's comments uttered so many years ago poured into my brain. I heard her words: "The air here is terribly unhealthy. Patricia Fleming and her sister had T.B." I didn't know then what she was talking about. I had attached little importance to it, except it was the dreaded illness from which people sometimes died.

For once, I was glad my mother was with me in the doctor's office. She held my hand. I cried and let her console me as we waited. We had been there for hours with various tests and X-rays. Mother said, "You know, I bet the doctor at the immigration office was from Pakistan. It's this damn National Health Service. You know all our good doctors have gone. We'll get a second opinion, that's what we'll do."

"Mother," I said, trying not to blubber. "It's what the medical examiner found out on behalf of the American Consulate, and he wasn't from India." I found myself consoling her. "It's all right; I'll be fine. Anyway," I added, "Indian doctors are just as good as British."

"Humph!"

To make things worse, I received a letter from my cousin, Ellie, saying that my Aunt Dorothy had died from a blood clot to the brain after her surgery. It was so sudden; I had had tea with her only two weeks ago. I remembered thinking about how fragile she was, but I never suspected that she had breast cancer because she wouldn't talk about it. No one talked about those things in those days. She had survived the surgery apparently, and when a blood clot went to her brain, it caused a massive stroke. I remembered how happy she was when I had brought her a bunch of Cowslips from Hadley's field. Now the realization that she would no longer be around for me to talk to over a cup of tea depressed me almost more than my own predicament. That night, I dreamed I was sitting on one of the high stools in the greenhouse, the one with the Freesias. It was a short dream, but when I woke up, I could smell the flowers. It was all so real.

My mother was eager to explain. "Oh, that's lovely. Your Aunt Dorothy was with you."

"She just died, Mother."

She smiled, "Yes, dear, but you will smell those flowers when her spirit visits you."

Meanwhile, I had received instructions from our doctor, arranging for me to go to the T.B. sanitarium in Brighton on the south coast of England. I couldn't believe this was happening to me. It was all so unexpected. I didn't have a cough, no outward sign of anything like T.B.

Two weeks later, Colin and I sat on a wooden bench in the corner of Leicester's draughty railway station, waiting for the southbound train to Brighton. He had his arm on the back of the seat, and he was stroking my hair. I laid my head on his shoulder. I could feel the rough surface of his tweed jacket against my cheek. I said, "I don't feel sick, and I don't know why I need to go to a sanitarium. It sounds like a terrible place. I bet the walls are Eau-de-nil, just like the walls at the mental hospital where my mother was."

"You're not sick, lass. The spot on your lung is small, and as the doctor said, Tuberculosis is curable now with the new antibiotics. You'll get better faster at the sanitarium, I'm sure. From the photographs of the place, it looks as though it's right on the beach. Three months will zip by, and then you'll be well."

"I wonder why they couldn't give me antibiotics at home and forget the sanitarium in some seaside place. It's not right."

"Because Dr. Marks told you, you need lots of bed rest. I don't think you'd get that at home or with your Aunt Olive. Do you?"

"No, I suppose not."

A voice echoed through the station from the loudspeakers. "The Brighton train departs in five minutes from Platform two. Platform two. Brighton train. Platform two."

"That's ours," Colin said. "Come on."

As the train pulled away from the station in a cloud of dense smoke, Colin lifted my small suitcase onto the overhead rack. We had the carriage to ourselves. As the train picked up speed, I studied the landscape flashing by. It was all so peaceful out there. Rows of small houses all close together, then a patchwork of green, then yellow fields separated by hedges. Fields of wheat, then one being plowed by a man on a tractor wearing a blue shirt and a funny hat. Life was going on everywhere around me, but here I was, all my plans gone out the window. It just wasn't fair.

Colin held my hand. "It's not going to be a bad thing putting our plans on hold for a while, you know," he said, "I'll be close by all the time you are in the sanitarium. I've decided to take a room in one of the boarding houses near the beach. Brighton is a great place to spend the winter." He winked and gave my hair a slight tug. "I can have a dirty weekend in Brighton."

I couldn't manage a laugh, but I had to smile. It was not uncommon to hear someone say that they were going to have 'a dirty weekend in Brighton.' The joke had begun in 1841 when the Prince of Wales was known to have taken his mistress there for weekends. Brighton is only a short train ride from London.

"How can you stay there?" I asked. "You have to be ready to leave in a couple of months."

"Don't be daft; I'm not going to America without you. I've decided you need me here, and that's that. When you're better, and your company gets you transferred to New York, then we will go."

"Oh, Colin, how sweet." I pulled away from him. "But, that's not right. I won't let you miss this opportunity to work for Bell Telephone. It would be silly."

Colin didn't answer.

I sat listening to the rhythm of the train on the tracks and the different sound it made as it went through the tunnels.

Suddenly, he sighed, turned, and took both my hands in his. "Look," he said, "there's another reason why I'm going to wait for you. Listen carefully, Amelia."

I looked at him. "What is it, Colin? You passed the medical. You've got a visa; you'll have a green card when you get to New York, so what's wrong?"

"Here is the problem," he said slowly, "when I signed those papers to get my status as a legal resident alien, there was a clause that I had to agree to." He let go of my hands to turn my face to his. "Look at me and listen. As a Legal Registered Alien with a green card, I would be eligible for military service. Do you understand that?"

"How could you be, Colin? You're not a citizen. How could they draft you into the military? You're an alien. See?" I stuck my fingers up above my head.

"A-l-i-e-n."

He turned away to stare out the window, "You don't listen to the news, but you do realize that America is on the verge of helping Vietnam, don't you?"

I didn't know because I didn't listen to the radio or read newspapers. "But," I argued, "you are not an American, and just because America is thinking of helping out another country doesn't mean much, does it. You couldn't be affected in any way." I could feel myself talking, chatting away to blot out what he was going to say to set me straight on events in another country.

"Amelia, it doesn't matter. If I have a green card, I will be drafted into service if they need me, Capiche?" Colin had been to Italy a couple of times with his friends. He often used that word when he was frustrated with me.

"I want you to go to America, Colin. Please don't miss this opportunity to work for a great company in something you are trained for. Okay? Okay?"

"Well, I'm asking you now to be sure if you really want me to go. The risk is that things will escalate in Vietnam. I'll have no choice but to go where and when I'm needed. I want to wait for *you.* I don't want to go without you."

"What will happen to the job with Bell if you don't go now?"

"They'll hire someone else."

"There you are, you see," I said it triumphantly as though I had won the argument. "There you are. I don't want you to stay with me if that is true. Why miss this opportunity."

"I suppose."

"Well, then! Just go and risk that they don't call you up. Anyway, I can't imagine that there will be a war in Vietnam. Are troops really being sent over there? I think it could be over before you even get settled there, don't you?"

"No," Colin said, more to the window than to me. "No, I don't think that will be the case at all."

Fourteen

Hildreth Sanitarium in Brighton faced the sea. Glass enclosed verandas had been built on to the front of the Georgian Mansion so that patients could sit in comfort on the front terrace and face the lovely view of the beach across the boulevard. My room was overlooking the grounds at the side of the house where lawns and rose-beds were carefully tended.

My room-mate, Sheila, a delicate girl of twenty-three, lived in Birmingham and had been at the sanitarium a month. It didn't take long before we were chatting comfortably with each other. "Is that your fiancé you're with, in the photograph?" Sheila asked.

"Yes, this was taken about a year ago."

"Is he tall?"

"Well, much taller than me, anyway. He's about six feet. He's such a lovely man, brown eyes, brown hair, and a nice body."

"Oh. Really," Sheila giggled, "Hussy!"

I threw a pillow at her. She tried to laugh but coughed instead — just a reminder of where I was.

After six weeks, they moved me to another wing facing the ocean, and visitors were allowed. I missed Sheila because she was still in the other part of the sanitarium. My father came with Aunt Olive to visit me. That was a real surprise. Maggi, whom I'd known since high school, was on holiday in Brighton and spent an hour with me reminiscing about old times and other girls we'd known at Folville School.

Colin arrived a few days later with a big bunch of my favorite flowers he'd brought from Uncle Walter. I bawled. "Hey lass," he said, "What is it? I thought you loved Freesias."

"I do," I wept. "But you know Aunt Dorothy died, and I think of her when I smell these. I'm just sad, that's all."

"Well, I came at the right time then to cheer you up." He sat down on the chair, placed carefully by the nurse beside the bed, and handed me a big fancy box. I knew what it was by the label on the lid, *C & A Modes*. We had been shopping together months ago. I had tried on a lovely blue wool suit with a little fur collar. I had told him six guineas was far too expensive, but now I was delighted with the gift, and I could imagine myself in it, with the white blouse he'd chosen.

Then he showed me his airline ticket to New York. It was dated April 30, 1961. I held it in my hands and studied every word. I wondered how long it would be before I owned a ticket with my name on it.

I smiled, "It's all very good," I said. "Wonderful."

It was good, I knew that. But, for some reason, and to this day, I will never know what made me depressed at that moment. Was it the fact that he was going before me? Was it a premonition that maybe I would never see him again?

One of the nurses brought us a cup of tea as we sat on the glass-enclosed veranda overlooking the boulevard and the ocean beyond. The window was open, and I could hear the waves pounding on the Shingle beach. Thin winter sun gave little warmth through the glass, and when I shivered, Colin pulled the blanket around me.

"They should have the windows closed on a day like today," he said.

"No, the idea is to have fresh air all the time. Last week I slept on the outside porch. It's part of the treatment."

"You're so pale, lass. You are getting better, aren't you?" I didn't tell him I had developed a cough, but the doctor had informed me that sometimes T.B. got worse before it got better.

"Oh, yes, I'll be out really soon," I said. "I'm just sorry I can't come to the airport with you to see you off, Colin."

I wasn't just sorry, I was heartbroken. On the day he left, I felt as though it was the end of the world. What if the plane crashed? What if he hated New York? What if he found someone else before I got there?

All the doubts about everything to do with Colin going away, and all that I had to do to get there surfaced in my mind leaving me anxious and depressed, but, true to his word, Colin wrote every week. He described the busy streets of New York with the skyscrapers that reached up and up, leaving a tiny space of blue in between. He wrote about his apartment and his office in Manhattan and the people he'd met at work. After a while, I felt I knew all the places he visited. When he sent me a photograph of himself leaning against a car. A streak of envy ran through me. Things were escalating too fast without me being there; the apartment, now the car! I should have been part of that. He'd written a note underneath the photo of the vehicle, "It's not new, but it runs well." Then a letter. "You will love it here, even though it's hot and humid now."

He wrote that he didn't take baths anymore. "Everyone has a shower in the States," he said.

I tried to imagine what a shower was like. No more weekly baths in the old portable bathtub set up on a Friday night in the kitchen where it was warm. I remember I was usually the last one in the same water after my sister and brother. It wasn't until I was in senior school that we had a bathroom with hot running water. It was a very tiny bathroom next to the Loo. The word Loo comes from the French words *Gardez l'eau*, which means, "Watch out for the water." In medieval times in Europe and Britain, chamber pots were emptied into the street. The maid or someone would shout out the window, *Gardez l'eau*. Probably sounded like "guard the loo." Not a pleasant thought. Of course, that does explain the detritus in the streets and the night soil men who collected it for fertilizer as my father had mentioned.

✳✳✳

Two months rolled by in a series of boredom and reading books, sleeping outside on the veranda, or in a chair on the lawn when it was sunny. It was July when I finally was told I could leave the sanitarium. The air was scented with roses from the garden and salt from the sea. A nurse who came to my room as I was packing announced that the hole in my lung was calcifying nicely, but I would still need the streptomycin injections that would be administered by my doctor when I got home.

My father had offered to come to Brighton to accompany me back. I told him I had to go to London to the American Consulate to show them my X-rays. It was imperative that they knew I was well again and able to go to the States.

It was all quite simple now, I thought. All my worries were over, and I would soon be flying over the Atlantic to New York. At least that's what I hoped as the steam-train puffed its way into London. I wore my new blue suit and the white blouse Colin had chosen. I had convinced one of the nurses to help me touch up the dark roots of my hair. I liked being blonde.

All I had to carry with me was a small overnight bag. I felt good, full of hope and confidence as I walked up the steps of the beautiful white building of the American Consulate with the enormous pillars and the gold eagle poised high above the entrance.

A young woman handed me a piece of paper with the number 63 on it and told me to take a seat in a room filled with people. I waited for more than an hour, watching folks sitting quietly or reading. I studied the walls lined with past presidents of the United States. President J.F. Kennedy was the last one.

A man came to the door, called out my number and introduced himself as Jason. I handed him my medical reports and the large manila envelope with my X-rays. Another hour passed before he finally reappeared to lead me down a long corridor to a small office where a tall man with dark-rimmed glasses sat behind an enormous desk. The name *Elliot Crawford* was stenciled in gold on a sign on his desk. I recognized my file open in front of him.

He looked up at me and smiled; I was conscious of his American accent, "I've read your report, and I've had our medical advisor look at your X-rays. I'll make sure you have all copies of these reports before you leave here today. "Now," he said, motioning for me to take a seat. "Now, you will have to find a sponsor."

I took a deep breath, "Well, my fiancé, Colin Hadley, is already there in New York, and he will sponsor me."

"Is he a citizen?"

"No, not yet, but he will be soon. He works for Bell Telephone Company."

"I see. Well, it's not as simple as that for you. Your disease complicates matters because you are still undergoing treatment. That means you have to have someone to take full responsibility for you and your health requirements and sign an affidavit to that effect."

"Well," I said again, trying to remain calm, "how can I find a citizen to sponsor me if I don't know anyone there?"

I must have looked confused because he took his glasses off, and after carefully placing them on the table, he looked down studying the folder and the papers in front of him, "You do *know* that anyone applying for a green card needs to be either sponsored by a citizen or have employment verified in the U.S.A?"

"I guess so."

"Yes?" Then he sighed and put his glasses back on. He wrote something on a sheet of paper and handed it to me, "Here. Your best bet is to work for a family in America. Many wealthy folks are willing to hire a girl as an au pair or nanny and be the responsible party. You need someone to sign an affidavit that you will not become a ward of the state. That means employment and health care. Do you understand?"

He obviously thought I was a little dim, and I felt foolish.

"I've given you a phone number and the address of a good agency in Herford. He closed the file. I wanted to correct his pronunciation and say Hartford, like heart, not Hertford like hurt. Americans, I thought, should learn English if they work in England.

He went on, "This particular agency hires maids, nannies, and au pairs for families in the States. I'm afraid that's your only way until you are well and able to travel."

"My job," I said, suddenly feeling desperate, "My boss said he would arrange for me to work in New York, what paperwork would he need for that?"

Mr. Compton sighed and leaned his elbows on the table. "I want you to listen carefully, Miss Norton. I know you are eager to join your fiancé in the States. However, because of your disease, even if you had employment, you must have someone willing to be responsible for you."

"Well, what can I do?" I could feel the tears pricking my eyes. "I have to get there soon."

Mr. Crawford closed the file. "Call the agency in Hertford. I repeat, if they can find you employment and that employer would also sign an affidavit for your health care, I would consider it. I cannot help you further. I'm sorry."

The younger man in the suit was already at the door, waiting to show me out. I turned to Mr. Crawford with the idea that suddenly presented itself in my mind. "I can go as a visitor?"

Mr. Crawford looked up, a puzzled expression on his face. "I wouldn't allow you a visitor's visa in your present condition."

I wanted to say, "I'm not pregnant, you know," but I didn't.

✳✳✳

Now I had to tell my parents I couldn't go to the States right away as planned. I had been so sure, so adamant in the face of their doubt. I stood outside the Consulate and tore up the paper Mr. Crawford had given me with the address and phone number of the agency for au pairs. That was the last thing on *my* mind. On the way to Foxby, sitting on the bus, I had a brilliant idea. Colin would have to come back to England. That was the answer. Now I felt a bit better.

Aunt Olive, unmarried and a retired teacher, rarely showed emotion to me, but she saw my face and came to hug me. "You've lost a lot of weight, my dear. Are you still not well?"

"No, I'm fine, it's just that …" I told her the tale of my day at the Consulate and the terrible news that I could not go to the States without a sponsor.

"Oh, dear," she said. She studied me for a minute before she shook her head, "Oh my dear. Surely England is not such a bad place to live, is it? You can go later. America will still be there."

"But it's not what we planned."

"Look, your father rang me this afternoon." She went into the kitchen. I heard her fill the kettle. "He's concerned about you. You were supposed to call him when you were back from Brighton."

"I know. I can't tell him yet, it's too embarrassing."

"Nonsense."

As she placed the tray with the tea things on the side table, she said, "There's a very large parcel in the hall that came from Colin yesterday. If you look at the postmark, you'll notice it took six weeks to get here."

I ran into the hall and brought the package back into the living room. I set it on the floor and just stared at it as I drank a cup of tea. Then I took it up to my bedroom. I shook it to see if it rattled. It was all so carefully wrapped; the ends folded neatly and evenly. Inside, tissue paper lined a pink box. I gasped when I lifted out a negligee, pale pink silk with lace trim and a nightdress to match. I had never seen anything so beautiful.

I laid it on the bed and stared at it before I noticed the folded sheet of paper in the bottom of the box.

Darling:

I saw this in Saks. I couldn't resist buying it, and it will pack easily so you can wear it for me very soon!

Tell that boss of yours to get off his behind and get the ball rolling. I need you here.

I love you, and I am looking forward to seeing you very soon.

I've moved into a bigger apartment with air conditioning. When you write, use the new address.

Love, Colin

Aunt Olive came into the bedroom, "What did Colin send you? Oh," she said, looking at the negligee and nightdress, "that is lovely."

"Now, how am I going to tell him I can't go?" I whispered.

I looked out of the window at the peaceful fields and the grazing sheep in the stillness of the evening. It was always so still at this time of evening in the country. England wouldn't be such a bad place to live. A house in the country would be lovely. Those thoughts consoled me for a few moments before I felt the dread of having to tell Colin. How was I going to approach him about his return, or, on the other hand, I thought, maybe he wouldn't mind a bit? Perhaps he would even welcome the opportunity to return.

"I'm going to have to tell him he has to come home, that's all there is to it," I said to Olive. This time I felt a little more confident. But the question remained, would Colin want to leave New York?

Fifteen

Of course, Colin would want to return, I thought, especially if he knew that I would not be able to join him right away. We would settle here in England. Maybe not Foxby; no industry here. I knew from what Colin had mentioned, that to find a well-paying job as a draftsman, you had to live in London. All at once, that didn't seem so bad either. Living in a large city had never appealed to me, but now I didn't care, as long as Colin came back. People commuted every day to and from London.

"Come downstairs for another cup of tea before you make the call to Colin," Aunt Olive said.

We went downstairs, and I sat quietly, wondering how I was going to break the news. "New York is five hours behind us," Aunt Olive said. "So…" she looked at the grandfather clock, "it's only two in the morning in the States, you should wait until six maybe to call."

✳✳✳

It seemed like an eternity waiting for hours to pass until I dialed the operator. "I'd like to make a person-to-person call to New York," I said.

A woman's brisk voice answered, "I'll connect you to an international operator; hold please."

It was a few minutes before there was a hissing sound and then the ringing of a phone, a different ring to an English telephone. A man's voice answered, "International."

The brisk voice again, "I have a person-to-person call for Colin Hadley at this number."

He repeated the number; it sounded as though he was in a tunnel. "Connecting now, hold please," again the hissing, then Colin's voice. He sounded strange, "Hello."

"Colin," I said, "It's me. Hello love, how are you?"

"Amelia. God, it's good to hear your voice. How are you? Are you home? Did you get my gift?"

"Yes, I did. It's lovely. It really is, thank you. But sweetheart, I have to tell you something." I felt so anxious all of a sudden I just wanted to get it over with.

"All right," he said, "I'm here, go ahead. Sorry about the bad line, but I'll listen. Are you well now, everything okay?" Colin's voice was coming and going over the air-waves, faint then clear.

I hesitated before I could say the words, "Yes, Colin, I'm almost better. But… but…but listen, please." I paused again, then it all came out in a rush, "You have to come home. I can't get to America without a sponsor."

Colin's voice faded away, "What did you say?"

Another hissing sound then silence. I raised my voice, "I said, you have to come back home. Are you there?"

"I'm here." Suddenly he sounded as though he was next door, "Did you say I have to come back?"

"Yes, I have to have a sponsor who will sign an affidavit because of the T.B. I can't be with you, Colin, not in America. Not for a long time."

Silence.

"Colin?"

"I can't come back, lass."

"Pardon. What do you mean? Why not?" I heard my voice slow down as I whispered, "Why not. What do you mean?" My thoughts were racing. My heart was pounding in my ears.

Colin spoke clearly, enunciating every word. "I've been drafted into the army. I leave next month. I got the notice last week. I didn't want to call you at the sanitarium. I was waiting until you got back to Foxby."

Suddenly the room was spinning. A strange lightness enveloped me. Colin's voice came again. "Did you hear what I said?"

"I don't understand, Colin." I managed, "What's going on? How can they do that, you've only been there a few months."

I heard him take a breath, "I have to go. I can't just leave. I'd be a deserter."

"You mean you have to stay in the army for a long time? So, what does that mean? Where will you be? Oh, you have to come home, please, Colin."

"Amelia, it won't be forever. It will be all right. I'll write and let you know where I am."

"You won't be going to Vietnam, though, will you? You can't do that."

"If there is a war, no matter where, you know I will have to go. There's nothing sure about Vietnam, not yet. Please be brave, and don't worry about me."

"Oh, Colin, what have I done?"

I was the one who persuaded him to go and now look at what had happened. For a moment, I fought the blackness, and then I succumbed to it. I felt myself falling into darkness.

I thought I would never experience real depression, but for several days I could not face the world; I could not get out of bed. I was suddenly overwhelmed with guilt. Mea Culpa.

The girls at work called me, so did Mr. Trevors, who said he was trying to negotiate with their affiliate company in New York. Yes, they could hire me, but with T.B., I had to have a sponsor. He had even been in touch with the American Consulate, who had sent him reams of paperwork, giving details of how to emigrate to the USA.

Aunt Olive invited my father and mother to Sunday tea. I'm sure she wanted to make me feel better. I was surprised to see my mother too, because I'd had very little to do with her since I'd been living in Foxby. Now she seemed genuinely sorry about my predicament.

Strangely enough, it was my father who made me feel bad. He said, "Well, Colin told you he might be eligible for military service before he went? If he's a permanent resident of the States with a green card, it's normal procedure. Did you think he would be exempt because he's English? And," he added, "Yes, I can understand if Colin is in communications, he would be one of the first to be called up with a situation like Vietnam, but who knows when that will happen. Nothing has been on the news about it. I would just wait for his letters. He's not there yet."

My mother said, "It was up to Colin in the end. He could have said no. You can't blame Amelia."

Colin called several times from boot camp in Fort Polk in Louisiana. I'd never heard the term 'boot camp,' but he told me it was to train men for the army. He emphasized what my father had said; he would be chosen to go if war actually broke out in Vietnam. His employment with Bell Telephone and his knowledge of communications would be a crucial part of the Army's role at the very beginning. At least Colin would not be in combat on the front where there was fighting. He would be safe behind the scenes. I found that of little solace under the circumstances.

I studied the map of America in the local Library and found Louisiana, trying to envisage his life there. He said it was very humid, not a pleasant climate to live in. I never did know what his job or his training entailed, and he didn't enlighten me. Then he phoned me to tell me he was being transferred to a military base in California. He said it would be a more agreeable climate than Louisiana. The strange thing was, he didn't sound upset at all. He said he was looking forward to being in California. How could he be so happy? The thought that they might be sending him to Vietnam filled me with dread. What was I supposed to do without him?

It was then I started to rethink going to the United States as an au pair. The thought horrified me, but I had been writing to Sheila, the girl who was with me at Hildreth Sanitarium. She had said she was home, but had some exciting news and asked if I would meet her in Brighton and stay for a couple of days.

I agreed, and a week later, we sat on the porch of a pleasant hotel, not too far from the T.B. Sanitarium, on the boulevard opposite the beach listening to the surf pounding on the shingle beach and breathing in the salty air of the sea.

Sheila seemed excited, "Guess what," she said. "I've found an agency in Hertfordshire that arranges for au pairs for America."

"Yes," I said. "Well, I've been told about that. But who needs to cater to these rich Americans who think they won the war for us."

"Oh my! You sound very unhappy. But, what are you waiting for?" she asked.

"I don't want to be a nanny," I said, "or an au pair, whatever that is."

"I thought you were serious about going to America."

"Not if it means running around after some spoiled kid or cleaning up after someone else. Do you want that?"

"Yep. If it will get me a green card."

"Oh, I don't know. It sounds awful."

"Too high and mighty, are you? I guess it won't look good on your C.V., will it?"

Her words echoed in my brain for a minute. Was that what it was for me, I wondered? Yes, I could hear friends now. "You*? You* went as a *maid."* It now seemed obvious; I had to accept the fact that if I wanted to get to the States, I would have to go as an au pair. But did I care? That was the question. It was only at that moment that I realized I did care what people thought of me. My father was to blame for that. The need to be superior had rubbed off on me. I was going as a maid to the States. Oh no!

I thought about it for a minute, then I nodded. It might be the answer to having a green card. I could be with Colin or near to him. "You're right," I said. "I'll come with you to the agency, just to see what they have in mind for us. I'm not saying I'll go anywhere as a maid, but I'll see."

We traveled together on the train from London. It was not a happy journey. I was doubtful I would be able to find someone to take responsibility for me in the United States, a land far away, where no one would know me or probably care. Why would they?

Sheila kept me from turning back. Only her enthusiasm to leave England encouraged me to knock on the door of the old mansion on a quiet street in the large city of Hertford. As in most large cities around Britain, many large old homes had been converted into offices.

An elderly lady, beautifully dressed in a dark suit and a blue and white striped blouse, met us. Her grey hair, coiffed to perfection, was an indication to me that she was serious about her job. She asked us to tell her all about our desires to get to America. Why did we want to go? After completing several pages of the application describing our own families, likes and dislikes, experience with children, and a host of other questions, she said she would contact families who were looking for English maids or nannies. "However," she told me, "since you require an affidavit from someone, it might take a little more time." Just my luck.

✳✳✳

During the next three months, few letters came from the agency in Hertford and, sadly, fewer from Colin. He was too busy with his job in the Army. It seemed that there wasn't a family anywhere in America who wanted to be responsible for me with my history of T.B. It was all very depressing. One family contacted the agency about me, and it looked promising for a few weeks, then it fizzled because I had no babysitting experience. In my teenage years, I can't remember any of my friends babysitting. Mothers didn't go out at night and leave their children with a babysitter. Fathers went out to the pubs, and I cannot ever remember going to a dinner restaurant with my parents. There were lots of cafés in Leicester, and afternoon tea in one of the large department stores was a real treat. Dinner out was never an option for my family. I suppose, looking back now, that was why the Gun Club dinner was so impressive to me. Just a glimpse of wealthy people dining out.

Finally, a letter came from Colin. He was now settled in a military base in California. He sent me the address and wrote that the climate was just wonderful.

Meanwhile, on the news, there were rumors about Vietnam. Things were heating up, although no soldiers were going from

America as yet. Surely, this was not something Colin would be involved in. He was not even an American.

It turned out to be May 1962 when the ground command structure in Vietnam was brought into play. Colin called me, but again he didn't seem upset. I could hardly keep the emotion that bubbled up in me. Would I hear from him while he was there? How would he send letters if he was out in some awful place? Colin was in another world from me even now at this military base in California.

When I spoke to Colin's mother, Ellen, she was trying to be helpful, I could tell. She said, "Colin's a big boy. He can look after himself."

It was the bravery of her thoughts that made me feel worse. Her comments only added to my misery.

When I heard from him four months later, he was in Hanoi. For God's sake, where was that? Little did I know at that time, it was not a good place to be.

✳ ✳ ✳

Another three months passed before I heard from the agency that Mr. & Mrs. Devereau had expressed a desire to see photographs of me, and my parents also. I don't know why. The Devereaus wanted a resume of my qualifications as a housekeeper. Huh?

I provided what I could about my background, waited, and hoped. Things were looking up when I received a photograph of the Devereau family, via the agency, with a short note that said, yes, the family in Chappaqua, New York, was interested in hiring me as a maid. I kissed the face of the man in the photograph. Being a CEO of a large corporation, I assumed he had taken the appropriate course of contacting the Consulate in London to secure my visa to travel out of the country, even though I was to be examined by a doctor in New

York when I arrived. I guessed that it was to reassure the American Consulate in London that I would not become a ward of the state. Such red-tape I had never thought possible.

I had had Streptomycin injections every week; the wonder drug for tuberculosis and many more lung diseases. Surely, now with that information and the sponsorship from the Devereaus, Mr. Crawford could not refuse me admission to the United States of America?

I spent Christmas with my parents. I did so enjoy the usual gifts of Black Magic chocolates with the red ribbon on the box, the orange, and the pomegranate. Things we had not been able to get during the war. I told my parents as we sat at the dining room table that I would be leaving England soon. They had refused to believe my intention to leave and go to America. What was I thinking? Mother had said, it was not right for me to quit my birth country and go to an alien planet where there were guns, and fast cars and goodness knows what else. It wasn't proper.

"I don't know how you will manage," she said.

"I'm going to be working for a wealthy family. You should be pleased. I'll be safe."

My father, looking at me over the top of his glasses, said quietly, "You'll be fine, dear." His words made me cry, and I wanted to hug him and say how sorry I was that I was leaving him. But, of course, he just held out his hand and grasped mine. "I'll take you to the airport when it's time," he said.

My mother sighed, "Well, you've always done what you've wanted to do, so I hope you find Colin and whatever else you are looking for."

Douglas was nowhere in sight. I learned later he was upset that I was leaving, and decided to visit some friends, so he didn't have to say goodbye to me.

Was it goodbye? Would I ever return to England to live? Would I ever see my parents again?

I packed my one suitcase at Aunt Olive's house. My father waved goodbye as I boarded a BOAC turbo-prop bound for New York City, with my X-rays in the large manila envelope tucked under my arm, wondering what on earth I was doing moving so far away.

The woman in the agency had explained in detail that I was fortunate to be going to a beautiful area near White Plains, New York, Chappaqua, I was told was a wealthy town where members of Congress and other important people chose to live. She explained that Westchester County was considered the crème de la crème of the whole area.

To work as a domestic in a foreign country was not my idea of enhancing my life, even if it was the most desirable place to live in New York. The realization that I was embarking on a journey to another country alone didn't hit me until I was halfway across the Atlantic. Shouldn't I be afraid of what I might find in America? Would the family I was going to be with turn out to be awful people? Or, would they be the genteel wealthy folk I so envied on all the American TV shows?

I suppose, if I had let all the doubts overwhelm me, I could have stayed where I was. No, I expected the roads to be paved with gold with glamorous families in beautiful homes.

I wasn't to know that the streets of America were not paved with gold, or good intentions, not from everyone anyway.

Part Two

America - 1962-1980

Your whole life lies before you,
Like a clean white sheet of snow,
Be careful how you tread it,
For every step will show.
-Anonymous

Sixteen

During the trip over the Atlantic, I remember the lady who sat next to me as though it was yesterday. Anna Blakely was her name. Never married, around fifty years old, she had spent her whole adult life as a high school teacher. She reminded me of my Aunt Olive with her clipped, precise accent. She was leaving England to become a personal teacher to the children of a prominent family in Boston. She said she could not stand living in the United Kingdom with things as they were now. It was interesting to hear her views, "Now isn't it a fact," she said, "that two world wars ruined England's economy. Yes?" She tapped my arm, "Of course you are aware that after the last war, the Labour Party introduced its comprehensive welfare state." She sighed, for a moment seeming to reconsider her words carefully before continuing, "You know I like the idea of free education, old-age pensions, and the National Health System. But of course, changes like that always have an adverse effect, don't they?" I don't think she expected me to answer because she carried on, "I suppose it was all well and good to have the Bank of England, public utilities under that same welfare system, but you see, without private and independent enterprise, people get discouraged. They think they might as well live on the dole. Why work when the Government takes care of you? Oh, dear, dear me."

I said, "Well, my fiancé said that's because England is a socialist country now."

"True," she said, "that's why it will be great in the States. They want private enterprise. You could even have your own business there. You can't do that in England." She sighed again. "Now we have a three-day work week, and capital punishment is banned. I ask you what is the benefit of that? No wonder all the power has gone from Britain. Can you believe we have attracted more than two million migrants with low numeracy skills to take the place of skilled workers?"

As she went on, I realized how ignorant I was of England's political situation. I felt illiterate. It made me wonder if my naiveté would get me into trouble. I decided I was too uneducated to vote anyway. I would be one of those people who is swayed by the media rather than thinking about it and analyzing it on my own.

I think I listened to the drone of the engines all night long. I don't remember if I slept. I walked up and down the aisles a lot. It wasn't normal for me to have to sit for hours and hours in the confined space of a cabin.

I do remember seeing the lights of Boston as we flew over to land at New York's Idlewild Airport.

Anna Blakely said goodbye. She didn't look as tired as I felt. When she had walked away and melted into the crowd, I realized I was among hundreds of people standing around in one room. Most seemed to be looking for relatives or loved ones as they emerged from the plane.

I stood for a while, looking around at the melee. How would Mr. Devereau be able to recognize me? Then I saw a man walking toward me, smoking a large cigar, and looking as though he'd just stepped out of the bar in an American Western. He came toward me, a broad smile glued to his face, and greeted me in a Southern drawl that fitted his image exactly. I thought it would be quite feasible for him to have a gun hanging from his belt under his jacket. He looked vaguely like the photo I had received of the family. Perhaps he recognized me from the recent photograph I had sent to the family, or maybe it was the tired and bewildered expression of a lost little girl who had just arrived on the plane from England.

✳✳✳

His friendliness didn't stop me from being nervous as I sat in the cream leather passenger seat of his Lincoln Continental.

It was dusk. In the darkening light, I could see dirty piles of snow at the side of the road. We were crawling behind a stream of red tail lights along a four-lane highway on the outskirts of New York. When the tail lights became less, I knew we were out of the city and in the suburbs of another town. Clusters of houses and small shops spilled light into the street for a few minutes, and then we were on a two-lane road winding through forests of tall pine and fir.

The clock on the dashboard read 6:10 p.m., but it was past two o'clock in the morning for me still on British time. I couldn't stop yawning, and I was hoping the anxiety I was feeling would go away, although Mr. Devereau seemed to want to talk, "So, Amelia, this is your first trip to the States, huh?" He puffed steadily on his enormous cigar.

"Yes," I said. "Thank you for sponsoring me. I am grateful."

"Sure, sure." He leaned over the wide console to pat my knee. "We must get you to the hospital in White Plains tomorrow. Make sure you pass our medical team. We'll do that first thing."

A huge diamond in his pinky ring flashed as he expertly flicked ash into the already full ashtray on the dashboard. I turned my head away as the smell reached me; it lingered in the car, although he did open the window an inch. He drawled on, "Robyn…Mrs. Devereau is looking forward to your arrival. We had to fire our last au pair. It sure upset the household for a while."

I wanted to ask why she was fired but decided it wasn't quite the appropriate time to do so.

He chatted about my trip and talked about the members of his family. They all sounded like very nice people. "Of course, you will be expected to help Robyn with our dinner parties. We do entertain a lot," he said.

I could feel my eyes growing heavy as I heard myself saying, "Oh dear, does Mrs. Devereau expect me to be a chef? I'm not experienced in that."

"I'm sure you'll learn. She's a great cook. Jeremy helps out with the serving."

"Who's Jeremy?" I asked.

"He's our butler, chauffeur, general handyman around the house." He chuckled suddenly, almost as though he was going to tell a joke. "He's Scottish, our Jeremy," he said, "and we couldn't understand a word for a few weeks. Even now, I have problems myself with that."

For a while, he was silent. I looked out of the window at the ever-changing scenery. Even in the dark, lights of one small town seemed to be joined to another in an endless line of buildings.

I had studied the photographs of the family I was about to join. Mrs. Devereau looked pretty, youngish with red hair. She was standing by a dark-haired, middle-aged man and two boys by the entrance to what looked like an English Tudor style house. The photo had not been a recent one, because unlike the photograph, Mr. Devereau now had white hair. He was talking again in his low drawl, "Now I'm retired, Robyn likes to get away on vacation every few months. You'll be there for the children, of course. Richard is twelve. He needs someone to keep him in line while we're gone."

I wondered how old Robyn could be if Richard were only twelve.

My question was soon answered as we pulled into a circular driveway of a house that reminded me of Kilby Manor just outside Foxby, which had been converted to a hotel somewhere back in the twenties.

Robyn Devereau stood tall in the doorway of what appeared to be a replica of an English half-timbered Tudor style house. The sconce lights on both sides of the double doors illuminated her like a model posing for a magazine in beige pants and matching blouse, which shone like silk in the light. A blue cardigan was draped around her shoulders. Her auburn hair was swept back into an elaborate chignon accentuating high cheekbones and a sculptured pink mouth.

I found myself being scrutinized as I tucked a wayward strand of hair behind my ear. I had recently touched up my dark roots to be sure I would look my best, but I had lost some of the bobby-pins that held my thin, fine hair up in a ponytail. After almost twenty-four hours of travel, I could only imagine my appearance was not very appealing. The woman offered her hand without smiling. "Have a good flight?"

"Yes, thank you."

"I didn't realize you were so petite," she said. "We'll have to get some new uniforms for you. The ones we bought for Sveta, our Swedish au pair, would hang on you like a sack."

"Uniform?" I queried.

"My girls always wear a uniform, blue, sometimes yellow, and a hat."

"Hat?" I couldn't hide my horror.

"We don't like to find hairs in our soup, you know." With that, she turned and went inside, leading the way into a dimly lit hall. She looked back to watch me pick up my suitcase, "Oh, for goodness sake, Jeremy will bring your luggage."

As we passed an open door along the hall, I stepped back to look inside the room. A young blond-haired boy was lying in front of a TV. He turned to look at me. I smiled at him and said, "Hello, you must be Richard."

The boy stared at me for a long moment before he stuck out his tongue.

"Nice boy," I murmured to myself as we continued down the hall, through a vast expanse of the kitchen, and up narrow stairs to a small two-room apartment.

I heard Jeremy before I saw him coming into the room behind me. His Scottish brogue instantly comforted me, "Whatever can you have in this soot case? It weighs a ton."

I turned to find myself face to face with a tall, slim young man with unruly sandy hair. "Hello, I'm Jeremy," he said.

I reached for his hand, "Pleased to meet you."

Robyn settled herself on the small sofa, beige. Like a loveseat.

Jeremy, on his way out, winked at me, "See you later," he said. I knew I had at least one friend.

"Now, there are just a few things we need to sort out," Robyn said, crossing her legs and leaning back, "just a few things."

"Excuse me, Mrs. Devereau," I said. "I know it might be inconvenient, but could I, er…would you mind if I made myself a cup of tea. It might wake me up a bit."

Robyn's face flushed as she sat up straight, uncrossing her legs. "We only have herbal teas in this house, dear. I'm not about to cater to your English whims. I do hope you understand that."

I sat down on a chair opposite her. "I'm sorry," I said. "I'm just so tired. It was a long flight." I decided at that moment I would buy my own tea. I wasn't about to drink herbal teas no matter what, and all at once, I felt drab and dull in front of this well-put-together woman. My confidence was evaporating.

"The quicker we get to the rules of the house, the better," she said evenly. Robyn leaned forward; her intense brown eyes held my attention. "I do not want you to fraternize with Jeremy in his apartment, which is at the other end of the house, not even during the afternoons after your duties," she hesitated, "or any other time. Is that clear?"

I wanted to ask why but thought better of it.

Robyn continued, "I have a few more things to say. Then you can go to sleep. This is a comfortable apartment for you, isn't it?"

I looked around the living room with its small square table, two chairs, and pretty sofa. I could just see the bedroom with a single bed and its bright yellow quilt and a nightstand. It looked inviting at that moment. I couldn't see the bathroom. "It's fine," I said. "Thank you."

Robyn sighed before she continued, "Clifford's son, Canyon, is shortly due back from skiing in Europe. She rose from the couch and went to stand by the window. After a moment, she pulled the blind down and turned to me, "Canyon is a very attractive man, and he tends to flirt with young women. It would be to your advantage if you were not overly friendly toward him."

She sounded so serious I just stared at her. "As you say, Mrs. Devereau," I finally managed.

Robyn flounced to the door. She stood in the doorway, her back to me, "I'll have a list of your duties for each day taped to the fridge. Clifford is taking you to White Plains to the hospital tomorrow, where you'll be examined by our own doctor. Then he'll take you to the uniform shop in town afterward. We must get you properly fitted out. She turned to me, "Mustn't we?"

I didn't think the question was directed at me, so I said nothing.

"We usually start our day at seven," she said, "so if you could make a note of that, I'd appreciate it." She smiled, "You sleep well now, goodnight."

When she left, closing the door softly behind her, I went to the window and lifted the blind. I looked out. Darkness enveloped the grounds except for a patch of light shining from a window of a small squat building close by. I opened the window and listened to the soughing of the wind in the trees. It sounded like the sea, and I was reminded of my time in Brighton at the T.B. sanitarium. When I closed the window, took off my shoes, and lay back on the bed, I relished the stillness after the hustle and bustle of a long day. Tomorrow, I decided I would talk to Jeremy. The scenario that Robyn had presented to me was intriguing. What was going on in the Devereau household? Who I could fraternize with and who I could not was quite a mystery, but with little energy left to think about it, I rose from the bed, undressed, washed my face in the small bathroom sink, and slipped between the clean sheets of the single bed.

I awoke to the darkness I had never experienced before. There was no light from a street lamp to send a sliver of light into the room — no light shining under the closed door. It took me a minute to realize I wasn't at home in my bed at Aunt Olive's in Foxby. I fumbled for the light on the bedside lamp. My small travel alarm clock read four-twenty. The house was quiet except for the hum of what I suspected was the central heating, and I suddenly realized the room was stiflingly hot. I was not used to heat in a bedroom. In fact, the two radiators my aunt had recently installed were in the hall and the living room only. "One wouldn't think of heating a bedroom," she'd said.

Everything was still and dark outside. I opened the window wide and listened again to the sound of the wind in the firs. I knew I wouldn't sleep any longer. I opened my suitcase, dumped everything on the sofa in the living room, and found my airmail writing pad and envelopes at the very bottom. I suddenly felt very much alone. What had I left behind me, and what was I expecting to find here, three thousand miles from England? At that moment, I questioned my sanity. The reason, I said to myself over and over, was to know more about Vietnam, to be closer somehow to Colin, to find out where he was.

I wrote to my parents, Aunt Olive, and Colin's mother. I told them about my long trip over the ocean, the lady I'd met on the plane, and what I knew about the family so far, which was not very much.

I had been writing to Pauline in Africa every week. Sometimes it took five weeks to reach her, so the news was out of date, but she wanted to know what I was up to.

Dawn crept through the room without me being aware of it. When I looked out the window, I could see trees, just tall green trees, evergreens — different from the undulating fields of Foxby and the occasional elm or oak, deciduous trees, which at this time of the year would still be bare and naked with thick branches that would hold a lot of snow in winter. And, outside my window at home in Leicester, I would have seen the smoke, haze, and factory chimneys. But this! This was paradise, and perhaps at that moment, I knew I would never be a city-dweller again.

I took my first shower. At first, I wasn't sure I liked the water spraying on me. After only baths in lukewarm water, it was very different. I soon found the whole experience of a shower soothing, and washing my hair was so easy. I could see now how it had made an impression on Colin. It brought to mind again our Friday night ritual at home, a metal bathtub, the same water, Pauline and Douglas, then me. It was a standard request of each other not to pee in the water.

At 6:30 by my clock, I dressed in my new sweater and skirt, nylons, and flat shoes. When I went downstairs to the kitchen, I found Robyn making breakfast for me. I was prepared to be ordered to help, but it wasn't to be, not that day anyway. The scrambled eggs served with lox, bagels, and cream cheese were delicious. I had never tasted lox before. It had been many hours since I had eaten anything, so perhaps that's why it all tasted so good.

At that moment, my heart warmed to Robyn just a little bit. This was the first day of my new life. So far, so good.

Seventeen

Mr. Devereau drove me to the hospital in White Plains. It was a large brick building that spread for two city blocks. For some reason, I anticipated something more like the T.B. Sanitarium in England. I had to remind myself that there were no sixteenth-century mansions in America that had been converted to modern-day living requirements.

My X-rays were given to a plump nurse with a pretty face and a sweet smile. I thought I was going to be examined, but the nurse nodded to Mr. Devereau, "I'll have the doctor look at these, and then we'll be in touch to schedule an appointment for an examination…if needed," she added.

Afterward, on a busy street, the uniform shop was well-stocked. It was apparent, by the vast selection of uniforms hanging on the racks, there was a need for outfits in this upscale area of large homes. Everyone had an au pair, of course. I was given two coat-like cotton uniforms: one blue, one yellow, complete with a hat to try on. I thought they were not at all bad-looking. They did wonders for my figure and the hat was just a shaped band of the same material that served to keep hair back from one's face.

Driving down the long driveway back to the house that morning, I had the chance to look at the house as it sat amidst evergreens of all kinds. Paths meandered around the neatly clipped lawns — not so different from our stately homes in Britain. A green and gold plaque was attached to the wall by the front door: *Fairview House.* It was an elegant house with its tall gabled roof, half-timbered walls with stucco in between resembling the fifteenth-century buildings in England.

As Mr. D opened the front door for us, he said, "Oh, by the way, usually, you will use the back door when you come in."

There it was, the reminder that I was the maid.

This time, I did take a moment to inspect the beautiful tapestries depicting hunting scenes that adorned the walls of the semicircular foyer, and the granite steps which led up to a wide carpeted hallway opposite the front doors. Rooms led off the hall on either side. The formal section of the house had a very large living room complete with separate clusters of comfortable chairs and small tables. A dining room with a highly polished wooden table and eight chairs on each side, plus end chairs with arms that were intricately carved with scrolls — all highly polished. A candelabra hung above the dining table with elaborate glass droplets that I assumed would have to be taken down and washed by me.

And so began my routine in the Devereau household. On Mondays, I was to clean and dust the staircase and upstairs rooms, Tuesdays were laundry days. Wednesdays, the best day I was told to clean the toilets and baths, plus the shower areas. Thursday was my day off. Fridays, downstairs dusting, vacuuming. On Saturdays, the kitchen needed extra cleaning in preparation for the parties planned, or gatherings in the library for some political conversation. Robyn often followed me around, showing me how she liked the cleaning done and not to forget the window-sills. I caught her running her fingers over the frames of the paintings quite often. She said I should always answer the front doorbell, the back only if she wasn't home.

I did have an hour off for lunch each noon, and I looked forward to that. At least I could prepare a sandwich in the butler's pantry and take it up to my apartment, which was relaxing after being under the constant gaze of Robyn. It was a relief when she was out at one of her philanthropic meetings in White Plains or New York. The afternoons seemed to pass quickly, and at four, I was expected to help prepare dinner to be served promptly at six.

When no one was home, I often sat in the day-room, which boasted a television and comfortable recliner chairs. The TV was always interesting to me, particularly the ads. Our BBC didn't include advertising. It was all very straight forward news and such.

Another place that intrigued me was the library. With a brick fireplace, and red leather-studded wing back chairs set around the room, I decided the aristocrats of England would feel right at home here in what would be called a smoking room, primarily for the men after a formal dinner for after-dinner drinks. Elegant dark-wood side tables beside each chair sported unique lamps with nude bronze female figures holding white pleated shades. I stayed there when I thought no one was around. There were so many shelves with impressive reading materials to browse. Also, it was my delight to explore the beautifully groomed grounds after dinner. I don't remember an abundance of flowers in the garden. Still, the lawns and topiary were immaculate, kept that way by Mr. Taylor, a quiet man who kept a low profile, refusing to have even a casual conversation with me. I wondered why that was. Jeremy and I would meet in the enclosed garden arbor at the back of the house to chat about Mr. Taylor and the family, I thought about Robyn's advice against any fraternizing with Jeremy, but I figured she didn't have to know. I don't remember her even being in the garden actually, or trying to check up on me when I went outdoors.

Jeremy had been with the Devereaus for two years. He said he didn't have any desire to go back to Scotland, and the family had been pleased to have him stay on.

I was curious about Robyn and the elderly Mr. Clifford Devereau, and I asked Jeremy if he knew how they had met. They seemed such an odd pair. She, with her high-society, butter-won't-melt-in-her-mouth demeanor, and Mr. Devereau, with his laidback southern drawl and equally laidback attitude to everything and everyone around him.

Jeremy said Robyn had been Clifford's secretary when he was in business in his office in Manhattan. He was the president of his large corporation and was still on the Board, where he attended meetings once a month.

I figured Robyn must be half Clifford's age. She was now fortyish, although I never knew for sure. I never saw her without makeup and beautifully coiffed hair.

Apart from the game room next to the library with a sizeable felt-covered pool table and one for table tennis, there were six bedrooms, plus the master suite that took up one whole wing. The king-size bed seemed small in the expanse of the sitting area with a chaise lounge and two armchairs. Clifford and Robyn had separate bathrooms and large dressing areas.

Of course, like most au pairs, my place was in the kitchen. It was huge with a center table, a large refrigerator and separate freezer. Every modern amenity possible, including a butler's pantry—the unique little space with a sink and lots of shelves for storing extra plates, cutlery, and such, had a lot of counter space and was next to the stairs to my apartment.

After a few weeks, I learned the routine of the household, experienced grapefruit for the first time, tried to like corn on the cob, but failed. Our corn in the UK is called maize and is used only for cattle feed.

I tried to understand these precocious, spoiled, rich children, who lived in such luxury compared to most British kids that I'd known. Christopher was fifteen and polite, although he was not about to have any conversation with me at any time. On Saturdays, he tucked himself away in a separate room that was part of the large basement. Robyn told me it would be best if I did not even attempt to try to clean that room, and when I ventured down there when everyone was out, I noticed a sign on the door that said NO ADMITTANCE – KEEP OUT. The door was locked.

I was not to know until a few weeks later when the door had been left ajar, that it was a professional-looking chemistry lab. In my mind, I could already envisage him as a scientist perfecting a cure for some terrible disease.

The twelve-year-old Richard was very rude. Many times, I had the urge to slap him. He stuck his tongue out whenever I looked at him, and on one occasion, he kicked me. I grabbed his shirt and held him captive for a moment. I whispered, "Don't ever do that again." He avoided me for a few weeks, and he never kicked me again. Luckily, I only encountered him on weekends. Both boys were used to having domestic help around the house, and they ignored me. They were both too old for babysitters, according to Robyn, for which I was thankful.

Jeremy drove Robyn to Chappaqua for her ladies' meetings once a week and knew her far better than I ever did. She treated me coolly most of the time, although I did learn a lot about cooking. I observed the way she prepared meals for dinner parties, which seemed to take place every Saturday night.

The groceries, including delicious bread, ordered by telephone, were delivered by Hugo, a dark-haired Italian. I noticed Robyn always greeted him herself, unlike the man from the butcher's shop, who was virtually ignored. It fascinated me the different faces and attitudes Robyn displayed to visitors to the house. She could be quite rude to delivery men, except for Hugo!

I had yet to meet Canyon, Clifford's son by a former marriage. I asked Jeremy if he'd met him.

"Oh, yes. He's a good-looking chap; I like him. I think he's a bit of a devil with the ladies."

"Really?" I asked, "Why?"

"I think he's the reason they fired Sveta, the Swedish au pair. She flirted with him or him with her; I'm not quite sure. You'll soon find out everything in this house is kept secret from the hired help."

His words *hired help*, made my stomach turn. It reminded me of the time I'd said to Colin that we would probably have a maid in *our* house.

I watched the television in my room in the evenings. I began to understand what was going on in Vietnam. It was depressing news since the communist forces had infiltrated Hanoi. I suddenly realized Jeremy was the same age as Colin, and I wondered why he was in this cushy position in the States instead of in the military.

"What about your military service?" I asked.

"Well," he said, "I've got some medical problems. They wouldn't accept me."

"Oh?" I waited, thinking he'd enlighten me, but he didn't.

He motioned for me to sit down. "At least we're here. We have our green cards."

"Right," I agreed, "It's true. We can stay if we want to."

"That's right," he said, patting my knee, "that's right."

✳✳✳

I was concerned that I had not heard a word from Colin since I'd been in America, and when pale green leaves suddenly appeared on the plane trees, buds on the horse chestnut, I realized that it had been over three months.

It was one early morning when I noticed Mr. Taylor, the gardener, busy weeding around a tree with lovely white blossoms. He was thin and agile as he almost jumped when he saw me. "I don't think you should be out back here," he said. "I don't want you to get into trouble."

"Hello, I'm Amelia," I said, intentionally ignoring his warning. "I used to work with my uncle, who was a market gardener in England. He used to make wedding bouquets of Freesias, my favorite flower."

"That's nice," he said, bending down again to scoop up some weeds.

"I love the way you trimmed those trees into shapes."

"Thanks."

"What's the name of this tree? I don't recognize it."

"Dogwood."

It was obvious this man was not about to have any conversation with me, which was a shame because I thought he must be lonely. I'd never seen him in a car, driving out of the driveway or anywhere. I had spotted him in different parts of the gardens, but he surely was a mystery man — another one to add to the mythical inhabitants of Fairview House.

Later that afternoon, I was upstairs cleaning the master suite when the doorbell rang with Westminster Chimes that swept through the whole house. It always reminded me of our clock in the living room. When I spotted a van in the driveway with *Western Union* written on the side, I raced down the stairs to open the door. A young man, neatly dressed in a navy-blue uniform, handed me a telegram. "Well, it came about three," he said as though I had asked him a question. "I brought it right out."

"Thank you," I said as I took the yellow envelope from his hands and closed the door.

I stared at it. It was addressed to me. Telegrams were usually bad news, weren't they? I could feel my heart beating faster. I had heard my mother had been ill. Aunt Olive was in her late sixties. It could be anything.

I went inside and sat down at the kitchen table, staring at the envelope. I didn't expect it might be something to do with Colin. I always believed no news was good news, and when I'd last written to Ellen, she'd said that the army did move men around to remote areas where the mail could take weeks, so there was no need to worry. Still, I trembled as I opened it. There, in the stilted printed lettering, were the words: *Colin Hadley. Stop. Reported missing in action. Stop. Call me. Stop. Ellen.*

I let myself sink back in the chair. "Oh no," I said aloud.

I closed my eyes and buried my face in my hands. I had to give myself time to think, not to panic. I must have sat there for five minutes before I realized I was not alone. I felt his presence before I opened my eyes to see in front of my face a gold chain with a cross. It belonged to a blond, curly-haired man who was leaning down to look at me. I made myself concentrate on pressed cream pants and a crisp blue shirt open almost to his waist.

A voice, "Hey there, why so sad?"

"Oh God," I said.

"Well, He straightened up, "No one's called me that before, but I'm sure you can tell me why you look so upset. Can I help?"

I thrust the telegram up at him. He took it, read it, folded it up neatly, and laid it on the table. "Brother or boyfriend?" he asked as he sat down at the table opposite me.

"Fiancé."

"Ah." He hesitated for a moment, "You know you shouldn't make this into more than it might be. Men at war are often thought to be lost. They usually turn up."

"Well, where could he be? It is Vietnam, you know." I fumbled in my pocket for a handkerchief.

"It's simple," he said, "call this Ellen, whoever she is." He rose quickly and carried the telephone to the table, leaving the cord stretched between the counter. "Okay," he said, "give me the number."

He obviously knew the house well because he went to a drawer and pulled out a notepad and pencil. By this time, I had assumed he was Canyon, the infamous son of Mr. Devereau. When I looked at him now, I could see how he would be labeled handsome with his blonde curly hair against tanned skin and very blue eyes. Too feminine for me with his long eyelashes. I compared him to Colin with *his* rugged good looks: brown eyes, brown hair, and tweed jackets.

"I don't know how to call England," I said, blotting tears with my handkerchief, "and I don't think Robyn would allow long-distance calling anyway."

"Give me the number."

I wrote it quickly on the paper he set before me. Without hesitation, he dialed all the prefixes, and I heard him talking to the international operator giving the telephone number of Ellen. I listened to the ringing of an English telephone. He thrust the phone in my hand and sat down at the opposite end of the table, watching me intently. I waited, listening to the ring-ring, ring-ring, ring-ring.

145

The operator's voice cut in, "No one is answering that number; please call later."

I yelled into the phone, "Let it ring; let it ring."

Finally, there was Ellen's voice, "Hello?"

"Ellen, it's me."

"Oh, Amelia, it's almost nine o'clock. I'm just getting ready for bed. Give me a minute." There was static on the line, but I could hear her moving about. I pictured her in the living room in her slippers and robe, making room on a seat laden with a stack of old and new newspapers; the living room I knew so well. "All right, now I'm with you," she finally said. "You got the telegram. Isn't it dreadful?"

"I can't believe it," I said, trying to talk normally.

"I wanted to know where Colin was," Ellen said. "You know me. I had to find out from somebody. I called the hotline for military men in the States. I had a devil of a job convincing them it was my son I was trying to find. Some clerk wanted to know who I was and where I lived and all that. I shouted at him, 'I'm his mother.' I suppose he believed me because he explained that it was suspected that Colin went missing with two other men. Apparently, headquarters had heard from Colin's commanding officer." I could hear the quaver in her voice.

What could I say except, "I am so sorry. It's my fault. I thought he told me he was *not* on the front line."

"I don't know either why he was there. But it's no good crying over spilled milk, is it?" I heard her blow her nose. "Nothing we can do."

"Nothing?" I echoed.

"Wait, that's what we do. Wait."

I heard a click as she replaced the receiver.

Ellen Hadley was not pleased with me, and she had every right. I lived with the guilt of having persuaded Colin to take the job with the phone company instead of waiting for me, which he wanted to do. Now there was nothing I could do about it.

Eighteen

When Robyn sauntered into the kitchen, her eyes widened, seeing Canyon sitting at the table with me. "I thought I heard voices," she said, holding out her arms to him, "Canyon!" A bright smile lit up her face, "When did you arrive?"

Canyon rose from the table and gave Robyn a long hug. "Robyn, Robyn," he said, standing back to look at her, "still as beautiful as ever." Robyn blushed and turned away, but she was flattered by his words. I noticed when he hugged her; she pushed herself against him. I wondered how fond he was of her. It seemed she really liked *him.*

Canyon handed Robyn the telegram. This man certainly seemed to take charge of things. When she read it, she looked at me and shook her head. "I'm sorry," she said. "I'm sure he'll be all right, though, you mustn't let it worry you too much until you know more."

That was the way it was left. All I could do was to try to forget it for now, but of course, I couldn't. Robyn wasn't about to let me off the hook for the day's work she had on the schedule for me, which was probably good because there was nothing I could do. I was to clean the silver and make sure the butler's pantry was clean. She said she had found stains in the sink in there.

I consoled myself with the thought that at least Canyon was sympathetic to my problem when he came over to me and took my hand in a gentle grip just for a minute. Robyn raised her eyebrows when she looked at me. She need not have worried; handsome though this man was, I had no intention of making a play for him, now or in the future. But he was an ally, and that was important to me at that time.

I had to force myself to stop dwelling on Colin and his fate, whatever it might be, although I lost my appetite completely, and that was sad because Robyn was a splendid cook. Everyone at her parties raved about her Italian dishes that I had never experienced in England. I realized how narrow my existence had been.

During the next month, my thoughts rarely strayed far from Colin, and I thought I would go mad, trying to understand how he could have got lost.

It was good that I did have to concentrate on work, even though cleaning was not exactly stretching my mind. I remember that one of my duties was to take care of the laundry. I finally managed to get the hang of the washing machine and the dryer. Aunt Olive had a tiny washing machine but no dryer. All the washing was hung on the line to dry. My mother's system was archaic. She had to boil water in a large brick copper, which is a large tub made of copper, with a coal fire underneath. The water was transferred to a ribbed metal tub, and the laundry would then be punched and twisted with what looked like a three-legged stool on a pole. The clothes were rinsed by hand in the sink and shoved through two rollers of a mangle. Then everything was hung outside on the line to dry. Monday was wash day in our house, and it did take all day. Now, I could pop the laundry into the washing machine and have it dried and ready to iron within a couple of hours. I ironed the boy's shirts and pants. And Mr. Devereau's were sent to the cleaners.

Meanwhile, I was aware that when Canyon was around the house, Robyn seemed happier. Even her demeanor was softer toward me when he sat in the kitchen talking to her. Perhaps she realized I was not a threat to her and her association with Canyon.

I found Clifford, the quiet husband, who now I referred to as Mr. D, seemed to be content to tuck himself away in his office in the mornings, oblivious to the comings and goings of the family. He spent most afternoons watching television in the dayroom. I always knew where he was because of the ubiquitous and nauseating smell of half-smoked cigars left in the ashtrays.

One early morning, deep in thought about Colin, I wandered around the perimeter of the house and ended up in the back part of the garden where Mr. Taylor lived. I noticed from my window that he often stood in the doorway of the small ranch style house with a cigarette stuck between his lips. I wondered what his past was and how he came to be here.

Today, the door was open; he seemed to study the lawns and the garden beds.

I had to pass by quite close, so I said, "Hello."

"Morning."

I thought that would be the end of it, but then he stubbed his cigarette out in a sand-filled decorative pot by the door. "I've got some Freesias in the greenhouse," he said.

"Oh, how lovely."

"C'mon. I'll show you. They're just about to bloom."

The greenhouse was small, but heated, and smelled just like I remembered my Uncle's greenhouses in Foxby. I breathed in the sweetness that filled the air. I wondered then how memories could evoke such feelings of sadness, joy, and all the things I'd experienced when I lived in Foxby.

Mr. Taylor busied himself, cutting most of the budding blooms and gave them to me.

"Thank you. What a treat. How long have you been at Fairview House?"

"Since she moved here with him," he said.

"You mean Robyn and Clifford?"

"Yes. Robyn's my sister."

"Your sister?"

"Yup, hard to believe, isn't it. But, you know that she wasn't always as she is now. I mean, she came from an impoverished background as I did, and, trust me," he hesitated, "she wasn't the jumped up snob she is now. She was just a secretary. Clifford took a fancy to her and bingo; suddenly, she was the lady of the house. But," he stopped to nod his head, "she'd promised she'd give me a job at the house as a gardener, and here I am."

Robyn was smart marrying so well. But, I gave Kudos to her for keeping her promise to her brother.

Of course, Robyn was usually the topic of conversation when Jeremy and I met after dinner in the garden. We decided that after divorcing Canyon's mother, Clifford married Robyn because of her looks. And, thinking we knew Robyn, with her taste for expensive clothes and furniture, we were sure she must have married him for his money. I didn't notice a display of affection between the two, but I imagined Mr. D, at eighty, was content to have the house running smoothly under her supervision. Although, I wondered, after seeing Canyon and Robyn together, if she had more than a stepmother's affection for *him* or was she just a flirt. I rather suspected the latter.

I had been at Fairview House for six months when I began to detect that Robyn had an admirer. Hugo, the Italian baker who delivered other groceries as well, became a contender for her attention. She was obviously flattered. I could tell by the way she dressed on Tuesdays, when he came to the back door laden with bags of food and excellent freshly baked bread, that something was going on between the two of them. At that time, I didn't realize that this man's appearance at Fairview House would portend a turn of events for me over which I had no control. An event that would change the course of my life completely.

✳✳✳

It was early June; the air was sweet and warm. I had been up and out at dawn, where I had found a Robin's egg on the ground. I wondered if they had Cuckoos here, although I had never heard one. Cuckoos lay their eggs in other birds' nests, then when the chicks hatch, all the other eggs are heaved out of the nest, and the host bird is tricked into raising Cuckoo chicks. They are not lovely birds, but the sound of the Cuckoo is very much a part of an English summer.

Back indoors, after I had cleared away the breakfast dishes, I went upstairs to make the beds. I heard the doorbell ringing at the kitchen entrance. Unlike the melodious front door chimes, the back door had a buzzer. The button tended to stick down, and unless the caller lifted his finger from it quickly, it didn't stop buzzing until the button finally popped out, sometimes minutes later.

I heard the brief buzz and Robyn open the door promptly. Hugo's accent was unmistakable. I went about my chores and thought no more about Robyn or Hugo.

It was noon when I went downstairs and into the kitchen. I opened the door to the butler's pantry. There, leaning against the counter, was Robyn with her arms around Hugo's neck. Her skirt was up around her waist, and I could only guess where his hands were. I didn't wait to find out. In horror, I closed the door and fled upstairs to my apartment. What was to happen now? Either she would ignore the event, which I hoped, or, oh God, she may want me to leave.

The thought entered my mind, just momentarily, that she could be a candidate for blackmail. How delicious to have the opportunity to blacken her name, but it was clear to me the obvious solution would be for her to invent an excuse to be rid of me before I could spread the word to her husband about her philandering. Yes, logically, she would fire me. She would have to.

Sure enough, half an hour later, there was a knock on my door. Robyn walked in and sat down on the sofa, crossed her legs casually, as she had done the first and last time she was in my apartment. She leaned back with one arm draped across the back and looked directly into my eyes. "You know I'm going to have to dismiss you," she said lightly. There was even a hint of laughter in her voice.

"Why?" I asked, trying to keep my voice even innocent.

"You know perfectly well *why*, dear."

I looked her, and as firmly as I could muster, and said, "It's none of my business what goes on in the house. Really."

I was back on stage for a minute, trying I suppose, to impress this woman. I put on my best British accent, "It's none of my business."

I could feel the intensity of her gaze. Her voice turned gravelly, "Do you think I was born yesterday?"

"But, it *is* none of my business," I said. "I don't even know anyone except Jeremy, and he wouldn't care what you do. It's not his business either. We both appreciate being here; you know that."

For a moment, it looked as if she was reconsidering, and then she confirmed my fears, "Look, dear, it is not going to work." It sounded to me as though she thought she was talking to an idiot. A conciliatory tone in her voice, "I know Clifford likes you a lot, and apparently, so does Canyon, so I'll write a good reference for you." She uncrossed her legs and sighed, "I think it's best for us all if I buy your ticket home to England. You fit better there anyway, don't you?"

"Oh no," I said. "I have nothing to go home to. What about my fiancé serving in *your* war? When he comes out of the army, I want to be here for him."

"I'm sorry," she said, rising from the couch. "That could be years. If he's lost, there's a good chance that he's been taken prisoner by the Viet Cong. That's what I've heard is happening. If that's the case, he most likely will not be released until the war ends, and that may not happen for a long time. I suggest you go home and pick up your life where you left off. Now wouldn't that be best?" Her voice was lower now, "There is nothing you can do here if your boyfriend is being held hostage in some god-forsaken country. You know that, don't you?" Her voice softened, and she smiled as she walked toward the door. "Now, I'm going to call BOAC and see if there's a flight to the UK in a few days. In the meantime, I would appreciate your cooperation in not spreading any rumors about me. I could let you go right this minute, but I trust you, and I'm going to write you a check for five-hundred dollars that will serve as severance pay, with the understanding that you tell everyone your mother is ill, and you must return to England right away. I'll make sure you travel in first class. How would that be?" If any other story gets back to Clifford, I will not give you the money, and I shall cancel your flight home. You'll be out of here and on your own."

I lay down on the bed and bawled. Not yet a year in America, and already I was to go back home, and it wasn't my fault. Plus, the thought that Colin may be a prisoner somewhere made me feel physically sick. It made me more determined to stay in America to find out more about the situation that Robyn had alluded to.

I had to find somewhere to live. I was homeless yet again. This time, I knew for sure I could not even think about escaping to Africa since I had received a letter from my sister only a week ago. Things had turned nasty in Ghana. There was a coup d'état. Pauline said the government of Ghana and its president, Kwame Nkrumah, had been implicated in the assassination of Olimpio, Togo's first President. She said they could be in danger since the investigation wasn't over. They could be banned from the country without any of their assets.

I knew that Richard had arranged for his income from Singer to be in a Swiss bank. I guessed that was the smart thing to do.

At the end of her letter, she'd said they were moving to Kenya on the East coast and that she was pregnant again.

I met Jeremy that evening at our usual seat in the garden. I reiterated that our conversation would be between him and me. I told him everything about Robyn and how I had found her messing about with Hugo in the Butler's pantry.

"No wonder she's fired you. I know she's a bit keen on Hugo. But, mum's the word with me. It wouldn't do me any good to get myself dismissed either, so you can rest assured their secret is safe with me." He chuckled, "Poor Mr. D. I wonder if he's aware of his wife's admirer. Maybe he doesn't care as long as she's happy."

He rested his arm on my shoulders. "Look," he said, "your situation needn't be as bad as you think. You wouldn't want to stay here in this house forever anyway. Why not get an apartment in New York? Think of it positively, you've got your legal green card now. You can come and go across the pond just as you like."

"But what would I do here?"

"You are a secretary, aren't you? What about your company in England? Didn't your boss there say he'd get you a job at one of the brokers on Wall Street? Isn't that true?"

I was too miserable to concentrate on what he was saying. "Yes, but how am I going to live while I'm waiting for Mr. Trevors to fix the job up for me here?" I said. "Five hundred dollars is not going to last long, is it?"

"Here's what I'm thinking," he said, taking my hand in his, "here's a plan. I have a good friend in Manhattan, Ronald Duluth. He's a photographer for a big magazine. I reckon if I told him about you and how pretty you are, he might want to photograph you. He'd pay you quite a sum."

"Why would he *pay* me?"

"He takes photographs for Playboy Magazine."

"What?" For the first time that day, I laughed. "Jeremy, I couldn't do that."

"Why not?"

"You mean nude?"

"It's big money, considerable money, just for showing what you've got. That's all I'm saying."

"Oh, don't be so daft, I don't have the face or the figure."

He turned to me to take my face in his hands, "Look, if I liked women, that way." Jeremy emphasized the words *that way,* "I'd have made a play for you myself. You've got a pretty face and a lovely petite figure. Don't underestimate that. I bet you look great in the nude."

I felt the heat rise to my face. "Oh, I don't think so. Anyway, I couldn't do it; I mean…pose without a stitch on."

"I bet you could if he offered you two thousand dollars."

"Two thousand?"

"And you wouldn't have to worry about him trying to get you in the sack; he's like me."

"You mean…?"

"We were partners at one time, not now. He found someone else."

"I had no idea about you."

"I hope not. I wouldn't want it to be obvious."

"Is that why you weren't drafted into the military?"

"Oh, no, no. I have asthma. I think I was born with it. I'm much better here, but in Scotland, I was a mess. I think I'm growing out of it. Anyway, back to you. I can ask Ron to find you an apartment. He knows Manhattan well, and if you decided to go for a photograph, and he likes what he sees, you should think seriously about it. The money will help until you get a proper job."

A proper job, now that was something to consider.

So, we had a plan, and I didn't tell Robyn I was not going home. She gave Jeremy permission to take the day off to drive me to the airport and pick something up she had ordered from Saks. On the morning of my departure, Clifford Devereau said how sorry he was to hear about my mother. I glanced at Robyn, and she was nodding. She said, "I hope she'll get better soon."

What a deceitful lady, I thought. She was still talking, "Canyon will be sorry to hear you had to leave us in such a hurry. He's away on an excursion in the Caribbean with some of his yachting friends."

✳✳✳

I stashed the first-class ticket safely away at the bottom of my suitcase, knowing that I could always change the date and use it for my return to the UK if things didn't work out.

Jeremy had arranged with Ron to meet us at an apartment he'd found in Brooklyn on Flatbush Avenue. I had never seen such an odd configuration of houses. Steps led up to a front door, and some steps led down to an apartment underneath that was to be mine. The hallway was dark, the living room small and narrow with hideous brown old leather furniture. The kitchen was just a counter, a sink, and an electric stove set back in an alcove off the living room where a sliver of daylight slanted through a mesh-covered glass window close to the ceiling. There was a wire grid over the window because it was just below ground level. My view was a concrete wall. A tiny bedroom at the end of the hall reminded me of the spare room we called the 'box room' at home.

The whole apartment was very drab and dark, a place I would never choose to live. There was no sign of luxury. It was the antithesis of Fairview House. But what could I do at that moment? Then I began to question why I was just sitting around in a horrible place, waiting for news about Colin. I decided I had to write to Ellen and find out if she'd heard anything about Colin being captured by the Viet Cong. It sounded very unrealistic to me. And, truthfully, I didn't believe it.

It was when I met Ronald Duluth that my destiny seemed a little better than I had first thought. He had an easy smile and seemed genuinely pleased to meet me. He certainly scrutinized me from head to toe, and I assume he was looking to see if I was the right material for a nude photograph. He reminded me of Canyon with his blond curly hair and blue eyes. His face was angular. His skin showed a pallor that indicated his delicate health, but he radiated warmth and friendliness that I needed at that time. I thanked him for arranging for the apartment for me, although I knew I really would not be able to stay in that dungeon for long. It seemed inevitable that I would have to get a job if I was to survive in New York. The question hung in the air. If I didn't find something, would I be forced to become a nude model? Another question remained. Would I be good enough to feature in a famous magazine like Playboy? If I was rejected when they saw the photos, would I end up in some sleazy magazine? My figure was not bad, good proportions, long legs for my height of five feet three, but only thirty-four 'A' bra, not exactly voluptuous. However, two thousand dollars would help to rent a more beautiful apartment. Already, I was warming to the idea. No one would know it was me. My name could be changed for the caption if they had to have a name.

A couple of days later, after trying to settle into what I now labeled the apartment, *The Dungeon*, I ventured into the city from Flatbush to Manhattan.

Nineteen

New York was sweltering in the July heat as I walked up the two steps to read the brass plaque on the door: 'Ronald Duluth, Photography.' I was about to push the bell when the door opened. A swarthy-faced young man stood there. He was stocky, well-built, with a shock of black hair that flopped untidily over his forehead. "Ah, you must be Amelia," he said, ushering me inside. "Ron won't be a minute."

He had an accent, and I asked him where he was from.

"Italy," he said. "Ever been there?"

"No, I've been to Greece," I said. "I went to Paris several years ago. Didn't get as far as Italy."

He swept his hair back with his large hand and smiled, "Wonderful place, Italy. Here we are. I'll tell Ron."

He opened the door to a small room off the hall. It was a few minutes before my eyes adjusted to the dark. I was in a warm cocoon surrounded by an unfamiliar chemical smell that permeated the darkness like incense.

Ron appeared a moment later and asked me how I was feeling. I told him I was very nervous.

"Oh, no worries," he said. He turned on a small lamp in the corner of the room. "We should get started." He nodded to me and took my purse from me to place it beside the lamp. "Here, when you're undressed, put this on, then call me." In one brisk movement, he reached up for a robe on a hook on the door and handed it to me. He disappeared behind a black curtain that separated the room from another.

As my eyes adjusted to the dimness, I could see the studio was equipped with cameras set up on tripods in all four corners. Spotlights hung in neat rows from the low ceiling, and I could only imagine the intense brightness of the lights when they were turned on.

I undressed slowly. I thought guiltily of what my parents and Aunt Olive would think of me if they knew what I was doing. I hadn't even written to tell them I'd been fired from the Devereaus. I suddenly realized that I had not given them a forwarding address. What would happen if their letters went to Fairview House? I was almost in panic mode when I thought about that. The Devereaus had no notion I was still in New York. They thought I had returned home. One of my father's quotes came swiftly to my mind: "*Oh, what tangled webs we weave when first we practice to deceive.*"

Ron's voice cut into my thoughts, "You ready?"

"I…, I suppose so," I said.

He appeared at once, and with deft long-practiced movements, he adjusted a camera here and there, peering down intently, his hand cupped around the front.

I stood in the middle of the room, hugging the shapeless robe to me.

"You're okay there. Just right where you are is fine."

There was a burst of light, and I shielded my eyes, still holding on to the robe with one hand.

"It's nice and bright," he said, as a smile illuminated his face. "You're all right now. Let's get that robe off." He walked to me and gently took the robe off my shoulders. "There," he said.

161

His angular features suddenly softened as he looked at me. He went to the spotlight and adjusted the direction, "That's better. Can you let your hair down? Maybe pull it to one side?" I'd always worn my hair up in a twist or pony-tail because it was so thin and fine.

I stood awkwardly, trying to pose before the camera's eye. I felt ridiculous.

"Hey," he smiled and lifted his head to look directly at me. "I know this is your first time. Jeremy told me he thought you might be a bit nervous. You can do this. Pretty girls don't usually have trouble showing off their —"

I cut him off, "Well, I do." I said, feeling my face flush. "I do."

"Right, well, let's start again." He turned back to the camera. "Just relax, that's right. Put your arms up over your head and push your breasts forward, that's right. Good, now tilt your head back a bit. Great, much better, nice."

I moved around quickly, getting the idea of what he wanted. The room was hot from the lights. The click, click, click of the camera filled my mind.

"Great stuff. Keep moving. That's good. Head up."

"Better," he said. "Yes, better."

I don't know what my expression was as he clicked away. But suddenly, he was lying at my feet, taking a photograph from the ground up. "This should be good," he said. "It will make you look taller, and we need to have some of you with props." He rose from the floor; then he looked around at the different pieces of furniture at the back of the room. "Let's see, I think the wicker chair, yes. You can sit with one leg over the side, reading a book. Then I think a classic pose on the chaise and one more with you with a gardening hat and that plant pot in your hands."

"Oh, not a hat," I said. "I don't look good in hats."

"From the back, then, eh? A shapely bottom with a hat. Provocative, don't you think? Let's try that, okay?"

He arranged me in one pose after another, then suddenly thought of something else and produced a blue towel, which he draped over my shoulder and had me hold a bath brush. He had all the props.

"You'll be impressed when the negatives come out of the darkroom. I'll make you look taller than you are."

As he walked to the curtained room, he said, "It'll be about a week before I can get to developing these, if you want to come back then?" He popped his head back through the curtain, "You ever see Jeremy these days?"

"No, I haven't seen him since he came with me to see the apartment."

"Ah."

"When did you two meet," I asked, suddenly curious.

"I was in Scotland on a shoot. I used to be with National Geographic, freelance, you know. I met him in a hotel bar in Edinburgh. We clicked right away. Pardon the pun. Nice guy. I miss him."

"You could have sponsored him then to come to the States, couldn't you?"

"I tried, but it meant getting a lawyer and all that. I wasn't wealthy enough at that time. And he didn't have a job. Yeah, you know they have a quota of how many Brits they allow into the U.S. It's not easy for you guys."

"I know that," I said. "Yes, I know that."

He snapped off the lights after I'd dressed. He looked at me and smiled. "Good job, young lady. Come back in a week, okay? We'll get to the paperwork then if I think they're good. Okay?"

I hesitated as I left the room. "You know I'm really not sure about this. What if my parents saw me in Playboy? I honestly have to think about it."

"Why don't you wait until you've seen the photos?"

"What'll happen to them if I don't want you to send them to the magazine?"

"If you don't want them to be published, you'll have to pay me. Or, I can peddle them to calendar makers."

"Oh, dear," I said.

He laughed as he showed me out, "You wait and see. I bet you will be impressed, and I think you'll feel better about it then. You do need the money, don't you? Even that takes time. There's a process to go through; I must warn you of that. It could be a few weeks."

The front door clicked softly shut behind me. I stood on his front step squinting into the brilliant sunshine. Heat shimmered on the pavement like a mirage in the desert.

I made my way back to The Dungeon. At least it was cool being underground.

How strange my life was in the vast metropolis of New York. I spent nights alone feeling sorry for myself and wishing I was back in England. I could still use the airline ticket to go back, but then the old feeling of not quitting made me want to accomplish something before leaving.

I decided the first thing I must do was to write home and let everyone know where I was. I went to the post office and bought several pre-stamped air letters; blue, thin, the lightweight paper that folded into three and sealed like an envelope. The four-day air was better than six weeks of surface mail by boat. I wrote to my parents, Aunt Olive, and Colin's Mum. I didn't know how to get in touch with Jeremy. I certainly couldn't write. His mail was always delivered to the house, and I'm pretty sure Robyn would know my writing and expect a letter to be mailed from the UK, not New York.

A week later, I set out to the studio, eager to see if my photographs had turned out successfully. I was still nervous about the whole idea of nude pictures. When I arrived at the studio on Seventh Avenue at eleven o'clock, I found the door locked. I knocked, but there was no answer. I waited around for half an hour, thinking it might be early lunchtime for some. I was just about to walk away when I heard an inner door open and close. When the front door opened, a pretty girl was standing there. She was blond, tall, and beautifully dressed in a short red dress with a fringe that came level with her knees. She brushed by me with scarcely a glance as I stepped inside. She looked like a model should look. I stared after her as she walked quickly down the street. Ron appeared from another room in the hallway. He saw me because he called out, "Well, come in, then."

The same smell greeted me as I walked past the door to the studio. Ron beckoned me to follow him to their living quarters. "Amelia," Ron said as he motioned me toward a chair, "What brings you here?"

"The photos?"

"Oh, Gee! Got to get to those," he said, tapping his forehead.

"They're not ready?" I asked.

"Nope. Got busy. Did you see the gal that just left? Big time model. Good stuff. But don't worry," he added, "I'll get to yours soon, I promise."

I knew if she were my competition for nudes, I might as well not bother to even ask for any magazine to publish me. I said, "She was about six feet tall."

Ronald must have read the skepticism in my face because he said, "I'm making you look tall. I told you that. Your proportions arc good."

Then he looked at his watch, "Hey, let's do lunch, just you and me, what do you say?"

"Okay," I said.

Ron took me to a little bistro on a side street. The air-conditioning was making me cold. It was a reminder that I should take a cardigan or coat when I went into a restaurant in New York. He ordered a green salad with chicken. I ordered the same. The dressing was very different from anything I had ever tasted. It was delicious.

We talked mostly about Jeremy. I told him how much I had enjoyed being at Fairview House with him as my friend.

Ron looked sad at that moment, his thoughts lost to me. He sighed, "Ah, those were the days. We had some laughs back then, Jeremy and me."

After lunch, he went back to the studio. I stood on the corner, wondering what to do next. On an impulse I decided to check out the Wall Street area, where, if everything had gone according to plan, I would be working.

I ventured down into the subway station. Here, the trains ran just below the surface of the street. In London, the tubes are a long way down. During the war, Londoners flocked to the underground stations at night with their blankets and pillows to escape bombing raids.

When I emerged from the station, the heat was intense. The humidity made me feel nauseous. As I walked along the narrow street where the tall buildings gave shade, I noticed most of the men and women were well dressed and carried briefcases. I followed a couple of men as they hurried through the revolving doors of one of the buildings. I stopped to check out the directory on the wall, and to my surprise, there, listed under Brokerage Houses, was: *Lerner Hutchinson Corporation, 3rd Floor*. It had to be the same company, the affiliate of Wycliffe Brokerage in Leicester. Was it too much of a coincidence? It certainly seemed so. But then, I thought, why wouldn't it be the right place? The address was correct. My heart quickened. Would I dare to go up to the third floor and ask for a job?

I was ushered into the elevator with several men. When the doors opened, the men stood back, waiting for me to leave; they all got out after me. A long reception desk was opposite the elevator doors, and in large print behind it was the name of the company. It seemed very grand to me, a whole floor for one brokerage. I asked the pretty dark-haired girl behind the desk who I could talk to regarding a secretarial position. She had a very pronounced New York accent when she replied, "You need Mr. Cornboyg. He might be busy, and you don't have an appointment, do you?"

"No, but would you check please."

She looked at me and seemed to roll her eyes. "Well," she said, "his office is at the end of the hall second door on your right. Just go and knock." It took me a minute to fully understand her. I thanked her and walked to the door marked, *Alex Cornberg*. It was Cornberg, not Cornboyg, as she'd said.

The secretary in his front office was an older lady with a friendly smile. "You'll have to wait a while if you want to see Mr. Cornberg. He's in a meeting right now."

I waited for almost two hours before a man appeared in a dark suit, rotund and red-faced, with a jacket that strained against his portly figure. I told him my name and the company I'd worked for in England. He beckoned me to follow him into his office, and after he'd sat down and rearranged folders and files on his desk, he looked at me. "Now," he said. "I think I know who you are. Let's see, your boss is Mr....?"

"Trevors," I finished for him.

"Yes, yes. David Trevors. I told him you'd be welcome to work here, with his glowing report and recommendation he sent on your behalf, but then I heard no more. Are you living here now? He didn't tell me."

"I know," I said, not wanting to go into a discussion about where I'd been since I'd worked for Wycliffe Brokerage. "I'm here now, though, if there's still an opening for me?" I held my breath.

He smiled and rose from his desk. "I don't see why not," he said. "Why don't you fill in all the hiring paperwork now in the front office, and then we can get you started next week. How would that be?"

"Thank you," I said, trying to keep from hugging him.

"I'll put you in Mutual Funds. Isn't that where you were before?"

"Yes, that would be lovely," I said.

He smiled at me and repeated, "Lovely."

It all seemed so simple to him that I decided that he probably hired secretaries and fired them often, so it was no big deal.

I spent the afternoon wandering around Battery Park and watching the activities around the water and out into the entrance to New York Harbor, trying to imagine all the immigrants who had approached the Statue of Liberty from other countries on boats just as nervous as I was — a new life for them too.

I finally found my way back to Flatbush Avenue and The dungeon. It was such a dismal place, but I was happy that my day had been successful. I had met Ron, and I had met my neighbor, whom I thought was rather odd. She was very friendly one day, but she ignored me the next time she saw me. I had to remind myself this was New York, full of strange people. But at least I had a job offer. Then I realized we hadn't discussed wages. I couldn't just call Mr. Cornberg and ask what my salary would be, not now, could I? I decided I hadn't been too sharp when I was in his office, so I put that out of my mind. I had a job!

I had just closed the front door when there was a knock. It was my odd neighbor. She handed me a telegram. "It's for you, came this afternoon."

I thanked her and took the telegram into my living room, turned on every light, and opened the yellow folded paper. It read: *Colin. Stop. Now believed killed by Viet Cong. Stop. Ellen.*

✳✳✳

If you've ever read a page in a book and then realized you had no idea of what you had just read, that was how it was for me at that moment. I must have read the words several times before the meaning sank in. Even then, I did not quite believe the words. This could not be happening. I read the telegram yet again, and all I could say was, "No, no, no." No tears, just agonizing, "No. No. No."

I found the bottle of scotch I'd been saving for special occasions and drank half of it until I was drunk and fell asleep in the chair. I woke up to a strip of daylight that slanted through the window below the street level. I sat there for a long time in a daze. Vague thoughts drifted through my mind about where I was and why I was sitting in a dark, dismal place. Then it struck me, out of the blue, a shock. Colin was dead. I yelled out, "Has anyone seen his body? If he was missing, how would they know he had died?" It sprang from nowhere in a wave of anger. How did they know? I really did refuse to believe it, and when I found a few new airmail letters stuck in a drawer, I sat down and wrote to Ellen. She must have some of the answers. Or, maybe, I should just go home to see her. I needed more answers about Colin. Undoubtedly, the military would not dare to say he was dead unless they knew for sure, but then again....

169

I took the airline ticket from its envelope, laid it on the table, and stared at it. I wanted to call Jeremy to tell him I was going home, but I had no telephone, and I was too hungover to go out of the apartment to walk to the corner telephone booth. It was all too much. I took some aspirin and went back to bed, feeling that the end of the world had come, and there was no point in living. I wanted to die.

It was early afternoon when I finally surfaced enough to feel hungry. I stood by the tiny kitchen counter, eating scrambled eggs on toast, then I went back to bed.

I finally woke to the now-familiar strip of brightness filtering through the high window. It was dawn. I dragged my suitcase out from under the bed and started to pack. Now and then, I went back into the living room and just stared at the wall. I couldn't cry. It was an unreal scenario.

Suddenly the whole room seemed to be crowding in on me. I had to get outside, take a walk, anything except to be in this place, alone. I dressed quickly, fled out the door and onto the quiet street. Even as the city came alive I walked, head held high. I walked for hours, not really thinking, just walking, my mind a total blank.

I found myself at the subway entrance, and soon I had boarded the train for Seventh Avenue and made my way to the Duluth Studio, where I hoped Ron would let me use his telephone to call my father. He was the one I wanted to talk to first. I would tell him I had failed, that Colin was dead. I would be coming home. I was to blame for his death. Mea Culpa.

It was almost impossible to make an international call from a telephone box. I didn't know how to do it, or how I would pay for it. How many coins would I need and all that?

It was a quick trip from Flatbush Avenue to Manhattan by subway to Ron's studio. Again, his friend answered the door. He invited me in and introduced himself this time as Bernado. When

Ron appeared, he said, "They're not ready yet, your photos," then he must have noticed my face. No makeup, my hair stringy and straight around my face.

"Okay now, what's this all about?' he said, "You look like hell."

"I know," I said. "I know. I just want to talk to you if you have a minute, and I need to make a telephone call to England, please. Colin is dead." I blurted it out. Even the words sounded alien to my ears.

"Whoa, back up there." Ron came to me, put an arm around my shoulders, and led me into their sitting room. "Let's get you some coffee." He nodded to Bernado, who went out presumably to make it.

"Thank you," I mumbled.

Their sitting room was cool, small, with a few pieces of antique furniture and a worn brown leather sofa. Bernado brought the coffee in on a silver tray. They both sat with me while I told them all about Colin and the telegram and that I had decided to go back home to England. They listened attentively and made comments, "How terrible for you. Oh, that's awful." They both agreed. "What can we do to help?" Bernado asked.

"Nothing," I answered. "I just needed someone to talk to."

Ron refilled my coffee. "I'll see if I can develop your photographs tomorrow. I can cancel one of my girls. I do want you to see them before you leave."

At that moment I didn't care about the photographs. I just wanted to go back home.

Bernado said, "You know, I think you should stay and take the job here. England will still be there if you don't like the work. I expect your ticket home is valid for a few more months."

"I don't know what the point would be, staying here now," I said.

"Well, what's the point of going back to England?" Ron smiled. "Think about it. You will have your family, sure, but unless your old firm wants you back, you'll have to look for work. You've got a promise of employment here. Why not give it a try?"

"Oh, I don't know. I can't live in that apartment you found for me. I'm grateful to you, but it's awful."

Ron said, "Ah!"

There was silence for a while. Then Bernado said, "If you do decide not to go home, I have an idea. You could stay with my mother in Rockaway. I bet she'd be glad of your company. She has a nice house close to the beach. Why don't I call her and ask?"

I shook my head, thinking about Aunt Olive and my parents. "Oh, I should go back. Please, can I use your telephone?"

Ron called the international operator and handed me the telephone. I was glad my parents were modernized with a phone now. When it began to ring, I felt tears suddenly coursing down my cheeks.

The ringing seemed to go on for a long time before my mother's voice came over the line. "Amelia. At last. We've been worried about you."

I was blubbering, "I sent you letters."

"What's the matter?"

I could hardly utter the words, "Colin…Colin was killed in Vietnam."

"Oh, no. Oh, God."

I heard her turn away from the phone, but her voice was clear, "Amelia's on the phone."

There was silence for a few minutes, then my father's voice, "Your mother said Colin is dead?"

"Yes," I could hardly say the words, "Yes, in Vietnam." Then I couldn't speak. I pulled a handkerchief out of my pocket with my left hand, holding the telephone away from my face while I blew my nose.

"You come home right now," my father said. "No need to stay there. Nothing you can do. Do you have money for the fare?"

But suddenly I didn't want to talk about going home. I finally managed, "I've got to go, I'll write. Bye."

Just as I replaced the telephone in its cradle, I heard my father, "Amelia?"

In front of me, on the table was a glass of shining brown liquid. Bernado said, "Drink this. You'll feel better."

It was brandy, and the harshness hit my throat like fire.

Ron said, "You know, I agree with Bernado. I think you're making a big mistake going home, anyway." He looked at the clock on the wall, "Hey, girl, I have an appointment I can't afford to miss. Stay here with Bernado, okay?"

It occurred to me I had barged into this place unannounced, and of course they had work to do. I should get out. I rose and apologized for coming.

Bernado said, "Please sit down. I'm serious about you staying with my mother. I know she would like to meet you. Please come with me this afternoon. Okay?"

I said, "Well, I suppose I could go out this afternoon. Yes."

The truth was I could not bear to go back to that dungeon.

"Good," Bernado smiled. "I take you. It will be good to see my Mom."

✳✳✳

Rockaway Beach is on a peninsula on the south shore of Long Island, in the borough of Queens. Bernado took me to the boardwalk first. The beach was crowded with young people; most looked as though they had spent a lot of time in the sun. Some bikinied women were playing volleyball. The net was strung between posts in the sand.

Zanetta Basile was small and dark. Her face was worn and wrinkled, but the smile lit up her face. Barnado called her Netta. She hugged him and me.

"Yes," she said in her pronounced Italian accent, "Of course you stay here. Come, I show you the room. See, it has its own bathroom. I cook the meals. You join me for meals, yes?"

"Yes," I said. "That would be wonderful."

I let myself feel comforted by the warmth of this woman and good smells that emanated from her kitchen. Somehow, I had the feeling that Netta Basile would be my savior, and she was.

For the first time since I arrived in the States, I felt at home. Netta was true to her word and shared her meals with me. She seemed to be happy to mother me. I think if she had not been there for me, I would have gone back home to the UK; there was so much sadness to deal with. I wondered if I would ever be free of the guilt. She listened to my story about Colin and my family. She helped me to cope with the terrible feelings and grief about Colin. The days I was in my dark tunnel when I didn't want to go to work, she encouraged me to face my job and my life as it was at that moment in time. "No, look-back," she said. "You have good future here. Just get on with every day and give it your best."

I liked the work at Lerner Hutchinson Corporation, although the trek in the mornings was grueling: train, then bus into Manhattan. At least I had found there was some sort of normalcy in the routine of getting up and having a job to go to. I had gained a friend in Netta and *the boys,* as she referred to Bernado and Ron.

The photographs were developed. Ron said if I gave permission, he would send six of the best to Playboy magazine. Somehow, it didn't look like me in those nude photos, especially the ones he took from the floor. I didn't think anyone would recognize me. I decided to say yes, providing he changed my name on any paperwork.

He sighed, "So…what name do you want?

It didn't take long for me to decide. My father told me that he had wanted to name me Julia, and I chose the last name as Lester; a different spelling than the city, although the pronunciation was the same.

"Is this the name you want to be called Julia Lester?" Bernado asked.

"Just for this photo," I said.

✳✳✳

Ellen called one day when I was at work. She told me it would be just as well if I forgot Colin and got on with my life.

I said she was ridiculous. "In fact," I said, "I have some doubts about Colin being killed. I don't believe it."

She said, "You should find a nice young man and settle down."

Could I accept the fact that Colin was never coming back to me? How could I just go on with someone else in my life? No, I thought, I had better resign myself to the fact that I would never meet anyone as wonderful as Colin. I would remain single and wait for him. I just could not accept the fact that he was gone forever.

Twenty

The Brokerage on Broad Street was a pleasant place to work. It all seemed very efficient to me, and although I thought about Colin every single day, I had to stop crying or thinking about him, especially during business hours. I consoled myself that this was to be my life for a little while. My income was good, and my living costs were minimal, thanks to Netta, although I was bored when the market closed at 3:30. I decided I needed to find something to do because our day began at seven, and I wasn't ready to go back to Rockaway at four in the afternoon.

Every day, on my way to the subway, I passed the McKinley Dance Studio. Memories of my dancing days came back to me when I heard the music that filtered through the open windows.

In the little studio at the *Granby Halls* in Leicester with Kevin, I had taken the classes and the examinations for bronze and silver medals, and now, I knew with my credentials, I would possibly be allowed to teach.

The boss, Mr. Udovin, was Russian. He said he would give me a try. I did not doubt my routine and dance steps, although when he whirled me around the floor in a two-step, the sequence was different. He was a strong leader and took charge. When he asked me to take the lead, I did. He hired me on the spot.

Teaching ballroom dancing at McKinley Dance Studio took my mind off of the sadness I still felt about Colin. It was only two hours from four to six, but it filled in my day nicely. I taught seniors, men, mostly. A young man I knew as Darin partnered the women. Waltz and Swing were my specialties and I sold a lot of contracts to customers who signed for six weeks for quite a fee.

I didn't realize until I'd been there a month or so, that Mr. Udovin expected his girls to have sex with him. According to Jasmine, a tall, willowy girl of nineteen, it was just par for the course. Those who were regularly trapped in Mr. Udovin's office with the door locked I suspected were victims of his desires. I was determined not to be caught in the same situation. I avoided him whenever possible, and he didn't approach me until one evening just as I had finished with my last student, he asked me to step into his office to show him the previous student's contract for a six-week course. I didn't think anything of it, and I went to his desk and stood by his side while he looked at the contract before him. He seemed to be looking at the deal with interest, and then I felt his hand slide down my back. He was lifting my skirt! I felt his warm hadn on my bare skin above my stocking top. "You disgusting creature," I said as I pulled away from him.

This man had photographs of his wife and children in beautiful frames on the walls and his desk. I felt the heat rise to my cheeks as I stepped away from his desk. He laughed, "You won't get your commission on these sales, girlie."

I turned and ran out the door, grabbed my purse and cardigan from my locker, and flew out the door, down the streets that had once been interesting and full of friendly people. When I slowed to a walk, I suddenly realized everything around me was dark and menacing. I became aware of the streets echoing with the noises of people and cars, the ubiquitous steam that sprang from the vents in the pavement. The hot, stifling city of Manhattan was suddenly a nasty place to be.

I had arranged to meet Margaret, my friend, whom I had met earlier at the Brokerage. She had found another secretarial position, but we still met once a week at a hotel bar on Lexington Avenue. When she arrived, I was already on my second glass of wine. I told her about Mr. Udovin. She said, "Oh, Honey, men are such pigs, but it's not unusual, this sort of thing. Lots of bosses expect it, you know. This shit happens all the time."

"I hope not," I said. For some reason I started to cry. But then, lots of things and situations set me into a crying jag.

"It's okay, Honey," she said, putting her arm around my shoulders. She repeated, "Men are such pigs."

Again, the thought of returning to England swept through my mind for a brief time. It was only the thought that I would be unemployed, and since Aunt Olive had died and the house was being sold, I would have to live with my parents, and that would not work. My life at Lerner Hutchinson was not unpleasant. Shorthand had morphed into audio dictation, which was easy. I was the ticker tape girl, reading the ticker tape around the walls when customers called about the stock market highs and lows. There were no computers in those days; phones were busy all day long.

One of the unmarried guys asked me out, I went for a drink with him, but he was a total bore. He was more interested in telling me all about himself — what he did at the brokerage all day, what his life was like, where he'd been, etc. etc. On and on. He didn't ask a single question about me, and I was to learn that a lot of men I met were like that; not selfish, exactly, but self-centered. It didn't bother me because I wasn't looking for a man anyway.

I found out that Playboy Magazine did not accept my nude photographs, and I was glad. It had been a worry to me, although I never saw them again and often wondered if Ron eventually threw them away. He told me he would not sell them to calendar makers, but I wasn't sure he was serious when he said that.

It was Netta who made me feel that life was worthwhile. She told me a lot about her childhood growing up in the big city, Florence. She taught me how to cook real Italian food, not just meatballs, and spaghetti. She said their main entrée was usually a meat sauce on a bed of polenta. She served veal, which I was not too keen on because of the way it was said the animals were raised. Her pizza was nothing like anything I had tasted before, either — no meat ever on it.

Sometimes Bernado and Ron came for dinner. They were pleasant Sunday dinners with me included.

One evening, when I had offered to pick up a prescription for Netta from the Rexall Drug on 29th Street, I met Joseph, the head pharmacist. Netta's medicines had to be filled once a month, and I'd called into the store for my cosmetics and toiletries, but I hadn't had the chance to talk to Joseph, who was six feet tall with black curly hair and an eager smile. He laughed a lot with his assistants. They seemed a happy bunch.

It was a blustery late afternoon, and it had just begun to rain. Joseph looked at me and smiled. His eyes seemed incredibly large behind his thick glasses, and I noticed his long, dark lashes swept the glass. I wondered if that bothered him.

I heard him tell the staff to go home because of the impending storm. When the doors in the back closed, he came to the counter and handed me the filled prescription for Netta, "You know it's going to be a nasty night out there. I'm going to lock up early. Do you want a ride home?"

The wind howled around the place, and I accepted gratefully. On the way out, he picked up an umbrella from the big ceramic pot in the corner, flicked it open, and held me close as we ran to his car.

I had never been inside a Cadillac before. It gleamed inside, and I presumed by that that it must be highly polished on the outside.

As he pulled over to the curb outside Netta's, he said, "My cosmetic girl is getting married, and I need someone in the evenings just for three hours, three nights a week. Do you know of anyone who might fill the bill?"

I told him I didn't know anyone locally, but maybe I could help for a while. The hours would suit me now. I wasn't at the dance studio, although I knew Netta always expected me to be home to eat dinner. I decided I'd give it a try. It was only five to eight in the evenings. The extra money would come in handy, too.

***

Joseph Levine was a caring man. He was outgoing and friendly to everyone in his store. Also, he was amusing with his silly expressions and jokes. Everyone loved him. He often drove me home if it was late, or the weather was terrible. When I walked the seven blocks back alone at night, I did feel frightened, although no one ever accosted me. But I welcomed his offers of a ride home. He was always such a gentleman, and he became a friend I could talk to about anything.

What bothered me was the fact that during the next six months, I thought about him, even when I was at work during the day. I looked forward to my evenings at the drugstore but reprimanded myself for the thoughts that sprang unwelcome to my mind about being with him. It was apparent my resolve to stay a single woman for the rest of my life was weakening. I told him about Colin and my mother, my family. He was a good listener and seemed eager to please me.

One evening, as he was driving me home, he asked me if I would like to accompany him to shul on Friday evening.

"What's that?"

"It's our Jewish church."

"Oh," I said, "I'm not religious in any way."

I didn't know any Jews, although it suddenly occurred to me that my mother would ask me to take something, apples or vegetables, to the Jewish lady who lived on the corner. Why label her? Why not say to the Christian lady who lived next door? Religion and race never crept into our family conversation. Everyone around us were the same, although I had never seen or met a black man until the Americans came to our park during the war.

I was reluctant to go to Joseph's church, or any church for that matter, but because he had asked me, and I wanted to be with him, I said yes.

It was fascinating to meet the people there. He explained that his parents, who were sitting two rows behind us, were Orthodox, but they liked the Rabbi at this shul, which was Reform. I didn't ask what the difference was, but I did wonder why he hadn't introduced me to them. I caught them watching me closely as Joseph showed me how to read the prayer book from right to left.

After the service, he excused himself to go to the restroom. I stood in the foyer, checking out the congregation as they left. I was surprised when his parents approached me. His mother smiled and touched my arm. "You like my son," she said. "I can see that, but I'm telling you now so that you won't be disappointed. He's engaged to be married."

"Really," I said. "Well, I'm just a friend from the store, nothing more."

His father said, "Hc shouldn't be bringing friends here unless they are Jewish."

"Pardon?"

They walked away. I was stunned. It was an interesting scenario, and when Joseph took my arm on the way to the car, I told him what his parents had said. I asked him if it was right about his engagement.

He was furious. "Don't take any notice, please," he said. "Esther is just a friend. I'm not engaged."

"Well," I said, "seems you need to explain that to your folks because they were serious."

"They're just old-fashioned," he said. "Think no more about it. They really can't rule my life; I am over twenty-one."

The Jewish service had fascinated me. I went to the library and checked out a book on Judaism. Since the catastrophe at a Baptist church in Leicester when I was fifteen, I hadn't been to any church, and I thought now that the Jewish teachings were interesting although rather complicated with the rituals and traditions associated with it.

As time went on, I was becoming more attracted to Joseph but determined to remain friends. I enjoyed his jokes; he made me laugh; he made me happy. I compared the physical appearance of Joseph with Colin, who was strong and muscular. There was a softness about Joseph's body that made me suspect that probably, as a child, he was plump. But he carried his extra weight well and always looked smart in white shirts and black pants. Even when I got to know him better, I realized he didn't like T-shirts or jeans.

From what he told me, his family was very formal in their day-to-day lives, almost to the point of being rigid about everything, and yet he seemed relaxed in his skin, confident and capable. He told me stories about his childhood and his early experiences as a pharmacist, the funny situations he'd experienced in college. Since I had started work at fifteen, I never thought about what I might have missed in college.

After a few months, our relationship grew into more than being just business acquaintances. Sometimes, we just sat in his beautiful red Cadillac with the blacktop and listened to *Moon River* and other songs of that era. We kissed a lot, although it never went much further than that. He took me to all the Italian restaurants in Brooklyn, and there were many. He would not go into a German restaurant ever. I understood why.

Colin's mother wrote to me regularly. I was reminded from her letters how sad she must still be. There lay the guilt. My guilt. I realized now that Colin would always be a bright spark in my life, but like a photograph that eventually fades, the colors of our togetherness were blurred, the colors muted. Memories were ever-present, but I knew I must take the chance at happiness with Joseph. I knew he loved me, and I loved him, not as I'd loved Colin, my first love, but it was wonderful to have him in my life.

Joseph came to Netta's house a lot. We escaped to my bedroom. I did catch her once or twice, giving me a look that conveyed disapproval, but I wasn't a teenager any longer. I felt it was my own business.

✳✳✳

Unbeknownst to me, Joseph had told his parents he was going to marry me. That didn't sit well with them, not at all. One evening, his mother came to Netta's house to speak to me. She had made it her business to find out everything about me, where I worked, where I lived. How long I had been in the U.S. She stood at the front door, "So, what do you want with my son?" she asked. "Please leave him alone. He will be married to Esther before too long. Do you understand? Nothing against you, but we don't allow non-Jews in our family. I hope you'll honor my request and do the right thing. Leave him alone."

I was shocked to hear words like that. Was it an arranged marriage? How could parents dictate who their son would marry? I didn't understand, but I certainly didn't want to cause problems for Joseph.

I closed the door after I watched her walk away. I knew what I had to do. I told Netta about it, and she said I was doing the right thing to let him go. "Family business," she said. "Best you stay out of it. So be brave and know you are doing right by him."

I didn't answer the phone calls from him all weekend. I expected him to come and check on why I wasn't answering his calls. Then, I decided he'd probably been to see them and had decided that his future lay with Esther after all.

On Monday evening, after work at the Brokerage, I went to the drugstore at my usual time, determined to accept his decision to break up with me. There was no point in making a fuss. Accept the inevitable and get on with your life, I told myself.

He came to me right away and ushered me into the back room. "Are you all right? I called the house, and Netta answered, she said you were sick and not going to be going out or accepting my calls."

I knew then he had not been to see his parents or decided to marry Esther.

"Come outside for a minute," I said. "Please."

"What is it?"

"Joseph, your mother came to see me, and she made it very clear that I was to leave you alone, and that's what I'm doing, so please let's not see each other anymore. You have Esther, a nice Jewish girl, your mother said." I knew that sounded like a somewhat sarcastic quip, but I felt I had to be calm, otherwise I would have cried.

Joseph shook his head, "What bull-shit. I've known Esther since I was a kid. She's not interested in me, and I'm not interested in her. My mother tries to run my life, but she can't tell me who I am to marry." He held my face in his hands, "You and I will be married. We shall just go away. We can be married anywhere, and my parents don't have to be around."

And that's how it was. He didn't ask me; he just assumed I would say yes and I was not going to tell him no. I gave two weeks notice at work. Joseph had things to arrange at the store. He said he would need that two weeks to get things sorted out and I should pack a bag and be prepared to leave.

I waited and wondered what was going to happen between him and his parents if they spoke to him during that time. Would he give in to them? But I needn't have worried. On Sunday evening, I was sitting watching television with Netta when there was a knock at the door. It was Joseph. "You ready?" he asked.

"You bet I am," I said.

I had told Netta our plans, and she had cried, but she gave me a long hug and wished me well. She shook Joseph's hand and told him sternly to look after me. "Capische?" she added.

✳✳✳

Joseph had packed three suitcases in the Cadillac. I had one. He planned to drive to Rochester. At one time, he had been offered a job there, and he said it was a great place to live. I didn't care where we went as long as we didn't have to stay in New York. In Rochester, we found a guest house on the outskirts in a suburb of Rochester, an area of ordinary homes. Still, the window of the bedroom overlooked

185

a beautiful garden, and I immediately liked the owner who showed us the whole house and garden and made us a cup of tea.

Joseph had talked about getting married at a temple. We searched the Yellow Pages and found one not too far away. "It'll be a short Jewish ceremony. Will that work for you?" Joseph asked.

"Of course," I said.

The Rabbi was very stern in his comments to us, and when we asked about marriage, he said he had no intention of performing interfaith marriages. "It just won't work," he said. "You have to be Jewish to marry in this Temple. Sorry."

"Well," I said, "why don't I become Jewish, then?"

The Rabbi looked askance, "Oh no, conversion takes a long time. There's a lot of training and studies. It is an honor to be a Jew, you understand."

I said, "Yes, I'm sure, but the question remains, how can we marry?"

"I would think any Registry office in Las Vegas would do it."

I was upset, "Huh, I bet a Christian church would not turn away an interfaith marriage."

"Then you must do that," he said.

Before I could tell him what I thought of him, Joseph took my arm. "Come on," he said, leading me outside, "Let's just have some fun for a while. We need a vacation. We can go to Niagara Falls if you like. It's magnificent."

It was. We spent an unforgettable week of sightseeing — a boat trip on the *Maid of the Mist* that ventured close to the falls. Even in my travels in England and on the Continent, I had never seen such an impressive sight as those falls.

I liked Rochester. Joseph even suggested we should perhaps rent a house there. I liked that idea, too, away from New York.

It was two o'clock in the morning when Joseph suddenly sat up in bed. He was listening to something.

"What's the matter?"

"Oh, my God," he said. "That's my car. Someone's driving my car! I know the sound of that power steering." He leaped out of bed and moved quickly to the window. I followed just in time to see the brilliant red of taillights turning onto the street from the driveway.

"Joseph, someone *stole* your car!" I shouted, "Call the police," I was frantic.

He sat down on the edge of the bed and held his head in his hands. "Yes, I will call the police," he whispered, "but I know who it is." He looked at me and shook his head."

"Who, for goodness sake. Who?"

"My dad."

It was true. Joseph called the police, and half an hour later, they called back. They had stopped the Cadillac and questioned Joseph's father, who told the police he was the owner of the car, and his son had taken it without his permission or knowledge, but that he would come back to the house to talk. He did.

The police followed, I suppose to make sure his statement was true. When the policeman left the scene, the three of us stood at the bottom of the driveway in the stark light from the street lamp. Joseph held my hand. His father was leaning against the car. He looked at me and then at Joseph. He said firmly, "Joseph, if you marry this girl, you will no longer be our son."

"What a terrible thing to say," I blurted out.

Joseph gripped my hand more tightly. His voice was almost a whisper, "So be it, Dad," he said. "So be it. Just let me have the car."

His father opened the door of the car to step inside, "Absolutely not," he said. "You have been spoiled, just like your sisters, and you will not have it. I'd sooner sell it."

I gasped. The car was Joseph's pride and joy. Every time we pulled into a restaurant, he would park it where we could see it out of the window. He carried a towel to wipe it down after it rained no matter where we were. I knew he loved that car as much if not more than me.

I was furious. "You nasty man," I yelled.

His father gave me a look that told me everything. Suddenly, I knew I had to put things right. I let go of Joseph's hand and looked up at him. I said sternly, "Joseph, you must go back to your family." I meant it.

He stared at me, his eyes wide behind his thick glasses. For a minute, he said nothing, and then his brow tightened together in a frown I had never seen before, "So you don't want me either?" His words were forced, as though he really could not believe what I had said.

I shook my head, "Oh no. That's not true, and you know it. I just want you to be okay with your folks. I want to do what's right for you."

He said quietly, "Then we'll be together, you and me. That's what is right for me." He turned to his father, who was already in the car. "Goodbye, Dad," he said. "Give Mom my love."

His father took off with a screech of tires. Joseph and I stood to watch the car until it was lost to sight. We said not a word to each other. That night, I slept with my arms around his big chest, and when he rose and went to the bathroom in the early daylight hours, I noticed his pillow was wet. I sat on the bottom of the bed and wept. Was this how it was to be?

I heard the shower running and then his voice, "Today we shall go back to New York." When the bathroom door opened, he emerged with the towel wrapped around his middle. "We'll have to go by train," he said. "I have a cousin in California; we can stay with her. I'll borrow some money from Bernie Lieberman. He'll do that for me." Apparently, Joseph had thought of everything during the night.

I knew in my heart, the sadness of the situation with his folks would haunt not just him, but me too.

Twenty One

Joseph's suggestion to leave Rochester and return to New York filled me with dread. He knew he could get a job as a pharmacist quite quickly anywhere. I would sooner have stayed in Rochester, but he pointed out we'd have no car, and he wasn't about to travel to work on a bus. I decided he had no idea how a lot of people managed their daily life going on the bus or subway. He was spoiled, as his father had said, always having a car.

We took a train to New York City. We didn't talk much. There wasn't much to say.

Joseph's friend, Bernie, and his wife, Sophie, made up a bed for us in their small spare room. It was a bizarre situation. I felt we were intruding, but in a few days, Joseph had located an agency that was looking for people to drive a car to California. In this case, the owner was elderly and was flying to Van Nuys. We had one week to deliver the vehicle to him.

I remember the black Buick, with soft suspension. It bounced on every bump. July was hot and sticky, and with no air conditioning, we traveled with all the windows open. I dangled my legs outside to try and keep cool. It seemed an endless journey of five hundred miles a day across the United States on Route 66. When we arrived in Oklahoma, the car over-heated and needed repair. What now, I wondered. I had visions of us being stranded, but as always, Joseph didn't panic. He called the car agency back in New York, who said we were lucky that there was an agency in Oklahoma. Eventually, we transferred our luggage into a station wagon. This car was destined for Los Angeles also, so we were in luck again. We drove away with the air conditioning blasting cold air, a treat when driving through the desert. The tiny town of Needle*s* was the ugliest place I had ever seen in my life. LA was the busiest, and I hated them both.

Joseph's cousin, Eva, and her husband, Sal, lived in Monterey Park. It was apparent they adored Joseph, but they seemed wary of me. I was a Shiksa, a non-Jew, a species not acceptable in their world. Yet, they did show respect because I was Joseph's sweetheart. I learned how to make knishes and challah, the delicious soft egg bread for Rosh Hashanah, one of the Jewish holidays. I liked almost all the dishes Eva made, but I certainly missed bacon for breakfast. Kosher cooking and their rules about pork, at least in the olden days, made sense. Although trichinosis is no longer something people worry about.

Luckily, we were able to stay with his cousin for a month while Joseph checked out every pharmacy from Alhambra to the coastal towns of Torrance, Redondo, and Manhattan Beach and all areas in between. He was not one to sit around and mope; he was enthusiastic about finding a place for us to live.

Within a month, he'd found a position as a pharmacist at Thrifty Drug Store in San Pedro. He knew I loved the ocean, and we searched for an apartment in Redondo Beach, where he had once visited. He said I would like it. I did.

Somehow, in the confusion of change in all things in my life, I had put aside the fact that I was not yet married to this adoring man. It was when we were exploring Mexico, just before he was due to start work, I suddenly remembered something was missing. It jarred my senses to realize what it was. I had missed a period. I never worried about that monthly inconvenience, but now it was of prime importance. What to do?

Of course, I didn't believe I could be pregnant. Yet, after another worrying week passed, I had to accept the fact that maybe it was true. What would people say? Pregnant and not married, shame on me. I could hear my mother's voice now, "Only bad girls get into trouble like that – isn't it shocking."

When I finally managed to tell Joseph my fears, he smiled. "Wonderful," he said. We shall get married here in Mexico. Why wait?"

Well, it wasn't quite the wedding I had once planned with Colin. We found a small registry office in the state of Tlaxcala in Mexico where we were enjoying the wonderfully historic buildings. It was a fast ceremony. I have no idea who the witnesses were, two people walking by I think. I had to believe that it was the only thing to do under the circumstances, and then I began to wonder if our marriage was legal in the States. Still, I had a marriage certificate, and I was convinced it didn't matter if it wasn't legal in the States; no one would ever have to know. From then on, I told everyone we were married in Rochester. A lie, that after a while, seemed to be true, to me anyway. When you tell a lie often enough, you begin to believe it.

Joseph seemed thrilled at the prospect of becoming a father. How lucky we are," he said. "Our first. We can have three more."

"Really," I said. "Will you be discussing it with me?" I was kidding of course. But, then, one morning, I discovered I was not pregnant. Joseph broke down and cried.

"It's all right," I said, "We have time. We've only just begun married life."

"You said you were sure you were pregnant," his voice had an edge to it, and for a moment, I sensed suspicion in his mind. Did he think I would say I was pregnant so he would marry me?

"I was looking forward to being a dad," he said.

"I'm sorry," I said, "I suspect it was because of all the stress that gave the false alarm. It happens sometimes."

Joseph was good with money, and he worked overtime when he could. It wasn't long before he had enough money for a deposit on a lovely apartment on the Esplanade in Redondo Beach. We had an ocean view. I went to the beach every day, and I took a lot of time to search for job opportunities close by, so I could walk there. Joseph found a used Thunderbird for me. I'd never driven a car in the States, but I did pass the test.

My life in Redondo Beach was idyllic, especially when I found out I was pregnant. This time I consulted a doctor in Torrance, and he confirmed it. Joseph was elated. I swam every day in the apartment pool in the center of lush landscaping with palms and bird of paradise plants and in the ocean when I had the courage. Joseph brought home salve that he had concocted at the drug store to rub on my belly every night. He said I would never have stretch marks, and I never did.

At Thrifty Drug Store, he made friends quickly. His workmates often came to the apartment in Redondo to sample his five-layer gateau. Joseph didn't drink alcohol, but he was a master cake-maker. He measured every spoonful of flour and sugar with the glass measuring vials he used at work. Of course, the cakes didn't do much for his weight. I could see now why he tended to have a little extra flesh around his middle.

When he would concoct a gin-fizz for me, it was quite a production. He served it to me on our silver tray with the words, "Only one."

He was very attentive to my needs. I wrote to my parents and told them they should not worry about me; I was pleased and secure in a relationship that was so wonderful it was almost too good to be true. At Christmas, Joseph arrived with a huge Douglas fir. We had to cut some off the bottom so it wouldn't hit the ceiling. He had never decorated a Christmas tree, and he bought far too many boxes of glass balls, tinsel and other things I would never have chosen. But this was his tree. All I could do was smile at his enthusiasm and love him for the wonderful man he was.

"We do the Festival of Lights," he said. "It's pretty but not like your Christmas trees. We have a menorah for the candles." He explained everything about Chanukah that I found delightful. That Christmas, we had a menorah and a heavily decorated tree.

The Ford Thunderbird was not the car I should have been driving. At only five feet three and pregnant, I could barely reach the pedals. If I went over a bump, the front of the car lifted off the ground and seemed to float for a few seconds obliterating my vision of the road. The soft suspension of this American vehicle was not at all like the hard-riding car in which I'd learned to drive as a teenager, and even with a couple of cushions, I was still too low in the seat for that car.

It seemed that Joseph wanted to fill our lives with everything he deemed necessary for a family to be complete, and one evening, he came home with a puppy, a miniature Doberman pinscher. She was a black and tan purebred, and she came with instructions to have the ears properly cropped and wrapped so they would stick up like a true Doberman. I thought that was a bit barbaric, but it was done. When she stuck her head under my blouse one day while I was holding her, I said, "Oh, you are Cheeky." That, of course, became her name. For some reason, Joseph decided two dogs were better than one, "Company for each other," he said. He arrived with another mini-pin, who became Tammy. Ah yes, Debbie Reynolds and the movie

Tammy and the Bachelor, in 1957. Even now, I can remember the words to *Tammy's in Love*. Funny how songs and music are reminders of times in our life.

One gorgeous sunny summer day, Joseph and I were walking on the beach. I took off running, splashing through the surf, and when I looked back, he was running too. I was way ahead of him, when I realized he had not kept up with me. When I looked back, he had stopped and was bending over. I ran back to see what was wrong. His face was ashen; his lips were turning blue, "We have to get back to the apartment," he managed. "I don't feel well."

He needed my help to get him up two flights of steps to the second floor. It was hard to believe this was the same man who always seemed to be the one to help people in any way he could; always the one to volunteer to help push a stranded car out of the way of traffic.

Being pregnant, I couldn't hold his weight. He knew he couldn't rely on me to hold him, so he held on to the handrail, hauling himself up step by step.

I was panic-stricken when he collapsed on to the floor of the apartment. I didn't know what to do. He had no doctor. I had an excellent obstetrician, but we never thought about Joseph. The manager called an ambulance and Joseph was admitted to a hospital in Torrance. The doctor who attended him was brisk. He turned to me, the stethoscope still swinging from his neck. "Your husband has a bad heart, you know. He shouldn't have been running on the beach." I, in my naiveté, had never wondered about the moments he had chosen to stop on our frequent walks along the pier in Redondo, or the park. I must have appeared like an idiot to the doctor when I said I didn't know anything about a bad heart.

The thought crossed my mind that that might have been the reason his parents had been so keen for us not to marry. Maybe they were trying to release me from the responsibility of marrying someone who had a congenital heart problem.

St. Mary's Hospital in Long Beach was one of the leading cardiac hospitals in the country. And, during the next examination, the Jewish doctor was brief in his assessment of Joseph's prognosis. He said, "Boychick, I'm happy to tell you there's a brand new procedure now, a replacement valve that can be inserted into the heart; *Starr Edwards ball* Valve, it's called."

He leaned forward in his chair to look directly at Joseph, "I would advise that you seriously consider this procedure. It's major cardiac surgery, but without it, your days will be numbered."

I took a deep breath. Joseph was twenty-six. He had a congenital heart problem, and he hadn't discussed it with me, ever.

When I asked him about it later, he said, "You wouldn't have married me if you had known that, would you?"

I had no answer to that.

To make things worse, when I asked the doctor how successful the surgeries had been in the past, he said, "That's a tough question. This mitral valve is new, and it depends a lot on the person. I would say with Joseph's condition, well, let's say fifty-fifty."

Fifty-fifty! Those words did little to instill me with confidence to take that step. I said, "No, then we will wait and get a second opinion."

"Just don't take too long," the surgeon said.

Now, Joseph seemed to be mindful of my safety and well-being. He didn't want to drive the car with me in it in case he passed out. He worried all the time about that. Then, another problem arose; the apartment manager told us that babies were not allowed; we had to move. As it happened, the apartment on top of a garage next door was vacant and available. It was old fashioned with gold wallpaper and terrible multi-colored shag carpet, but the rooms were large, and there was a huge deck out front that overlooked the ocean. All along the Esplanade, houses were being replaced with modern apartment buildings, so we knew it was temporary, but it was beautiful to see the ever-changing moods of the ocean from the window.

Joseph was reluctant to think about open-heart surgery knowing the risk involved. He stood for hours on the deck staring out to sea. He said he was just thinking. I didn't want to sway him one way or another, because I wanted him to be well when I had the baby. Then one day, he said he'd decided to have the surgery.

"Right," I said.

"You don't want me to have the surgery?" It must have been the way I'd replied, because he was upset now.

"I'm frightened, Joseph."

"Oh, Honey, I'll wait until after the baby comes." He took me in his arms, and I could feel his heartbeat against mine. It made me want to cry. It was all so unfair. A lovely man with such a cloud over his head, and there I was asking him to wait. What if something happened before the baby arrived? It could not be worth thinking about, but I was terrified, and I even said a prayer to someone, whoever was supposed to listen. I knew I would not be able to look after him and a newborn at the same time. I was no nurse. Even the sight of blood made me feel faint

✳✳✳

One early September evening, there was an earthquake. California had many shakes, but this one was strong, and my two mini-pins shot out the open front door, down the steps, and out onto the street. They had never run away before. I ran down the steps and out into the street. I finally found them at one of the apartment entrances way down the block. That night, I went into labor, and my daughter was born early the next morning. She was a week early. Joseph was with me all through the birthing, telling the nurses what to do. "Give her more Demerol," I heard him say two or three times. I'm sure they were irritated with him for being there, but I was happy.

When the doctor finally brought my daughter to me, he said: "Congratulations, she has ten little fingers and ten little toes." Then he hesitated, "but she has to have surgery immediately, I'm sorry to say."

"What do you mean, surgery?"

I was filled with dread at what he was going to tell me.

"It's necessary, that's all. Your husband wants to be the one to tell you."

I just wanted to hold my baby. She was so pretty with a lot of hair. I have never bought into the theory that all newborns are beautiful, but she was, and one of the nurses had brushed her hair up into a curl.

Joseph couldn't speak for a little while. When he finally did, it was to tell me that our daughter was born with a congenital disability, which would mean she would never be able to have children. That was the moment my heart began to break into pieces.

Twenty Two

Looking back now, it was Joseph who carried me through a terrible time. He dealt with everything. He arranged for the after-surgery care of our daughter and me. I was no use at all. Post-partum depression was never far away. Plus, we had yet to name our daughter. I was convinced all through the pregnancy that I would have a son, and it was going to be David. We had given very little thought to a girl's name, which was, of course, a little naive. I had always liked Jennifer, and since Joseph had wanted his Aunt's name, Esther, we compromised. Our daughter was named Jennifer Esther in the Jewish Temple.

I did remind Joseph that his intended wife (according to his parents) was Esther. I was joking, and he laughed, but I often wondered if Esther and Joseph had had a meaningful relationship.

Joseph now seemed confident that he was going to have the open-heart surgery, and was convinced it would all turn out well. With fifty-fifty still floating through my brain, I wasn't so sure, and the second opinion did not change his mind. He wanted to see his daughter grow up, and that was that. I think we were both convinced now that Joseph would die young without this complicated surgery.

At this point, I knew he should call his parents to tell them all that had happened. He had never been in touch with them since we left New York, and sadly, they had made no effort to contact him either.

I thought it was not right. How could they just disown their son? It was beyond me, but then I didn't know the rules of their religious beliefs, and if this was an example, I didn't think Judaism was what I wanted to believe in.

When I told him I was going to call them, he was so angry. "Don't do that, don't call them, please. Remember, they were the ones who disowned me."

I said, "I thought Jews were family-minded, watching out for their own and all that. You have to make amends with your family, Joseph," I said. "You can't go on like this."

"You don't know my parents, Amelia."

I felt a chill descend on me. The open-heart surgery? It was all so new. Not much had been done in the medical field at that time for bypass surgery or valve replacement. It was a nightmare, and in my post-natal situation, I thought the worst was to come. My depression deepened. It was hard to function. My friend, Thelma, came to see me. "You know, Amelia, you have to be the strong one. You have to pretend to be calm. You have a newborn to look after, and you have to breastfeed her with joy, not depression. She will know. I'd heard that anxiety sometimes influenced mothers and their milk. This did not seem to affect my milk production. I had to express milk every day for the milk-bank, which was an unpleasant procedure, to say the least. Someone came daily to collect it in the sterilized bottles provided.

Jennie did not sleep through the night very often. Up to now, Joseph had been the one to get up for her. I decided I should be the one. I took her in the car-bed and drove around the block to get her to go to sleep. It never failed.

If only I had my sister to talk to, I thought. Pauline was in Kenya, better than Ghana she'd said, but now there were terrible problems with the Mau-Mau terrorists who were attacking the British settlers in the Rift Valley, just north of Nairobi. She said one of their Shamba boys, a Kikuyu, who wouldn't join the Mau-Mau when he was asked, was taken away in the middle of the night. She said she believed they killed him. It seemed Pauline was now living in danger surrounded by tribes with vicious intentions to wipe out the elite British who had taken over their country.

I told her to come to the States to stay with me. We had room for her and the children. I needed her. I wanted her advice and companionship, particularly regarding Joseph, who was changing from a happy-go-lucky-person to a depressed man with the weight of the world on his shoulders. He worried about me. He worried about Jennie. But now, with his mind made up about his future, his confidence in his doctor's advice to have the heart surgery remained intact. Doctor Ivens at the Long Beach Hospital had told us that since we had planned to go to England to see my parents that we should go as soon as possible. "Do it now, Boychick," he said. Go now. Come back and have the surgery." It was on Joseph's mind that he might die tomorrow and leave us without anyone. I canceled the trip.

Joseph wrote to his parents. I never saw the letter, and I did not ask to read it either.

We waited for their response, wondering if they would ignore it. He was agitated for a few days, and not talking much. We lived in a silent world until a letter came back. He finally smiled. They would be coming to visit. Imagine my thoughts. I was an outsider in their world. I had no right to marry him, and surely they thought I had no reason to have a child with their son.

The date for the surgery was set. All the concerns of his parents coming to stay; the operation itself, my sister's problems dominated my daily life. On top of it all, I had developed a bad toothache, but I couldn't go to a dentist, not now.

Joseph's parents flew from New York one week before the surgery. It was March. Surprisingly, they were gracious to me, very loving and attentive to Jennifer. I was relieved and I tried to fade into the background while they were with us. I wanted Joseph to love his parents again and for them to love him. It was not about me this time.

Joseph's cousin, Eva, was at the hospital; her mother and father, Joseph's Uncle Louis too. It was evident, by his demeanor, that Joseph was glad to have his family around him. I didn't care how they felt about me. I was content to be at my husband's side.

I learned that for the surgery, the heart would be stopped, Joseph would be connected to a heart-lung machine. This machine does the work of the heart and lungs during any open-heart surgery to this day.

My former neighbor at our apartment, Edith, agreed to look after Jennie, who suddenly had to be bottle-fed with my milk expressed early in the mornings for her daytime feeds.

My parents now had a telephone, and I had called them to tell them what was going to happen on March 17, St. Patrick's Day. At six a.m. at the Long Beach Hospital.

We gathered around his bed every day for three days before the surgery, and he was given a special diet and pre-surgery meds. Joseph was in good spirits, laughing and joking with his family, and when the morning of the surgery arrived, he handed me his glasses on the way to the operating room. As I bent to kiss him, he said cheerfully, "See you in a few hours, Honey."

But it wasn't just a few hours. Six hours later, one of the nurses came to the waiting room where we were clustered together, not speaking very much, just glancing out our watches and the door waiting for news. When a nurse came in to ask if anyone with O Positive blood who could donate to the surgery, we looked at each other in amazement. Surely, this was unusual, wasn't it? Didn't they have a blood bank? It was all very bizarre.

The nurse in charge was reluctant to take my blood because of my recent pregnancy. Joseph's uncle volunteered. Luckily, we were both O positive. Then, over the loudspeakers, came an announcement, "Requesting Blood donors, O Positive immediately." Could this really be happening? Surely, this was unreal. I kept visualizing Joseph attached to this device with his heart removed. I remembered what the surgeon had said about the heart-lung machine that did the work of the heart and lungs when the heart was stopped during an operation.

At seven p.m. that evening, Joseph had been in surgery for thirteen hours. I finally went to the hospital chapel to pray. Praying to someone you couldn't see was never logical to me. Now, I was about to do it. I had a raging toothache; I felt weak from giving blood so soon after birth. My breasts were swollen, and milk leaked through my bra and blouse.

I sat in the chapel in a stupor. I said aloud, "Dear God, I know I have never believed in you, but if you are there, please let my husband recover. It will be proof to me that you exist."

My prayers were interrupted by a voice over the loudspeaker. "Will Mrs. Levine, please come to the Administration Office?"

Three surgeons stood up as I walked into the small room. Their faces were as green as the scrubs they still wore. After a moment, one of them spoke, "I'm sorry, Mrs. Levine, he's gone."

Like a crazy woman, I said, "Gone, gone where?"

One of the surgeons led me to a chair. "We tried for so long," he said, laying a hand on my shoulder, "but his heart was too calcified to hold the valve. We tried."

At that moment, I wanted to block everything out. All I could say was, "No." I rose quickly and fled out the door, down the corridor out into the grounds. I kept running in circles until Joseph's Uncle Louis suddenly appeared in front of me and stopped me. I was still shouting, "No." I remember he slapped my face hard, then held me to him before leading me back into the hospital. I said, "I want to see him."

One of the nuns said, "No, dear, that would not be a good idea."

I must have screamed that I wanted to see him, because suddenly I was looking down at the lifeless body of the man I loved. That was the very worst thing I have ever experienced. I knew beneath the sheet that covered his body there would be a ruined chest. I kissed his cold forehead and whispered, "I love you." I would remember that moment forever.

When I've mentioned this to people since that day, they all say that would never be allowed to happen today, not for me to see my dead husband in the morgue just after surgery, but it did happen on that terrible St. Patrick's Day so long ago.

On the way from the hospital, with Joseph's father at the wheel, we sped through the city in silence. The sun was just setting and illuminating the buildings with a glow of pink. We stopped at traffic lights, and I opened the window to try to get some air; it was hard to breathe. On a wire above the road, a little bird sang so beautifully. Even above the noise of the traffic, I heard it. I rolled the window up quickly, thinking how could any bird sing at a time like this? On a day like this, how could it? I can still see that little bird, its tiny body outlined against the orange sky.

I managed to call my parents. It was early morning in England. My father answered the phone. Before he could say anything more than hello, I blurted out, "Joseph died." I wept into the phone.

There was a silence before my father said, "Yes, I know."

"How do you know?" I managed.

"Your mother woke up just after three this morning, Amelia. Strangest damn thing. She sat up and said, 'Joseph has died.'"

"I don't understand. Oh my God, how would she know?"

"It was about seven your time in the States, isn't that when he died?"

I thought back about the time I was in the chapel and realized it would have been that time when the heart-lung machine was disconnected, and Joseph would have taken his last breath. My mother knew before I did. It was then the memories came back. Of course, my mother talked to the dead.

✳✳✳

The following day passed in a blur for me. Edith was still babysitting Jennifer and said she would continue to feed her, but it had to be formula now. My milk had stopped. At that time, I apparently told Edith I didn't want to live any longer, not without Joseph.

I don't remember raiding the medicine cabinet that night.

When I woke up in a hospital bed, I was facing the sour expression of my doctor, "Why would you do that, Amelia? I thought you were stronger than that."

"Why don't you just bugger off and leave me alone?" I said. "Who do you think you are to tell me how I should feel?" Dr. Stilling sat on the bed and reached for my hand, "I know you are angry, Amelia, but you can't just disappear, you know. Joseph's parents have arranged for the shipment of Joseph's body, and they are with him now on their way, flying to New York."

I was furious. How dare they take him away? But they had. A few days later, I flew alone to New York, wishing the plane would crash.

I stood with the family at the gravesite at Wellwood Cemetery on Long Island. He was buried in their family plot, and that was that. There were no flowers. Joseph loved flowers. Everyone threw stones on top of the grave. It was all very bizarre. Afterward, as is the custom at Jewish funerals, we sat 'Shiva.' The mirrors were covered with cloths — neighbors brought in food. The talk was constant among the Levine family and friends. I was ignored.

When Joseph's father told me to join him in the hall for a minute, I had no idea it would be to say to me something that shook me to the core. If they had been discussing it during the time I sat with them in the living room, I hadn't heard the words, "We are going to adopt Esther," he said quietly.

"You mean Jennifer?"

"She'll be Esther from now on."

Before I could say anything, he continued, "Look at you. You should never be a mother. You aren't fit for it. Wouldn't you rather be free to follow your own life rather than be tied down with a child?"

"You? Adopt Jennifer. You?"

"Yes, I think she would have a perfect life with us. She will be raised as a Jew, because our son would want that. You do see that, don't you?"

"Yes, I suppose so," I said.

"Good, then that's settled. You are doing the right thing by her, just remember that." I found myself nodding. I didn't care. What did I have to offer her, and how would I manage without a husband? Being a single mother was not what I wanted.

In a day or two, a lawyer had drawn up the papers and called me into his office. He asked the Levines to leave us alone for a minute and motioned for me to sit opposite him at his desk. He hesitated before speaking, seeming to study my face. "You do know," he said, "that you will not be allowed to see your daughter ever again."

"Why not?" I asked, trying desperately to understand.

"Because you would want her back." He looked at me intently, "It would not be fair for Mr. and Mrs. Levine, so you must be sure before you take this step."

I sat there for a long time in a daze. Suddenly, I came to my senses. Of course, I could not let my daughter go. Never could I be parted from the only thing I had left of Joseph.

The Levine's were heartbroken, "Our son is dead because of you," they said. "We could have taken care of him. He was under a doctor's care in New York." On and on, the incriminations surfaced from these two bewildered parents.

The thought came to my mind at those moments, watching their lives crumble, that I was leaving a trail of distraught parents.

If Joseph had not married me, would he have lived? Undoubtedly, they had always been aware of his condition. He had been born with a bad heart. Maybe they were right.

Was I responsible for the death of yet another man in my life? If so, was there ever going to be an end to the guilt? Mea Culpa.

Twenty Three

After three weeks in New York, I was back home in Redondo Beach. My friend Thelma had met me at the airport. On the way back, I told her what had happened, "I almost let them adopt my daughter."

The words echoed in my brain for a minute. What was I thinking?

Thelma said, "I'd never have spoken to you again if you had done such a thing. Jennie is your only child."

"I know, I'm a mess. I can't think straight."

"It's just not like you. I know you are struggling with the grief of Joseph's death, but you must keep on living for Jennie. She has no one else but you."

Despite my resolve to just get on with things, my life still did not seem real to me. I started to hallucinate, imagining Joseph's face in the wallpaper. I could see him often in the bedroom or living room. If I saw a man driving a car who looked like him, I had the notion of following the vehicle. I was in total denial.

I tried to keep my imaginings about Joseph to myself, since, even to me, it did seem weird. I had the distinct feeling he was watching over Jennie and me; I was sure of that. I knew I was getting like my mother when I started talking to him. When I mentioned that to Thelma, she said, "You know you need some help."

A week later, she announced that she had made an appointment for me to see Dr. Robert Devour, a psychologist, who had an office on a side street in Torrance.

"That's stupid," I said.

"No, it's not. I worry about you, you know."

"Why?" I said, "Do you think I might off myself?"

"Well, you did try it once."

"Oh, don't be so daft. That was then. I couldn't even think of it, not now."

"Nevertheless," she said, "please, go see this doctor."

Thelma drove me to Dr. Devour's office and told me she would be back in an hour to pick me up. She even waited as I reluctantly went inside the doctor's office.

There was no receptionist in the foyer. I stood for a minute, wondering what I was supposed to do. Someone's voice from down the hall was faint. I couldn't make out the words; then, a black Labrador appeared from the direction of the voice. My love of animals far exceeds my admiration for people, and I greeted the dog with a "Hello." He responded with an enthusiastic wave of his tale. The voice came again, louder now, "Is that you, Mrs. Levine? Follow Eddie; he'll bring you to me."

I followed the dog down a hallway to a room lit only by a small table lamp. A man sat in the recliner chair in the center of the room. He was not at all what I expected a therapist to be. His clothes were disheveled, and even in the dim light, I could see his socks were mismatched. He wore dark glasses. Oddness emanated from this man, and I stepped back, suddenly afraid. Only then did I realize he was blind. I heard myself take a deep breath. He must have heard it too because he leaned forward and patted the seat in front of him. "It's all right," he said. "I need you to be very close to me while we talk. Is that okay with you?"

I sat down, and he immediately reached for my hand. "Now," he said, "tell me about you. You have some problems you'd like to share with me. Is that right?"

I could feel tears sliding down my cheeks, "No, I don't have any problems. You do. You're blind," I whispered.

The man threw back his head and laughed, "I've been this way for a very long time. I see everything just the way it was, with so much beauty in the world, how can I ignore it in my memories."

Well, that did it for me. My tears came uncontrolled. I couldn't speak. He didn't either for what seemed like a long time. Then he said, "I believe there are tissues on the table beside you."

Now I felt foolish. I just wanted to get away from this man. I pulled my hand away and rose from the chair. He said, "Please, let's get on with this. You are paying me for my time, and I'm here to help you."

Dr. Devour listened. I talked. I talked about Joseph, about Colin, my mother, my brother, and my dad, the relationships in my life before I came to the States, and since then, "I'm to blame for all the problems in my family, you know."

"You must be important, then," he said.

"What do you mean?"

"Don't you agree that it's a little bit pompous to assume that you are responsible for the problems of others?"

"But it's the truth. I've made so many bad decisions."

"And you will make a lot more. But, you must learn not to take everything personally, or blame yourself. You are and were a victim of your brother's sexual advances, yes, but in that instance, you became a warrior and got away from it. You took the correct action. Even if your mother thinks you should not wear red lipstick, or bleach your hair, and your father tells you you're not as good at math as he was, you must learn never to be offended by anyone who criticizes you unkindly; it's because they are unhappy and want to have power over you. You *must* love yourself and shrug off the unhappiness you now feel. You see, it's not fair when unkind comments are said to you or blame you, because, as sensitive as you are, you suffer, but *they* don't. So why fall for their ploy? Do you understand?"

Before I could answer, the soft ting-ting of an alarm clock sounded from a corner shelf.

Dr. Devour squeezed my hand before releasing it, "I'm sorry our time is up, but I want you to listen carefully to what I'm saying. You know it's not logical or rational to think that you are responsible for your mother's suicide attempt, your brother's sexual advances, Colin's death, or Joseph's. I want you to think seriously about the logic of your thoughts. You are not to blame. As I said earlier, it is rather pompous of you to think that way. To dwell on the past as you do is very harmful to you. I will see you next week."

It may have been easy for him to tell me I wasn't logical, but trying to imagine myself positively was certainly not in my thoughts at that time. My weight was now low for me, one hundred and five pounds. I was thinner than I had ever been in my whole life. I was flat-chested. I had no periods anymore. I had dried up inside and out. My grief for Joseph was different from what I felt when Colin had disappeared. Perhaps, underneath it all, I didn't believe Colin was dead, there was hope. But, Joseph? I had seen his dead body in the morgue. It was final.

I believe, at that time in my life, it was Jennie who saved me from dwelling so much on the guilt I truly felt. She demanded my attention as most babies do, and I gave it to her. I received a 'widow and child's benefit' of three-hundred-and-fifty dollars a month, and I knew we were not going to starve, but it was the dunning letters that arrived from the hospital that bothered me. Phone calls at six o'clock in the morning asking that the bill for the open-heart surgery be paid. I was nasty to the poor girl at the credit department since the bill was now well overdue and had been sent to the collection department. I said, "He died during surgery. Why should I pay?"

The problem, of course, was that we had no health insurance for Joseph. His military status had been 4F, which told it all. Then at Thrifty Drug Store, where Joseph had worked for a year, the employees had a whip-round and presented me with a check for a thousand dollars. I was overwhelmed by their generosity. They said they had loved him and missed him because he made everyone laugh with his silly jokes and his infectious laugh. The thousand dollars was sent to the collection department, and I presume the balance was paid off because I heard no more from my creditors.

I found a part-time job as a receptionist in a dental office. Edith once again stepped in to help look after Jennie until my dog, Cheeky, my oldest mini-pin, became obsessed with keeping anyone away from Jennie in her crib. Edith said, "You know she growls and bares her teeth when I try to pick Jennie up; I'm afraid it's either the dog or me, one of us has to go." Fortunately, Anne, down the street, said she'd be glad to take the dogs while I worked. I had such good neighbors.

I was still going to see Dr. Devour once a week. One of the things he imparted to me was that all the burden of guilt would eventually ruin my life if I didn't change my thoughts.

I said, somewhat defensively, "Well, that's how I am."

"Your life has been traumatic," he said. "You must learn to accept the things you cannot change."

It was at that time that my British friends, Audrey and her husband Don, suggested I go back to England for a while to be with my family. They insisted they pay for my airfare, and I could not dissuade them.

In those days, for infants, BOAC provided Sky Cots that hung from the ceiling of the plane. Jennie slept peacefully over the Atlantic.

Surprisingly, it was a joyful reunion with my mother. Our relationship had always been tenuous at best. At this point, I didn't want to upset her routine or step on anyone's toes. I thought before saying anything to her and tried to keep the conversation light.

My brother Douglas, had moved into my old bedroom, and I was glad that I was able to comfortably say, "I've arranged to stay with Ivy."

✳✳✳

Ivy had been a good friend since Folville Girl's School, and we had kept in touch. She had a son, Wayne, a year older than Jennie. Her husband was in Canada on business when I'd called her, and she said she would be delighted to have me as company.

I met my father quite often since Ivy lived just around the corner. Usually, he and I sat in the back garden with a cup of tea. I could tell he was worried about me, "You're so thin, love. I wish you could go out more now you are here. Enjoy some trips into the country. Why don't you and I go to lunch next week at the Rothley Court Hotel? You know the restaurant there is superb."

I laughed, "Oh, Dad, you mean on the back of your motorbike like we used to do?" I was a pillion passenger on his big motorbike for many trips to the countryside when I was a teenager. He still liked the excellent machines and could describe each make and model in detail.

"Why not?"

My father smiled when I didn't answer him. He said, "I bet you miss your car, don't you?"

I nodded, "Well, it is easier to travel with a baby in a car. I see mothers here dragging a stroller on and off buses, and it makes me wonder if I could do it."

"What do you mean, *stroller*?"

"Ah, yes." I laughed, "I mean push-chair. They call it a stroller in the States."

He thought for a minute before he rose. "Come with me," he said.

I followed him to his workshop that smelled of sawdust. It brought back memories of when I was little and would stand and watch the curls of wood that came off the lathe as he worked. He showed me the intricate carvings he was doing on three sets of bellows for his siblings. They were extraordinarily beautiful and his designs.

He poked around under one of the shelves and came up with an envelope. "Here," he said, "take this and buy that car you want. You could use it while you are here and then have it shipped back to the U.S. duty-free." He hesitated, "I'd appreciate it if you didn't tell your mother about this, please."

"Oh, no," I said. "I can't take your savings."

"I've never given you anything. I want you to have it."

I hugged him and thanked him. I didn't look in the envelope, but it was thick, and I knew there must be a lot of pounds he'd obviously set aside for something. But what? Not me. I was sure of that.

When I discovered how much money was in the envelope, I wondered why he'd given it to me. There was a lot, and it wouldn't have taken too much more to buy a house. In the sixties, you could buy a house in the UK for six hundred pounds. It had always irked my mother that she lived in a council house. He knew that well enough because she reminded him all the time.

After discussing what car he would suggest I buy, he said he thought the Volkswagen 'Beetle' was very good and affordable. I thought that was strange since it was a German car. A lot of Brits didn't buy German products after the war. Of course, being the pragmatist he was, he thought that was stupid. If the product was good, why not buy it, and since he thought German engineering was brilliant, who was I to argue?

I flew to Munich. I took a train to the factory at Wolfsburg and ordered a VW to be made for America with a left-hand drive.

The car made all the difference to me, although having a car with a left-hand drive and driving on the left side of the road was strange and a little scary at times. But, having a car was freedom, except that very few people owned automobiles on Winstanley Drive. No one had a garage. When the council houses were built in the late 1800s, there were no cars. My mother said she didn't remember vehicles in Leicester until 1910 or thereabouts. I now wondered why there were no garages in the newer council estates. To this day in England, most houses in the suburbs do not have the luxury of attached garages. Some owners have cleared their front gardens to accommodate a small car. Vehicles line the curbs in some busy cities causing chaos at rush hour.

The bus stopped directly outside our house, and there was no room for any vehicles to park on the street, so I parked my car in the nearby Co-Operative store where there was a space outside for delivery vans.

We went on lots of trips in that Volkswagon. My father and I went to Rothley Court for lunch. Rothley Court Hotel in Leicestershire is full of history associated with the Knights Templar and is mentioned in the Domesday Book of records. The lovely gardens surrounding the place are beautifully kept with fountains and statues reminiscent of the formal gardens still in manor house gardens in the UK. The chapel with its leaded-glass windows is a major attraction in the area, not to mention the classy restaurant that attracts tourists from all over Britain.

I drove to Cornwall with another old girlfriend when Ivy agreed to look after Jennie. Cornwall is in the West of England. Delightful villages nestle in the countryside among gently rolling hills and moorland, and fishing villages line the coastline, which in places is wild and windswept, with a history of pirates dating back to King Arthur and the Knights of the Round Table. Delightful cliff-top walks surround the sheltered coves and fishing villages. It is paradise, at least to me.

After six months, I decided to ship the VW back with me on a Holland America cargo-passenger ship that was to call at Panama, Haiti, and Bermuda. In those days, Cargo Passenger ships, with more than fifty passengers aboard had a doctor. That suited me because of Jennie.

The VW's engine was steam-cleaned at the docks before being loaded on the cargo-passenger ship in Southampton with about a dozen other vehicles. All the cars on board were classic or vintage: Rolls Royce, Daimler, Jaguars, and MG's snuggled up against my small VW Beetle. All vehicles were destined for Los Angeles or ports en-route.

As I stood at the rail of the large ship and watched the tender vessel swing away with my father on board, he tipped his hat. I must have wept for hours, just wondering if I would ever see him again. Was this to be our last farewell?

✳✳✳

Our journey was to take five weeks. I was the youngest person aboard that vessel except for a fourteen-year-old girl who loved to take Jennie in her stroller along the decks. The ship's doctor, a pleasant Dutchman, often asked me to join him on deck to sip brandy in the balmy evenings as we approached the Panama Canal. It was Christmas, hot and very humid. The ship was pulled slowly through the locks by thick cables attached to electric mules. That's what they called them — sort of like tractors.

The doctor was happy to tell me all about the canal. He said it was completed in 1914 and that it connects the Atlantic and the Pacific Oceans across the Isthmus of Panama. The complicated machinery can lift a ship 85 feet up from one lock to another. The three sets of locks, massive concrete structures 45 – 55 feet thick, can only be opened when the water level on both sides is equal. He said the port of Cristobal in Panama now connects a maritime route between the Caribbean and the Atlantic. "A great time saver for ships," he added.

On this trip, cars were unloaded in Haiti and Bermuda. Bermuda is a fascinating island and the oldest British overseas territory in North America, dating back to 1707 when England and Scotland were joined, thus creating the Kingdom of Great Britain.

Jennie was thirteen months old and just learning to walk. Fortunately, I had thought to bring a harness for her so that we could go on deck. A cargo-passenger ship is not like the glamorous cruise ships where the top deck is built for comfort and lined with glass and metal for the railings. This Holland-America line commercial ship was crude in that respect, with considerable gaps in the railings where anything that wasn't anchored firmly to the deck's surface in rough seas could fall to the ocean far below.

When we finally docked in the Los Angeles harbor, to my horror, I saw, when the car was unloaded by the large crane and swung over the side to the dock, the tires had been swapped, and the headlights smashed. I could only assume it had happened while we were docked at the port of Cristobal in Panama, where my car had inadvertently been unloaded and was in the dock overnight. In any case, even though the insurance paid for the repairs, I never liked the car after that. I sold it soon after returning to Redondo Beach. I remember sticking a 'For Sale' sign in the window of the car, and when I wound the window down, the sign stuck inside the door. I often wonder if the new buyer ever found it.

When I think about that six months in the UK, I realize it had been a time of renewed faith in myself. I would manage alone with a child. I do wonder now as I write this story why I returned to the States, except I did have a lot of friends who had stood by me all the time, and I missed them all. I also knew that I would have to have a place of my own if I was to stay in England. Sharing with Ivy was great, but I knew her husband would be shortly returning, and then what would I do? I was also aware that I had done so much to acquire my green card. Why throw that away?

I returned to America to work as a part-time receptionist at an Optical Company in Redondo Beach. During that time, my father surprised me by coming to visit Redondo for a month. He had never been out of England. I was delighted and flattered he chose to come to see me.

We went on a long road trip to Bryce and Zion Canyon National Parks. There's nothing like those places in England, and my father was in awe at the glorious colors in Bryce Canyon. Although England has a lot of open countryside, it's not the same. When we returned to Redondo, I asked him what one word he would use to describe what he had seen, and he answered, "Vast."

Arranging my story chronologically, I encounter moments of discomfort, just writing it down. Perhaps all of us have had times in our lives that we wish never happened. Meeting a man named Reuben Malkovich is one of those periods in my life I would rather forget.

I had recently been taking lessons offered at the Temple to become Jewish. I became a regular member on Friday evenings, and I always seemed to be sitting directly behind a man who looked, from the back, a lot like Joseph with the yarmulke sitting atop his thick, dark hair. After the service, it became a habit to walk together to the meeting hall for refreshments.

Reuben talked about his job a lot. He was a computer engineer at IBM, apparently one of the first in the computer industry. He was well-paid. He drove a Saab and had a truck with a camper on top that he'd built himself. I liked the fact that he was an outdoorsy sort of man.

After a party or two at his apartment complex in Torrance, we became good friends, although there should have been a red-flag warning for me when he made it clear that, if we went out, I would need a babysitter for Jennie. There was always the problem of babysitters for me in the evenings; since Edith had moved to the Bay Area to be with her daughter, I now had to rely on Thelma's daughter or another neighbor.

Reuben was very attentive, buying me gifts and making me feel attractive. He said he liked to camp in the high desert areas like Corona Del Mar and confessed he had spent many weekends there in a nudist park in the past with a woman friend. When he asked me if I would go with him, I immediately said no. I could not imagine parading around without a stitch of clothing. Then I remembered I had been photographed in the nude, although I never did know what happened to those photos.

Reuben said it was protocol to go with a partner or be married if you attended the nudist park. He said he really would like me to try it. Finally, I told him I would try it, but Jennie would have to come along. He said, okay.

Surprisingly, I began to enjoy the feeling of total freedom. Couples with children rented a cabin, or they camped in a lovely parklike setting, which is what we did.

Jennie was soon playing happily with the other children. Some of the rules were interesting to me. Not every woman went around totally nude, sometimes shorts and a skimpy top or just shorts. I never witnessed any improprieties between men and women. Without clothes, there were no class differences. I knew there were doctors and lawyers and office workers there, people from all walks of life. Everyone could be equal, except that some of the bodies were not as equally attractive as others. That's for sure. One of the things that I did love about the place was that you could take a shower so easily. Hoses were looped and wrapped to hang from some of the trees in the park. Just bring soap and a towel, enjoy the hot water, sometimes too hot. Wait a few minutes, and you could have a cold shower. The place was well kept with gardens and an Olympic-size swimming pool. Modern cabins were all around the perimeter. The campsites were in a separate area.

I loved nights outside the camper on a sleeping bag on the ground. Looking up at a sky full of stars was magic. We were a long way from the civilization of L.A., and the milky-way was so clear and bright in the wilderness dessert of Corona Del Mar. I suspect that urban sprawl has influenced the views of the night sky now. I'm sure it's not as isolated as it was then.

Reuben paid Jennie very little attention, but I reasoned that he wasn't her father, so why should he.

We met mostly at weekends, and I did enjoy being with him, especially on those weekends in Corona. I don't think our sex life dominated our relationship as it had done with Joseph. Reuben seemed to enjoy my company, although I found him to be rather intense, not a fun person, far too serious, too careful with money. He was so knowledgeable about most things, with a high IQ, and I admired that, although I was soon to realize that his scientific knowledge was excellent but not his understanding of others, at least not of me.

When he announced that his company was sending him to Ashland, Massachusetts to be a trouble-shooter on some new computer software, I expected him to leave and tell me he'd see me sometime in the future. I was surprised when he asked if I would go with him.

I told him I couldn't give up my apartment just like that.

He said, "It's only for six months, maybe less, and you won't need to spend a dime of your own. You can save your widow and child's benefits. Wouldn't that be good?"

I thought seriously about that. What would be the harm in going for a few months? I even added up what I could save during that time. I suppose, with that in mind more than anything, I said yes. He was delighted and helped me put my stuff into a storage unit in Redondo. I stored my car in Thelma's garage, gave the notice to leave my apartment, and two weeks later, we traveled to the East Coast in his Saab.

Twenty Four

The Massachusetts winter had turned into spring. Snow had left a soggy landscape on the grounds around an apartment complex that Reuben had found before we had left Redondo. The small town of Ashland was not within walking distance of the apartments, which were isolated from any commercial buildings or any other houses for what seemed to me like miles around. After the mud around the area had dried up, it was a green and pleasant place, moist with the smell of new growth different from the salty air from the sea in Redondo.

Reuben left early every day to drive to his office in Boston and I thought I would be lonely, but the nice thing about living in this enclave of apartments was that the couples were all around my age, and most had children. For the first time since Jennie was born, I was living close to young families. The camaraderie was terrific. Jennie made friends with Susan, a pretty four-year-old, the daughter of Nancy and Paul Woods, who lived in the apartments across the lawn area. Paul was an intern at Boston Hospital. Nancy and I got along nicely and spent days together, either sewing, knitting, or trying out new recipes. She had a car and took us to Boston quite often to see the historical places I'd only read about. I enjoyed parties and teas with the other women who were deeply involved in the political situation and the fact that Richard Nixon and Hubert Humphrey were battling for the Presidency. This was causing concern among a lot of folks in the apartment complex. Also in the news at that time was the Vietnam War. My thoughts often turned to Colin, and I still wondered what had become of him. It was then that the doubts and the guilt surfaced to darken my days. It all seemed so long ago and yet only yesterday. And here I was with a man I barely knew filling in the spaces of my life.

When Reuben announced that the project at his work was held up and extended and we could not return to Redondo yet, I told him that I should go back, but again, Reuben convinced me that my bank account was growing. I knew even though what he said might be true, this life was not what I wanted forever. And, it was when I noticed Reuben's possessiveness toward me that I began to feel smothered and I began to work out how I could move out quickly without causing too much hostility from him. He even invited his parents to stay for a week to meet me. I guessed he was trying to prove that they were different from Joseph's parents, and that they were very accepting of a non-Jewish girl for their son, who had never married. His mother and father were affectionate with Jennie and made a fuss of her, bestowing presents on us both. They asked about Jennie's father, and I showed them lots of photographs, but they never hesitated to sing Reuben's praises, continually telling me how good a son he was and such a good wage earner. "A very good husband he would be," they said.

I had already accepted the fact that Reuben tolerated Jennie at best. Our living together was a temporary situation in my mind, and when one small incident occurred, I decided that it was time for us to go our separate ways.

I was standing at the window watching Jennie and Susan playing in the little plastic swimming pool on the lawn. Jennie stepped out of the pool when Reuben arrived. She ran toward him with her arms outstretched. He walked right past her, didn't even see her, so engrossed in his thoughts he ignored her. I shall never forget her face as she turned to run into the house to me. That was the start of incidents that I noticed more frequently, and when I received a letter from my father telling me that my mother had had a stroke, I knew I had to go to see her, because I was really concerned about her and how my family would cope. Plus, it was my opportunity to leave Reuben. That evening I told him about my plans.

His voice was harsh when he said, "I thought you didn't get along well with her."

"True, sometimes," I said. "But she's ill, and maybe I can make it up to her and be the sort of daughter she would admire before she dies. It's very important to me, I know you understand. And, I'm sure my father would want me to be there."

Reuben took my hand, "I don't want you to go, Amelia," he said firmly. "You are saving a lot of money, you know. It's your job now to stay with me."

A prickle of fear ran up my spine. I shivered and withdrew my hand. "My job? Are you buying my time?" I asked.

He laughed, "Hardly."

I could feel the heat rise to my face. I wanted to say more but kept my mouth shut. Now I really wanted to get away, but how could I break off this relationship without causing a row? I had to play it cool, I knew that, but since I had already booked tickets for us to go to see the Ice Capades in Boston, I figured one more week would not hurt. The company was there for only a couple of weeks, and I thought Jennie would love it.

"I have no desire to see dancing on ice," Reuben said, "Why would you?" He sounded annoyed.

"Oh, come on," I said. "It'll be fun for Jennie. It will be a nice birthday present for her. Just something special for us all before I leave."

"You are leaving then?"

"Yes, Reuben. I did tell you about my mother."

"Well, how're you going to get to the Ice show?"

"If you don't want to drive me or go with me, I'll ask Nancy. Or, there's a bus that goes to Framingham. We can transfer to another one from there to Boston. You don't need to bother."

"What time does this thing start?" he asked

"Seven o'clock."

Reuben snorted, "It's too late for a five-year-old. It will be nine o'clock before it finishes."

"It's just once. She'll love it."

He looked at me and seemed to be deep in thought before he said, "I'll take you. I can drop you and Jennie off at the ice thing. There's a guy I know in Framingham; I'll go see him, then I'll come back for you afterward."

"You will? Oh, that would be super."

"Sure, I don't mind," he said. It was apparent he had no desire to go, but for some reason, he was trying to placate me.

"Thank you," I said.

I wore my black skirt and a pink silk blouse with a cotton jacket with pink flowers on it and high heels that I hadn't worn for a long time. Jennie was in her prettiest blue and white dress. We left the house at six. It was a forty-minute drive.

Reuben was quiet as we drove into the parking lot close to the big ice rink where the Ice Capades were performing. I thanked him for driving us, got out, and closed the door. Before I could reach for the other door to take Jennie out of her seat in the back, he took off, weaving around the cars in the parking lot like a madman.

I was speechless. Perhaps this was a joke, and he would come back laughing. But he didn't. Had he kidnapped my child? That's what ran through my mind at that moment. Reuben wasn't that crazy, or was he?

I waited for a minute or two, not quite believing that he had left me standing outside in the huge parking lot of the Boston Garden Ice Rink. Now I did want to call the police if I could find a phone booth. Then I wondered if *they* would believe me. What could I say? "Oh, I've been living with a guy, and he just kidnapped my child?" It sounded lame to me, so I opted to find a taxi and go home as quickly as I could.

Fortunately, a couple drove into the parking lot a minute later and told me where the taxi stand was outside the train station. The woman looked at me quizzically. "Are you not going to the show?" she asked.

I couldn't explain everything, so I just said, "No, changed my mind. Got to get home, emergency."

I'm sure she must have wondered about me and the emergency, but I didn't want to stand around to chat.

She looked at me for a second, "Oh, hop in," she said. "We can take you."

I thanked her and was glad I didn't have to walk in my high heels.

By the time I had found a taxi and arrived back at the apartment, it was almost eight o'clock.

I pounded on the door. No answer. I saw a light in the living room and knocked on the window. My child was in there with him, and I wanted her out. I'd have to go to Nancy's to use her phone and call the police; I was prepared to do anything.

Reuben opened the door. Even in the dull light of the hallway, I could see he was angry, and I could smell beer. Without a word, he turned and went into the living room where the TV was loud. I rushed upstairs to find Jennie fast asleep. I sat on the bed, reliving the scenario I'd imagined during the ride back to the apartment. Why had he been so mean? It didn't make any sense to me.

Breathing a sigh of relief to see Jennie safe and sound, I undressed and got into bed, already working on a plan to leave in the morning, but I was afraid. I did not know this man. Be calm, I thought. Don't make an issue of what had happened. Suddenly I was aware of him in the room. He came to the side of the bed and bent down. "You don't decide things in this house," he said, leaning over to breathe in my ear. "You purposely disobeyed me. I'm paying your way while you're here don't forget."

When he drew back, I noticed his face was flushed. Anger flowed from him. For the first time, since I was a child, I saw an aura, his aura, vicious, red, turmoil, like a snake winding up and up and all around him. I took a deep breath. "Reuben," I whispered. "I do thank you for supporting me, but you know I do need to go home and see my mother, whether you like it or not," Sweetly then, "I must go."

He frowned and turned away, then in one swift movement, he lifted his hand, made a fist, turned, and pounded my face catching me in my left eye. I flinched and grabbed the sheet to protect myself. Oh, God! He stripped away the sheet and hit me again.

I couldn't scream. I was shivering uncontrollably. I lay still just waiting for the next blow. I'd fought my brother off me, but this was different; there was a rage in this man's actions. I was terrified. I closed my eyes, feeling a searing pain in my eye. My head felt as though it would explode.

Suddenly, there was silence. I opened my eyes. He was gone from the room. I heard him run down the stairs; then, after a minute, he charged out the front door. With my heart pounding in my head, I darted to the window and saw the Saab racing down the street.

I can't remember how I dressed or what I wore. I could feel wetness creeping down my cheek. My eye was already closing shut, and my face burned.

I pulled my suitcase from the cupboard, slinging everything I could think of into it. Clothes for both of us. I left all my personal stuff behind. All the photo's I'd brought with me of Joseph and Jennie.

I went to her room and woke her up, "Come on, sweetheart. Get up."

"Mummy?"

"It's okay, come on, love."

We ran over the grass to Nancy's house, and I knocked on the door. "Oh my God," Nancy said as she ushered us inside.

Paul bathed my eye and put a bandage on it. He told me I should go to the hospital tomorrow and that he would take me. I told him I just needed to get away.

Jennie and I slept on their couch or tried to, and first thing in the morning, I used Nancy's phone to call a travel agent for a flight to L.A. I called Thelma, and she said she'd pick me up. I didn't tell her much about why I was returning so quickly, and she didn't ask.

I flew back from Boston to L.A. with a patch over my eye and dark sunglasses. The bruises I could not hide.

Thelma insisted I stay in her guest room for a few days until I felt I could gain control and feel better. I kept the dark glasses on. Even the light bothered me. I wanted to get to England quickly, escape maybe to my father? He would make everything right.

Thelma drove me to the immigration department in L.A. In those days, green-card holders or non-citizens had to pay U.S. taxes before they left the country, especially if there was no return air ticket.

She and her family were at the airport gate to see me off.

Two days later, I called Nancy and Paul to thank them for all the lovely times we'd had together and for all their help. Nancy told me that Reuben had burned all my stuff on the front lawn. All my photos were gone.

✳✳✳

Leicester had changed since I was a child. All England had become smokeless, and chimneys no longer spewed smoke into the air. Where there had been smog that hovered over the city, now hills emerged, visible behind a skyline of buildings etched against a blue sky.

It had been two months since my mother's stroke, and the paralysis on her left side was not as noticeable as it had been, according to my father. I noticed her words didn't come out quite right sometimes, but apart from that, she seemed fine. I could see that my father's arthritis in his shoulders and his hands was painful, although he never complained. He walked bent over and struggled to open doors and go upstairs. I asked him if I could take him to the doctor to see if there was something they could do for him. He said, "Don't worry about me, love. I'm getting old. That's all."

Although I was wary of Douglas, I knew I had to let go of the past. He probably regretted what had happened. What I did notice was that he had done his best to look after my parents. I hadn't been around, neither had Pauline, so I was grateful to him. I could see the house needed cleaning, and the garden had been left neglected. The borders of the lawn, once bright with pinks and marigolds, were now just weeds. The grass was not looking good and needed mowing, but I wasn't about to say anything. Keeping the peace was my objective at that time. Douglas was doing his best.

I stayed in the small bedroom with Jennie. It was a tight squeeze in there, and again I knew if I planned on staying in England, I would soon have to find somewhere to live on my own.

One morning after breakfast, my father handed me a letter that had just arrived from Thelma. Inside was another sealed envelope, and I recognized Reuben's writing.

I opened it carefully.

Dearest Amelia:

I am so very sorry for what happened. I didn't mean to hurt you.

I don't want to go on without you, and I'm now back in Redondo. Please come back to me. Forgive me. I love you.

Reuben,

P.S. I will kill myself if you don't come back.

I wrote back.

Go for it. I'm sure someone will send me your obituary from the newspaper.

I never heard from him again.

The Estate Agent in Leicester told me there was now a new block of flats in Oadby, a village not too far from the city. I could lease a flat but it would have to be for three years. It had central heating. I was impressed. My folks had no heat except for the coal fire in the living room.

I remember when I was about seven, just after the war ended, it had been one of the coldest winters in history when the snow lay on the ground for weeks. It seemed everybody on our street ran out of coal at the same time. Forests had dwindled, so we never had the luxury of logs to heat the house, and fuel was in short supply. There had been a strike among the miners.

In the newspaper, my mother read that coke would be available to those who wanted to haul it themselves from a local factory. Coke is a by-product of coal used for smelting iron or industrial furnaces. There was no shortage of industrial furnaces in Leicester, one of the richest cities in England. But how to fetch the coke was a problem for my family — no car. Few families had that luxury. My father was at work, so my mother, with me in tow, walked to the ironworks two miles away with my old pram and a spade. We queued for an hour. My mother chatted with other neighbors about food rationing and swapping butter for eggs and such. Eventually, we were next in line. Mother lifted as much coke as she could into the pram with the spade.

Coke is lighter than coal, but not that light, and on the way home, the pram, which had sunk visibly from the weight, suddenly lost a wheel and tipped over. The precious coke spread out across the road. I remember I bawled. Mother stood there and said quietly, "Oh, bloody hell!" It was typical of my mother. She could swear when the need arose, and this was one of those days.

I think we sat on the curb, although I'm not sure why, but when our neighbor boy came along dragging his home-made wooden box on wheels, it was a welcome sight. He helped my mother scrape up the coke, and we made it to our house intact. My mother gave him sixpence and a piece of cake. That week we had heat in the living room fireplace.

The flat I rented was ultra-modern on the outside, but inside, it was just a shell. There was no fitted kitchen with lots of counter space, as is usual in America, no large refrigerator either. But then most people shopped daily for fresh produce and meat. My parents never owned a fridge. We had a meat safe, just a metal box cupboard with a mesh on the front, and a marble slab in the pantry for cheese and milk that was delivered daily.

For the first time in my life, I shopped for furniture: high-backed swivel chairs for the living room; a glass-topped rattan dining set; and I paid for the kitchen to be revamped with built-in cupboards. I had enough money to buy everything I needed.

Jennifer was attending the infant school in Oadby village. It seemed strange to see a five-year-old in a uniform: grey tunic and light blue blouse with a blue-and-white striped tie. As far as I know, it still is the rule in England. School uniforms render all children equal, without the accouterments of social standings.

I went on the bus to see my folks once a week. One day I accompanied my mother to the cemetery where her mother was buried. I had visited my grandmother's grave many times when I was young, and my mother still made her monthly sojourn to keep the gravesite free from weeds and leave flowers. Due to the burgeoning population, and the churchyards now filled, cemeteries were built on the outskirts of the town. The Burial Act of 1852 allowed the city to buy public land to use as civil graveyards. Old gravestones in ancient churchyards have always fascinated me, and Leicester, being a Roman town, boasts many pagan and Christian burial sites. Bones still are being discovered in and around this medieval city during digs. The skeletal remains of King Richard III were found beneath a parking lot. King Richard died during the Battle of Bosworth on August 22, 1458, the last significant battle of the War of the Roses between the royal houses of Lancaster and York, before Henry VIII became king in the House of the Tudors.

At the cemetery, my mother arranged a bunch of daisies in a metal pot on her mother's grass-covered grave. She hesitated before she moved along to another small monument. I read the headstone, 'Baby Elizabeth Rush, Born June 10, 1919, Died July 15, 1919.' I said, "This baby was only a month old. Did you know who it was?"

Without a word, she turned to me and took my elbow and led me to a seat. She sat back and looked around before turning to me. She sighed, "I suppose it's time you knew the truth."

I perched on the edge of the seat, leaning toward my mother and waited.

"You know," she said. "I should never have married your father. I was in love with another man. His name was Jack Rush."

It was the heyday of the twenties. My mother, Victoria, was a guest at a ball held in a large stately home. With her dark hair, eyes the color of a summer sky, she was the center of attention. Her beige flapper dress jangled with beads she had patiently sewed on the bodice and the bottom of the knee-length skirt. Her silk stockings and elegant strapped shoes showed off her shapely legs to perfection. Her dance partner, Claude, was not a good dancer, and she excused herself and escaped to the balcony where she found an unoccupied chair. A man was standing by himself in the corner of the balcony, watching as she closed her eyes for just a second, taking a breather from the loud music and the crowds inside the house. She crossed her legs and looked around at the formal gardens before she caught a glimpse of the man with bright red hair and a beard watching her. She felt hot from his stare, and a tiny dribble of sweat made its way between her breasts. Since Claude had monopolized her attention from the beginning of the evening, she didn't think it was rude to leave him chatting with the host. Glancing again at the man in the corner, she felt a moment of panic. Then, with a smile, he came to her. She flushed under his gaze.

Without a word, he led her back into the house. They spent the rest of the evening, and every evening for the next year, together. She knew he had made enough money somewhere, somehow, to own a beautiful car and accompany her everywhere she wanted to go. He never told her where he had lived before coming to Leicester or what his business was. They went to all the dance halls in the city and never sat one out. They made love in his room at a posh boarding house. Victoria assumed he would ask her to be his wife.

One evening, out of the blue, he said his business in Australia needed him for a while. Jack told her he would send for her when he was settled. He didn't explain further, and she trusted he would keep his word. She waited for his letters, and when she finally received one postmarked New South Wales about a year later, she knew, at last, he wanted her to go to him. The letter had taken eight months to get to England. Inside was a short note, 'Jack had an accident at the gold mine. He'll be in touch.' The signature at the bottom read C.J. Boyl.

"Gold mine!" I said, "Goodness. You never knew?"

"No."

"And who was C.J. Boyl?" I asked.

"I've no idea."

I sat and pondered what she'd said, "Perhaps Jack couldn't read or write, did you ever think of that?"

My mother was also deep in thought. "Well," she said, "I suppose that could be true. I never saw him write anything."

"What about the baby?" I asked.

"Oh, I found out I was pregnant just after Jack left. My mother sheltered me from all the prying eyes of the street neighbors, but it was awful."

"I am sorry," I said. "So what happened to the baby? Why did she die?"

"I can't tell you that. I never discuss it. It's too painful for me. But at least you know about your father and me. We were both on the rebound. It was never a good match."

It was apparent she had finished the conversation, so I asked, "So you didn't ever hear from Jack again?"

"No."

"Goodness, a gold mine. How strange you never knew."

We didn't talk on the way home. I suspect we were both thinking about her story. I was very curious to know how the child had died and anxious to understand why my mother would not reveal it, and, indeed, I was bewildered by her sudden confession of a past love. Then I remembered my father's story about Violet. My mother was right; they were both on the rebound.

Twenty Five

That afternoon, sitting quietly with my mother enjoying a cup of tea, I thought about this man named Jack, who had led my mother on a merry chase. Or had he? I tried to imagine him in Australia in a gold mine and asking his friend C.J. Boyl to write a letter to my mother. Could it be true that maybe he could not read or write? It was a puzzle and sad that we would never know.

I looked around at all the things I remembered in the living room. It was all so familiar. Just as it always had been. Even as a child, I remembered the same pictures on the walls, the shiny black upright piano, and the alcove where once the sewing machine had its place. It was comforting to find the sameness in everything, a permanence that one does not find in the States, where everything seems so temporary, except, I was now used to old buildings being replaced by new ones, furniture changed to keep up with new trends, and homes sold after only a few years. I had become very used to modern houses with attached garages, plus wide roads even in the small towns.

In England, buildings are preserved. Families live in the same home for thirty or forty years, some all their lives. The roads are narrow in country villages, and although lots of people own cars, there are very few homes still with garages, unless they are separate and tiny. People don't seem to desire newness in all things, or a different environment every five years or so. There's an old saying among the older generation, "If it's good enough for my dad, it's good enough for me."

The furniture in my parent's house had been reupholstered by my father years ago, but it was now looking very shabby. I began to imagine new furniture, plain wallpaper instead of the paisley design. The worn beautifully patterned Axminster rug with its faded reds and blues would look great with plain wallpaper, and yes, the curtains could be a coordinating color. I visualized a three-piece-suite in neutral beige. I could see it all in my mind's eye. I was excited. The thought sprang to my mind quickly, and without thinking further, I turned to my mother and said with a smile, "How would you like a new three-piece suite? I could buy you one."

She looked at me, and I saw the same look in her eyes. I remembered when I visited her in the Tower's Mental Hospital. She said icily, "You keep your Yankee dollars."

I was stunned. I had, in one sentence, ruined my relationship with her once again. I had pushed aside any thoughts that perhaps their furniture held special memories. I was the one who should have apologized for my ignorance, but she never afforded me the chance. Once again, the chasm between us opened, never to be closed again.

I stayed away from my parents after that episode for weeks at a time. I wasn't bored, but I was missing my apartment in Redondo with an open view of the ocean.

I liked my flat where I had now been living for six months, but to look out on the parking lot didn't exactly thrill me. The apartments across the way were identical to mine, and I was often drawn to the window to see people coming and going to their cars. I learned their routine. The girl directly opposite always wore long skirts. It was a time of the mini-skirt, so she stood out as someone very different, with dark hair swept up in a ponytail. She always carried a huge

237

handbag. Then there was a young man who lived next door to her. I saw him walking to his car at eight every morning. Once, he glanced my way and waved. He was tall, dark-haired, and carried a briefcase. He was always smartly dressed in a suit, a pastel-colored shirt and a tie. Undoubtedly, he was handsome.

After Reuben, I was determined to live without a man in my life. I purposely stayed away from the places I'd frequented during my teens in England. I did miss the ballroom dancing and thought briefly about joining a club. Britain has always held dance clubs at the local dance hall studios. It is a great place to meet people.

I discovered Jennie's school was the best place to meet women around my age, and I was fortunate to know two women who became good friends. They arranged a party for Jennie when she turned six. We often met for coffee in the village, and I began to feel at home in Oadby.

One warm sunny day, I was walking along the narrow street in the village with Jennifer in her stroller when a car pulled up beside me, "Need a lift?" It was the dark-haired young man from the flat opposite me.

"Oh, thanks, but we like to walk."

After he'd introduced himself as Mark and I told him my name, he asked if I would like to have a drink with him one evening.

"Sounds nice," I said, "but I'd need a babysitter."

"Oh, no worries, I know someone."

About a week later, he knocked on my door with a young girl who was eager to babysit. Her name was Rosamund. She was sixteen and as sweet as her name. She also appeared to be sensible, and I decided I had to trust her. She made my life much easier and I was introduced to her parents who turned out to be wonderful friends to me and Jennie.

I joined Mark often in the local pub, and I noticed he drank a lot, but since I never intended this friendship to go anywhere it didn't bother me. He was a sales representative for a large pharmaceutical company and traveled to all the local doctor's offices. The interesting thing was that Jennie seemed to approve of our relationship, always asking where he was. When he brought her the gift of a hamster in a very fancy cage, it seemed to seal the deal of their friendship, until the animal got trapped in the bars of the ladder and hung itself. Jennie was devastated. So was I, but Mark came to the rescue and bought another hamster in a plain cage.

He was twenty-five, I was thirty-two. After I had vowed that I would not get entangled in another relationship, here I was again. When Mark asked me if I wanted to meet his parents, I said it was a little soon for that, I feared he expected more of me than I was willing to give at that time. Still, when he suggested a trip to the small town of Leigh-On-Sea in Essex, I gave in. At least we would be by the ocean for a few days. I needed to breathe the salty sea air. It would be a treat.

His mother and father owned a bungalow in the small coastal town on the East coast of England, where the low tides leave fishing boats high and dry until the tide rescues them again six hours later. Mark's father was a minister at a local Baptist Church. This man was patient and loving to his wife, and I figured he didn't need to know that I was not religious, and fortunately, he didn't even talk about his church. He was apparently delighted his son seemed to have found someone, and he encouraged us to leave Jennie with them if ever we wanted a holiday alone. I began to appreciate having a father figure for Jennifer and grandparents who adored her. When Mark suggested a holiday in Tunisia for Christmas, I was happy he included Jennifer in his plans.

In the early seventies, new resorts and hotels were springing up in isolated spots along the Mediterranean coastline of Tunisia. Tunis lies between Algeria and Tripoli in North Africa. It became a city eight hundred and sixty-nine years before the birth of Christ. There, the sea shines green and blue; the narrow streets wind around mosques, minarets, and historical buildings; date palms line the avenues where camel markets are held, and spices from all over the world are sold. The mixture of Moors and Arabs embodies a colorful past.

At our hotel, chickens roamed around the outside of the resort, and grass-roofed Palapas lined the beach directly behind the hotel. In the large foyer, there was an enormous Douglas fir, imported to make tourists from Christian Europe and England feel at home. Unadorned, the tree looked odd amid the potted palms and exotic plants. I decided the tree ought to have snow. I had brought a bag of cotton balls with me and I asked if I could spread them out along each branch. The manager was puzzled. In his broken English, he said he'd never seen snow and had no idea what sort of a tree it was. But by the time I had finished, the tree looked as though it had grown in a forest of trees in winter.

The Christmas dinner was rather different in its presentation. I thought it was amusing when the sliced turkey came as course one, then the dressing as course two. Even the potatoes were served separately. A loud-spoken English lady at the next table leaned over to me, "Isn't it awful," she said in her broad Midland's dialect. "Fancy serving Christmas dinner like this." She shook her head in disgust.

I turned to her and smiled, "Well, if you wanted a typical English dinner, you should have stayed at home."

To me, being in a very different world than my own, was not only fun but an eye-opener as to how other countries survive in their daily living. All travel is educational to me.

At this hotel, most of the breakfasts were scrambled eggs with very orange yolks, served with grainy bread and date jam. Delicious. Other meals were mostly couscous, with lamb and carrots, which is typical North African fare.

We went on a camel ride in the desert outside the resort. Our group was expected to dress as Bedouins for the day. The garb wasn't very flattering, but I didn't want to spoil the fun. Unfortunately, my camel was in heat, and Jennie's camel was forever trying to mount mine. Finally, a man whom we'd met at the hotel, Don, who was used to riding camels, rescued her quickly and hoisted her up to sit with him. My "she" camel went berserk and took off with me on it among high pear cactus, with the male camel running after us. All I could do was hang on. Riding a camel is not like riding a horse, believe me. I suspect it created much amusement for the onlookers.

One thing I remember clearly was the day at the spice market. Men in white robes sat cross-legged in a line on rough wooden boards on the ground. Their teeth were yellow, and they spat tobacco into the dirt. Each man had a pair of scales in front of him. I asked one man if he had saffron, which of course, is very expensive in the States because it's from the three stigmas of the saffron crocus. It is hard to grow and harvest. The man nodded and asked me to put an American quarter on one side of the scale; then he filled the other side until the scales balanced. The saffron pile was enormous. Saffron is light as a feather. I told him all I needed was a little to take back with me. Years later, I still had lots of saffron.

It was quite a unique experience wandering through very narrow cobbled alleyways, admiring lovely hammered copper jugs, pots, wonderful things unknown in Britain. The Moroccan rugs hanging outside the tiny storefronts were costly. A storekeeper, seeing my interest in the hand-tying of the rugs, came out to greet us and immediately asked me if he could touch my hair. Women with blonde hair are unique, apparently. This man whispered something to Mark as we left. I asked Mark what that was all about. He said the storekeeper had offered five hundred camels for me! Mark had told the man to make it six hundred, and he'd consider it a done deal.

✳✳✳

I was happy with Mark in my life at that time, and knowing my daughter was being educated in England was satisfying because I thought the school system, at that time, anyway, was far better than in America. Although, based on my memories of my early years in school, I'm not sure why I determined that to be true. In the fifties, when I attended the local primary school, it was basic reading, writing and arithmetic that were emphasized. Handwriting was taught daily in those days, and knuckles were rapped if we didn't do well in cursive. We had a school nurse and a nit nurse. Hard to imagine the weekly inspection of head-lice in those days. There were no gym-clothes for us. We had to strip to our underwear for exercises in the large hall. I'm sure I never thought about the smells of sweaty kids that must have lingered in that hall where so many other things took place. We were given eye tests, hearing tests, and vaccinations for German measles, all at the school.

Education in England these days is streamed and divided into stages based on age. Primary school is between the ages of four and eleven when the SATs take place. A secondary school is eleven to fourteen, then lower sixth at age sixteen, and upper sixth for seventeen and eighteen-year-olds. Independent schools are known as

Public schools, which must be confusing to Americans. 'Grammar schools' were initially attached to Cathedrals and monasteries teaching Latin, which was the language of the church. With the introduction of universities in the late 12th century, a grammar school became the entry to higher learning.

Cathedral schools in England closed when King Henry VIII destroyed all the monasteries. Grammar schools became part of the modern education system and remained as the gateway to a college education at the age of sixteen.

When I graduated with an 'O' Level (ordinary level) at fifteen, it was not an option for me to gain my 'A' (advanced level and college, because my parents needed me to pay room and board. I had to go to work. The thought that I had never had a college education made me feel inferior when I first came to the U.S. Even my parents had assumed I would never amount to much because I'd attended a Secondary Modern School.

But now, back in the UK, I applied to the City's Education department to take my 'A' Levels at the local Grammar school. It was an exciting year attending classes with sixteen-year-olds. I emerged with my certificate in English and History which would qualify me to attend a college even if I was well over thirty.

In the meantime, Pauline had been asking me to visit her in Kenya. I was thrilled to be able to travel anywhere, but to Africa, well, that was fabulous. With the school year finally over, I left Jennie in Mark's capable hands and flew alone to Nairobi. I was amazed at the number of hours we traveled over the Sahara to East Africa. We kept up with the sunrise all the way over the dessert.

Nairobi in Kenya is a marvelous place. Pauline and Richard's house on Livingston Drive had beautiful mahogany floors polished by the Shamba boys almost every day. I thought of the boys as the silent people. They walked the halls of the house with bare feet. It was a little unnerving to realize that suddenly I was not alone, not unless they were wheeling the tea-trolley along the hardwood floors, which made quite a racket.

In the bedroom, my sister warned me not to leave anything close to the windows because of 'pole burglars.' Like Hawaii, there was no glass in the windows, just bars. It was easy for someone to hook a purse from inside using a long pole with a hook on it. Just like the one I remembered in school to open and close high widows.

Pauline's five daughters were all beautiful. Confident and smart; world travelers. English boarding school education for Louise, the oldest girl, who was named after my grandmother. She was born in the UK. All the others, in Africa.

I went alone on safari to the famous Treetops Lodge in Nyeri, Aberdares National Game Park, where Princess Elizabeth had visited the day she became Queen of England on February 5, 1952. As I read the plaque with the date on the wall of the lodge, I thought about that day in England. The broadcast stations were silent except for a few words every half hour: "This is the BBC London. The King is dead. Long live the Queen."

Because I was alone on safari, I sat in front with the driver in the Zebra Wagon. I asked him how he liked Kenya; now the British had left them to their own devices. He told me he much preferred his English brother bosses to the Africans. They were much kinder, he said.

Kenya gained independence from the British in 1963. Now, ten years later, the street names had been changed from British to Kenyan. Princess Avenue became Kenyatta Avenue, and so on. However, there was still the elegance of the old era of British colonialism in the Norfolk Hotel in Nairobi, where we often had dinner. It was a world of elegance and charm in that hotel.

Pauline's husband, Richard, took me to Nakuru Lake, where hundreds of flamingoes gathered and waded through the shallows, a blanket of pink. That was a sight I will never forget — or the smell!

✳✳✳

While I was away in Africa, Mark was offered a job as a sales rep for Bass Charrington, a large, well-known brewery in England. It would include a move to Hampshire in the south of England. The company would be paying for a rental house in Dibden Purlieu, close to Southampton and the New Forest, one of the most beautiful areas in England. Of course, the New Forest is not new. William the Conqueror dedicated it as a Royal Hunting Ground in 1079. It still belongs to the crown and to the verderers, or commoners, who have ancient grazing rights for their cattle. Wild ponies still wander freely through the small country villages, and they have the right of way on the roads. Vehicles must wait until the ponies have walked lazily through the streets. Everyone knows the rules, and I've never witnessed any problems. You just can't be in a hurry.

Southampton is a medieval city with the remains of a city wall and a fortress. It is a bustling seaport, home to the QEII at that time, and the departure point for the Titanic. I found Southampton perfect for serious shopping because it was just a short ferry ride across a stretch of the water from the village where we now lived.

Jennie was eight years old when Mark and I were married. It seemed the right thing to do at the time. He was such a good father to her, and to find such gentle grandparents who wanted so much to be involved in her childhood was remarkable. Mark's parents were precious to me. But it was clear that Mark was becoming an alcoholic. I could see the signs but do very little about it. I can only believe that his job at Bass Charrington did not help one bit. He had

245

to have a pint with the proprietor of each public house he visited, I suppose.

I decided it was time for me to find employment, not knowing how we were going to end up if Mark lost his job. He was not as reliable as he once had been. It was awful to see him when he had been drinking.

I applied to a boating company at the docks in Southampton and was lucky enough to land a secretarial position at Blue Funnel Cruises. My office was above the entrance to the pier, built in the late 1800s, it was Victorian architecture at its best and worst. Great ornate scrolls of concrete adorned the arched doorways, upon which hung large wooden boards displaying signs and notices of various boat trips around the docks, or to Portsmouth, or across the Solent Water to the Isle of Wight.

My boss, Mr. Bertram, would yell up the stairs to me in my small office at the top of the narrow stairs. "Queen's in." His voice rang between the concrete walls of the ticket office below. At that time in Southampton, the *QEII* used the long dock. Her great hull dwarfed our boats docked nearby. When she arrived after her transatlantic voyages, four tender vessels escorted the Queen and then swung away in wide arcs, all piping in unison, a sharp thrill, whoop, whoop. The Queen would answer in her low voice, one long, low, single horn, triumphant.

Blue Funnel Cruises was owned by two partners, Henry Bertram and Bill Holmes. Bill was a robust chap with a rubicund complexion. On his nose was a very large mole, from which sprouted one single hair. This affliction of his became a fascination of mine. When I talked to him, it was hard to concentrate on anything else. It was comforting to be with Henry, who was slight of build and had a wonderfully aristocratic, fine-boned face, as pale as Bill's was red. Henry had inherited Blue Funnel Cruises from his father. Bill was a hired boatman. It was a mystery to me why they became partners because their criticism of each other was sometimes cruel. Henry, ever mindful of Bill's flurries of activities, which included overbooking passengers or sending boats out half-empty, would shout at Bill, who was generous to a fault for making promises that could not be kept. He and Henry would get into a shouting match. Bill would complain that Henry was a mean old bastard, and Henry would call Bill a zealous old buggar who couldn't do anything he was told.

Old Fred had been the owner of a small boat for twenty-five years. He would take visitors around the harbor. Every day he stood outside of the entrance to the pier. He would cup his hand to his mouth and shout to anyone passing by, "Any more for the Skylark?" Then he beamed as the rumble of the turnstile filled the air. Every clickety-click meant another shilling in his pocket.

My job at Blue Funnel Cruises was to contact bus companies and tour agencies all over Britain advertising cruise trips to the Isle of Wight in summer. Our largest vessel, *Solent Scene* carried a hundred passengers, and at high tide we would sail the Beaulieu River to take passengers to Lord Montague's Motor Museum at Buckler's Hard. All of Lord Nelson's ships were built there during the sixteenth century, using the huge oak trees that were abundant in the forest at that time. Today, there are no trees in the area.

Life at Blue Funnel Cruises was never dull. My desk, chair, and file cabinet took up every inch of space in my office. Henry or Bill would stand on the narrow staircase to talk to me, but I never felt isolated or lonely. From my small circular window, I could observe the coming and going of ships from all over the world. Large liners docked close by with their flags snapping in the wind. Oil tankers passed by en-route to the refinery at Fawley and the Red Funnel Ferries plied back and forth across the Solent, a stretch of twenty-two miles to France before the Chunnel existed. The hovercraft sounded like a bumblebee as it slid down the ramp to the sea, and the hydrofoil spumed its way to France every day. I could see them all from my window.

✷✷✷

If you remember earlier in my story I mentioned my desire to go to college. I found the opportunity when I learned that Blue Funnel Cruises operated only in the summer months. At last, I was able to attend the Art College in Southampton, which offered a certificate in Fashion and Textile Design. That included pattern cutting, which posed a problem because that year, Britain became metric. Yards became meters, a drastic change when pattern cutting is involved since there is a significant difference between a meter and a yard. A meter is almost four inches longer, which made math in design hard for me. Pattern cutting is all math. However, I was good at drawing and loved to create designs that looked good on normal girls, not just models who were six feet tall and slender as a reed. I also knew how to draw details for construction necessary in mass production. The order of sewing pieces that go into an elaborate evening dress is not complicated, but it must be thought through very carefully. I liked the process, not realizing that in the distant future, I would own my own company as a designer of silk lingerie.

Many people believe that home economists study cooking only. It isn't so. I would later belong to an organization with the designation, HEIB, an acronym for Home Economists in Business.

I was enjoying my college course when I received a letter from the Immigration Department in the States telling me I had violated the rule of being away from America for more than a year.

Somehow, the date had slipped by. I had to decide where I wanted my domicile to be, England or America?

What a decision to throw at me, just when Jennie was due to go to a high school, and she was looking forward to that. I had to consider that by whisking her away, she would have to go to a middle school for a year in the States. America is a year behind England.

I was worried about Mark. He was such a good father to Jennie, and we still spent a lot of time with his folks in Leigh-On-Sea, but I could not envisage him living in the USA without his favorite pubs. Rightly or wrongly, I decided to return to the USA. I had to apply for a re-entry visa, which took a few months and more anguish in convincing myself I was making the right decision It upset my father, I know. He loved to visit us in Hampshire and he adored Jennie. She was mad at me, and Mark was lost. It was such a sad time for us all, and looking back now, we should have stayed in England.

✳✳✳

Meanwhile, Mark had decided that he would join us later in the States, so Jennie and I traveled to Leicester on the train from Southampton to say goodbye, once again, to my folks. When the taxi arrived outside my folks' house in Leicester, I could see neighbor Bette in her front garden.

"Hi Bette," I said. "How are things with you?" I gave her a long hug. We had always been good friends. She held me close for a minute, and I told her that I would be leaving England in a couple of weeks to return to the States. She stepped back from me, and I noticed a strange expression on her face. I said, "Are you all right?"

She paused, "We have to move, you know. We've rented another house on Gooding Road."

"Well, that's exciting, isn't it?"

"We didn't want to move."

Her hesitation made me curious, "So why move?"

"It's your brother, Amelia!" she said, turning away. "He exposed himself to Lisa when he was in the backyard. Lisa is only sixteen; she was frightened. We all were. We have to move."

"Oh my God," I said. "I… oh, that's awful. Oh, dear. Oh, dear. Did you tell my mum and dad?"

"How could I?" she said briskly. "Your parents rely on Douglas for everything. Your mum dotes on him; you know that."

For a minute, words didn't come easily. Betty interrupted my confused thoughts. "And there's more," she said. "He's a peeping Tom, your brother. All the neighbors know about him."

I stared at her, unable to believe or even comprehend that Douglas could be the one to cause such travesty in such a close-knit community of friends and neighbors. If what Bette was saying was true, then my whole family would be shunned. How could I deal with that? Suddenly angry, I said, "Why didn't one of you go to the police, for goodness sake?"

She answered quietly, "I couldn't do that to your folks, Amelia. It would ruin them."

"Then I will call," I said. My teeth were so tightly clenched I could hardly utter the words, "I'll have to."

"You mean you would call the police about your own brother?"

"For God's sake, Bette, think about it. He could rape somebody. Don't you see that?"

"He's your brother, Amelia!"

"I know," I said. "I know."

I regretted the call immediately. I even gave my name. I had no idea why I did that. And worse, how was I going to approach my parents. They would have to be told.

I went to see my father, who was in his workshop at the bottom of the garden. His face went white when I told him about Douglas. He sat down on his high stool, laying his hands flat on top of the workbench and closed his eyes. An odd look transformed his face. He suddenly opened his eyes and looked at me over the top of his glasses, just as I remembered he had looked at my mother when she had had too much to drink. It was total disapproval, not of what I was telling him, but of me. He said, "We will take care of it."

"But you won't," I blurted out. I could feel my whole body shaking. "You just want to sweep anything unpleasant under the carpet."

"Did you tell your mother?"

"Not yet."

I watched my father silently as he placed all the tools in the drawers, everything straight and neat on the top of the work table. He looked suddenly old, pale, small, and insecure. I had done that to him at that moment.

I left him knowing that I had to be the one to talk to my mother. I doubted he would be able to tell her the awful details.

She was sitting in her chair, smoking. I approached her defiantly. "Our Douglas is a Peeping Tom," I blurted out. "He exposed himself to Lisa next door. I called the police. Bette must move away because of our Douglas. She's too nice to tell you, but all the neighbors know."

My mother's face turned bright red, but she didn't back down. She hissed, "Don't you dare to say that about your brother." She stubbed out her cigarette angrily, crushing it in the ashtray.

"Mother, I called the police."

"You don't know anything, do you?" I thought she was going to spit at me. "If only you knew how that poor little boy was treated back during the war, packed off from home with a label tied to his coat, then waiting in some drafty village hall to be picked out by a family who would care for him until the war had ended? No, they didn't treat him well. I can tell you that. Whoever they were, they must have abused him. It's no wonder he is as he is."

"What do you mean, abused?"

"I don't know what they did to him, but I know he's not what he should be. I've seen the photos in his bedroom…and the sleazy magazines. He's sick, but it's his business, not mine or yours."

"Well, this is your business, Mother," I whispered. I thought I would tell her about how he had exposed himself to me and the other sexual abuse that was hard to talk about, but I could not utter those words. Instead, I took a deep breath, "Douglas needs help. He's a Peeping Tom."

My mother turned away, "I don't believe you. You are a trouble maker, always have been, and you should leave now. I don't want you here. You come here with your Yankee ways of superiority. Thinking you are better than us. Best you go back there."

"Mother," I said quietly, trying to ignore the barbs thrown at me, "Bette is the one who told me about Douglas."

Mother continued as though she wasn't listening. "You were trouble even before you were born. I had no intention of getting pregnant. You were to blame for me having to be back with your father and live here, in this blasted council house."

At that moment, I knew no matter what I said she wouldn't listen. "Yes," I said. "I'm to blame for a lot of things that are not right. But you have to take care of Douglas now. It's important. He's in a bad spot with the law."

I walked out of the house, away from my family, knowing, once again, I had put my foot in it. This time it would change everything in my life. I knew it, but it was too late for me to make amends. I had given little thought to punishment or what happened to peeping toms, which is, of course, a type of voyeurism. In the U.S., it is considered sexual harassment.

In the UK, at that time, psychiatry was the answer, and from what little information I later garnered from my father, Douglas had to see a psychiatrist every week for a year. Bette and her family moved away.

✳✳✳

I've always thought I could handle my emotions as well as anyone else. Yet, sometimes I've felt like an outsider watching a game of sports, being part of the audience, seeing all, but not involved with the action. This time, knowing that I could not take back the words I had told the police about my own brother, I knew I had caused misery and confusion. My family, with their old-fashioned ways, lived in a world without sexual overtones — a society when the BBC censored its programs to preserve the dignity of the people and the country. My parents had always avoided unpleasant things that went on because it could never affect them, they thought. Now, they labeled me an imposter in their beliefs. I was the one who was wrong in their eyes.

I realized I could not ever heal the wounds that I had created between my parents and me for my actions in this catastrophe.

I went back home to Dibden Purlieu in Southampton. It took a week or two to pull myself together enough to complete my plans to return to America, but I had no choice. I had to return pronto with my re-entry visa, which is not issued without a lot of paperwork back and forth to the U.S. Immigration Office.

Mark tried to lighten my mood; he was always a help to me, but mostly he hid away in the pubs. Even he preferred the company of his mates when I was in one of my 'dark tunnels' as he called it. How

253

could I explain anything to Jennie about my past with my brother? How could she or anyone know that the call to the police on that fateful day would change my life and hers in ways that I could never have imagined? No one could see it from my point of view, that I had saved my brother from becoming a rapist or worse. He was a danger to others, I thought. No one knew him or his past. But I did.

✳✳✳

I had to try to concentrate on my future place to live in the States — somewhere with seasons, I thought. I had heard that Oregon was much like England in its climate and would be most likely to have the same flowers and fauna I had loved. There is nothing more beautiful than spring in England, where fresh, new, pale green leaves of the beech woods shelter blankets of bluebells in the damp earth beneath.

On one of our last evenings in England, I spread a map out on the table and suggested to Jennifer that we close our eyes and stick a pin into a place in Oregon that might be our destination. With the pin in hand, Jennifer closed her eyes, and her pin landed in Brookings, Oregon. "Well," I said, "I wonder what's there."

I went to the local library and checked out a tour book on the northwest coast of America. Brookings seemed to be a nowhere kind of place as far as industry, especially in my limited field of fashion. I read about the Stretch and Sew Company based in Eugene, but after the word 'polyester' appeared, I declined. It was a time when the polyester fabric was all the rage, but it was a dirty word in 'couture' fashion. Natural materials were in vogue in the better circles.

I didn't know where we would end up or what I would be doing. That, it seemed, was to be my *modus operandi*. I was never to know what was to come next in my life.

Part Three

1981 – 2003

The moving finger writes and having writ moves on.
Nor all thy Piety nor Wit shall lure it back
Nor all thy tears wash out a word of it.

The Rubáiyát
Omar Kháyyám

Twenty Six

Back to America once again, and during our flight over the Atlantic, I mused that I could forget the past. I could be reborn with a different philosophy on life and change my ways forever. I didn't like myself, but I could change, I thought!

We ended up in Portland, Oregon. I knew there would be more opportunities for me to find work and, hopefully, a decent place to live.

At the Holiday Inn, a friendly young man at the reservation desk suggested Lake Oswego as a place we might begin to look for a house to rent. It was there that I met Meredith in a real estate office. She mentioned she had a daughter just as small as Jennie. My friendship with Meredith became vital to me. Her daughter, Karen, seemed to want to take care of the little girl from England, who, unbeknownst to me at that time, was having a tough time adjusting to a new home, new school and a different way of life. She was destined to attend a middle school in the States, even though she would be entering high school had we stayed in England. It did prove to be an advantage because she was ahead of the class curriculum.

I found a job in Beaverton, selling Singer, Pfaff, and Viking sewing machines. The owner of the store was a very upstanding Christian. He was kind to me, often inviting Jennie and me to share a meal with his delightful wife and two children. The problem was that he used his religion to sell the machines. It was as though, to do honest business you had to be a Christian. Every time he talked to a customer about buying a machine, he came out with the same words, "You know I would never lie to you about how good this machine is because I'm a Christian." I didn't say anything, but I didn't like it.

At the middle school, Karen introduced Jennie to her friends, who were all smart. At least I thought so. Karen was small and pretty, but tough. She watched out for Jennie. I noticed that Jennie's English accent disappeared once she started school. She wanted to fit in with the others. The skirts she had worn as a school uniform in England soon gave way to jeans and T-shirts.

The only occasion that made me sad during that school year was when she arrived home with a question I found hard to answer.

She said, "What's wrong with Jews, Mum?"

She had been sitting next to a boy, who, when hearing her last name of Levine, said, "Oh, I don't want to sit next to a Jew." I was horrified to hear that.

It was an eye-opener for me. I hadn't ever experienced anti-Semitism in my own life. I never knew how she handled that incident afterward, except Karen told the boy to get lost whenever he was around. And as far as I can tell, she didn't experience that again at that school. If she did, she never told me.

During that year, Mark arrived from England. He was trying to stop drinking, he said.

He and I went to check on high schools in the area. In Portland, the schools appeared well run, but I noticed some of the boys lounging around in the halls waiting for their next class were smoking. Lakeridge High School in Lake Oswego was more structured, or so it seemed to me, and more to my liking of what a learning institution should be. The school had an excellent reputation for preparing students for college with higher GPAs than any other school I had researched.

We had to find a house to rent in Lake Oswego so she could attend Lakeridge. It was a low ranch-style house with a large garden that the owner kept immaculate. We were so lucky to find it just minutes from the high school.

***

It soon became apparent that Mark could not do without his Scotch or vodka. I felt sorry for him, trying to understand why he couldn't quit. I tried to adapt to his routine of drinking, but after six months, when his visitor's visa ran out, he had to return to the UK. In those days it appeared the U.S. Government kept tabs on anyone with a visitor's visa. I was sad, yet relieved if that's possible. I looked back on the years we had traveled to exciting places, and often thought of his parents and how wonderful they had been to Jennie. I kept in touch with them for many years, and when we heard that Mark's father had died, it was very upsetting.

When I filed for divorce, Mark did not stand in the way. His mother wrote, saying he was still drinking heavily and that he was living with a woman he had met before he moved to Leicester and met me. I hoped he had found help for his alcoholism, which had ruined his chances at various jobs for which he'd applied. I wondered if his new friend was now supporting him. I just wished him well.

Jennie's new friend, Karen, was in the same class. They both loved to study. Jennie complained that she needed a car. Designer jeans had to replace the ones I made for her. After all, the purchased jeans had a distinctive logo! I tried to convince her that studies were more important than cars or clothes. But she won out on the jeans. She was a treasure in my life. I wanted her to be happy.

✳✳✳

I had been attending a University Women's Forum, where I met Rue McCready. She was as unique as her name. Tall and very attractive, she told me she was a manager at an auto leasing company in Beaverton and that they were looking for another girl in the office. Was I interested?

Cars had never been something I thought a lot about, but she suggested since I had the secretarial experience, I could at least give it a try. However, it was the antithesis of fashion design or sewing machines. It seemed my directives as to my career at that point were slightly skewed, just go along with whatever comes along appeared to be my motto. At Barry Warren Auto Leasing Company I was welcomed into the office by a group of women who were known as 'the harem.' Barry Warren was an imposing character. At six feet five, he towered over all of us except Rue, who, though not quite so tall as he, dominated the room with her leadership qualities. I admired her and her ease of dealing with the men who ordered cars, and who were, without a doubt, part of Barry's 'Old Boys Club.'

Rue left the company soon after I began to work there. I missed her guidance. Now there were three of us who seemed to be enthralled by this big boss-man regularly seen on TV ads whose name was recognized around town or wherever he went. Everyone knew Barry Warren. He lived in a beautiful home on one of the canals of Oswego Lake with all the accouterments necessary to be a member of the boating club. He had a speedboat on which we harem girls were often invited for a spin. Parties were held at his house, catered by the best restaurants in Lake Oswego.

I decided that one of his attractions was the fact that he spoke so lovingly about his second wife, who had died in a boating accident on the lake. I wondered if we women liked him so much because of this sweetness remembering her. He had two boys who lived with their mother, Barry's first wife. The youngest boy attended Lakeridge High School, same as Jennie. His older son was rarely mentioned, and I soon discovered it was because the lad was gay. He was not allowed to visit the house, which bothered me. I didn't understand that.

I did learn from Jennie, who saw a lot of Barry's younger son at school that Barry did not like children, and that was the cause of a divorce from his first wife. So, despite the charisma this man exuded, he was not as loving as we had supposed.

When I learned from the office gossip, that all the harem girls, except Rue, had at one time or another been seduced by Barry, I decided I must be wary of him and his charm. I was just an employee, after all.

I had been with the company for a year when I was promoted to Barry's personal secretary with my own office. When he learned that I was going to England for my vacation, he seemed very interested in where I was going and what I was going to be doing. I explained in detail that I was going with Jennie and her friend, Karen, to see Mark's mother in Leigh-On-Sea; then, I was going to Southampton to visit my former boss, Henry, and his wife, Pat.

"Aren't you going to visit your family in Leicester?" He asked.

"Not a chance. Unfortunately," I said, "They hate me."

He laughed, "I'm sure that's not true."

Even though this trip was obviously to visit friends, Barry was not put off. One evening he took me out to dinner and explained that he would pay for the whole trip, airfares and all if he could go along with us. He said he had never been abroad and wanted to travel with someone who knew it well.

I immediately said, "No, absolutely not."

Then I changed my mind when he said, "We can go to France as well. I'll rent a car; we can travel all over, even go to Germany if you like."

Well, what could I say to that? I mean travel to places I'd loved! The excitement of travel for me always exceeds logical thought.

When we arrived at Southampton, Henry's wife, Pat, immediately succumbed to Barry's charms. I could tell he worked his magic on her in no time, so I left him there in their care while Jennie, Karen and I took the train to see Mark's mother.

She was delighted to see us and cooked all the lovely dishes I remembered so well, calories no object. Mark was apparently living with his former girlfriend but didn't want to see us.

By the time we got back to Southampton to pick up Barry, he had made himself at home with Henry and Pat. He had arranged for them to visit him in Lake Oswego. What a cheek, I thought.

Being in France was quite an experience. We had not made reservations at any hotel, and we ended up in a *pension* in Paris. It was a three-story crooked house located on a bustling boulevard. Jennie and Karen were given a room downstairs, and because we didn't speak much French, it was awkward trying to explain that Barry and I needed separate bedrooms. After a frustrating half-hour, we finally had to give in and were given the last and only room upstairs in the attic, with a small window that overlooked the Eiffel Tower. The room had nothing other than a small sink and a double bed. The bathroom was down the stairs. Sharing a bed with Barry was an adventure that I need not explain. I was hooked.

Twenty Seven

When we returned to the States, Barry announced that he wanted me to move into his home on the lake. I reasoned that we might get on well in bed, but it did not guarantee our association was a lasting one. I thought about the experiences of some of his past loves that I'd heard about early on, and I was unsure of his sincerity so I opted to stay in my small rental house in Lake Oswego. However, it seemed this man was not about to be put off. Within a couple of months, he invited me to have a short vacation with him in one of his condos in Hawaii.

It was my first time in the beautiful climate of Maui. We went to the best restaurants, skinny-dipped in the evenings in the condo pool, and made love on the balcony. I didn't want anything more at that point and when we returned to Oregon and the work-world of car leasing, I felt as if I had been in a different world. Nothing would ever replace the feeling of the magic of that time in the sunshine in Hawaii.

I've never been good at deciding what makes a man sexy or sensual, but Barry Warren had the key to success with women in the bedroom and I still can't quite make out what exactly it was about him. He was terrific to me, and the lovemaking was the best I'd ever experienced. Of course, I had to accept that it was pure lust, not the kind of relationship I wanted.

After a week in a happy place, I was faced with a reality in its worst form.

A telegram arrived from my father saying that my mother had died. I was shocked. He hadn't even written to me to say she was ill. Barry found some Scotch in his private cupboard. He held my hand while I cried into the glass; there were so many things left unsaid to my mother and so many regrets; a lot to be sorry about. It was too late now, too late. After the last incident, I didn't think I could make it all right with her anyway, considering my father had written to me only recently to tell me not to send any more flowers via *Interflora*. "She won't have them in the house knowing they are from you," he'd said. Well, that told the story in its entirety as far as I was concerned, but I knew I had to attend her funeral. I didn't want anything more to apologize for.

When I rang my father to say I was booking a flight home, he told me that Pauline was on her way from Africa. Arrangements were made for Jennie to stay with Karen and her family, although she argued that she was old enough to look after herself while I was gone.

I arrived in Leicester in the rain. Pauline told me that I was welcome to stay with her in the house she and Richard had purchased years ago for when they came from Africa on leave each year.

After the funeral, and the quiet gathering of long-lost relatives whom I had seen only once or twice in my life, Pauline and I talked for hours about my mother and how our memories of her differed so much. Pauline said she would like to go to the Towers Mental Hospital to find the records of our mother's stay there. I wondered why, but she said she wanted to know just what had happened and what sort of treatment Mother had experienced.

I told her I would go with her, although I said, "They won't have records of that time so long ago, Pauline."

"You're wrong," she said, shaking her head. "They keep them all, and I'm going to find out what Mother said in those hypnotic sessions and what the electric shock treatments accomplished."

I learned that the Tower's Hospital was the first Borough Asylum opened in 1869. It was originally an old manor, Victoria House.

I was surprised to find out my mother's records *had* been kept. Pauline and I had permission to peruse the files. We had to give our ID and the reason we were interested in our mother's time in this place. The woman in charge said we could ask questions anytime.

You might wonder from earlier on in my story if I remembered those Eau-de-Nile painted halls of that day in 1944. Yes, of course, but now the hallway was bright and light with offices on each side.

The file about my mother was thick. With my mother's name and address and long patient number were the words: Auditory Hallucinations and Guilt. I wondered what exactly that meant. Pauline and I waded through the papers. Each entry hand-written by a doctor who had talked to her. Her answers to his questions were strange. She was a very complicated person with all her past fears.

I found a separate file of papers in a folder. Headed: Hypnosis Session: There were questions, and my mother's answers right before my eyes.

Q: I want you to go back to your first memory as a little girl. Where are you now?"

A: I'm outside playing whip and top.

Q: Is anyone there with you?

A: No. I'm walking down the street and playing all the way. I can hear Mum calling me. Now I can hear the bell.

Q: What is the bell for?

A: The curfew bell. It's nine o'clock. Oh, they're here now. They're coming for me. Those horses and the men. They're coming for me. Ohhh!

The doctor had then made a notation: *The patient was distraught. Session discontinued.*

There were pages for each session. I turned to the last page under the heading. *Conclusions:*

The patient believes in her previous life; she was a little girl in medieval times when there was a curfew at nine o'clock at night. There were horses pulling drays with wooden barrels. One of the men had hauled her up on to the cart. She struggled and was able to get away.

I remembered the conversation I had had with my father about it, and he had mentioned that children out past curfew were often kidnapped and taken away by the night soil men to work on the farms.

Pauline called my attention to another file. The psychiatrist had asked my mother to write down what had happened to her baby she had conceived with Jack Rush. In her spidery hand, she had written, "*I was coming down the stairs with my baby in my arms when I tripped and fell to the bottom. The baby was dead. I killed her.*"

✳✳✳

Those words haunted me during the flight back to America. My mother had confided in the doctor her worst nightmare. To lose a child and believe you are to blame. As I sat in my office at Barry Warren Auto Leasing on my first day back from the UK, I thought a lot about my mother's funeral, the time spent in the office at the mental hospital looking through all her medical records.

I remember reading somewhere that it had been a common complaint from soldiers who returned from war who were left with the noises of a battle that haunted them forever. Some doctors thought it was schizophrenia or auditory hallucinations. Still, as the years of medicine improved, it seemed that the new word for it was mysophobia: hearing things that are not there and why it sends the victim into an extreme fight-or-flight response.

I talked to Barry about it during lunch. He said, "I think all of that is absolute nonsense. Why delve into your mother's life when you have me? Instead of thinking about stuff you cannot change or do anything about, why don't you give yourself a break. Come on, move in with me, enjoy my house on the lake and forget all this weird stuff. You know there's nothing you can do about it."

I said, "Oh, Barry, I do thank you, but I'm just fine."

"Well, I am serious, you know," he said. "I'd love you to come and live with me. Of course, you would have to foster Jennie out. You know I don't like kids."

"What are you talking about?"

"I know how you feel about your girl," he said, rolling his eyes, "but Holly, who I met in Hawaii, had no qualms about fostering her daughter out so she could move in with me."

I was astounded. I couldn't resist my answer. I said, "You are one pompous prick. Do you really think I would give my daughter up for you?"

He laughed. My English sarcasm and sense of humor always amused him, "She'd be fine, and you would enjoy being with me. Why don't you give it a try?"

"Barry, you are totally out of your mind. Anyway, if Holly was willing to give up her child to be with you, where is she now?"

"She was from Canada, and she had to go back. We still keep in touch."

266

"Ah hah," I said. "Well, you can keep your home for another woman, just know it won't be me."

He patted my behind, "But we can still date, right?"

"You mean so we can sleep together?"

He grinned, "That would be great. Why not?"

The twinkle in his eye that had caused so many women to fall into his arms almost made me forget that he was a selfish bugger, not wanting Jennie if I moved in with him!

I shook my head, "Hey, we can go out sometimes, but that's all."

"Well," he said. In that case, there's a party at Brian's house on Saturday. I'd like you to go with me. Okay?"

"All right," I said. "I guess I'll just meet you at his place."

Barry did not turn up. It was not like him to miss an entrance at a party.

I phoned his house. No answer.

After a while, I began to be concerned. Maybe he'd taken the boat out on the lake and fallen overboard. I started to imagine all kinds of scenarios and I mentioned my concern to the host.

He said, "I wouldn't worry about Barry Warren if I were you. A couple of years ago, my wife's friend fell for him in a big way, and when he'd finished with her, she was so upset she went up to Mount Hood and never came back."

"You mean she got lost skiing?"

"No, she committed suicide because Barry had dumped her."

I said, "Oh, no. Do you really believe that's true?"

"Yes, my wife knew Rhonda was seriously involved with Barry. She loved him and said she didn't want to live without him; she told that to Marge. Of course, it's not a bad way to go — if you know what I mean, but I certainly wouldn't trust him, Amelia."

I asked for another glass of wine. I thought the story was a bit over the top. Would a woman do herself in over Barry Warren? He was a known womanizer. He was fun to be with. Good in bed. But I couldn't imagine anyone trusting him when it came to love.

After noticing the late hour, and still no sign of Barry, I phoned again. No answer. I decided I had better go to his house. All the lights were on. I knocked on the front door expecting him to tell me he'd forgotten about the party. A minute later, I heard a woman's laughter echo down the hall from the bedroom. I stayed for a minute more and then heard her again. He hadn't forgotten the party. He'd forgotten me, or at least he'd found someone else to entertain him in the manner to which he was accustomed. I obviously didn't fill that bill any longer.

The next day at work, I didn't mention it. After all, I had been just his 'next in line,' which led me to an idea, "Hell hath no fury as a woman scorned."

I found some large metal buttons, the ones you see for sports and special events, and I covered the buttons carefully with white cloth, sewing the fabric securely at the back. In black pen, I wrote five letters on the front: BW then underneath FFC. The acronym stood for, Barry Warren Formerly Fucked Club. Our Company letterhead read: Barry Warren Friendly Finance Company, so the buttons would not offend customers. All the girls in the office wore the buttons, we were all part of the same obsession for this man. I now knew why all his buddies in the old boys club referred to us as his harem. What suckers we women are.

When I was offered a job at another leasing company, I took it. I was expected to contact companies who used fleets of cars. The investment tax credits were supposed to encourage big companies to lease all their vehicles from us. Cold calling all day and every day nearly drove me insane.

I soon discovered that the guys in the office doing the same thing as I was doing were paid more than me. I complained to the boss accusing the company (more or less) of discrimination. They must have disliked me for that, and a couple of months later, when I couldn't bear even the thought of going to work another day, I gave my written resignation. They didn't ask me to stay. I wonder why.

Twenty Eight

Scrambling to find a job in something familiar, I saw an ad for an experienced seamstress at Martin's Bernina Sewing store in downtown Portland. I applied and waited.

Mr. & Mrs. Martin were very particular about the girls who demonstrated their expensive machines, and with my degree and experience, I fit the bill. After a few months of learning their demonstration techniques, I was sent to Steckborn in Switzerland to learn more about Bernina machines and maintenance. I loved the work, and I loved the owners. I was lucky to eventually become a store manager at the Mercantile Village in Lake Grove, an area close to the city of Lake Oswego. It suited me down to the ground, and my teaching career took shape with sewing classes every week, which were well attended.

I did a lot of business in that store, and I was happy every day working with people who loved sewing clothes and craft items. I had a following with all my classes and sold lots of accessories for sewing. Mr. Martin showed his appreciation by slipping a hundred-dollar bill into my pay packet sometimes if business had been exceptionally good.

My sister wrote to me from Kenya and told me that Richard was ill with malaria for the third time. His usual doctor was an Italian who was away on vacation, and she had no choice but to have a local African doctor attend to him. Not a good idea, because Richard was not well-liked by the Africans who worked for him. She had told me that he had been threatened more than once with Voodoo from the Shamba boys — Voodoo comes from the religion of *Vodou* practiced in Africa, Polynesian countries, and from Medieval England when people stuck pins in a doll to create a hex on someone they didn't like.

Richard died just shortly after his illness, and Pauline and her daughters blamed his death, not on malaria, but a hex. However, I clearly remembered my parents' response when Pauline had announced she and Richard were going to Africa, way before they were married. My mother had said, "Malaria, white man's grave." Now it came to be true. To add to Pauline's unhappiness, Singer Sewing Machine Company told her she could no longer live in Africa because Richard was gone. She had lived there for almost thirty years. She and her family had to return to England, and she was not happy.

I urged her to apply for a visa to America. She said she would try. But again, finding employment would be a problem for her. How many Montessori teachers were needed in the U.S?

✳✳✳

Jennie graduated from Lakeridge High with a 4.0 GPA. Now the question of where she would go to college was of prime importance. From my perspective, the problem was, which one could we afford? I had a lot of questions about that, and I did a lot of research. I was a single mother with not much income, at least not enough to support a child in college.

I applied for the Pell Grant and got it. I went to the U.S. Bank and asked for a scholarship for her. It worked. Her scholastic achievements made it possible.

She said she didn't want to attend Lewis & Clark College, which was close to us. So we toured California. Berkeley was too liberal, she said. Stanford too large. Pepperdine, Seaver College, on the coast in Malibu, California was perfect.

I worried about the church affiliation because Pepperdine is Church of Christ, and with a name like Levine I wondered if she would be accepted. I need not have been concerned, her GPA meant more to them than her religion. I was impressed with the university because they didn't press her to go to invocation every morning.

During her second year at Pepperdine University, Jennie went to Heidelberg, Germany. A syllabus was offered to good students. I had grieved when she left Oregon to attend Pepperdine, and now she had gone to live in another country. It was awful. I couldn't just drive to California to spend a few days at the beautiful campus in Malibu. She was in a foreign country far away, and I remember spending the year while she was away just waiting for her letters.

Without Jennie, I was finding the house in Lake Oswego lonely and isolated, and when my home-economist friend, Barbara, asked me if I would like to share her large home in West Linn, close to Lake Oswego, I agreed. She was a member of a church singles group and urged me to go with her. I told her I could not belong to any church. It would have been very hypocritical, I thought.

She had met a nice man there and couldn't understand why I didn't want to join just to meet someone.

I wasn't desperate to be involved with a man anyway, not after Barry and his shenanigans. Not to be outdone, however, Barbara invited the singles group to the house for a party. I was introduced to John Evans. He was tall and elegant in his well-cut clothes, but I felt sorry for him because he had heart problems. Association with someone with a bad heart did not bode well for me. After Joseph and his death due to a heart disorder, even the mention of heart problems made me shiver. In any case, John was very religious although he did not talk about it much or proselytize. He visited the house with the group and often stayed behind to talk to me about music. He was a sweet man and a gentleman and had a pleasant tenor voice.

He told me his mother was a concert pianist, and he liked classical music, which we discussed at great length. Sadly, I began to realize he was never without a glass of wine or Scotch in his hand. Oh, I was wary of that. I had had my fill of being around an alcoholic, but eventually, he and I became good friends. He was so caring in his way with me, and even though he was thirteen years older, perhaps at that time it's what I wanted. I was lonely. He said all he needed was friendship. There was very little sexual attraction between us, so friendship was good.

John had been married twice before and had a son, Jerome, who was at the Airforce Academy in Colorado Springs. I thought it strange that there was no correspondence between them, but he never seemed to want to talk about it, and I was not to know until much later that his former marital problems regarding his son would become mine.

A year later, when John asked me to marry him, I suggested it would be better to live together just to see how things worked out between us. He told me that it would not be proper in the eyes of the church. We went to see the pastor at the Lutheran Church to ask what he thought. After talking to me, he was not keen on the idea of us marrying at all. He suggested that with my ignorance and unacceptance of their church, or any religion, our relationship would have little chance of survival, but it didn't stop coming to see me. His tenderness toward me was wonderful, and without the sex, it meant that he was interested in me and not just that.

I felt guilty arranging to be married while Jennie was away, but Barbara organized the whole thing. It was taken out of my hands completely.

We were soon ensconced in John's small condo in Lake Grove, near the Bernina store where I worked.

Alas, within a year of our marriage, John had a heart attack and had to retire from his job at Consolidated Freightways, in the Workers' Comp department, a position that required a lot of attention to detail working with large amounts of money. I think that did not help his health problems. The retirement benefits were excellent, and he seemed happy to be the housewife while I worked. He cooked the meals, cleaned the house, and made me tea every morning.

I taught classes in French Draping, and my classes were popular. I wrote articles for sewing magazines, which brought in a little more income. But instead of being satisfied with what I was doing, I decided to form my own company designing and manufacturing silk lingerie. I would be a successful designer, I decided. However, we did not think it through properly. We didn't consider the seed money that would be needed. I was in love with my designs, and John was very supportive of my endeavors, but I had no workroom. When he suggested we buy a house with an extra room to use as my workshop I was delighted. But in the middle of real estate negotiations, John had to have by-pass surgery. It took months for him to heal, and during his recovery, it seemed that his past problems with his two marriages surfaced. He talked about it all the time.

John had married his first wife when he was nineteen. They had a son, Jerome. However, he had always suspected she had been unfaithful to him, and when their son was born, he knew or decided

274

that the child was not his. This idea, though completely unfounded, led him to a decision to leave her and his son, who was eleven years old. I could not imagine how a child of that age would feel, and I tried to explain that in my view, the child would always think of him as his father. Except to John, Jerome was the spitting image of his best friend, Alan.

Married again, this time to Lucy, a pretty woman with a great singing voice, she delighted in making John more aware that Jerome was not his son. She pointed out quite often with photographs that Jerome looked like Alan, a cruel lady indeed.

John and Lucy adopted a baby girl, Amy, but even that did not keep them together. Divorced, Lucy was not about to let John be part of Amy's life, even though he wanted to be. Now, after many years, he was feeling guilty about his son and his adopted daughter, with whom he had lost touch completely. I'd already suggested he get a blood test to find out for sure if he was Jerome's father. There was no DNA at that time, just blood tests. He refused. I suspect because he didn't want to find out for sure that he was not Jerome's father.

I decided I had to try and fix things between him and his son. I made inquiries at the Air Force Academy and contacted Jerome, inviting him and his family to visit us. Something had to be done to heal this relationship, I thought.

Jerome and his wife and children were delightful. They came to see us and stayed with us in our large home in Portland. Still, even after all the meetings and good times, in my husband's mind, Jerome, even with his sweet wife and four children, was a reminder that there had been an unfaithful wife. The relationship once more was over. Eventually, we lost touch even though I continued to write and ask for photos of the children.

Meanwhile, I was absorbed in my lingerie line to include loungewear. I used more fabric and more time to complete each garment.

Norm Thompson department store at the Portland airport became my first customer, but to complete two dozen garments took far more time than I ever imagined. It was fine making the pretty samples to show, but trying to mass-produce became a nightmare. I was introduced to Barley Jones, a young black man who had been sewing in a factory in California for years. He parked his car in our driveway every day and worked from nine to four o'clock to complete the order for Norm Thompson. His presence didn't sit well with the neighbors. At first, Rose, from next door, told me his car was so old it looked terrible in the driveway. Next, I heard that it was because he was black, and a black man in the neighborhood just wasn't good.

I told them I was sorry they felt that way, but Barley would stay. I was surprised that we had *that* kind of people in the neighborhood. Discrimination had never been something I thought about at all. Anti-Semitism had reared its ugly head in my life, but not this.

I had explained the situation to Laurie, my friend, who had often helped at the Bernina store. She surprised me by suggesting that she and her husband Dick, become my partners, "We've been thinking about it for a long time, Amelia. We would be happy to help you out, and Dick suggested the large warehouse at the Kohl Business Center in Beaverton might be ideal. It's new, and they want tenants. At least you won't be annoying the neighbors."

Of course I was delighted. It was the answer to my problems. John and I had invested our entire savings, and now Laurie and Dick spent an equal amount. We were able to purchase Juki machines made with unique feet for sewing silk.

I bought silk-jacquard from Japan and China and hired five Korean girls who did such an excellent job with their small fingers handling the slippery fabric so well. We had individual cutting tables and equipment, plus all the accouterments necessary to mass-produce.

The quality of our garments was excellent, and having been a couture designer, I knew the difference between good quality sewing and the not-so-good mass-produced lingerie in polyester silk for a far lower price.

We hired a rep who included my line in with three others.

I was busy from early morning until very late at night, filling orders and rarely had time to write to my sister and her family. Pauline had applied for a job with a Montessori School in Lake Oswego, but it took too long, and by the time all the red tape was completed, the school had hired someone local. Having employment arranged in the U.S. was necessary before the magic green card was issued. I knew the twins were already in America on visitor's visas. Tonia had married an American serviceman and was living in Florida, so she was all right, but Glenda was illegal because her visa had run out. One day she phoned to ask me if she could come and stay with me for a while because she needed a favor. Even though I was too busy to have a house guest, I said yes, wondering what she was up to, to ask a favor of me.

I met her at the airport, marveling at how beautiful she was with her dark hair, pretty face and figure. On the way to the house, she said, "I'm in real trouble, you know. I'll be deported, and I need to find a husband quickly here in the States. I know you can help me with that."

I thought she was kidding, "Glenda," I said, "I'd love to help you, but I don't know a fella who would want to marry a girl just so she could have a green card and stay here. You'll have to go back to

England and apply for a legal entry like your mother is doing." I added, "Just marrying someone wouldn't work."

"Yes, it will," she argued. "I can establish residency with their credit cards and stuff. That's how it works."

I reiterated that I didn't know a guy who would marry a stranger just to give her legal residence, then the thought struck me like a bolt of lightning; Barry Warren knew a lot of guys in his old boys club. He could steer me in the right direction, at least.

I called him, not sure he would be happy to hear from me since it had been a few years since we had parted company. But he was his usual charming self, assuring me that it was so good to hear from me and that he would love to have lunch and talk over old times.

With tongue in cheek, I told him about Glenda. Did he know of anyone who might wed this beautiful girl just to sponsor her? I quite expected him to laugh, but he said, "Let me think about it. Why don't you bring her to the office next week?"

Well, he took one look at Glenda and said, "I'll marry her myself, to hell with introducing her to one of the other guys."

I remember laughing at him. "Barry, you're thirty years older than she is."

He said, "I bet she won't mind about that."

I told Glenda if she liked the man at first glance, she might as well go for it, since it wouldn't last long, knowing Barry. At least she would have a marriage certificate and credit cards in her new name, plus all the other perks that would make a green card possible if she could stand him for a few months.

She agreed, and a month later, Glenda married Barry in Hawaii. They stayed in his lovely condo in Maui, the same one he and I had shared.

Barry now had the perfect wife, at least for the moment, no children to worry about, and the satisfaction of being with a stunningly beautiful young girl. He gave her all the things she wanted: money to spend on clothes, parties, and the luxury of living in a house by the lake in an upscale neighborhood in Lake Oswego.

They went to Hawaii often, and to my amazement, they went to England and stayed with my friends, Henry and Pat, in Southampton. Barry still oozed charm apparently and was welcomed by them. That really did irk me.

Interestingly, later, John and I enjoyed many dinners with Glenda and Barry at the lake house. I went there sometimes on my odd days off and helped Glenda improve her cooking skills. That was a strange experience; she was where I had been with the same man. The weird thing was there were still photographs on the wall of Barry and me during our trip to England. I thought that would bother Glenda, but the pictures stayed. She worked at his office at the front desk. The harem girls were gone, but there were a couple of men who took their place. Glenda probably did wonders for his reputation with her looks and his money. My prognosis that their marriage would probably be over in a couple of years was wrong.

Now, by this strange twist of fate, Barry Warren and I were related.

Twenty Nine

Jennie had returned from Germany and was settled in her third year at Pepperdine. Tuition was high, and she had taken out a student loan, but in 1985, when President Reagan stopped student loans for high-income families, it put me in a terrible position. John was not rich but not poor, either. In any case, with the costs of my business expenses, I had given little thought to the fact that we did not have enough money for her to complete her fourth year to graduate. It was heartbreaking to have to tell her that she would not be able to graduate from Pepperdine. I dreaded the call.

To my surprise, when I finally broached the subject, she said, "Oh well, you know the university needs good students, and I guess I am one according to my GPA. Statistics are important to them. I will tell the dean about your situation. No worries, Mum."

I couldn't believe her response. I wept when I received the letter from the University. She had a full scholarship to complete her last year. I knew then she was savvier than I would ever have been at her age. The Jewish term is Chutzpah.

Jennie graduated Summa Cum Laude and remained at Pepperdine as 'Year in Europe Coordinator' for four more years. Pepperdine now offers International Programs in Argentina, Italy, Germany, Switzerland, England, China, and Washington, D.C.

When she called to tell me that she had been in academia all her life so far and she was leaving Pepperdine for a new career, I was worried. What would she do? She was fluent in German, and had majored in communications, but what sort of employment would she seek? I need not have been concerned. She had applied for a position with a title company in California and had excelled with her leadership qualities. She was a valued employee. She had made a lot of friends, some of whom were realtors, her clients. One of them was a lovely young man, Brent Preston. He was very good-looking and a successful realtor. Even from the start, it seemed they were meant for each other. It wasn't long before they were planning their wedding to be held in a beautiful home in Agoura, California.

I missed seeing Jennie and Brent regularly in California. When she announced they were heading for Colorado, where, with Jennie's background, a job was created for her at a major title company, I knew I would miss being part of their life. I had always encouraged her independence and ability to stand on her own two feet, and now she now rarely asked me for help. Instead, I began to rely on her for advice and encouragement in my business.

✳✳✳

Pauline lived in England, reluctantly though after Africa, and she wrote to me often. She told me my father was not well at all and getting worse every day. I told her I would go to see him for one last time. How could I not go? She said he needed hip surgery, which he declined at eighty-four, and that he did not leave the house because he could hardly move, the arthritis was so bad.

Jennie said she would go with me, and on the way over the pond, I had what I thought was a brilliant idea. We would hire a wheelchair and take my father to the lovely park that he and I had so often had enjoyed together when I was little. I conjured up a whole scene of my father sitting comfortably in the wheelchair as we strolled around the park, talking about the changes and how things were now. He would remember the flowers around the old manor house that had once been my school. He would comment on the types of trees and the wildflowers in the wooded areas. I could see it all in my mind's eye.

Once in Leicester, after the long flight and train journey to Leicester, we rented a car. Jennie said she'd drive and had applied for an International driver's license, so we were legal. Still, she was very wary driving on the left side of the road and she took her time. To our annoyance, we discovered we were impeding the speed of those behind us who wanted to get somewhere quickly. There were horns and hoots and then someone gave us the finger as they passed. It wasn't funny, but I had an idea. We eventually found a newsagent shop that sold typing paper. We joined several sheets together with tape and I wrote in big bold letters: Caution, American Driver. We stuck it in the back window. It did the trick. People actually gave us thumbs up when they passed, or smiled.

We picked up a wheelchair from one of the medical supply places and drove to Winstanley Drive feeling pleased with ourselves.

My father and Douglas welcomed us and Douglas went into the kitchen and came back with cakes and tea. I was anxious. I could see that my father was having trouble getting around, even moving from the sofa to the dining table. I wondered why there was not a bed downstairs and a porta-potty or something that would accommodate him and make life a little easier. After the tea, Jennie went back to the car and came back in with the wheelchair. My father was still seated at the dining table. He said, "What's that for?"

I said, all aglow with enthusiasm, "Well, I thought we could go to the park like we used to do. You know, take a stroll around the old school. See some things you and I haven't seen for years. Have some good memories."

He stared at the chair, then looked at me over the top of his glasses, "You expect me to sit in that thing and go outside?"

"Yes," I said, "don't you think it's a good idea? It's the only way you can get around comfortably."

His face turned bright red, "I won't sit in a wheelchair with a rug over my knees. People will think I'm old."

I wanted to laugh but stopped myself. "Dad," I said, "you are old. We are all getting old, whether we like it or not."

At that moment, my brother piped up, "He won't go outside in a wheelchair. Lots of folks have suggested that, so why do you think you could make it happen? Why don't you go away and leave us alone? Every time you come here, you interfere and spoil things for us."

I stared at him, unable to believe his words.

Jennie said, "Come on, Mum, let's go."

I looked at my brother. It took a lot of control as I said, "Can't you see how difficult it is for Dad without a bed downstairs? He can't get to use the bathroom upstairs. He needs a bed down here and a porta-potty, or something."

Douglas spat out the words, "I help him get up the stairs to the Loo and bed."

"He needs a nurse to help you look after him," I shouted.

"Just get out."

We took the wheelchair back to the medical supply place and bought a bottle of Scotch, which we drank at Pauline's house. I was furious, hurt, and frustrated.

When the phone rang later that evening, I was surprised to hear my father's voice, "Amelia, I think you should apologize to your brother for what happened today."

I apologize to him? Shouldn't it be the other way around? But I didn't say that. Instead, I managed, "Everything will be all right, Dad." Then I put the phone down and had a good cry.

We went back to see my father again during the week we were there, but it was a strained visit. I was glad to leave.

Two weeks later, he died in the hospital from congestive heart failure. I was able to leave a message with the nurse who was attending to him in the hospital. I told her to tell my father I loved him very much and everything would be all right with Douglas and me. I hope he got the message, but I could never be sure. At least Pauline was with him when he died, and I was so glad about that.

Once more, we were back in the USA.

My lingerie was selling well. I had increased the line of designs, and I had begun to make larger sizes: more fabric, more time. I had the patterns sized at White Stag in Portland; they had all the equipment to make metal patterns for the cutting process. My Lingerie was becoming well-known, except it became necessary to send out past-due notices regularly. I had no idea until that time how many businesses worked on credit and were often reluctant to part with their money, even long after receiving the goods. Money became tight for us because all our bolts of silk were paid for C.O.D.

Then one winter, we hit a big snag, one from which we were never to recover. My order of silk from Japan was held up at Seattle Airport because the quota was filled for the States. I had no idea that America could import only so much silk from other countries.

The fabric was unavailable for three months. We were doomed. We would be a season behind and could not fill orders. I started to have nightmares every night and went through the days in a blur of indecision. John and I had not taken a salary in the three years we had been at the Kohl Business Center. I went to the bank to ask for a loan of seventy-five thousand dollars. The manager implied that I had two strikes against me. I wasn't a man, and we hadn't been in business for five years. I went to the SBA (Small Business Administration) and asked for their advice. Nothing was doing there. My partners offered more money. I declined; they had already helped so much.

When a woman friend approached me and said she would buy the company from me and I could work for her, I turned it down. Too proud to let it go to someone else. How stupid I was. I argued, "I am the designer. I have to be in charge." As they say, "Pride comes before a fall." And fall we did.

I woke up one morning and decided I must stop the angst that had invaded my life. I had to escape this triangle of the emotion of realizing that my ambition of being a designer of note would never happen, and making money, well, that was a laugh! I had disappointed John and my partners. I walked into the workshop and announced the closing of the factory. I gave the workers a week's notice plus severance pay. At a sale later, we sold what little remained of the silk for a dollar a yard. We sold the machines and all our fixtures. I still wanted to pay back Laurie and Dick, something I could not do. It bothers me still.

John and I were bankrupt. He hated debt and was beside himself, even considering having to go to a lawyer to set up a Chapter 13, where we would have monthly payments for a long time. I felt my life was over. I was almost fifty years old and a failure. I wanted to run away; I didn't want to face another day. Of course, there were a lot of people later who asked why we had not become a corporation, meaning we would not have had to go through bankruptcy. Helpful to know or think about that afterward. Yes, in hindsight, we could have been a limited liability company, an LLC, which would have protected our assets. As I said, I just didn't think it all through.

I knew John had always worried about our finances, and I said, "You know we could live in another country for much less than we do here."

"Where do you suggest?" he asked.

"Portugal," I said. "That's what we should do, live in Portugal. A lot of Brits go there to retire and to Spain." The view of the bay and the beach, the villa where I had stayed in Portugal with Colin, suddenly appeared before my eyes.

"You mean for good?" John asked.

"Well," I said, "let me do some research on living costs and call a couple of letting agents over there. You know it's only two hours from England, and we could always end up there. I'm still a British citizen, and it is cheap to live there, too."

"It's the weather in England," John said, "Remember when we visited, it rained every day."

"True, I think the weather is much better on the Continent."

"If that's what will make you happy, we'll try it."

Poor John. I never realized until later how selfish I was to ask him to leave a country he loved. I had disregarded that he, in his sixties, may not want to be uprooted for good. He was a home-body. He didn't like to travel anywhere unless it was close to home. But he went along with my plans. We had an estate sale. He sold his lovely Japanese Screens and antique furniture. The house sold too. He must have been so sad, but he didn't grumble. If he did, it went unnoticed by me, so intent was I on moving away. Mayflower Movers came to the house and packed our personal belongings in large wooden crates, ready to be shipped to Honolulu for storage until we were prepared and settled. It had taken a while with paperwork back and forth, but we had contacted the Portuguese Consulate and arranged for permission to live there permanently. They were used to ex-pats moving there, and it didn't seem to be a problem. John's retirement income from Consolidated Freightways was transferred to a bank in Portimao on the southern coast of Portugal, the Algarve.

Thirty

When we arrived at the airport in Lisbon on a chilly winter's day, there were armed soldiers everywhere. We were shut inside a bus and thoroughly frisked before they let us out into the cold evening. Not a good start, I thought. At that time, it was standard practice to search everyone, no matter who you were or where you had come from.

John had developed a cold. We stayed in Lisbon in a charming private hotel for a week. It was inexpensive, and for me, quite delightful discovering the narrow winding streets with washing strung across from one side to the other. On the window ledges, canaries in cages sang and filled the air with birdsong. I found the green wine delicious, *Vinho Verde*. Restaurant food was also inexpensive.

The villa, in a luxurious resort on the edge of a cliff, was much too large for us. There were four bedrooms and a huge living room with one small electric heater. We could not understand the language. No one seemed to speak English, other than the ladies in reception. Of course, I had been on holiday with Colin in the summer; this was winter and just as cold as England. I did find an excellent library in Portimao, and some books written in English. One of the history books was interesting because it gave some history of Portugal. The Romans occupied southern Portugal before the Arabs came and named the area Algarve: *al-garb,* meaning west. It is the west coast of the European Continent. The monument of Henry the Navigator is on the westerly end of the coast. He was the chap who sent sailing expeditions to Africa's west coast during the age of discovery and the Atlantic slave trade.

The Arabic influence was particularly evident in the chimneys all around Portugal. However, the chimney in our place did not work worth a damn. The fireplace smoked every time we tried to light a fire with logs. As the manager said, "These places are really for summer, you know."

The nights seemed long and cold, and we were three miles from the nearest town of Portimao. We were isolated from civilization. When the water ran brown from the faucet in the kitchen, I tied a nylon stocking on the tap, but it didn't help, and since the tiny on-site grocery store did not open until April, we had no choice but to walk to Portimao to buy bottles of fresh water. We'd turned the rental car in, deciding it was too expensive while the weather was bad.

Now, you may wonder why we even stayed there after discovering all the annoying things like lack of heat, having to walk miles for water and food, and being pretty much alone in the resort. Of course, we'd been told over and over it was meant for the summer holidays, so we had to accept the situation and manage. In the winter, it was much cheaper than in the summer months, and if John thought it was all terrible, he didn't moan about it.

We did take the opportunity to travel to Lisbon on the coach that went through forests of cork trees, which I'd read about. Cork comes from the cork oak tree. The layer of bark is called *phellem*. It is stripped from the tree in late spring and summer. The bark is harvested every nine to ten years, and while the tree is growing more bark, the quality improves. Trees can be harvested for up to two hundred years. It is considered one of the essential commodities, and the workers who harvest the cork bark are highly paid. It is illegal to cut down a cork oak, even if it's dead.

I noticed that beyond the cork forests, closer to the city, there were, as I've seen in a lot of European countries, enclaves of people living in poverty in their cardboard shacks. Tourists tend to ignore the poverty that lies beyond the glamour of a European city.

Portugal has its share of glamour, beautiful castles like Sintra, and fascinating places like the Sandeman winery famous for sherry, brandy, and Madeira. Portuguese fortified Port wine is produced exclusively in the Douro Valley in Oporto, north of Lisbon.

Our diet, when we were at the villa, consisted mostly of fish from the local boat owners in Alvor after we noticed the sides of beef and pork hanging from racks covered in flies. I didn't even trust the meat in the grocery stores. Inventory was always low for one thing, and it was then I realized that's why everything was so inexpensive; it was still a third-world country. We participated in the weekly sardine dinners held on the quay-side, where locals and tourists sat at the long tables enjoying the local *Vinho Verde* that flowed like water. and, there was always the British Pub, where Penny, the owner, provided terrific fish and chips. We became part of the local community. It was nice to know there were a lot of Brits in the Algarve, just a two-hour flight over the Atlantic.

When we were there, I noticed that close to the new resorts, there were half-finished buildings. People ran out of money to build houses because there were no home-loans. You either had the cash, or you didn't. But if the people were poor, the Catholic churches with their glorious gold and ornate interiors were not. They were very well attended.

Now, things have improved drastically. Portugal ranks among the top for expensive accommodation and elegant gourmet restaurants.

For us, when spring arrived, blanketing the cliff-top with yellow Shamrock, we were ready to explore further afield. John looked better than he had in ages and said he felt like a new man. Perhaps the lack of meat and more exercise than he'd ever had in his life did the trick. That summer, we rented a car and went to Spain, which is about thirty-six miles east of Portimao. The Costa del Sol is full of beautiful resorts, very touristy. Marbella, Mijas, and Nerja. But the village of Rhonda way up in the mountains was fascinating, and our hired guide, Christopher, told us about the influence of the Moors and the Muslims in this fifteenth-century town with colorful mosaic courtyards and crooked streets with beautiful gardens behind ornate wrought iron gates.

Granada is a busy city. John drove like a pro avoiding the bicyclists, hundreds of them, and small cars racing around in no particular lane. The Alhambra in Granada is a Moorish settlement full of fountains and beautiful courtyards, a reminder that royalty lived there in the thirteenth century.

We chose to stay in a parador that was once a castle owned by King Felipe III in the small village of Lerma high on a hill just outside of Seville. Paradors were set up by the government to help offset the horrendous upkeep costs of palaces and castles. In Portugal, they are called pousadas. This parador in Spain housed one hundred and thirty-three guests according to the brochure. The food was Tuscan and included lamb, partridge and quail. In the village, there was a small café that looked interesting, and I suggested it would at least be warm, even though after the enormous lunch we were not hungry. It was siesta time, and we were alone in the place, which was just as cold as outside. I said, "Oh, Frio, Frio. It's cold in here." The proprietor, who nodded to us as we came in, obviously heard my comment. Within a few minutes, he arrived with a large metal bowl of hot ashes which he placed underneath the table. "Calorie," he said. *"Calorie."* He was right. It was hot.

As the year progressed, I thought John was adapting to our new life. He looked forward to movie night at the Alvor Hotel, just a mile along the road to see American movies. The movies had subtitles in Portuguese of course, and eventually I learned enough of the language to get along just from reading the subtitles.

Little did I realize, underneath John's bright outlook on life, he was missing America, and when a letter came from a friend in Ashland, Oregon, and he read that his mother was very sick, he said he had to return to the States. I suspect that although John never talked much about his mother, she must have been on his mind a lot. She had always been a healthy woman, so this was an unexpected turn of events, but John now reproached himself, "I shouldn't have left my mother at her age. I don't know what I was thinking."

"Oh, John," I said. "I persuaded you. I'm sorry. I dragged you out here without thinking of your mother at all."

He said, "Oh, I would never have wanted to miss this wonderful adventure with you, so don't feel bad. I agreed to come here, and it has been great, but now I'm going home. You should come too."

I said, "I can't go back to face our debt from the bankruptcy. Not yet."

"It was nice for a vacation, Amelia," he said, "but I do miss my Monday Night Football and a lot of other things. I'm responsible for my mother's estate and all that. And you've forgotten I'm almost fourteen years older than you. I don't have the energy to keep going and going. I just want a peaceful place to live in America."

Of course, he was right. I hadn't given thought to medical facilities in Portugal. Hospitals were few and far between in the Algarve, and the British Hospital for ex-pats was in Lisbon, so far away. Dragging a man who had heart problems, often in need of assistance, to another country was stupid.

At this point, I knew I had to let him go without me. I did not want to return to face the chaos I'd left behind with my business. In Portugal, we were well-off. In the U.S., we would be back to square one. I did wonder how I was going to manage without John's income, which he was going to stop sending to Portugal. He needed it all in the States.

I wasn't used to being alone in the large villa, and I had many days when I thought I was crazy to stay on my own, but when I went to see Penny in the pub one evening just for something to do, I sat next to a man who I had seen there before. He was editor and publisher of a local free newspaper. I told him I loved to travel and that I had written articles for a few sewing magazines back in the States. He looked at me and smiled, "Why don't you write a column for the newspaper?"

"Really?"

"Yes, go ahead — about fifteen hundred words. You know, write about the area and the things tourists can do while they are visiting. You'll have some legwork to do, but if you visit local restaurants and pubs, you can interview people. Let's see how you do. I can't pay very much, but it might help."

I was delighted. It was just what I needed to fill my days without John. I walked everywhere. I found new friends, new places, and described the restaurants and their menus. I wrote profiles on the owners of the small boutiques and English restaurants. Like everywhere abroad, ex-pats found places to gather to catch up on what was going on at home and to speak English.

I tried to be more conversant with the Portuguese merchants, so I used Spanish several times when ordering coffee or a meal. One waiter said to me, "It would be better if madam spoke English." So much for my efforts trying to learn their language! The proud Portuguese do not appreciate anyone attempting Portuguese or speaking Spanish. The language is similar, but not the same.

Writing for the tourist newspaper was fun, but as with most papers, the pay was mediocre. I had to think carefully about what I could do to sustain myself for at least a few months more. Then, I had an idea from Penny at the pub. She kept a lot of books for the Brits to swap, and had often said she wished she had some fun clothes to sell since the boutiques in the hotels charged so much for their summer cotton wear. I told her I could make some shorts and simple tops. Would that work? She said yes.

I borrowed her old Singer sewing machine, took a bus to Lisbon to buy fabric, and after trudging the streets to locate a fabric shop, I stood with the proprietor trying to explain in Portuguese what interfacing was. It must have been quite hilarious. "You know," I said, using my hands to explain, "stiffening for the waistband, and the edge of pockets?" Finally, after many puzzled looks, the storekeeper led me to a tiny back room filled with bolts of fabric, cotton damask, silk, beautiful stuff. I found the interfacing fabric tucked underneath a bolt of colorful floral cotton. I bought the whole bolt of that, too. The proprietor beamed, and I was satisfied I could make some adorable shorts, some with pockets, some without, and simple tops to match.

Within a month, I had a line of what I called 'Sunwear.' It was easy for me to design paper patterns, and cut and sew the garments at the table in the large living room of the villa. Even the small boutiques purchased the shorts from me, and orders began to pour in. Again, like the lingerie business, I was just one person trying to fill orders. I kept going for another six months, spending all my time at the sewing machine with the occasional night out at the pub. I missed talking to the proprietors of the restaurants and other places to write articles for the newspaper.

At that time, a friend of mine from Portland, Oregon, wrote to me and told me she would love to come and visit; did I have room? I wrote yes since the villa had four bedrooms.

She was such good company, and we traveled on an organized tour to North Africa via Gibraltar, which has been controlled by the Brits since the 1700s. The famous Rock of Gibraltar has miles and miles of tunnels excavated into the limestone. During WWII, Britain controlled almost all naval traffic into and out of the Mediterranean from the Atlantic. Gibraltar is also home to the Barbary Macaque monkeys that have no fear of humans. They are everywhere.

A small vessel took us to Tetouan, one of two major ports in northern Morocco. A bus took us to Medina, the old town, and as I was snapping photographs of the Arabs who lined the street, my camera was snatched out of my grasp. "No photographs!" The tour guide who had just boarded our bus was firm, "I give it back to you later," he said.

There were so many unfamiliar sights and smells. A guide marched us through the streets where mosques and minarets lined the square; orange blossom filled the air, as did the singing voice of the *muezzin* calling for prayer. Cats were everywhere in the streets, on the walls, well-fed and friendly cats. In the Kasbah, we enjoyed a dinner of couscous and carrots with lamb, while a belly-dancer entertained us.

The conquistadors from Spain influenced Morocco, but the men garbed in white robes, women in black, were a visual reminder of the Muslim way of life.

A couple of weeks later, when my friend had left, I knew it was time for me to return to the States.

John had written that his mother was still frail and needed him. He did not live with her but close by. He was renting a room in a condo that was owned by an elderly lady. He spoke highly of this lady, and from what he said, she appreciated his company. Hmm!

Thirty One

Mayflower still stored our belongings in Honolulu. We had never shipped them to Portugal because we had always been in the furnished villa, and now we were back. At least it made me aware that our possessions were just stuff we did not need. However, it was like Christmas unwrapping all the bits and pieces we had packed almost two years earlier.

Now, living in Ashland, I could at least pretend I was far away from my previous life in Portland and my business failure. We visited John's mother daily in her little pink house by Lithia Park. She and I became close. I sat with her and talked about her career as a concert pianist.

I was sad when she died at age ninety-four in the Ashland hospital. She left us enough money to buy a lot in a new subdivision in Jacksonville, Oregon. But the bankruptcy was still a problem. Chapter 13 bankruptcy can remain on your credit report for ten years. How would we get a bank loan to build the house?

The subdivision was filling up, and I was disappointed that we would not be able to live in that very desirable neighborhood. There was still one lot left.

I was crying on Patricia's shoulder; she was my beautiful neighbor who met me for coffee twice a week. She said, "Honey, you should buy that lot you want," she said. "I'll loan you the money to have a house built."

"You are kidding?" I said.

"No, I'm a businesswoman, and when you sell, you will pay me back with interest. It's a win-win for all of us."

We signed the paperwork that was drawn up by her lawyer. Our dream house would be built. We figured it would be our last house since we would have it made to our specifications.

John and I studied floorplans and changed things around. It was all very exciting to watch our house being built from the ground up. I planned the landscaping with flower beds and shrub borders. It became the beauty spot of the area with a garden full of flowers all year round, a fountain and low brick walls, just like the cottage gardens I so admired in England.

What a shock when Patricia took ill, and her family moved her back east. The loan had to be paid back, pronto. Properties in the area were not selling well, and some were on the market for a long time. Later, I was sure that we could have waited, but I was worried about Patricia's family and how they would feel. Negotiations were not even considered at that time.

We were left with very little to spend on another house, and we had no choice but to rent a condo, this time back in Ashland.

I must say however, it was pleasant to live close to the Shakespeare Theatre and know about the plays. Once again, we participated in all the cultural things we'd loved in Portland. We adopted a lovely black Lab that became very important to John, while once again I scarched for employment.

Life goes on with so many twists and turns, but I felt as though I had probably had more jobs than a lot of women my age. This time I found a travel agency in Medford who hired me. It seemed a perfect occupation for me because of my extensive travel, although my initial experience with the United Airlines software to book flights was a nightmare. The owner suggested I could specialize in selling just cruises and tours. Joni would make the airline bookings. It suited me. She booked the air travel for the tours I organized. I met a lot of wonderful travelers during that time, and I wrote articles for a local magazine and loved it. At that time, airlines had decreased their commissions to travel agencies, the cruise business was taking over. I enjoyed the "Fam" trips—familiarity trips—to various destinations and learned about the different cruise companies, whose mega-ships held up to three thousand passengers or more that were becoming popular. My travel articles brought in a little income too. I wrote a monthly column in the local newspaper and read scripts and ads for the radio. My employers liked my British accent. I became a "voiceover" again, just like when I was in the player's group for radio drama with the BBC many moons ago.

✳✳✳

Our life seemed to be based on managing finances, although I liked my job at the travel agency.

Pauline had found a job in Florida, and she lived close to her eldest daughter, Louise, who had been in America for three years. Pauline visited Glenda and Barry quite often in Oregon at their Lake House, and until Glenda realized that her child-bearing years were disappearing, things ran smoothly. Barry did not want children, and I was saddened to hear that he and Glenda were divorcing after twelve years of marriage. They remained friends, however, until she met and married a young upcoming interior designer and had a son.

In the meantime, the owners of the travel agency retired and asked if I would like to buy the business. I couldn't afford it, and my airline booking partner, Joni, said she and her husband had plans to move back to California. I was offered a job with another travel agency, but it entailed booking airline tickets. I had no desire to start that again, and when a friend of mine in Ashland suggested real estate as a perfect career for me, I decided to go for it. A few of my friends were making good money. At least I could give it a try, I thought. Of course, I was told there would not be a paycheck every month and it would be up to me to earn a commission. I had to concentrate on the real-estate examinations in Portland, and not being good at math had left me in a bit of a dither. Still, I passed, not by much, but a pass nevertheless, and I was fortunate to be hired by a privately owned company in Ashland. Most companies were part of a large franchise like Remax or Century 21, but I liked the owner of this small office, and it felt a lot less intimidating to me than the larger offices in the area.

I made a three-fold flyer with a photo of me and an outline of my marketing plan. The broker had helped me put it together, and it looked entirely professional, I thought.

With flyers in hand, I walked my farming area door to door. I didn't know how I was going to get listings without making myself known. For two months, every day, I walked the streets and knocked on doors giving out the flyer. One morning, having walked what seemed like miles, I knocked lightly on the door of a charming newish home on a pleasant street. The door opened a crack, and a hand came out, into which I thrust the flyer. I introduced myself to a closed door and thought no more about it until I got to the office. A woman had called and left a message to call her. She was Japanese. She said she had read my flyer and was impressed. She asked me to list her three new houses. They sold within a few months. I was fortunate. I always added more ads than the company provided, perhaps that did the trick, or the fact that business was brisk in the real estate market in Ashland, after a slump in 1994.

As I grew older I lost the ability to see auras around people, but when I was showing property to clients, I often sensed there had been a lot of anger in the house by the former occupants, or if something sinister had happened, like murder. Although in Oregon, it's not necessary to disclose a death, if a buyer asked me, I would tell them what I knew and advise them to investigate for themselves. It was inevitable that sometimes a person died in the house from illness or old age, but most of my buyers were not upset by it. I was often surprised when showing the house, the buyer, usually the woman, would mention bad vibes or good feelings. So it wasn't just me.

I had one very interesting client, Margery. About seventy years old, she had been a pilot in her younger years and was very intelligent when she spoke about her many businesses. The only problem was, she had moved several times in Ashland because she said people were living in her attic. She said she heard them talking all the time. They apparently followed her from house to house. She asked me often to listen to the people 'upstairs.' No matter how I tried to convince her that no one was there, she said she had to move again because they were following her. She even persuaded a company to install TV cameras in the attic of one of the houses. That did it for me — companies taking advantage of the woman was unacceptable. I called her doctor. "She's being treated for schizophrenia," he said, "but she won't take her pills." So much for that. Margery and I enjoyed tea together quite often. She invited me around to be there at her house for a party because she said, she'd won fifty thousand dollars from Publisher's Clearing House, and they would be presenting her with the check that afternoon. She'd bought hundreds of magazines from them. It was awful to see her disappointment. I'm sure a lot of older folk fall for that promise.

I had been introduced to Margery's niece, who lived in Montana. I felt it was my duty to call her and tell her about her aunt. I said, "You know, "I could list and sell a lot more houses to her because of her condition. I think it would be wise if you were closer to her." She said of course she would find a suitable retirement home for her. I was glad about that and eventually, I found a friend who was willing to drive Margery with her dog to Montana to join her niece.

❋❋❋

During those years with the real estate company, John had three surgeries.

The interesting part of it, apart from the trauma associated with illness and recovery, I learned that after each surgery, he needed his Scotch. He was addicted, and I had done a lot of research on the effects of sudden withdrawal from it. I made sure I was there to give him Scotch after each surgery. The nurses allowed it because, as one of them told me, "he could die with DTs" — delirium tremens. Despite John's need for his Scotch every day, his health improved after he had a pacemaker installed to regulate his heart. He loved his Monday Night Football on the TV, and we had a wonderful group of friends with whom we spent a lot of time, either on short trips to local beauty spots, or to a show, often for dinner. We took turns preparing gourmet meals and became social members of the country club.

We had a music group, eight of us, where we each chose a piece of music. John would start singing from some stage musical we'd seen as a group. He always remembered the words and kept us all paying attention until the end of it. He was the person chosen to be MC at the shows we produced at another friend's house. James Manley had been with a film studio in California for thirty years as a special effects man and photographer, long before the digital era. His home was like something from another world: movie star photographs all around the walls. It was always show-time at his house with his lovely wife, Sylvie.

∗∗∗

When John mentioned that he had a sore on his leg that did not seem to heal, I was not unduly upset. But I should have been. After all his surgeries, I thought this was something that could easily be fixed. I was wrong. It turned out to be a squamous cell skin cancer. It was a mess.

We went to the hospital to see a surgeon who suggested that cancer must be removed, but because John was so thin, it would require a skin graft from his thigh. No problem, we thought. An outpatient operation, in at 11:00, out by 4:00.

I was in the waiting room at 3:00 and waited until the nurse came out and said it would be a while longer because John was having trouble with his oxygen levels. Next thing I knew, he was to be admitted to the hospital. They could not allow him to go home, even though he had come as an outpatient. "He's just not ready," the nurse said, "but he'll be fine." He wasn't fine. John was moved to the hospital from the out-patient area, where he struggled to speak clearly. I could tell he would have been better off at home, but since the doctor said it was better to be where they could keep an eye on him, I told him he must stay just for the night. He hated the hospital, and I promised he would leave in the morning. I went home without him. During the night, John had a stroke, one from which he would not recover.

My son-in-law flew from Colorado to be with me. We watched John die. He did not seem to know we were there, but just in case he did, we played classical music in his room. I quoted the Lord's Prayer and sang his favorite hymns. Only then did I realize I had not given him his usual Scotch after the surgery. Never even thought about it. Did that add to his demise, I wondered? Was I to blame for his death? In my estimation, John died, not from the stroke or cancer, but delirium tremens. A man dying in a care center is tough to watch.

I wasn't up to making any arrangements for his funeral. Brent took care of everything. The funeral in the church in Ashland was well attended. I loved seeing the familiar faces of friends in almost every pew. Except, a youngish man was sitting behind me who seemed familiar, but I couldn't place him. It was John's son, Jerome. I had not seen or heard from him in fifteen years. Brent had found his name and address somewhere, and his phone number — hard to believe. Jerome thanked me for looking after his dad, and at that, I burst into new tears. I wanted so much to talk to him, to keep him around for a few days, but he left right after the service. I heard from him only once more. He said that although he was now a colonel in the air force, he was going to join a church ministry. One wonders how his childhood and his on-off relationship with his father had influenced that decision.

I had arranged for a memorial service in Albany, Oregon, where I knew John had friends who kept in touch. I put an ad in the local paper there.

On a bleak winter day at the Masonic Cemetery in Albany, we gathered around the gravesite and listened to the short eulogy given by the Lutheran church pastor. After everyone had gone, I noticed a stranger who lingered by the grave, "I don't know you," I said. "Were you a friend of my husband?"

"Well, not exactly a friend," the man answered, "but I knew him when he was a state cop."

"Really? That was a long time ago."

He held out his hand, "I'm Joe Gordon. I was Joey when your husband met me."

I repeated the name over in my head. John had told me a lot of stories about his time in the state police. I had written about a lot of his escapades during the time he was with the police, and suddenly the name Joey popped into my head. I remembered who he was.

John had been a State Trooper in Albany. It must have been around 1955 when his patrol in Oregon took him to out-of-the-way places like Brownsville and Sweet Home, small farming communities off the beaten track, just outside Albany.

On an early bright October morning, he was driving along his usual route, when he noticed a group of women clustered in the center of the road. One of them knelt beside the body of a young girl. The woman was beside herself, frantically trying to revive the little girl.

John approached the group, "What happened here," he said as gently as he could.

"It's my daughter," the women sobbed. "She went out early before school to pick a pumpkin. She was on her bicycle. Our church is having a pumpkin carving competition. A car ran into her, knocked her off her bike. Now she's dead."

John asked her to step back as he knelt to inspect the little girl. "What's her name," he asked.

"Jessie, my Jessie. Oh, who could have done such a thing? They just drove into her bike," she said incredulously.

John looked at the small crumpled bike lying a few yards away in the middle of the road.

"My brother gave her the bike last Christmas," the woman said. "He put a basket in the front so she could help me with shopping."

"How old is she?"

"Twelve, only twelve. Oh, who would just drive away after this?"

Before John went to his car to make all the necessary arrangements to have the body picked up and taken to the hospital morgue in Albany, he turned to the distraught mother, "I will try to find out who did this," he said.

After everyone had gone, and the little girl was taken away, John stayed behind to see if he could fathom why the bicycle was in the middle of the road. Usually, bike accidents occurred in poor visibility at the side of the road unless this girl had swerved into the middle of the road for some reason.

He walked slowly up and down the road looking for any clues; he didn't know what it might be, but someone had caused this fatal accident, and none had been reported. He had checked. It was a hit and run.

He kept walking up and down until he spied something shining in the center of the road, a piece of jagged metal about the size of a quarter. He stared at it for a moment. Then he knew what it was, a piece of the grill from an automobile.

Sitting in the car, turning the piece over and over in his hand, he decided the person who knocked the girl off her bike was probably driving to work on an early shift. But where, what work? A factory. The mill!

He drove into the parking lot of the paper mill and walked up and down between the rows of parked cars.

At last, he saw what he was looking for; an old black Buick with a small piece of grill missing about the size of a quarter. He bent down; it fitted precisely.

With the piece still in his hand, he went to the office and asked the supervisor at the desk who owned the Buick in the parking lot. The man said quickly, "Oh, that's Burton's car, but he's not here today." He looked thoughtful for a minute, "You know what, his son

Joey sometimes comes to work in his dad's car. He's a bit of a troublemaker, that one. I 'spect he drove it this morning. Anyway, why do you ask?"

"I just want to see him, please," John said. "Would you go and fetch him, now, if you don't mind."

Joey was a pimply-faced boy, thin and pale in a shirt that hung crookedly on his slender frame.

"Come with me, Joey," John said, motioning for Joey to follow him to the parking lot. "This your car?" he asked.

"It's my dad's."

"I understand he's not here today. Did you drive it this morning?"

"What if I did?"

"I'll ask the questions. Now, let's start again. Did you drive this car this morning early around six-thirty?"

"What if I did?" the kid answered again.

"I'd like to see your driver's license, please."

Joey hesitated, "I don't 'av no license. I'm only fifteen. My dad said it's all right to drive, as long as I'm careful."

"But you weren't careful this morning, Joey, were you?"

"Whaddaya mean?"

"You knocked a little girl off her bike, almost ran over her, didn't you?"

"I don' know nothin' about that. It wasn't me."

John stared at the young boy for a long moment, "Are you sure it wasn't you, Joey?"

"I'm telling you it wasn't me."

"The little girl was only twelve. She was on her way to pick a pumpkin at Stokes' Farm. You were driving this car, and when you hit her bicycle, this little piece of grille fell off. You drove away without stopping. You didn't look back. You didn't tell anyone. I found this on the road where you hit that little girl on her bike. Look, Joey, it fits this grille."

The boy looked again, and his face turned white.

John put his arm around Joey's bony shoulders, "Come on, son," he said. "Come on, tell me what happened. You are in trouble, you know. No driving license, and you ran into a girl on her bike. She's dead, son. Do you want that on your conscience for the rest of your life?"

Joey took a deep breath. His voice broke," I was playing wiv er,' you know from side to side of the road. I didn't mean any 'arm. I swear."

Johns squeezed the boy's shoulders gently, "I know. I know," he said, "but let's take care of it, shall we. The law has to be obeyed; you know that. You have to be responsible for your actions."

"What will 'appen to me?" Joey cried.

John pushed the boy gently into the back seat of the patrol car and sat down in the driver's seat. "I think we'll have to leave it up to the judge," he said.

Now you might think that is the end of the story, but it's not. Not quite.

I studied the man carefully as he came forward to look down at the inscription on the gravestone.

I'd had words carved into the top of the shining granite stone: *He lived with a Melody in his heart and a song on his lips.* It seemed appropriate.

I smiled at him. "I think I know who you are," I said.

"You do?"

"John told me a story once about a boy named Joey when he was on patrol somewhere near Sweet Home."

The man nodded, "Had to be me I guess, when I was fifteen. When I saw John's obituary in the paper last week, I wanted to pay my respects to him."

He turned away from me, and when we both looked at each other again, I could see tears in his eyes. He said, "Yes, I sure remember your husband. Officer John." The man stood there, his hands in his raincoat pockets looking down. I couldn't help myself as I reached up and hugged him briefly. I whispered, "He remembered you too, Joey."

For the next few months, I was in one of my dark tunnels; those times when the sun fails to shine in my world of guilt that has always plagued my life.

I blamed myself for not thinking about the Scotch after John's surgery. I felt that the outpatient surgery for a cancer cell on his leg was very different from open-heart surgery, and it would not be as dangerous. The thought that he might die never occurred to me. I'm convinced, rightly or wrongly, that the Scotch would have saved his life once again, just as it had done the four times before. But it was too late now. He was gone, and my life was without purpose.

Thirty Two

Real estate was up and down in the market. Some years I wondered how I managed on very meager commissions with no salary. But, it was good for me in the long run financially. Twelve years passed quickly, and I made so many friends of former clients and office personnel. I was busy all day, and somehow the evenings alone didn't bother me. Jennie and Brent had moved to Oregon, and I found a lovely home for them in the Rogue Valley. I knew they would love the close-knit community of Jacksonville, the small historic gold mining town set among the lush green hills of southern Oregon.

Having Jennie and Brent living in the same state was terrific. They surprised me with a sixty-fifth birthday party. A big; 'do' at their house with lots of friends.

When everyone had left, Jennie presented me with an airline ticket to England, "Happy birthday, Mum," she said. "I heard about an air-fare that was too good to miss. I bought a ticket for you. I thought April was a good time of year to go and see your brother."

"Douglas?"

"I think it's time you went to see him and try to make things right between the two of you."

"Oh, Jennie, It's too late to say very much to each other."

"Well, just go anyway."

"I'll go to see him in Leicester before I go to Hampshire to see Mary." I reminded Jennie of her school years there and that we had made a lot of friends with whom I had kept in touch.

When I phoned Pauline to tell her I was going to Leicester to see Douglas, she said, "Oh, that's good news. Yes, try to make amends, Amelia. He's not in good shape. He's almost blind from diabetes that is ruining his life. I'm sure he'd love you to call on him. He must be lonely."

I hadn't told her about my teenage years with my brother, but she had heard about the time I called the police to report him as a peeping tom. She hadn't spoken to me for months because of that. She too, had wondered how I could call the police about my own brother. Sometimes I think I paid too much for that call; the total separation from my family! Was it worth it? Did it change him? One must wonder.

Anyway, I wrote a letter to Douglas saying I would be arriving in April just after Easter and would like to see him. I said I would phone him before leaving the States to confirm my arrival time at the house.

I didn't receive a reply to my letter but didn't expect it. I figured he wouldn't want to see me either. It would be awkward for both of us, I figured. However, Pauline called me two weeks later, "I wrote to Douglas, and I called the house," she said. "There was no reply. I'm worried. Have you heard from him? I sent him an Easter card. He didn't send me one, and he usually does. There's something wrong."

I said, "It is strange, I suppose. He hasn't answered my letter telling him when I'd be arriving."

Pauline sounded really anxious, "I wish there was someone we could call to see if he's okay. You know, a neighbor, or someone."

"Pauline," I said, "I don't know anyone now, not since Bette left. Let's just wait. I'm sure he's okay."

"Right," she said, "That's what we'll do, just wait."

At that moment, I was jogged into the past by her words, "Right, just wait, that's what we'll do." It was when Colin was reported missing in Vietnam. His mother, Ellen, had said those same words."

Two days later, Pauline phoned me again, "Amelia, I just can't wait to find out if Doug's okay. I called the hospital. He's not there. We have to do something." She sounded desperate.

I said, "Tell you what, I'll look up Social Services in Leicester on my computer, and I'll contact the Society for the Blind, also. They can send someone to look in on him. Okay?"

"Great, thank you. That will relieve my worries."

It was past midnight when I finally managed to locate the number on the internet for Social Services in Leicester, which is handled by the National Health Service. The operator gave me the phone number of the Society for the Blind. A lady with a lovely voice answered, "It's all right, my dear. I will have someone out to your brother's house today. Now give me that address again."

It was then nine o'clock in the morning in England.

A couple of hours went by, and I wondered what was going on. Was there someone at the house talking to Douglas? Yes, that was it. He had just been busy, perhaps.

When the phone rang, I expected the person to tell me everything was okay. A man introduced himself from the local police department in Leicester, "Ma'am, we found your brother."

I said, "Oh, Good. Is he okay?"

"No, I'm sorry. He's deceased. Looks like he died in bed."

I couldn't speak for a minute.

"Ma'am?"

"Oh, well, I …okay. Thank you for letting me know. Oh dear, when do you think he died?"

"Well, by the number of letters on the mat near the front door, and the dates on the envelopes, I would say before Easter. About three weeks ago."

"Three weeks. How could that be? How awful! Oh dear, how…how did you get in?"

"We had to break the front door down. It's being boarded up right now."

"I wonder why the neighbors didn't notice his absence," I said, trying to recover my wits.

"We did check, Ma'am. Mrs. Mitchell next door said she thought he was in the hospital. It wasn't unusual for him to be gone for a few weeks at a time."

"Will there be an autopsy?"

"Not unless you suspect foul play."

There seemed to be nothing more to say. I thanked him again and called Pauline in Florida. She was so upset. "I knew it," she said. "I knew something was wrong. Oh, poor Doug."

I said, "Pauline, you perhaps should think of it this way. He didn't suffer. He just went to sleep and never woke up. I think that's ideal."

She didn't reply.

✳✳✳

Now, with Douglas gone, I wasn't sure why I needed to go to England. It was always great to have a destination, a place not visited before, or one that I loved. What was the point of going back to Leicester? I hated the place.

Jennie said, "Well, go to Foxby, Mum. See how it's changed from when you were there. It will give you a chance to renew those good memories."

I thought about it for a long time. Could I really go back there after so many years? But then, how could I waste a ticket so graciously given to me.

Pauline called me and told me her daughter, Louise, was going back to England to sort out Douglas's belongings. I thought about her having to go through all the long-kept treasured correspondence, and the photographs that I knew were probably still there. My parents kept every letter from my sister. I knew that. Then again, perhaps they threw all mine away. It wouldn't surprise me.

When a large envelope arrived from my niece a day or two before I was due to leave for England, I sat down and went through everything. My parents had kept all my letters, photographs, birthday, and Christmas cards.

I sat and wept for a long time. It must not have been easy for them to know that both of their daughters had left, not to live around the corner where they could visit their grandchildren, but to flee the country for greener pastures. They must have thought about Pauline and me a lot during those years. Perhaps they read and re-read all our letters—from Africa, some from America, different parts of the world, and wondered what our lives were like, just as I had done when Jennie was in Germany. It saddened me to think that I had never had the opportunity to tell my parents that I loved them, despite our differences, quarrels, and misunderstandings.

I must have looked at all the photos and letters several times before I noticed the yellow, faded envelope, with an Australian postmark. I stared at it, not remembering it. On the front of the envelope, addressed to my mother and printed in bold black lettering were the words:

Miss Victoria Adelaide Veasey
12, Gray Street,
Leicester, England.

I turned it over a couple of times, wondering why Louise had sent it to me. It must have been mixed up with the other things she'd sent. I opened the envelope. The one page of a thick paper faded slightly to parchment yellow, had a heading:

C.J. Boyl & Sons, Lawyer
Port Phillips, Victoria, Australia

Australia? Jack Rush! I hadn't forgotten my mother's lover from years ago. I opened the envelope very carefully. The handwritten note read:

Dear Ms. Veasey:

Mr. Jack Rush has informed me that he had been delayed in returning to England due to an accident at the gold mine. He is currently under advisement at Victoria Hospital and will be informing you henceforth of his whereabouts in Australia.

Truly yours,

C.J. Boyl, Lawyer.

Mount Alexander Goldfield Project

My mother had not mentioned that C.J. Boyl was a lawyer. At least I didn't remember that.

Thirty Three

Changing flights at Chicago O'Hare airport was always traumatic for me. Either I had to run to catch my connecting flight to Heathrow, or I had to wait hours and hours. I finally boarded the Boeing 747 at 7:15 p.m. I hate red-eye flights, and as usual, I was exhausted the next morning, arriving at the start of another day. It was slow going through British customs, and once out on the street, I was not prepared for the hustle and bustle of London's rush hour traffic. I struggled to keep up with the crowd of pedestrians heading for the underground trains. Steep elevators coming up and going down were packed with businesspeople and smartly dressed women. They swooshed past me, efficient in a long-practiced jog-trot, briskly clip-clipping to the bottom of the moving stairs. I stayed on the right side of the escalator, with my suitcase balanced precariously one step below as the stairs slid noisily down into the cavernous depth of the white-tiled tunnel.

I paused to study the wall map. The 'You are Here' lettering was almost worn away with constant fingering. I searched to find St. Pancras Station, where I could catch the train to Leicester.

I tried to focus on the labyrinth of tube stations, all in different colors. A man's voice piped up from behind, "Where do you want to go, lady?"

"Oh, er…St. Pancras." I turned to see a tall, white-haired man in a raincoat.

"It's the blue line you need. Change at Leicester Square." He trailed his finger along the route, "There."

Before I could thank him, he had disappeared, swept away among the crowds.

A few minutes later, I was standing on a platform among the multitude of bodies. Within minutes there was a strong gush of air along with the train that suddenly appeared from the tunnel. Engines throbbed loudly, double doors rumbled open. I was carried inside by a surge of people and barely able to keep my balance as the engines were revived. The doors closed quickly and immediately opened again. A man shouted over the intercom, "Please do not obstruct the doors, thank you."

Once again, the doors clanged shut, and with a long sigh from the brakes, we were off, hurtling through blackness for a few minutes before slowing to a halt at the next brightly-lit station.

✳✳✳

I was the only one on the bus to Foxby. The road wound silver through the countryside. Beech trees with fans of pale-green leaves lined the fields beside the road. Elms, waiting to burst into bud, stood dark and stately along the banks of streams still running swiftly from late winter rains. When I think about the population of England and the amount of countryside still green and beautiful, it amazes me. England, with 53 million people, comprises 94,000 square miles and fits easily into the State of Oregon, which has a population of 3.5 million in 98,380 square miles. And yet, small villages in England stand isolated among the 1,500 miles of the greenbelt. No one can build on the green-belts around the burgeoning cities of Britain. The British Government set the rules for controlling urban sprawl in 1935. Greenbelts provide space for agriculture, forestry, and leisure, and to protect the historic villages and towns from merging into each other.

The bus sped along Main Street and lurched to a stop in front of the *Bull's Head.* "Last stop," the driver said. I stepped off the bus on to the wet pavement. Brakes hissed, and the doors rumbled shut behind me.

I stood for a moment to watch the bus turn around by the old school, a low brick, U-shaped building, with iron railings around the playground. Colin and I had run sticks along the railings. I remember the sound: ducka, ducka, ducka, ducka. Now, above the entrance, a sign read, *Bingo Every Saturday Night.* Well, things *had* changed.

The bus left a trace of diesel hanging in the damp air. It reminded me of Manhattan and the daily bus trips to and from work at the stock market before I left New York for California with Joseph.

Shops still lined Foxby High Street. The names had changed but not the street, which still curved through the center of the village. There were two new houses next to the Pub.

In England, not all pubs have accommodation, but I knew this one did, and once inside, I was greeted by a tall young man standing behind a dark wooden counter, "On holiday, then are we?" His broad Midlands dialect sounded odd to me.

"Sort of," I smiled. "It's been a while."

"Did you live 'ere?"

"Once I did. I left for America when I was twenty-two." I smiled, "A long time ago."

The young man showed me to a room, which he described as "the biggest one at the Inn."

I sat on the side of the double bed, finding the mattress comfortably firm. I decided a nap was necessary before I explored the village.

The tall young man brought me tea as I'd asked, "Everything all right, Miss?"

"Fine, thank you."

I stood by the window, sipped the tea, and watched a young girl pushing a stroller across the road toward the post office. Her hair was a mixture of henna, bleached blond, and purple. Her faded jeans were halfway down her backside, revealing an inch or two of white skin. When I lived in Foxby, I remembered girls around her age wore dresses or skirts and pretty blouses or sweaters.

Venturing outside into the cool of the late afternoon, I stood at the corner of Gregory Lane. St. Giles Church, with its Saxon tower, still loomed over crumbling gravestones, but the cottages along the lane were gone, replaced with elegant two-story homes on a wide paved road. No hens clucked around pretty gardens; no cows plodded up the muddy lane to Hadley's Farm. I wondered if the fields still lay beyond the gate. Perhaps, I thought, with a shudder, there's just a long road of new look-alike brick houses with cars parked outside.

Relieved, when I turned the corner, I spied the gate at the very top of the lane. I remember the old wooden one had a rubber tire nailed to it, so it didn't disturb the residents. Back then, the gate would close with a thud. Now it clanged shut behind me.

I looked toward the bridge over the canal. The wind sighed, and scudding clouds cast shadows, light, dark, light, over the tall waving grass, just like it used to be.

Colin and I used to walk to the lock-house by the side of the canal two miles further along, and then we'd sit on the edge of one of the arms of the lock to eat his mother's homemade cake. Everything always tasted better outside. I also remember that was where Colin had talked non-stop about our future in America. He had picked me up and twirled me around, "America, here we come."

If only it had been that simple.

My attention was drawn to the drone of a tractor in the field next to the farm. I wondered who owned it now, and who would be on the tractor preparing the wet ground for a summer crop of wheat.

I could just see the field next to the farm where the scented Cowslips grew. There it was — the whole field, yellow and shining in the sun. I felt the sudden urge to pick a bunch and was glad I had worn my sensible lace-up shoes. I trudged through the wet grass to breathe in the scented air.

The tractor was close by now. I shielded my eyes to see a man as he sat perched high on the seat. I couldn't see him very clearly, but I heard his voice, "Hello. Finding what you want?"

"Is it all right if I pick some Cowslips?"

"Go right ahead, m'dear. You just visiting, then?"

"Yes, it's been a long time since I was in Foxby. I love these flowers. Can't remember seeing any in the States."

"The States, eh?" I heard him shut off the engine. He shouted, "Hey, I keep cows in this field. Just watch where you walk."

I laughed. Then I saw him open the gate and close it carefully behind him before plodding toward me.

I had picked a long stem and held it up to my nose, "Lovely," I said as I studied the bloom of pale yellow cups.

The man stared at me as he took off his hat. His hair was white. His skin was weathered and brown.

I said, "Cowslips always remind me of a Shakespeare poem. Something like, 'Where the bee sucks, there suck I, In a cowslip bell I lie.' I think that's how it goes." I laughed, "Something like that."

He nodded. A smile crept across his lips. He said, "How about, 'the Cowslips tall, her pensioners be; In their gold coats spots, I see.'"

"Right," I said, yes, that's Shakespeare too."

The man stood awkwardly, fiddling with his hat. He finally said, "You don't recognize me, do you?"

I looked more closely, "I'm sorry," I said. "I don't."

"I know who you are, though."

He smiled, and I realized there was something very familiar about the smile.

Suddenly he laughed, "Amelia?"

"Colin?" For a moment, I felt nothing, then I inhaled sharply, feeling the ground sway beneath my feet. I was looking at the man I still dreamed about, had loved. I tried to speak but couldn't. I thought I was going to pass out. His face was suddenly in a mist, and blackness was descending upon me.

He stepped forward to hold me steady. "Come on," he said. "Let's get you a cup of tea."

He led me away from the field and steered me unsteadily into the cluttered living room of the farmhouse to an armchair by the fireplace. When I was finally able to concentrate and focus on the room, it was a shock to realize nothing had changed. Newspapers were spread untidily on the chair. Everything as I remembered it. Only the absence of Ellen struck me as odd. She should be here somewhere.

When a sudden chill swept through the room, I shivered. I glanced toward the door where I thought I saw a movement. No one was there — just my imagination.

I watched Colin light the fire already set in the fireplace with coal and kindling. Then, with a nod to me, he went into the kitchen. I could hear him filling the kettle. I sat staring into the crackling flames of fire, wondering what was happening. I was numb. I looked again at the door, almost willing Ellen to be there. When the door swung open, I gasped. Colin came into the room, "Oh, damn door, gotta fix the latch." He went back into the kitchen and returned with biscuits and tea on a tray and set it carefully on the stool by my side, then he seated himself on the worn sofa and watched me. We didn't talk. I couldn't get my brain to cooperate. He leaned forward in his chair. "You are okay?" he asked.

I looked up, "I think I saw your mother just now."

"What? You saw Mum?"

"I… oh, just my imagination, I guess."

"Well, she's here a lot. I'm sure of it. Don't let it bother you. So, how are you, lass, still married?"

"Married? It took me a moment. "What? Oh, oh, he died."

"I'm so sorry."

I'm not sure why anger swept through me at that moment, but it did. "Colin," I said, trying to keep my voice even, "when did you get out of Vietnam?"

"Well," he hesitated. I got out in seventy-three. I lived in France for what…er…six years, I suppose. Why?"

"Seventy-three?" I tried to remember where I was in seventy-three. I sat and thought about it for a minute or two, and then I remembered. I was with Mark, and we had taken a trip back here on the narrowboat. I was pretty sure of the year. Could Colin have been back from Viet Nam then? The thought bothered me. "So, why didn't you try to find me?"

"Didn't come back here until eighty-four, when I bought this place," he said as he poured tea. "I went to see your folks. Douglas told me you were married. That's all. That's all."

"Why didn't you contact me then, Colin? No one told me you were alive. Douglas didn't tell me you had been there, and that you were alive. No one did."

His voice was soft, "I told them not to tell you, Amelia. Why would I interfere with your life? Really, can't you see that from my

322

point of view? They understood. And what would have been the point? For goodness sake, can't you see that?"

I watched the clock on the wall; the pendulum swung back and forth. The minutes ticked by. I finally spoke; my eyes never left the clock. "The thing is," I said, "Didn't you ever think I might want to know you were alive? You could have found out from my parents where I was even when you were in France, when you first got back."

Colin sighed deeply, "My past was muddled, Amelia. You must realize that, and anyway, you wouldn't have wanted to see me then." He handed me a cup of tea, "A buddy I'd met in the prison camp said he was going to live in France for a little while, and I joined him because I couldn't think of what else to do. I was messed up."

"What do you mean, messed up?"

"It's complicated…"

I waited.

"How prisoners were treated, and all that goes on in their mind afterward…. I mean, getting out didn't mean you just forgot about what had happened." For a minute, he drifted away, closed his eyes. Then he sighed again and smiled, "Anyway, can we talk about you? I don't understand why you're so angry."

"Because…because it would have relieved my guilt, that's why."

"Guilt?"

"Don't you know how much I hated myself for making you go to the States, and then you were in the military, and then Vietnam. Then I heard you were missing, and then you were dead. You were dead, Colin! In my mind, all these years, I've blamed myself for you going to America. I had killed you in a way." Suddenly, tears spilled uncontrolled down my face. I had no way of stopping them.

"Hey, hey," he reached for my hands and held them still. "Amelia, I was young and so excited about leaving England. You

323

were not the one to blame for my going to America. Please, get that into your head right now." He held my hands tightly, "Listen, lass; it's all too long ago. Look at me. Now I'm okay, but I was over the edge then. I was held as a prisoner for a long time. You have no idea how it was."

"Oh, Colin, I don't understand. You were in communications, behind the scenes. How come you were in danger?"

"I'll tell you sometime, not now. Not now. You know it was only by chance I came back to Foxby just to see how the farm was. It was for sale since Mum died. Long time. Needed repairs everywhere. I bought it."

"If only I'd known you were alive," I whispered. "It would have made my life happier."

"But you've had a decent marriage, a good life, haven't you?"

I nodded, "Yes, and I have a lovely daughter. She gave me the ticket to come here this time."

"I'd love to meet her, you know."

Outside, the birds were gathering for the night in the elm tree. For a while, their chatter filled the dusk with noise. Then it was quiet. I said, "I'd better get back to the Inn. It's getting dark. Perhaps we can talk tomorrow." I was too emotional. I just wanted to be alone.

Colin rose, "Oh, no. You are not getting away that fast, lass. Not this time. Tell you what. I'll freshen up a bit and walk with you down to the pub. They do a nice cottage pie, and we can have a good old chat. How's that?"

I nodded. Without talking, we walked arm in arm down the narrow path to the gate. I stopped to look at my Aunt's and Grandmother's house at the top of the lane. They both needed painting. The side yard, which was always so beautiful with flowers, was now just concrete slabs for cars. The lane was not as I remembered, but the air was fresh, and my mind cleared. There were so many questions to ask, but Colin wouldn't talk about Vietnam.

He'd asked Douglas how I'd finally got to the States. Now he wanted to know who I had been married to, all about Jennie. So, I told him about my travels, the countries I'd visited. How I now lived by the Pacific Ocean on the west coast of America. I did all the talking.

Colin said, "What about your mother? She was always the nervous lady, wasn't she?"

"You are right there, Colin. You knew she had been in that mental hospital, of course. That was when I stayed with the Moores' here in Foxby. A few years ago, after Mother died, Pauline and I went back to the Towers Hospital to see what her treatment was all about. We never really did know what caused all her problems, you know. We found a lot about her past, but some things are still not clear."

Colin rose from the chair, "Hold on, let me get another pint," he said, "How about you, wine?"

"Oh, no, thanks. I think two is my limit."

He came back with the beer and set it on the table. He rubbed his forehead, closed his eyes, and sighed as he sat down opposite me."

"Are you all right?" I asked. "You look tired, and since I'm here for a few more days, perhaps we can meet tomorrow."

"No, I get headaches, that's all. I'm okay. I need to talk to you, you know." He smiled, and his eyes softened as he studied my face.

I said, "Colin, don't look at me like that. When you last saw me, I was nineteen. I'm sixty-five now."

"Hey, lass. I only see the girl I loved very much. She hasn't changed."

His words made me start the waterworks again. He handed me his handkerchief. It was clean and white.

I sniffed, "You still use real handkerchiefs?"

"Of course," he said, "and I iron them."

We both laughed.

"So, what about your Mum?" he asked.

"Well, you know she was a bit strange, talking to dead people and all that, but she often complained that she heard a bell in her head when she was worried or stressed, and she said she heard horses running. It was all in her head. Poor woman."

Colin rubbed his eyes and sat silently for a while, "My buddy in France used to wake up in the middle of the night quite often, telling me someone was firing a gun outside. No matter how I tried to convince him there was no one there, he obviously could hear it in his head. When he saw a doctor, they said it was Schizophrenia? I think it was just the war that did that."

"Well, I read a report from one of her hypnosis sessions at the Towers Hospital. It was all there in black and white. All the questions from the doctor and her answers. Under hypnosis, she said she remembered when she was a child living in the city; the curfew bell was at nine o'clock, and then there were horses pulling drays with big barrels, and what was worst they caught up with her in the street and shouted for her to stop running. I thought she must have been remembering the street cleaners, drays with barrels of water and horses, or something like that."

Colin took a swig of beer, "You do know the history of chamber pots being emptied into the streets, though, don't you. All that nasty stuff in the gutters in England before toilets. It was logical that the local farmers collected it and used it for fertilizer. They were called the night soil men. I guess they were not allowed to pick it up until after nine o'clock at night. There was a curfew warning bell that meant the residents should get home. If kids were found wandering the streets after nine o'clock at night, they were often kidnapped — taken away to work on the farms."

"Yes, my father told me, but I'm not sure I believe her about a past life."

Colin leaned his elbows on the table, "I do. In solitary confinement, I think I went on trips into my past life. It's absolutely possible. And, like your mother, I used to talk to my dead relatives. I really believed they heard me. At least it gave me comfort. I don't think your mother was nuts. People who have the gift of contacting the dead are just very sensitive souls, anyway, back to Leicester's folklore. My mother lived in Leicester City before she married my dad and came out here. I remember her telling me about the nine o'clock horses. I thought it was just a ploy to get kids to come home."

My mind had skipped back to Colin, "So," I said, "Why didn't you go back to New York when you came out of Vietnam?"

"It didn't appeal to me in the slightest. I do like England better, and I was offered a job with British Telecom."

I looked around the pub. We were alone, and the bar was being tidied up. "It looks like we are being thrown out," I said.

He walked with me to the front door of the inn and kissed me gently on the cheek. "Night, lass," he said. "Let's meet at the bridge tomorrow, okay?"

I watched him walk down the street. He turned and waved before he disappeared around the corner.

✳✳✳

The next day was sunny and bright as I walked through the fields to the bridge. I still could not quite believe that Colin was alive and well. When I saw him coming from the farm wearing his tweed jacket with the leather elbow patches, I realized nothing had changed.

We both looked down at the water beneath the bridge. He quoted aloud, "*All along the backwater, through the rushes tall, ducks are a dabbling, up tails all.*"

I said, "You don't forget anything, do you."

He hugged me close, and his lips found mine. I kissed him back. He hugged me for a long time. When he released me and stood back to look at me, he said, "Would your daughter mind if you moved back to England? We are getting on, you know. Might as well make the best of what years we have left together. What do you think?"

The question hung in the air. I had all I wanted in America. But then, all at once, I wasn't sure what I wanted.

"I would like you to come and live with me, you know."

"Really?" I stared down at the water below. "It would be a big move for me, though," I said. "I mean my whole adult life has been in America. And my daughter! I ...just don't know about leaving her. I can't imagine being without her."

"I understand," he said. "Okay," he grabbed my hand. "Shall we get an ice cream in the village?"

I smiled. The part of me that was making me anxious was gone. His lightness enveloped me, "You bought me ice cream when I was a little girl," I said.

He laughed and took my hand, "I remember. Hey! I was thinking of getting some traveling done while I'm still able to get around a bit. I just received a brochure about a tour of New Zealand and Australia. I'll show it to you. The fares are not bad, and I think you might like it."

I laughed, "Oh, Goodness, Colin! You've got my number, knowing how much I love to travel." The thought of Australia led my thoughts to the note from C.J. Boyl I now had in my possession.

We sat on a wooden bench near the duck pond and ate our ice creams. I told Colin the story about my mother and her former lover,

Jack Rush, who had supposedly owned a gold mine in Australia; he sat quietly listening. I mentioned the note saying Jack had had an accident at the mine. I finished by saying that I'd love to know who the lawyer was.

Colin turned to me, "If you think there's any truth in that story, we could look up the name when we get to New South Wales."

"My, my! Now we are in New South Wales?"

"It's just a thought. You know I was in communications. We could easily find out who C.J. Boyl was."

"Wouldn't that be something," I said. "To go to Australia and find out about the gold mines in the 1900s?"

"Yes."

I laughed, "You can't be serious?"

He didn't answer. At the farm, he cooked a delicious meal; roast beef and Yorkshire pudding. We talked until it grew dusk. Colin turned some lamps on around the room.

"You know I'd better get to the inn now," I said, yawning. "It's been a lovely day."

"Hey, lass, why don't you stay the night with me?"

I wanted to say yes. To make love with Colin had been a dream for so many years. Just to have him by my side would have been enough for me, but I thought I knew men, and it wouldn't be that way. My body was not what it used to be. No, I couldn't let myself relax with a man now. I tried to say, "I'm not what I was." Or, "It has been too long." But instead, I said, "I'm sorry, not tonight."

"Does that mean you don't want to be with me anymore?"

"No, that's not it. I just don't know. Give me time."

"Okay," he sighed. "I'll walk you back to the pub."

As we walked quietly along the path to the village, Colin said, "I love this time of night.

"Yes," I said, "Everything is so still."

Colin was speaking softly, "*The curfew tolls the knell of parting day, the lowing herd wind slowly o'er the lea. The plowman homeward plods his weary way and leaves the world to darkness and to me.*"

"Grays *Elegy*," I said.

Colin took my hand, "Life in the country. Right, lass?"

I looked at him and noticed the twinkle in his eyes and the smile that I used to love so many years ago. When I turned to look back at the farmhouse outlined against the darkening sky, in the half-light, the field of Cowslips shone as though it was filled with sunshine.

Lightning Source UK Ltd.
Milton Keynes UK
UKHW020406031221
394997UK00010B/2794